KINGS OF MIDNIGHT

· J.Q. Anderson

To my family: my husband, my boys, and my girl.

You are my angels, my haven, and everything that is right and amazing about the world.

And to Marilyn. You never stopped believing in me.

KINGS OF MIDNIGHT

BOOK ONE
OF
THE MIDNIGHT SAGA

PART 1

THE SHOE

Chapter 1

That morning, the morning of the pointe shoe and the speeding car, the morning I met Him, didn't start any differently. Life chuckled at me from above, nothing tipping me off on how it was about to mess with me. Big time.

I held my half-eaten toast between my teeth as I pushed open the foyer door while shrugging into my parka. Strapping my dance bag across my back, I hurried through the streets of downtown Buenos Aires. The damp air from an earlier rain filled my lungs as I jogged—away from work—steam building inside my parka. *You don't have time for this*, my roommate's voice rang in my head. *You'll be late. Again.* But on a rebellious—and childish, I admit— impulse, I was doing it anyway. Even though I knew she was right. Even though that morning in particular I should have been at work early because the artistic director would be posting the casting for my favorite ballet, *Giselle*.

I had exactly twenty minutes to pick up my much-awaited custom pointe shoes and make it to the theater on time, or I would get grilled by my teacher, Madame Vronsky.

My feet complained from the long hours en pointe, but even after a year with the company, I still felt a high as I rushed to work every morning. Being part of the permanent ballet of the Colón Theater was every Argentinean dancer's ultimate dream and, in my case, also the first step toward my future career as a prima in New York City. New York was the grand prize for me, a future far away from Buenos Aires and the shadow of my own mother's brilliant career as the country's most beloved prima ballerina.

I rang the doorbell of the old building, catching my breath. Anna's small frame appeared almost immediately, as if she had been waiting behind the door.

"Camila, darling. Come on in," she said, ushering me inside and away from the morning chill.

"Sorry to come so early, but my schedule's crazy. I have no free time anymore."

I followed her into the small foyer, and the familiar smell of wood polish welcomed me. She reached into an armoire I had always believed was magic. It was neatly stocked with Anna's irreproducible works of art. I let my bag drop to the floor, watching impatiently while she retrieved the treasure I had been dreaming of for days: a pair of her special edition, hand-embroidered pointe shoes. I took them in my hands and grinned. Closing my eyes, I pressed them to my nose and inhaled my favorite smell in the world: satin and leather.

"They're beautiful," I whispered. And they were. Pale pink satin from Italy, carefully embroidered with the finest silk threads in elaborate patterns. Nobody made ballet shoes like Anna. At seventy years old, she still ran her own workshop. The wait list was normally several months long, but I had lucked out because Anna was my mother's favorite ballet shoemaker during her days as a prima. It also didn't hurt that my father was Anna's doctor and she had him on a sky-high pedestal. So as soon as I had asked her, Anna had squeezed my order in. I handed her the money I had been saving for the last three months and kissed her tissue-soft cheek. "You're the best, Anna. I gotta run. Take care, okay?"

"Let me get a sack for you. These are more delicate than your regular shoes. You don't want to put them in your bag with all your other things. The fabric is pure silk, it stains easily."

"I'll carry them in my hands. I need to go, okay? You don't have to get me a sack."

"No, no. One more minute won't matter."

Wanna bet?

"The new girl moves my things around. It's driving me crazy." She browsed through one, two, three drawers.

"Anna..." I fidgeted. Jesus, at this pace, Madame would have my head.

"Ah. Here." She opened a pale pink silk bag, and I quickly slid the shoes in, then followed her to the front door where, with unhurried movements, she eased the lock. "Say hello to your parents for me, will you?"

"Will do, Anna. *Chau.*" I dashed out, shouldering my ballet bag as I clutched the precious sack in both hands, flexing the shoes back and forth. I couldn't wait to try them on. Before wearing them, I would have to go through the whole ritual of breaking them in: bend them, buff the points to give them grip, pull out the inseams, and quarter the shanks to mold them to my feet. All without damaging the precious embroidery.

Needles of wind prickled my cheeks while I waited at the traffic light to cross 9 de Julio, Buenos Aires's iconic avenue, the widest in the world. The city's pulse quickened, a sulky dragon waking from a too-short slumber. I pulled the shoes out of the bag and admired them. Holding them in my hand, I darted a quick look at the now green light and hurried across the massive width of pavement. A passing body bumped my shoulder. I was almost at the other side when a woman in a crisp suit heading my way pointed behind me.

"*Querida*, you dropped something."

Instinctively, my fist tightened on the one—shit!—shoe I was holding. I whipped my head around and my heart constricted. The other shoe lay innocently a third of the way behind, a small wedge of pink on a sea of asphalt. Shit. That shoe was unique, and it cost a big chunk of my salary, plus the waiting time. My eyes flew to the light.

Adrenaline surged through me as I sprinted, every one of my limbs tensing to win the race against the tidal wave of incoming traffic. Without pausing, I bent down, scraping my fingers against the asphalt, and hooked the rim of the slipper. Behind me, an explosion of horns blasted, and I tripped forward with my hands tightly clutching the shoes. I squeezed my eyes shut, bracing for the impact, but the force of a tornado scooped me up and whirled me away.

"Are you *insane*?" snarled a deep, husky voice that went with the tornado.

I blinked through the shock, panting. As the world came into focus, my brain registered the pair of ash-colored eyes locked on mine. They were wide with annoyance, yet absolutely stunning, a cloud of powder blue, or was it silver?

"What the hell?" he said, now sounding less annoyed and more concerned.

"What?" I muttered, still trying to pin the exact color of his eyes.

"Did you seriously almost kill yourself for a *shoe*?"

Reality hit at once and I straightened out of his muscular arms, clutching the pointe shoes in my hands. *Safe.* "These are important," I murmured, securing them inside my bag that was somehow still tucked under my arm. I took an unstable step, and a shard of fire burned through my ankle. Shit. Not now. I let out a tense breath, clenching my teeth at the old injury. Nothing I couldn't handle. But the slightest twitch in the wrong direction could make the day's rehearsals unbearable. Pain shot up my leg when I took another step, and I winced.

"You hurt your ankle." He grabbed my arm gently, his tone impatient.

"Yes, but no," I said, cringing at the pain. I had no time for any of this. I looked up at him to send him off but stopped as I fully took in his appearance. Rebellious strands of raven hair framed the angular, perfect features of his face. His eyes narrowed a fraction, the furious silver of his irises blazing against sun-kissed, olive skin. A soft, five-o'clock stubble shadowed the square lines of his jaw. *Damn.* He was fucking beautiful. A mix between a superhero and something darker, an X-Man. My heart stuttered.

"I'm fine," I muttered, shaking off the trance. A sudden panic struck me, and I glanced down at my watch. Shit. I was late for the cast meeting. I flinched inwardly at the thought of Madame scolding me for my tardiness. I would much rather deal with my throbbing ankle than her. But as I took a step, pain burned through my ankle. I groaned in frustration.

"Here," he said. "Don't put your full weight on it." He held my arm gently and arranged it over his for support. I opened my mouth to protest, but when I took a step, the pain was significantly less. This was helping. "Careful." He pressed me against him to let a guy having a heated phone conversation pass us by. My whole body shivered at the closer contact with him. "This city's forgotten its manners," he murmured, looking down at me. Concern flashed in his eyes when he saw me frowning, though it wasn't at him, but at the sudden hormonal frenzy inside me.

"You okay?" The deep, raspy tone of his voice rippled through me, and I nodded. What was this? I didn't let myself swoon. Not even by ridiculously hot guys like this one. I didn't have time.

"I'm late," I said, pulling him with me to keep the weight off my ankle as I hurried.

"Will you slow down?" His hand clasped my arm more firmly. It was a bit comical: me half limping and him holding me to slow me down.

"I can't," I blurted. I darted a desperate look at him, and he was smiling in resignation. A small dimple had formed on his cheek. It was sexy and adorable. Dammit, I didn't like that he was so good-looking. It made me nervous. Yet, I was strangely enjoying his persistence and unnecessary concern for my safety. "You really don't need to escort me."

"Guarding instincts are intact. That's good. Come on." He nodded.

Arguing with him was wasted time. Plus, he gave long strides and we were moving fast. I let myself relax a fraction, using his arm as support as we navigated through a thickening mass of morning workers who seemed to have just realized they were going to be late for work.

"What's your name, crazy girl?"

"I'm *not* crazy. That shoe is one of a kind. And it costs a fortune."

"I can only imagine if you were willing to kill yourself for it."

"You ran into the street too."

"I did. To save *you*."

I thought about that as we awkwardly limped and hurried, dodging bodies in suits. He seemed at ease, as if going out of his way to help a complete stranger wasn't a nuisance at all. Didn't *he* have a boss? I was grateful, though. My ankle was warming up and already felt stronger. I would have to wrap it up before class, but it would be okay.

We stopped at the last light, and he pulled me closer. I resented the way my stomach swam at the heavenly scent of his body wash. He was tall. I peeked up at him and our eyes met. His were simply breathtaking. Like they had come up with their own color and didn't give a shit if it existed or not. Everything about him was confidence.

"Thank you," I said—I realized—for the first time.

He nodded.

"I'm fine now." I pulled my arm away gently. "Work's right over there. I'm good."

"You sure?"

I glanced at the theater doors as Karina and Paula ran in. They were always late. Crap. I set off to cross even though the light was still red, but his hand was quicker and gripped my arm tightly, growling as a car blazed by.

"Christ, girl. You *are* crazy," he barked.

I pulled my arm away. "I'm *not* crazy. I can't be late."

He clutched my elbow, forcing me to stop. His eyes pinned me down with a stern glare. "*Nothing* is worth getting killed for."

"You haven't met my teacher."

He shook his head in exasperation, and I let myself smile at the small victory as I glanced at the *still goddamn red* light.

"Really my work is just across the street," I said. "You can brag to your friends over how you saved a crazy girl from her death. Now go, I don't want to make you late for work."

He studied me for a second and ran a hand through his hair, a beautiful mess in perfect disarray, and I wished I hadn't noticed those tanned, roped arms under rolled-up sleeves. His mouth curved into a lopsided smile, and a million butterflies I didn't know existed inside my stomach fluttered their wings. *God.*

"All right. Be safe, okay? It was nice meeting you, crazy girl."

I blushed furiously, and my usual steel armor suddenly felt like a child's paper costume. I nodded, and forgetting about my ankle, I bolted to the theater entrance, desperate to escape him and the tornado of sensations whirling inside my rib cage.

Chapter 2

I pushed through the side door to the Colón Theater and took the stairs two at a time, minding the pain, which by now had scaled way down. A surge of unfamiliar electricity buzzed through me as the still fresh image of the beautiful stranger flashed in my mind. My heart protested, and not from physical exertion. I shouldered the swinging door, annoyed at the distraction. There was only room in my heart for one person, and that was already one person too many.

Yes. For the last year, I had been ziplocked in the vacuum of unrequited love, and as miserable as that made me, I didn't have eyes, or time, for anyone else. So how could a total stranger suddenly unhinge me like this? A *panty-scorching* stranger. Still. Maybe my body was retaliating for never wanting anything except Marcos and what went on inside the theater walls.

Down the hall, the door to the studio was still open, a good sign Madame wasn't there yet. I hurried over to the announcement board. No casting announcements yet. That would explain the delay. It wasn't uncommon for Madame and Federico, the artistic director, to discuss casting right up until the roles were posted. A lucky break.

Exhaling in relief, I ambled to the studio door, a smile escaping my lips as I walked in. Even though I walked through these same hallways every day, I still felt spellbound by every detail of this environment: the photos of famous graduates lining the walls, the piano melodies that accompanied the classes drifting through closed doors. Outside the studios, dancers stretched and warmed up, contorting their limbs in ways regular people would think unnatural. Even in the early hours, the air was heavy with the familiar mix of sweat and the waxy scent of aged wood.

This was my life now. My world. For the last year, I had danced here eight hours a day, five days a week. I had pushed myself beyond my limits to make it here, and my reward was a road ahead that promised nothing less but to be brutal.

From the first time I put on ballet shoes at the age of three, I had felt compelled to prove to myself as a dancer. At first, I wanted to be just like Mamá. To three-year-old me, she was a princess, a perfect combination of elegance, grace, and classic beauty. But as I grew older, Mamá's fame became my own personal curse. As one of the most renowned prima ballerinas in Buenos Aires, she had a brilliant career that included the best ballet companies in the world: places like the Royal Ballet in London, the Paris Opera, and exclusive productions in Russia. The only missing star in my mother's impeccable legacy had been the Manhattan Ballet Company in New York City. She had danced there as a guest prima and had joined other ballet companies in New York, but for one reason or another, she had never been offered a permanent job with Manhattan Ballet. Although Mamá didn't dwell on this out loud, I knew deep inside it had left a sense of unfulfillment in her. Manhattan Ballet was nothing less than the most prestigious ballet company in the United States.

So, naturally, becoming part of Manhattan Ballet became my life mission. It was not only my top career goal, but my emancipation from my mother's fame and concrete proof that I had what it took to dance among the best. I wanted to prove to the world, and perhaps to myself, too, that I was much more than my mother's daughter: *the Navarro girl*, as everyone referred to me at auditions. Every day I fought for the inches that would lead to a prima role in New York City. And with every inch, my dream of dancing in the Big Apple became a little bit closer.

I scurried into class and was immediately welcomed by the bright warmth of the studio. Relieved that Madame was nowhere in sight, I wiped the sweat off my face and spotted my two best friends, Natascha and Marcos, stretching out by the barre. Friendships were not easy to come by in ballet companies. We were each other's competition, and often one person's failure meant an open opportunity for the rest. My seniors, Natascha and Marcos had been principals with the company for three years. I danced mostly in the corps de ballet, but in the mornings, we were in a couple of classes together.

I dropped my bag next to Marcos's. From the floor, Natascha—or Nata as I called her—eyed me up and down, the soles of her slippers pressed together as she pushed her knees to the floor.

"What took you so long?" She frowned. "You're flushed." Even though she had lived in Buenos Aires since she was twelve, a hint of a Russian accent always filtered out when she nagged me, which as my roommate, she did often.

"I got held up," I said. I felt Marcos's curious eyes watching me from the mirror, but I didn't look up. Nata kept her eyes on her reflection as she stretched into a perfect split.

"Held up by what?"

A gorgeous stranger. "Stuff, I don't know," I mumbled, peeling off my sweats and fishing inside my bag for my old ballet shoes. I couldn't lie for crap, and she would grill me if I mentioned bumping into a hot guy. She suddenly looked up and her cerulean eyes brightened.

"So? Do you have them? Let me see."

I pulled the shoes out of my bag and handed them to her. She held them carefully, as if they could break in her hands, and we both admired Anna's outstanding work. They really were beautiful.

"I almost got killed today because of those." The words had escaped before I realized.

"What?" Nata's head snapped up. "Why?"

"I dropped one as I was crossing 9 de Julio, and I ran back to get it."

"You *what*?"

"You're shitting me, right?" Marcos chuckled.

I grimaced. "Marcos, I never got that expression."

"It means, are you fucking kidding? You jump into traffic for a *shoe*? Um, sorry to break it to you this late in the game, love, but we get those for free here."

"*You* get them for free. I won't until I become a soloist. And this is not *just* a shoe." I snatched the shoes from Nata's hands and tucked them back inside my bag. "You try dancing in Anna's shoes and tell me you wouldn't jump into traffic for them. Besides, these are unique. Anna hand-embroiders them herself with silk threads you can only get in Prague."

Marcos shook his head while I slipped my old pointe shoes on and quickly tied the ribbons around my ankles. They were almost dead now, and I should've invested in a new regular pair instead of depleting all my savings to buy Anna's. I would have to Jet Glue these to keep them alive until I got paid. Worst part was I wouldn't even get to wear Anna's. They were a gift to myself for when I got my first role as a prima. It was stupid, I knew. But it was my own dangling carrot, and I needed it.

The class filled with dancers taking their spots at the portable barres. Nata glanced at my battered shoes and clutched my wrists to pull me up. Her perfectly drawn eyebrows puckered together.

"I worry about you sometimes."

"Don't. Besides…" I smirked. "I made it right on time for Madame's daily *dose*." I nodded at the door where our ballet instructor stood in conversation with another teacher. "*Navarro, wake up! Your form is sloppy! Don't annoy me, girl!*" I spat out in Madame Vronsky's thick Russian accent. Nata and Marcos laughed, and the mood lightened.

Then Madame entered the room.

She began lecturing with her usual stoic, imperturbable demeanor. A legendary teacher in the company, she had been a prima with the Royal Ballet and, like my mother, was one of the most glorified dancers in ballet history. We were all intimidated by her presence and extremely proud to be under her tutelage.

She walked among the dancers as they stood en pointe, slapping their limbs into place and grimacing at the most minute imperfections.

"Carla, back!" she barked. Carla instantly straightened her back.

We craved attention from the teachers—especially Madame Vronsky's. Getting corrections in class was a good sign, even if it meant criticism. Anything was better than being ignored. Lucky me, Madame had made a sport of pointing out my mistakes. Like everyone in the company, she reminded me daily that I was taking up a spot at the Colón's permanent ballet, and also like most, she called me by my last name. The message was clear: I was the daughter of Inés Navarro, nothing more. But it made me want to work harder, longer.

I followed the warm-up routine and felt Madame watching me closely, her piercing green eyes missing nothing. By now I had learned to read her. I knew every look, every one of her gestures and what they meant. Most of them alluded to the fact that I could do better, but every so often she gave me the slightest nod, a smidge of approval, and those scant moments made the daily uphill battle worth it.

My thoughts went back to the events from the early morning, and the chemical frenzy I had felt in the arms of that stranger. I could still see his eyes, so intense I was sure he was able to see right through me. A warm sensation swam in my belly. I switched legs and found Madame standing behind me with her lips pressed in a thin line.

"Navarro, pull your ribs in. Are you sleeping? You look like you are asleep. *Come on.* The audience does not pay to watch you sleep." She eyed the new, gray leotard I had bought at a thrift shop and scrunched her nose as if she were smelling something bad. "That is not your color, girl," she said. "You must wear black or navy blue. Your bosoms need to appear more discreet, Navarro. Ballet is elegance. Always."

She then moved on to her next victim. I felt my face burn as I exchanged a quick look with Marcos, who couldn't keep a straight face. I narrowed my eyes. *Cocky bastard.* Marcos was not only naturally gifted but also obsessed with ballet. Like, for real. There was nothing else. No one else. To him, dates with girls had an expiration date of a single night, and I had never seen him with the same girl twice. Not that I held it against him. To most of us dancers, the rest of the world was just the leftovers of a full day of classes, rehearsals, yoga, physical therapy, and ice packs. But Marcos took our ballet-dominated life to a whole new level. Madame loved it: him, his passion, his talent, all of it. And she never, *ever*, harassed him.

Our teacher continued wandering around the class repeating in singsong, *"and one, and left, and two, and up, and stay. Stay, stay. Like this, longer. And one, pa pa pa, and two..."* She paused by Nata, arching an impressed eyebrow. It always amazed me to watch Nata at work, even during warm-up classes. She was flawless. A physically perfect ballet specimen, yes, but the most impressive thing about her was how, despite the glorious gene package she'd been handed, she never took anything for granted. Her family had immigrated from Russia with practically nothing and had built a successful business from the ground up. With every role she was given, Nata worked tirelessly until all imperfections had been erased. Her moves looked effortless, precise, even during transitions and impossibly difficult steps. As a true Russian, her body and determination had been carefully crafted for ballet.

Nata, Marcos, and I had first met during my initial tryout at the Colón. It was for a summer intensive, and my ticket to finally get into the most sought-after ballet program in South America.

I was beside myself and couldn't control my nerves. I had dreamt this moment every day since I could remember, and now here I was, waiting for my turn among a few dozen others, all looking more collected and prepared than me. I watched a girl's audition, and my stomach slowly fell. She moved flawlessly through her variation, a combination of complicated steps carefully planned to impress the panel of judges. My breathing shallowed as panic filled my chest.

I couldn't do this. I wasn't ready. Shit.

With my heart racing, I stood and hurried to the door. The hallway was deserted and too bright as the walls began closing in on me. Shit. *Shit.* I pressed my palm against a closed door, panting.

"Are you all right?" a voice behind me asked.

I shook my head no.

"What's wrong?"

I shook my head again, unable to formulate the answer, and looked up at him. He was tall, dressed in black tights and a black T-shirt, and the epitome of the male dancer. His warm, caramel eyes waited.

"I think I'm having a panic attack," I said in short, shallow breaths.

"Are you auditioning?"

"Yeah…no." I shook my head. "I don't know if I can."

He watched me for a moment, surely wondering what the hell I was doing at the Colón if I was having a panic attack at the first audition. I was wondering the same thing.

"Wait here," he said, then turned around and disappeared behind a door. A second later, he was back, holding a small square in his hand. "Come." He put his hand on the small of my back and opened a door behind me, which led to a vacant studio. "What's your last name?" he asked.

"Navarro," I said. "Why?"

He frowned. "Are your related to Inés?"

"I'm her daughter," I murmured. "But don't…I don't want people to know."

He shook his head in disbelief. "Well, auditions are alphabetical, and they're on J right now, so we have enough time."

"Enough time for what?"

He gave me a dashing smile and scrolled through his phone. "You have to forget about the audition and remember what you love about dancing and connect with that. This may do the trick. It's cheesy, but stay with me, all right?"

Juan Luis Guerra's "*Me Sube la Bilirrubina*" blasted through the small square he had placed on the floor, a portable speaker.

"What—"

He stepped facing me and took my right hand in his, wrapping his free arm around my waist. His face was inches from mine, and I was suddenly spellbound, breathless.

"Let go," he whispered and began following the tropical trumpets of the Caribbean melody. It was lively, loud, fun, and one of those songs that when it plays, you just *have* to dance. I followed him on the salsa number he improvised. He was a magnificent dancer, confident, free, and for a few moments, I forgot where I was and I became his partner. He made it so easy that if anybody had been watching, they would have thought we were partners, rehearsing. When the music ended, I was panting. He smiled widely, showcasing slightly crooked teeth. He was undoubtedly the sexiest man alive.

"Better?" he said.

I nodded. "Yeah." And as I said it, I realized it was true. The panic was gone, and all I felt was the freedom I always felt when I put on my dance shoes.

"Good," he said. "Now go in there and kick some ass."

In a trance, I hurried to the door, and as I opened it, I turned my head. "Thank you. What's your name?"

"Marcos." He winked. "Go."

I waited for my approaching turn, closing my eyes and holding on to the sensation left by the dance with Marcos. In that moment it felt like a sign. As if the universe was telling me I shouldn't give up.

A dancer stepped from behind me. She seemed a couple of years older than me, experienced. Her skin was ivory and her hair a furious red, tightly wrapped in a bun. She smiled warmly at me. It wasn't unusual for dancers to watch the newcomers' auditions. Hundreds of sylph-like girls from all over the country came to Buenos Aires every year, hoping to be chosen for a role that could earn them a spot in the Colón's permanent ballet company.

"Are you next?" she said.

"Yeah." I sighed. "You?"

She explained she was waiting for an audition for an upcoming tour, and I immediately recognized her, though she looked much younger without makeup. I was standing next to Natascha Zchestakova. She was a prima…the top spot. A pang of envy flashed through me as I glanced at the panel sitting behind a table in the center of the room. Their faces were blank, distant. They appeared bored and unimpressed by the unbelievable talent I saw in the room.

"Navarro," Federico called.

Natascha gave my hand a squeeze. "*Merde*," she said, the signature good-luck wish in the ballet world, and smiled. "You'll do great. I saw you warming up. Just watch your feet. Federico pays close attention to that."

"Thanks." I swallowed hard. Inside my chest, my heart hammered in anticipation.

Federico waved for me to approach, frowning at the list he was holding. He then looked up at me. "Are you Inés's daughter?"

"Yes, sir." I locked my jaw, holding his gaze.

"She didn't tell me you were coming. How wonderful to have you here. How is your mother?"

"Fine. She's fine." A low mumble buzzed in the back of the room, and Madame quickly hushed them. I had forbidden Mamá to tell anyone about my audition for this exact reason. Fire burned inside me as I took my place. I closed my eyes, summoning the feelings from the salsa dance with Marcos.

From the center of the room, I gazed at my reflection in the mirror before I began, studying the frightened ballerina staring back at me. Pulling every muscle against gravity, I let out a slow breath, repeating to myself: *You were trained for this moment.* This was it. The opportunity I had been rehearsing for my whole life.

In the seconds of stillness preceding the piano, I straightened my shoulders, fighting back my nerves, and stood in fifth, one leg in front of the other, waiting for the music. In the mirror, I spotted Marcos standing in the back, smiling at me.

"*Merde*," he mouthed.

Two weeks later, I got the good news. I had been accepted into the summer intensive that potentially could earn me a permanent position in the cast. Nata was the first person I called. She said we had good karma. She also had gotten the prima role on the tour.

The summer was harder than I could have ever imagined. The nails on my big toes bled constantly, until they finally gave up and fell off. At night, my ankles screamed from the hours spent en pointe. I wrapped them in ice, clenching my teeth until I was numb. Every morning, I mended my battered body, stretched through my yoga routine, and started anew. And no matter how miserable I felt, I never let Madame see my pain.

Nata was my rock, encouraging me and giving me pointers to endure the evolving physical torture.

Those first days with the company were long, merciless. The only reward was knowing I was breaking through new physical and mental barriers. A snapshot of what my future could be.

It was the last day of that summer, when a thin envelope from the Colón Theater finally came. With trembling fingers, I opened the letter. I didn't get past the first line before it all blurred. A contract in black and white to join the permanent corps de ballet. I wanted to scream, but my throat was thick. There it was. I was finally holding the beginning of my dream in my hand.

My parents' home in the suburbs meant a forty-five-minute commute in a jam-packed train, and my days at the theater started early. Nata saw the dark circles under my eyes after the first few weeks and seemed genuinely worried. She lived in a small penthouse a few blocks from the theater and insisted I moved in with her. I had stayed over a few times before, but I had no money for rent, and I was no freeloader.

"You can't do this if you don't sleep," she nagged in between classes.

Then one day, Madame snapped at me in front of the class for being late. I had gotten up early as usual, but the subways were on strike, and even in a taxi that cost me a fortune, I was fifteen minutes late. At the break, Nata pulled me aside.

"That's it. You're moving in with me," she growled. "And I will hear nothing of it."

Sharing an apartment with Nata meant abiding by her strict rules of punctuality. And I wish I could say I got better as the months went by. But I had inherited the gene of complete untidiness from my father, and no matter how hard I fought it for Nata's sake, I was always missing something crucial as we were walking out the door. It drove Nata crazy, and the morning of the casting announcement was no different.

"I'm not kidding, I will leave without you," she yelled from the hall while I scrambled to get the last of my stuff in my bag.

"Coming," I yelled.

"You are a typical third child. You have the Youngest Child Syndrome. Nobody will cut you slack here." She shut the elevator door and assessed her makeup in the mirror.

"I'm not the youngest, my brother is," I said, even though she already knew that. I searched my bag. Where the hell was my other leg warmer? Shit, I could've sworn they were both in here yesterday. I smelled the one I had in my hand and made a face. Nata caught me from the mirror and shook her head in defeat.

I was more disorganized than usual, and I blamed it on stress—and not on the images of the stranger with clear blue eyes, that had been haunting my thoughts since yesterday. Rehearsals would begin as soon as casting was posted. *Giselle* was my favorite ballet, but also one of the most challenging productions of the season. Many roles would be assigned, and that meant new opportunities for getting noticed. So in the last two weeks, the atmosphere in the company had been...tense to say the least.

As Nata and I made our way through the hallway, my stomach immediately knew what was going on. A cloud of dancers hovered around the announcement board.

Nata squeezed my wrist and whispered, "It's out."

Chapter 3

"Let's go see what we got." Nata grinned. Of course, she was grinning. She would get the lead as Giselle. I, on the other hand, would be lucky to get a row-leading role in the corps.

"You go. I'll let you surprise me." I feigned a smile and she nudged me.

"You're so self-deprecating. If you want them to believe in you, you have to start with this." She tapped my temple with her index, then calmly made her way to the board.

I stood a few steps behind, chewing on my lip. She was right. But it was tough to envision a clear career path to New York when I was consistently cast as another faceless tutu in the background.

Nata's head suddenly turned toward me, her eyes wide. Cutting through the group, she moved cautiously to me.

"Surprise, surprise. You got Giselle?" I smirked.

Her hands gripped my shoulders. "Yes. And you, my friend, are the understudy for Queen Myrta."

"Right."

"Camila!" she snapped.

I frowned, all the air leaving my body at once as I scanned the faces of the dancers behind her. Two girls from the corps scowled at me.

"You're not joking."

"Of course, I'm not joking."

"Holy shit," I mumbled. Inside my chest, a Brazilian Carnaval exploded.

Marcos was leaning on the studio door frame, arms crossed at the chest, a wide grin stretching his mouth.

"You did it, Cams." He pulled me into his arms, and the world came to a stop. Every one of my cells was suddenly awake. I blushed furiously, feeling myself liquify. His smell, his warmth. It was all lethal. "Drinks later?" he said, kissing my temple as he pulled away. "We have to celebrate this one."

"Yeah, later. Let's go." Nata ushered us to the studio where most dancers had already gathered.

Federico stood beside Madame, facing us from the mirror. He waited for the commotion to settle as everyone took a seat on the floor.

The epitome of a retired, decorated dancer, Federico was dressed in his usual black T-shirt and slacks, leaning back on the barre. His silver hair was the perfect length, somewhere between disciplined and artistic. His mouth was curved slightly at the corner, as if he were enjoying a private joke while those piercing blue eyes of his watched us with devilish amusement.

"Settle down, people. Time is an expensive commodity and we don't have much. We will begin rehearsals for *Giselle* right away. Madame and I have chosen the cast carefully, so if you're surprised or in any way disappointed with your role, I suggest you get over it quickly and put your energy in the work you have ahead. I will hear no complaints nor tolerate any grudges or attitude. Understood?"

I studied the other dancers' faces. Several looked down, some with disappointment, but everyone nodded. For productions like *Giselle,* there was a lot of work to be done and no time for grudges. Besides, what was the point?

Federico briefly explained the schedule's basic logistics. The demands of a production this large were extensive, so the company had two casts to accommodate the numerous performances. Dancing in First Cast was a privilege; it meant performing on both opening and closing nights.

I still couldn't breathe. I had a standard role in the corps with First Cast but had also been given the understudy for Queen Myrta, an important solo role. Normally a principal would understudy, but nobody questioned Federico's decisions—it would mean professional suicide.

Everyone took their places at the barre for the morning class with Madame Vronsky. As he headed to the door, I hurried to catch up with Federico.

"I...Thank you. I'm so surprised, and grateful. I promise I'll make you proud."

He nodded. "There's a lot you haven't shown us yet, and I'm confident the best is yet to come. It's in your genes." He smiled warmly, then walked out. A familiar weight pressed down on my chest at that last sentence. Madame paused beside me as she made her way to the front.

"Genes mean nothing, Navarro. You will have to work very hard. I hope you are well aware of that," she said in a chillingly calm voice. "Now, I suggest you take your place at the barre before somebody else claims it."

"Congratulations, Navarro," a girl who was slightly my senior in the corps line said from behind me.

"Thanks." I took a cleansing breath and thought of Nata's words of wisdom. *I* had to believe I could do this. Straightening my back, I strode to my spot with my chin up. *Yes.* I would prove to Madame I belonged here. Whatever it took, I would do it. And I would show Federico that regardless of my genes, I was the best choice for the role of Queen Myrta. All I had to do was radiate grace in every single movement to make it look perfect and effortless. That was key. Madame always said things like "The public pays to see perfection."

The day was a marathon: classes followed by rundowns of complex schedules, then rehearsals with the new choreographer where expectations were quickly laid out. Diving into the assigned roles as fast as possible and full focus during the first days were critical.

The last class ended, and the room buzzed with activity as the dancers dispersed, hatching plans for the night.

I was stretching one last time when I caught a glimpse of two Russian principals in the hallway. The Russian Ballet was on a one-week tour in Buenos Aires and was using the Colón's studios to rehearse. I was dying to meet them, especially because my childhood idol, Irina Baranova, was the prima on the tour. I had tried casually running into her between rehearsals earlier that week, but in the theater environment, the Russian principals kept to themselves and didn't mingle with the locals. Maybe I could get Nata to introduce me. I glanced over. She and Marcos were deep into the evening logistics with Diego and Carla, two new principals, discussing a new bar in Palermo Hollywood.

I listened to them absentmindedly, unwrapping the ribbons from my ankles. I honestly didn't get how they had it in them to go out after a brutal day like today. I winced as I plucked a blood-blotched piece of tape off my toes. They couldn't pay me to move another muscle. My plans for the evening were a shower and zoning out in front of the TV.

"Let's check out that new bar first. Then we can loop back and hit the Roxy." Marcos flicked damp strands of chestnut hair off his forehead. "That way we'll also skip those stiff-ass kids from Zona Norte. Nico works the door tonight, so we'll get in after two for sure."

Carla rolled her eyes as she slipped into her sweats. "Marcos, you're such a snob. Besides, if Nata and I go, we can get in *anytime*." She gave him a smug grin.

She was right. A dancer in a short dress and killer heels was a VIP pass anywhere. Plus, Carla and Nata were ridiculously hot. It was a given they would get in wherever, whenever they wanted.

Marcos eyed me from the mirror. "What do you think, Cams?"

"I think…it's Tuesday and you guys are planning to meet at two in the morning. That is so off my chart right now."

Marcos tsked his tongue in dismissal and went back to the planning. As principals, these guys were used to partying and being up for class the next day. I, on the other hand, was a nobody with a lot to prove, so I only went out on weekends and carefully planned my hours of sleep.

"Nata. Your vote decides, then," Marcos said.

Nata rolled up her leg warmers and tucked them into her bag. "Hm. The Roxy *is* lame before two a.m."

"Fine. Get Cams to come. Her social life worries me." Marcos smirked.

"Nope," I said. "I'm going to bed."

"Bummer. Chicks dig me even more when they see me with a hot girl. Guess these two hens will have to do."

Nata stuck her tongue out at him, and Carla kicked him as she walked past. He gave them that smug-bastard grin of his and kissed my head before throwing his dance bag over his shoulder and heading out.

I watched him go, and the familiar longing coiled in my stomach.

Marcos Sánz. Sigh. I had vowed long ago that I wouldn't date people I worked with, and Marcos was a threat to that vow. An experienced principal, Marcos was also the most sought-after dancer in the company. I was fascinated by the aura of greatness that radiated from him. His presence was striking: a dizzying combination of devilish arrogance and flawless grace. Confident and charismatic, he could instantly dissolve any girl's resolve by flashing his South American-Zeus smile—which he did all the time. After that first day at the auditions, he had become my best guy-friend. Not my choice, but I went with it.

A sweaty towel hit me on the face, snapping me back to the present.

"Hellouuu? Come along, Cami," Nata said. "You need to get that skinny ass out. How will you meet the man of your dreams if you never come out with us?" Her deep blue eyes mocked me from the mirror.

Clenching my teeth, I threw my leg warmers and towel in my bag as fast as I could. I had already met the man of my dreams, and I really didn't need new visuals of him making out with other women.

"Come on," she went on, her tone softer at the realization she had put her foot in her mouth. "We're going for a quick drink downstairs, and then everyone goes home to shower and get ready."

"Thanks, but I'm sitting this one out. My feet are killing me. You guys go. I'll take a cab home."

The moment I stepped out into the damp evening, my plan to grab a cab evaporated. Shit. Rush hour. The streets glimmered in a sea of scarlet dragonflies blinking to a distorted symphony of horns. Ignoring my throbbing feet, I tossed my dance bag over my shoulder and set off to trek the ten blocks to my apartment.

By the time I got home, I was chilled to the bone. The blisters on my feet reminded me that walking home after work was never a good plan. I kicked off my sneakers, peeled off my sweat-drenched clothes, and stood under a scalding shower, letting the aches and fatigue melt away.

I was getting into my pj's when Nata stormed in. While she showered, I heated up Thai leftovers and set the plates on the kitchen counter.

Dinner was our usual time to catch up on the day's happenings. Now that the excitement had begun to settle, she asked how I was doing with the understudy news.

"I'm super thrilled and a bit terrified. Myrta's so cool," I said, squishing the last morsels of rice under my fork. "The ghost queen of the dead damsels. Hungry for revenge." I smiled, but when I looked up at Nata, she was watching me with a pensive expression. Shit. I could never hide my feelings from her. My smile vanished and I exhaled. "Okay, I underplayed the terrified bit. I'm freaking out. It's not only my first understudy for a principal role, Myrta is a *huge* deal. She's dark, cryptic, and I feel like in order to fully get into it, I have to understand her first."

"Are you wishing you had your heart broken?"

I shrugged. "You know I've never been in a real relationship. Marcelo Cavallieri in high school doesn't count."

"*Of course* he counts. He broke your heart."

"It was a long time ago. I actually cared more about the humiliation of being dumped than I did about him."

"I see...so you're wishing somebody broke your heart for real?"

Nata wasn't aware of how I felt for Marcos. Yes, I was familiar with the heartaches of unrequited love...but Myrta was also all about rage and revenge.

"Honestly, it would help at this point. I'm desperate. Federico's betting his chips on me, and it's obvious Vronsky has reservations about that decision. I feel the rope around my neck."

"Cami, you are always your own worst enemy. Federico knows what he's doing. You should trust that."

"Giving the daughter of Inés Navarro a crack at it?"

Nata rolled her eyes. "Stop. You know it's not uncommon for him and Vronsky to debate about who gets cast. She'll come along. Whoever your mother is, you have what it takes and work harder than most of the principals in the company. She knows it."

She left to get ready for the night out. While I did the dishes, I thought about Federico and wondered if his decision to cast me as Myrta had been an impulse, or if Nata was right and he actually saw potential I hadn't discovered yet. I needed to nail this part. It wouldn't be easy, and it certainly didn't help that so many of my coworkers would be perched on a wire waiting for me to screw it up.

Nata walked out of her room twenty minutes later, looking like a badass comic heroine. She was wearing a platinum, skinny dress and strappy sandals. Her waist-long, red hair was pulled back in a high ponytail, a single brushstroke of furious copper.

"You sure?" she said. "You have time to change still."

"Totally, one million percent."

She blew me a kiss, and I waved her off, glad to have the place to myself. Cuddling in a blanket, I surfed through the TV stations and stopped at *Man of Steel*. Perfect. Nothing like an evening with Henry Cavill to take my mind off everything.

I jolted awake, disoriented, and rubbed my eyes. What time was it? The rattling vibration of my phone against the coffee table jabbed at my nerves. Glaring at the screen, I snatched it up. Nata.

"What."

"Oh, cool, you're awake." Her high-pitched voice blasted through the phone, making me cringe. A high tempo beat pulsed in the background. "Come over to the Roxy. It's crazy here tonight!"

"Jesus, Nata. I was sleeping." I sighed heavily so she could hear my irritation.

She ignored me and went on, "and oh my God, we met these Brazilians, and man, can they dance. Get over here. Now."

"I'm in my pj's, and it is two a.m. on a Tuesday. There's no way in hell. Are you out of your mind?"

"Irina is here."

I straightened. "What?"

"I don't know how long she'll be here. Hurry!"

I was fully awake. Irina Baranova, my childhood muse was at the Roxy.

Nata kept rambling, a bit buzzed, "I can send Alexei to get you. Grab anything you want from my closet." Her slurry voice filtered through the deafening music.

"I'll take a cab. See you in a few." I hung up.

It was almost two thirty in the morning when the cab dropped me off at the Roxy. Nico stood crossed armed, blocking the door, and flashed a wicked smile at my solo appearance. He was Marcos's cousin, and the kind of guy you wanted to know if you lived in a city like Buenos Aires, where nights were not an end to the day but a magic playground with a gazillion possibilities waiting. Without the right connections, there was no chance to get into the places that make the nightlife famous, like the Roxy. So, to us, Nico was our golden key.

His smile grew as I approached. "Hey. Camila, right? Looking sexy tonight. Here to give all those fools a run for their money? I warn you, Marcos showed up in very good company."

"Cut it out." I half chuckled to hide the way those words stabbed me. "Marcos and I are *not* together. Where is he?"

"He went in with Nata and the others about an hour ago. Came to check on him?" He winked.

"Yup. That's it. I came to pull him out by the hair."

"Second level!" he said as I walked into the club.

My favorite thing about the Roxy was the energy you felt the instant you walked through the door. The music vibrated from the walls, and you immediately became a part of it. There were three different levels—each with its own DJ and bar—so if you went from one floor to the other, both the music and the crowd changed completely.

Nata was surrounded by a group of what were, without a doubt, professional dancers. The Brazilians? As I got closer, I recognized two members of the Russian Ballet. The scene was beautiful and hypnotizing. They moved to the beat of the music, wrapping around Nata in sensual, effortless moves.

A few feet away was Marcos. Nico hadn't lied. He was sandwiched between two girls in tiny dresses who looked determined to win his attention. The old dagger in my heart sank a little deeper. I looked back at Nata. She had clearly made a new BFF and was now tangled around him. When she saw me, she hurried my way, tugging her boy by the hand.

"Cami, this is Teo. Teo, meet Cami, my best buddy."

Teo hugged me warmly and gave me a soft peck on the cheek. "*Eai tudo bom?* Great to meet you." He winked. His mouth stretched into an infectious smile every time he looked at Nata.

"Great to meet you too." I nodded, then turned to Nata. "Where is Irina?"

She gave Teo a soft peck on the lips. "I'll be back in a sec."

"Moving fast, are we?" I said as we reached the upper level. She dismissed me with a quick flick of the hand.

In the dance floor, Irina's platinum hair lashed about as she whipped her head to the beat of the music. Nata tugged me by the hand as we rushed over, nearly bumping into her.

"Irina, this is Camila. She's going to be a principal with the company soon," Nata blurted in her tipsy state.

"Nata!" I growled between my teeth. She pinched my back, her way to tell me to shut up.

Irina pulled me into her arms, a bit tipsy herself as she slurred something in Russian. She then held my face in her hand, crooning something else I couldn't understand. Her eyes were glassy, her breath laced with sugar and rum. She then gave me a sly smile and bit her lip. I blinked, unsure what to say.

"She just invited you to her villa in the south of France," Nata said into my ear while she gripped my arm to pull me away. "We'll be back," she said to Irina, who got lost in her dance again. Nata dragged me back to the Brazilians.

"Nata, you made me come all the way here, and I didn't even get to talk to her. Jesus, what's the rush?" I shouted in her ear. Nata shook her head, then turned abruptly, causing me to bump into her.

"She was hitting on you, big time. Be glad you don't speak Russian."

"Who cares? I just wanted to meet her. We could've invited her to the bar to have a drink with us."

"Maybe later this week. We'll get her after one of their rehearsals. I'll figure something out. But you need training before facing a Russian prima."

A Foo Fighters song started playing. Before I could protest, Teo and his friends gathered around us and quickly took command of the floor. I was suddenly surrounded by Brazilians and had a mojito in each hand. For a little while, I let myself go and not agonize about my self-imposed curfew. Brazilians have the power of making you believe there's nothing in the world worth worrying about. I closed my eyes and surrendered to their spell.

After a few more songs, I decided it was time to go. I was parched and needed water. I spotted Irina dancing with two skeletal girls who had to be models, and I debated whether I should give it another try and make getting out of bed worth it. But Irina leaned to one of the girls and kissed her on the mouth. Oh, *Do not disturb*. I set off toward the lounge…and the exit.

A crowd of sweaty bodies spilled over the bar. Tomi, the bartender, acknowledged my gesture and handed me a water. He waved off my intent to pay, so I blew him a kiss and scurried to a quiet corner. Leaning against a column, I people-watched as the fatigue from the long day crept up my legs. My watch said 3:00 a.m. Crap. Every second I was here meant lost sleep. It was time to give up on Irina and go home.

"This is a cool place," said a husky voice beside me. I turned my head to see if he was talking to me. A guy in a ponytail stood a few steps away, watching the crowd with a beer in his hand. He smiled when our eyes met. He was kind of scrawny, dressed in leather pants and a black T-shirt, but he had a sexy, badass thing going. His arms were toned and heavily tattooed. He looked like the bass player in a band.

I gave him a quick nod and looked away, letting him know I wasn't in the mood for making friends. These guys were all after the one-night fling. He took a step closer and I straightened up, ready to split.

"Can I buy you a real drink?" He nodded at my bottle of water. "Are you here with someone?"

"Yup. Here with friends. This is my last drink, thanks. I'm going home." As I downed the last of the water, he stepped closer and rested his hand by my head on the column, effectively trapping me. I pressed myself back against the bricks, and he smiled seductively, his slightly crooked teeth an understated weapon.

"You are beautiful. Don't leave." His chestnut eyes darkened, every inch of him exuding seduction, but the musky scent of his cologne was way too strong. It reminded me of bug repellent.

I ducked under his arm. "I'm not interested, okay?"

"How do you know?" His eyebrow arched.

"I just know."

He opened his mouth, then tensed when he looked past my shoulder. His expression hardened.

"Shame," he murmured, his eyes still focused on something behind me as he slowly straightened and turned away. I watched him go, intrigued. *What a night.* I turned to leave and slammed into a wall. *What the—* The wall stepped back and I jumped. *Holy fuck.* My whole body froze at the pair of eyes locked on mine.

Those eyes.

I couldn't hear the music anymore. The people, the noise, the lights—it all faded into a blur. The only thing that was one hundred percent sharp in HD was the hot stranger from that morning standing in front of me. He smiled, sending a tornado to my stomach.

"What are you doing here?" The words snapped out of me before I realized them.

"The same as you, I suppose." This time he smiled fully. His voice was deep, magnetic. I felt it everywhere. Shit.

"Right…" I said, glad it was dark. My face felt like a burning meteorite.

"I see you've got both shoes with you now. That's a good sign."

Snarky bastard. Like I needed another one of those around. My mouth fell slack and I snapped it closed, wishing I could wipe off that smug expression of his. He looked yummy in jeans and a gray linen shirt, sleeves rolled up in that way that hinted at those roped, tanned arms. Ugh. Why did this guy unhinge me like this? I tilted my head, reining in my wits.

"Helpful *and* funny. Charming combination." I gave him a saccharine smile.

He let out a throaty laugh, showcasing perfect teeth. I narrowed my eyes. But, damn, that same strange electricity from the moment we met tingled under my skin. It was unnerving. He was probably used to having this effect on every girl.

"You shouldn't be wandering alone. Aren't you here with friends?" His tone was commanding, almost sulky.

I frowned. "Excuse me?"

"You are tempting fate."

I scoffed. What the hell did that mean? Why did this guy think I needed babysitting? We locked eyes for a moment. The changing lights in the darkness cast shadows on his sharp features, making him look sexy, powerful, *and exasperating*.

"You're just bait for guys like that."

"Guys like who?"

"Ponytail Guy." He nodded. "He's in one of the bands that played here tonight. He's no good outside music, I would stay clear."

"Would you? Well, thank you, but I'm perfectly capable of taking care of myself."

He looked in the direction the guy had left, and something chilling crossed his eyes.

"You shouldn't be here alone," he said. "Find your friends." Then he simply turned and disappeared.

I stood there, speechless, feeling like I'd been sent to the principal's office. Fuckdammit.

I stormed back to find Nata and Marcos. I couldn't figure out why I was mad, but I was. Really mad. Marcos snatched my hand, pulling me to him. *Augh, Marcos.*

"Play along," he said, brushing his lips against my ear. His breath was warm, tickling my neck with the fresh scent of mint from the mojitos. His arms enveloped me and I immediately unhinged, the incident with Mr. Rude and Bossy forgotten. I closed my eyes, spellbound.

"Is she looking?" he whispered in my ear.

"Who?"

"The blonde with the red dress, behind me."

"I don't—"

"How about the other one? The brunette? Maybe I should ditch them both. This is too much work."

"Marcos, you're an infant. Look at them, they're both totally into you. What more do you want?"

"Shhh…Stay here with me, like this." His lips found my neck again and pressed a soft kiss, sending shivers everywhere. This night is cursed. I tried to break away, but his arm held me securely against him. "Wait."

I sighed in defeat, leaning my forehead against his. I could seriously not pack any more into one day.

"Marcos…"

"Yeah, yeah. We are friends," he whispered. Then he flashed a devilish grin. "That blonde wants me. You want in on a threesome?"

"Dude, you're all sweaty. Gross," I said and pushed him away. He narrowed his eyes, biting a smile. I knew that look. Payback would come my way later.

This is how it was between Marcos and me. He teased me and I let him. Even though he wasn't in love with me, I knew he loved what we had as much as I did. While he went through girls like an ATM machine spitting out bills, our friendship stayed stable. I told myself that was enough for now.

All the aches in my body screamed at once. My head pulsed with exhaustion. It was half past three and I needed sleep. I spotted Nata, who was still all over Teo, and gave her a quick wave. She said something into his ear, then cut through the crowd.

"You're not thinking of going home by yourself, are you?" she shouted in my face. The pounding music throbbed in my head.

"It's fine." I yawned. I was used to coming and going alone, even at night. As the middle child in a family of four and growing up in the city, I wasn't afraid to fly solo.

"No way, I'll come with you. Just give me a minute." She turned away.

"No," I said, grabbing her arm. "I'll get an Uber, or Nico will get me a radio cab. I'll be home in five minutes. You're having fun. Stay. Really, I'll be fine." I squeezed her in a quick hug, then gestured for her to go.

She hesitated. Nata always worried about me going around alone. She was sort of a safety freak, and it clearly ran in the family. Her brother, Sergei, and his friends were always hovering in the background. They were a peculiar bunch, the Russians. Skinny, pale, angular jaws with five o'clock stubbles. Sunken eyes like they had been up all night. But something in the way they looked at you warned you to keep your distance. Sergei looked like he could kick your ass even though he was small and wiry. I felt safe when they were around. From a distance, they seemed like friends hanging out together. Nata's father was a diplomat and ran an import business of some sort, so she always had protection. I suspected there was more to it, that the usual guys she kept around were on a payroll. Nata never said much, and when I asked, she was always vague. "Pappa is careful. That's all," she would say. I didn't give it much thought. Even *I* knew running a successful business in Buenos Aires could be...legally complicated. As far as I was concerned, sharing a killer apartment downtown with my best friend, cheap rent, and the added bonus of a bunch of badasses watching your back were a super sweet deal.

That night it was Alexei shadowing Nata. He was new and looked like a redheaded giant, too hairy in all the wrong places. He had a permanent scowl and eyed everyone suspiciously. Nata gestured toward him.

"Alexei will drive you and come back after."

"No thanks. I'll just have Nico get me a cab."

Nata rolled her eyes. "Will you stop being difficult? Alexei is *fine.*" We both looked at him just in time to catch him check his teeth on his phone.

I smirked. "I think he should stay with you."

Nata laughed. "Okay, but you swear, and I mean you *swear* you'll have Nico call you a cab. Don't Uber at this hour and *do not* walk alone."

Chapter 4

I elbowed my way out through the bodies still packed at the door. I felt bad for them. No way they would make it in. The basic rule for nightclubs was that if you didn't get in within the first five minutes, you'd better try elsewhere. I slipped into my leather jacket and glanced over at Nico, shielded behind a cloud of hovering girls. They always fit the same profile: scarlet lipstick, impossible heels, indecently short dresses offering a generous view of natural or enhanced cleavages. Anything they could use to wear down a bouncer's guard.

Uber had a thirty-minute wait, and getting to Nico would require some work, so I figured it would be quicker to get my own taxi. Just a block away around the corner was the taxi stop we always went to when we came here. Pablo, the owner, was a Peruvian guy in his fifties who reminded me of my father. He had seven kids and always made sure Nata and I got a safe ride home. He only hired drivers he would trust with one of his kids.

I set off in a fast walk, an old Serú Girán tune fading behind me. Damned heels. My feet throbbed and I wanted to kick my shoes off. A mound of trash bags piled up on the sidewalk made me think better of it. Just as I turned the corner, heavy steps approached from behind me. A shiver flew up my back.

"Hey, wait up," a husky, deep voice called. I doubled my steps, but he quickly caught up with me. "Hey, it's me. From the Roxy."

I turned my head and a vague sense of relief washed through me when I recognized Ponytail Guy.

"Oh...um...what...what are you doing here?" I asked without stopping. I could see the lights from Pablo's taxi stop ahead.

"Do you need a ride?" He quickly matched my pace.

"Huh? No, thanks, I'm good."

"Really?" He stepped in front of me, forcing me to stop. "I can't give you a ride? I mean...You're alone." He tilted his head. Cold fear rose up my back. I scanned the deserted street behind him. Shit. In the young hours of the morning, the city had fallen asleep.

"There's a taxi stop at the next corner. I'm good, really," I said, stepping around him. A heavy mist saturated the air, and I pulled up my collar to block the chill.

"Babe, I have a car." He followed, again. "We can go out for a drink. It's not late."

I sighed in irritation and hurried, but he stood in front of me again. Motherfucking night. Damn Nata, Irina, and the Russians.

"Dude," I said, managing a steady tone to hide the panic swelling in my chest. "I told you before. I'm not interested. I have an early day tomorrow, and I'd rather take a cab." I dodged him, but his hand caught my elbow.

"One drink. I promise I'm worth it."

I pulled my arm away, but he was strong and gripped me harder. Our eyes locked and his pupils darkened. A new surge of panic quickened my pulse.

"Let go right now or I'll fucking scream," I growled through my teeth.

He smiled, amused.

"Let go." I tugged away from him, but he yanked hard on my arm and wrapped his free arm around my waist, pressing me against him. I pushed back, but he locked me in his arms, blocking my attempts to get free of him.

"Don't be such a tease, baby. Though it would be fun to tame you," he said too close to my face. His beer-reeking breath brought a wave of nausea to my stomach.

"Fuck you," I said, seething, adrenaline charging through me. Fear traveled through my legs, and I prayed they wouldn't give.

"Well...that would be my pleasure." He laughed, pressing me tighter against him. He was hard, and it sent bile up my throat. *No.* I was small but strong, and I knew a couple of self-defense moves. Summoning all my will, I stomped on his foot as hard as I could, digging my four-inch heel into his Vans.

"Ow!" He loosened his grip and, pushing back with all I had, I shoved my knee to his groin. He screeched, keeling over in pain. I bolted forward, but he launched himself at me from behind, yanking my hair. I let out a yelp. He wrapped his arm around me while his other hand covered my mouth. His palm drowned my scream, and I couldn't breathe. I fought him off as tears of anger and frustration streamed down my cheeks. But my attempts to get him off me were futile. His hot, putrid breath panted against my neck. I thought I was going to vomit.

"You fucking bitch," he gasped against my ear. I squeezed my eyes shut and felt him smile. "You're mine, now."

"You have exactly one second to get away from her," a low voice growled from behind. Ponytail Guy startled, his grip relaxing. He turned to face the— oh my fucking god—hot and unnerving stranger from the nightclub—and the street that morning—Jesus, rescuing me—again? Relief washed through me.

"Palacios. What the fuck do you want?" Ponytail Guy said, tightening his grip on my arm.

"Step away, Danny. Now."

Ponytail Guy—Danny, chuckled. "We were just having a chat."

"Well, it's over." The stranger—*Palacios*? But to me he was The Guy— watched Danny impassively. Anger flashed in his eyes as he assessed me. "You okay?"

With Danny's hand still covering my mouth, I nodded.

"Let her go." His voice was low, guarded. "Now."

"I don't think so. Besides…I'm getting goddamn tired of you calling the shots, Palacios. In fact, I think it's time you fuck off." Danny let go of me abruptly and pulled a utility knife from his pocket, snapping it open.

I swallowed the tightness in my throat and stumbled back, panting. Without turning, his hand caught my arm again. The Guy's eyes locked on that hand and narrowed.

"Danny," he said in a contained voice, "I'm not going to tell you again. Don't make me have to teach you manners."

"*Manners*? Without your bodyguards? That, I wanna see. Let's go, Palacios. Show me what you got." He abruptly let me go and I stumbled back. My heel caught a crack in the sidewalk, and I fell, rolling my ankle. Shit. Hot pain lanced through my leg, and I prayed I hadn't sprained it as I dragged myself away from them, clutching my ankle. The Guy's gaze followed me, irritation flashing in his pale irises, then went back to Danny.

"Go home," The Guy said in a controlled voice.

"I don't think so." Danny pounced at The Guy, slicing the air with the knife. The Guy swung back and dodged the blade without even moving his feet. He wasn't armed but didn't look at all intimidated.

"Fucker." Danny snarled. He aimed the knife at The Guy's stomach, but he wasn't quick enough. The blade didn't come close to touching The Guy, who stepped forward and, with a swift move, gripped Danny's wrist, forcing him to drop the knife. Before Danny could react, The Guy kicked the weapon away. He was calm, in control. He also seemed…annoyed.

Danny swung his free fist at The Guy's face, but with another stealth maneuver, The Guy turned him around and wrapped his arm around Danny's neck. Danny tried forcing his way out of the headlock but couldn't move at all. His face was flushed, the veins in his forehead popping out with rage as The Guy gripped him firmly, waiting him out. Danny's eyelids grew heavy, and after a few seconds, they fully closed and his body went limp. I watched with a mix of horror and fascination. I had seen people do that in movies, but I never knew stuff like that actually worked in real life.

The Guy let Danny's unconscious body drop to the ground, then turned his attention to me.

"You okay?"

I nodded.

"You hurt your ankle?"

"Um…yes. Is he…?"

"Just passed out. Your ankle…" He nodded. "Is it the same one from yesterday?"

"Yeah. It hurts, but I don't think it's sprained." I tried standing, but pain blazed up my leg. Shit. Maybe it was sprained. Fuckdammit. I couldn't be injured. Not now.

"Let me help you." He leaned down, easing my arm over his shoulder. He was much taller, so I had to adjust my arm over his and wrap it around his neck. A wave of that familiar body wash slammed over me, and my eyes instinctively closed. His body radiated heat, and I shivered at the contrast with the cold of the pavement. He held me in place as I tested my weight on my foot. A new wave of pain spread up my leg, but it was bearable.

"Can you walk?"

"I think so. But I need to ice it."

"That fucking scumbag," he muttered. "What are you doing walking alone at this hour, crazy girl?" His tone was soft, concerned. "There are assholes like him everywhere in this city." He sighed in frustration.

"You have to stop doing this," I said.

"Doing what?"

"Scooping me off the street," I said in an attempt to shake away the tremors inside me. Adrenaline still pulsed through my limbs.

"I promise to stop scooping you off the street if you promise to stop ending up there."

"Deal."

"Deal." His hand held me firmly against him. He was strong, and the muscles on his back were rock-hard. The warmth from his body against mine was comforting. He turned, heading in the direction of the club.

"What are you doing?" I halted, clutching his shirt. He looked down at me and frowned.

"I'm taking you back to the Roxy, to your friends?"

"Oh, no, no. I don't want to go back there."

"Why?"

"Because my roommate will flip out and make a huge deal out of this. I'd rather go home. I just need ice, and I'll be like new. I was heading over to the taxi stop in the next corner. I know the owner there."

He hesitated for a moment, then fished his phone out of his pocket and pressed it to his ear. "I'm at the corner of Humboldt and Córdoba." Without another word, he hung up.

In less than two minutes, a black BMW pulled over and skidded to a stop. A large shadow emerged from the driver's seat. He reminded me of Nico guarding the door at the Roxy, his massive frame discernible even under his leather jacket. He rounded the car and paused, glaring at Danny's unconscious body on the ground. His gaze flew to me, then to The Guy.

"Who's that?" He nodded to Danny.

"He's in Charlie's band. *Was*, after tonight."

The bodyguard scowled. "I could've taken care of him."

"It's fine. He went down easy." Just as he said that, Danny squirmed about as he came back into consciousness. The bodyguard took a step toward him.

"Want me to call the boys?"

The boys? Fuck, who was this guy?

"Nah," The Guy answered. "Not worth it. Have Tano take him back to the club. I'll deal with him later."

The bodyguard made a call that lasted less than thirty seconds while The Guy stepped to the car and opened the back door. I peered up at him. Whoever he was, there had to be a damn good reason for him to need a bodyguard. A shiver ran through me.

"You're safe with me. Let me take you home," he said in a soft tone, reading my thoughts. I stared at him blankly.

"Um…Thanks, but I think I'll get a cab."

He frowned. "Why?"

"I just…" I sighed. "Look, I can't get in your car. I don't know you, and I've maxed out on stupid decisions tonight. I'll get a taxi at Pablo's stop over there."

He ran a quick hand through his sable hair, and even the way he did that was sexy. "Okay." He gave a quick nod to the muscleman behind me. "Wait for Tano, then meet me at the taxi stop on the corner."

In the small office, Pablo leaned back in his chair with his feet on the desk, earbuds in, watching a soccer game on a little TV that had seen better days. He straightened when he saw us, his eyes fleeting to The Guy. I felt relieved at the sight of a familiar face.

"Good evening." Pablo shook The Guy's hand, then turned to me and placed his hand on my shoulder. "Camila, *princesa*," he said, looking from me to The Guy as if to assess the situation. "It's late."

I forced a smile, but inside my heart was still pounding. I just wanted to go to bed.

"Hi, Pablo. It *is* late. Any drivers ready?"

Pablo's expression fell. "Not for another hour. I sent everyone home because Tuesdays are slow. I'm so sorry. I'll call you a radio taxi?"

"Why don't you let me take you home?" The Guy said.

I looked up at him and chewed on my lip.

"Look," he said. "I know you're shaken up. But I assure you, you're safe with me." His tone was confident, kind. Regardless of how insane this all was, I did feel safe in his presence. But I didn't trust my own feelings tonight.

"Thank you. You've done enough." I glanced over at Pablo. I knew he would intercede and say he would take care of my ride. But to my surprise, Pablo simply smiled.

"Camila, I've known Mr. Palacios for a very long time. You wouldn't be safer anywhere else. Let him take you home." He looked up at him. "She's like a daughter to me, this girl."

The Guy nodded, then said to me, "Are we good then?"

"Okay," I said.

At the curb, the black BMW waited. The Guy opened the door and slid in after me as I gave the driver my address.

We rode in comfortable silence. Exhaustion weighed me down, and I rested my head back on the seat. The car was warm, comfortable. It smelled like leather mixed with traces of his cologne.

"You okay?" he said softly.

"Sure. Actually, I had him, till you showed up." I smiled and he mirrored me. His mouth was sexy, dashing. "Anyway, thanks."

"Someone like you shouldn't walk alone at night. You need to be more careful." The tone of his voice was firm but gentle. "You'll feel better after you've slept."

A mix of emotions whirled inside me. Tears prickled under my lashes, and I nodded. God, *sleep*. A luxury at this point. I would be up in less than four hours. I rubbed the exhaustion from my eyes, eager to push the thought away. "You were calm back there," I said. "Even after that guy pulled out a knife. You weren't worried?"

"No."

Damn. Who was this guy? Everything about him exuded authority and confidence. The silent, but palpable demeanor of someone used to being in charge. Even in my current state, I found it sexy as hell.

Part of me wished it had been true that I could've handled Danny. I wanted to be able take care of myself without anyone's help. Maybe I should start taking boxing lessons. But when? My brain hurt.

"You had some impressive moves," I said. "Are you a black belt or something?"

"I am," he said. He didn't make it sound smug. Just a simple fact being stated.

"Well, I'm very impressed. And glad. Thank you." I smiled weakly.

We got to my place a few minutes later, and even though I knew I would pay for this long night tomorrow, something about him held my interest captive.

"This is me," I said. He followed me into the foyer.

"How do you feel? Do you need anything?" He squeezed my shoulder gently.

"A bed, a shower, ice packs. Oh, and…my night back would be awesome."

He half smiled. "How's your ankle?"

"I'll be fine. It's always my left one. It just needs ice." I looked up at him, racking my brain for words that would make this moment last longer. His eyes blazed, an uncharted hue of pale silver. He tilted his head, and a few disheveled strands hung over his forehead. I curled my fingers, fighting the urge to touch him. And that face. Holy shit. It was as if Michelangelo had sculpted a bad boy of a future era. Beautiful and dark. A perfect contradiction between good and evil. It then occurred to me that for the first time in over a year, someone other than Marcos had sparked my attention.

"Ok, then." He sighed, snapping me out of my daze. "You should lie down and rest. And no wandering alone at night anymore."

"I won't," I promised. "Look, I know that both times we met contradict this, but I'm normally smarter when it comes to my safety."

"Good." He nodded. "Try to get some sleep. And let's stop running into each other in these kinds of situations," he said with a hint of a smile.

"Thank you so much." A sudden impulse to wrap my arms around his neck and press myself against him washed through me. Our eyes met. *Don't go.*

As if he could read my thought, he pulled me into a careful embrace and kissed my forehead. My body trembled. I took a long breath, letting his scent fill my lungs. It was a mix of suede, lavender, and soap. What was it about this beautiful, enigmatic stranger that lured me in with a force I had never felt before? I didn't even know his full name.

X-Man, you have to have a name.

He squeezed me gently and broke away. "I better go. You need to rest."

"Wait," I snapped, suddenly aware I was clutching his shirt in my fist. The muscles in his chest were like granite under my knuckles. "Your name?" I cringed at how desperate I sounded. A cryptic smile played on his lips. It went straight to the pit of my stomach. Fascinating how he could change my breathing pattern with just a smile.

"I'm Sebastián."

"Sebastián." I tasted the word, letting it linger in my mouth.

"Yours?"

"Camila."

"Nice to meet you, Camila." He watched me for a moment, then reached in his pocket and pulled out his wallet. "Call me if you need anything," he said, handing me a business card. How formal. I took it between my fingers and caressed it. The paper was white linen, his name engraved in a black, minimalistic font.

Sebastián Palacios, Arquitecto.

An architect...It didn't at all fit with the image I had put together of him so far. Why would an architect need a bodyguard? He yanked me back from my thoughts when he kissed my cheek, sending chills down my neck.

"In you go," he whispered.

He waited for me to step into the foyer, then turned away and slid into the passenger seat of the BMW. I watched him go with a mixture of exhaustion, pain, and a strange thrill at the effect he seemed to have on me.

On the ride up in the elevator, my thoughts swirled around the events from the last half hour. What a bonehead move it had been to leave the Roxy alone. And how did...Sebastián know where to find me? Wait. Had he followed me out too? My head ached, and I closed my eyes, wishing the pounding away.

I stepped into my dark apartment, dreading being alone, though I knew Nata wouldn't be long. Locking the door behind me, I headed to the shower to wash away the past hour, or at least part of it.

It was almost 4:00 a.m. when the sound of a lock turning woke me. Nata and Marcos walked in with a bag of food, the warm smell of baked cheese instantly filling the apartment. Marcos usually crashed on our couch on the nights we went out together. I had fallen asleep in the main room sofa, waiting for them, the images from the ponytail creep haunting me. Marcos ran to the bathroom.

"Hey," I said in a raspy voice.

"You're still up." Nata set the bag onto the kitchen bar. My empty stomach growled.

"Yeah, I had a headache." I watched her unpack a salad and grease-blotched boxes while I eased back onto the couch. Everything was right because Nata and Marcos were here. Nothing could penetrate the bubble where the three of us existed.

"Man, what a night," she said.

"You have no idea," I muttered.

She glanced over at me and frowned, abruptly stopped opening boxes. "Why are you icing your ankle? Did you *fall?*"

"I did, but I'm okay. It's just my bad ankle."

"What happened?"

I darted a look at the takeout. I wanted that food. I *needed* that food. I rubbed my eyes. "I'm fine. I was just…going to get a cab when this guy started following me, saying he wanted to give me a ride."

Nata rushed over and sat beside me on the couch. "Dammit, Camila. You should have taken Alexei."

I let out a defeated sigh. "I know, I'm sorry. I didn't think I would need him."

"So, what happened?" she said. Marcos had emerged from the bathroom and was pouring himself a vodka.

"What happened to whom?" he said.

"Camila, she fell and sprained her ankle."

"It's not sprained."

Marcos approached, his jaw locked in that way it did when someone pissed him off. "What the fuck, Cams. Tell me what happened."

I gave them a quick rundown of the events and how Sebastián had ninja-ed the asshole down and left him unconscious, then escorted me home in a taxi.

Marcos flexed his knuckles. "We'll figure out who this Danny asshole is. I'll fuck him up, babe."

"That's sweet, but right now I'm hungry, and I don't want to talk about him. Can you just bring me an empanada?" I forced a smile.

"I should've come home with you." Nata shook her head in irritation, heading back to the kitchen bar.

"I'm fine, you guys. Really, it's not a big deal." I looked up at Marcos. "Any cheese ones in that box?"

He handed me a plate with two empanadas and sat next to me, tossing a bundle of crumpled-up napkins between us. "Careful, they're hot."

I gave him a grateful smile. I never had to explain much to Marcos. He leaned down and kissed the top of my head, then scooted closer so our bodies were pressed against each other. Tears threatened, but I held them back. I just wanted to curl onto Marcos's lap and have him lock those muscular arms around me, making me feel safe. I ate slowly while he devoured his food, his ruffled hair flopping onto his forehead. Nata brought her salad and sat beside us.

"I don't like that you walk alone so much," she said, stabbing lettuce angrily with her fork. "I'll talk to Sergei. I'm sure one of the guys can hang out with you for a few days. I would feel better."

"What? No. And please, just stop ragging on me, all right? It's so late. Besides, I have Marcos," I said, kissing his shoulder. "He can be my bodyguard."

Marcos grinned. "Anytime, babe. Always ready." Tossing his empty plate on the table, he slid his hands under me and lifted me onto his lap, squeezing his arms hard around me and startling me into laughter.

"Stop!" I squirmed, half wrestling away from the incredible feeling of being in his arms. Ignoring me, he leaned back against the cushions, pulling me with him. I winced. "Marcos, ouch." He gave me a wet kiss on my cheek, tightening his grip to lock me in his arms. "Get your slobber off me." I giggled. He laughed and didn't budge. And just like that, it all felt normal again.

He slid me back onto the couch and winked at me, leaving me bereft and longing for the brief, enveloping warmth. One of my favorite things about

Marcos was his ability to lighten up any situation. You could always trust him to give it to you straight, but once he felt the point was made, he did or said something funny, and the mood would totally change. I worried he would want to find the guy that followed me. Marcos was instinctively protective and didn't let things go easily.

I admired his profile as he relaxed next to me on the couch. Everything about him was masculine, the square lines of his jaw, even his rebellious, sandy brown hair, a bit overgrown like he needed a haircut. Despite all the suffering I put myself through in the last year, I couldn't imagine my life without him in it. Even if his feelings for me were not what I fantasized.

He re-wrapped an ice pack on my ankle with expert precision. Then the three of us snuggled up in front of the TV. My head was heavy, and I curled against Marcos's bicep as he flipped through the channels. The earlier wave of adrenaline was replaced by deep exhaustion, and I drifted into the familiar comfort of being squished on the couch with my two friends. This is where I felt the most normal. Marcos and Nata were my family. My eyelids finally won, and I surrendered to Morpheus's spell as a surreal montage of images flashed in my head: Sebastián…an architect…with bodyguards. Deep in my mind, an unsettling feeling swam in circles like a shark in a tank.

Chapter 5

The next morning was a bitch. My body felt as if it had been pulled apart and put back together wrong. Exhausted from the long night, I stretched on the bed and cursed at the overall stiffness that overpowered me. Fortunately, only a residual dull ache was left from the pain in my ankle, nothing I hadn't dealt with before. Dancing through injuries was a reality all dancers endured.

I dragged myself to the kitchen and popped three Aleve to face the long day of classes and rehearsals ahead. A note from Nata tented the salt and pepper shakers. She and Marcos had already left for an early meeting with the principals, so I had the apartment to myself.

In the bathroom, a good embodiment of a zombie bride taunted me from the mirror. My eyes were bloodshot from the mojitos and rimmed with purple. I buried the exhaustion under concealer as best I could and slowly dressed, wishing I could crawl back into bed. Damn me for getting carried away by the dream of meeting Irina and whatever the fuck else. I had been totally irresponsible. The variation we were rehearsing that afternoon was a complex one, and it would demand every ounce of my concentration.

In the theater, I hurried down the hallway and snuck into the studio as quietly as I could. Madame Vronsky was looking through a notebook and didn't see me come in. When she did look up, her emerald eyes met mine full on. I nodded a greeting and peeled off my sweatshirt, pretending I didn't notice her look burning a hole in my back.

On its own accord, my mind drifted while my body followed the class routine it knew well, Madame's voice a background conductor marking the tempo: "...and up, and one, two, pa, pa, pa, like this, girl, not like that. And up, and higher, Emilia wake up, and up, and two." She walked around, making corrections with her usual stoic expression. As soon as the class ended, she called me to the side while everyone else dispersed.

"What happened." It was both a question and a statement.

"Sorry? What do you mean, Madame?"

"I *mean,* what happened to your ankle?"

I blinked at her like a dumbfounded idiot. Shit. Did anything ever escape her?

"Well?"

"Oh, um. Nothing, it's very minor, Madame. I'm okay."

She pressed her lips in disapproval. "Listen to me carefully. You are the understudy for a principal role now. I need *that* to be your priority. Even when you are not here. That means your life changes. It adapts to this"—she gestured at the air—"and that means outside the studio you stay away from anything that could cause physical injuries. Do you understand me?"

"Yes, Madame."

"Today are the first rehearsals with the corps. How do you intend to dance for all those hours en pointe with an injury?"

"I'm watching it, Madame. I assure you, I'm okay." Our eyes locked for a moment, the ire in hers fresh, letting me know just how royally I was fucking this up, how I was proving her right. *You're not ready*, girl. She then set off toward the group gathering for the corps rehearsal. For the next four hours, we would work with the choreographer while Madame sat to the side, watching everything closely.

Breathing through the heaviness in my chest, I hurried to the back to change into pointe shoes. A few of the girls exchanged looks, muttering under their breaths. I ignored them and proudly took my place at the barre, letting them know I gave zero fucks what they thought.

The morning dragged, and it was difficult to concentrate or ignore the growing pain in my ankle. I had underestimated the injury, and after three hours en pointe, it was throbbing. I was behind on my tempo, and Madame snapped at me, making it clear she was about to lose the last of her fragile patience. I promised myself I wouldn't give her another chance to lash out at me, but whenever I put my full weight on my left foot, I inevitably screwed up. Again. Fuck! Had I sprained it? Please, no.

"Navarro, if you can't keep up, I may have to replace you. I don't have time to waste. You are slow this morning and disrupting the other dancers."

"I can do it," I blurted, panting. Her intense eyes narrowed a fraction, and I swallowed, my mouth dry. She took a step closer.

"You are well aware," she said in that controlled tone that froze most dancers into place, "that I don't share Federico's view of your 'potential' and 'the magic of genes.' What I see is a sloppy dancer in the corps who has a lot to work to do. The fire may be in you. But even if it is, you haven't learned how to manage it. A principal is always in charge of her emotions and her body. Your mind is not here today because you are injured."

"Madame, I apologize," I said with my face burning. "I will give today all my focus, I promise. It's just… my ankle. I may have pushed it too hard."

She arched an eyebrow.

"Can you continue?"

"Um, yes," I said, shakily. Could I? Madame shook her head slowly, the deep sage background darkening.

"Getting ahead is not only a matter of physical discipline. It requires maturity, a mental and emotional commitment. Your passion in here is raw and inconsistent. Until you learn how to own it and care properly for your body, you will be at best worthy of a spot in the last line of the corps."

Anger burned furiously within me. I said nothing, holding her gaze defiantly. Drawing in a slow breath, I took my place in the line, ready to prove her wrong.

"What's up with you today, Navarro?" a dancer behind me said. There was no malice in her tone.

"Old injury," I said.

"Madame's in a mood too. I swear, we need to find that woman a boyfriend. Can you keep going?"

Frustration swelled in my throat. "I'll try."

The music started again. I followed the variation diligently, coaxing my body into cooperation as I concentrated on each note of the Adam's motif for the Wilis. *One, two, up, two.* I cringed through the pain, focusing every cell into keeping up with the tempo. I managed to do it without losing the pace or fucking it up. Then, as we held the final arabesque, time stopped. My ankle screamed with pain as it balanced my body's full weight. The seconds passed excruciatingly slowly. *One, two, three...* How much longer? Sweat beaded my forehead. A spear of fire stabbed my ankle and it gave abruptly. I dropped to the floor. Fuck. *Fuck!* My eyes flew up to Madame, and her scathing look delivered the speech I didn't need to hear. Turning away, she whispered something to her assistant's ear, then went on with the rehearsal, directing her attention to the other dancers. Her assistant approached me diligently, her face drawn in concern.

"Camila," she said. And for a second, it was comforting to hear someone call me by my first name. "Why don't you take the afternoon off? Madame tells me your ankle's injured. Maybe go see the physical therapist downstairs?"

"What? No, I'm okay. I just need to ice it." I panted, wiping the sweat of my face. She gave me a small, empathetic smile.

"Go rest."

Tears rushed to my eyes and I swallowed them. Her expression softened.

"Look," she said in a lower voice. "The corps will be working on act one for the rest of today. That's a small part for you. We're finished with the Wilis choreography, and rehearsals for Myrta don't start till tomorrow. Go take care of that ankle before it gets worse."

I looked at her for a few silent seconds. Shit. *Shit.* I was being kicked out? I darted a skeptical look at Madame. I was no quitter, but she had a point. I hated that I had proven her right. So much was at stake for me, and the lack of sleep and this injury weren't helping. But I couldn't *leave.* What if she demoted me?

"Camila, sweetheart," the assistant pressed, "go get well."

"She'll replace me."

"She hasn't done that yet. Come back ready tomorrow."

With the weight of my teacher's rejection pressing on my shoulders, I stepped out into the blinding sun. It was slightly past noon and I felt out of place. I had never walked out of a rehearsal in the middle of the day before, and it was disorienting. My head was heavy and my ankle throbbed with every step. I didn't want to go see the physical therapist on staff. What if he said to stay off of it for a few days? That would immediately get to Madame, and I would lose my role as Myrta before even dancing a single step. No, I would take care of this on my own.

Putting as little weight on my foot as possible, I slowly made my way to the corner to hail a cab to go home, nurse my ankle, and bury myself under the covers to erase all memories of the morning. Madame's cold green eyes barged in my thoughts. Why was she so hard on me? Would I always live under the shadow of Mamá? My phone startled me when it buzzed in my pocket. I frowned at the screen. Papá never called in the middle of the day.

"Papá, what's up?"

"Oh...honey. I was going to leave you a message. I hope I didn't interrupt class."

"No, you didn't. Is everything okay?"

"Yes, yes. I just need a favor. I'm getting on a plane to give a conference in Córdoba in two hours, and your mother left her laptop in my car. I would leave it with my secretary, but she's at home sick and I'll close up here when I leave. I was hoping to bring it to you during lunch? I'm sorry to bother you, honey. I know how busy you are."

"It's fine, Papá..." I said. "I'm actually leaving work right now. My ankle is bothering me, and I need to ice it before it gets worse."

"Oh..." he said, taken back. "I have a few things to finish up, but I can come by on the way to the airport."

"No, I'm getting in a cab right now. I'll swing by your office on my way home."

"Are you sure?"

"Yeah, it's fine, Papá. You need to leave and I just want to get home and rest."

Papá's office was in Puerto Madero, a contemporary neighborhood bordering the Rio de la Plata. An oasis where the top architects and cutting-edge designers in the city lined up for a chance to recycle old warehouses into ultramodern offices and lofts. New restaurants popped up weekly, competing for the eclectic tastes of wealthy investors claiming a share in one of the most iconic areas in town.

The Universidad Católica Argentina stretched along three consecutive lofts overlooking the river. I paid the cab driver and inched toward Papá's office in the Bioethics Department, my sour mood slightly lifting in anticipation to see my father. He was on the phone and waved me in from the other side of the glass door. Ending his call, he rounded the desk to wrap me in his arms. For an instant I was seven years old again.

"Camila, honey. It's good to see you." He pulled back and his eyes studied me with concern. "Are you all right?"

I squeezed my arms around him, swallowing the tears as I pressed my face to his crisp cotton shirt. "Bad day. It's good to see you, too, Papá."

"Things getting tough at the theater?" His endearing tone made it harder to keep my emotions in check. As the husband of a famous prima, Papá more than understood the struggles of a dancer.

"Yeah." I smirked. "Madame's not much of a cheerleader. You know."

He nodded. "Let me look at that ankle." He pulled out two chairs, and I sat on one while resting my foot on the other. Papá examined my ankle, probing here and there carefully, asking me if this and that hurt. "It's not swollen. Looks like a minor sprain. I can get you in for an MRI if you want to be sure. Regardless, you'll need to ice it, take something for the pain, and stay put for the day. Take these," he said, reaching into his briefcase and handing me a small container of painkillers. "Anti-inflammatory, for the pain. You know the drill. No more than one every five hours, always with food."

"Okay, but I just want to go home. I don't need an MRI."

Worry settled on his face. "Call the office if you change your mind. They'll schedule it for you. Take care of yourself."

"Yeah, I will."

He kissed my head and reached over to the desk for the laptop. Mamá would stop by my apartment later if she needed it.

Outside, I hugged him good-bye, lingering for a few long seconds. He helped me to a bench where I could rest and call a cab. I urged him to go so he wouldn't be late for his flight.

Papá left and I pulled my phone out, relaxing on my bench on the boulevard that lined the coast. The morning had been a ghost ride through a nightmare, and I hoped the second half of the day wouldn't suck as much as the first. Papá had a magic theory that no matter how badly your day had started, your luck was sure to turn around at noon. A clean start. I desperately hoped that was the case. I hated sulking and refused to open the door to my insecurities. My temples pulsed painfully. Had last night really happened, or had it all been a dream? The images thrashed around in my head: Irina, the Brazilians, me in Marcos's arms, dancing, Nata and her new guy, then that creep following me...and Sebastián...

I put my foot up and lay back, turning my face to the kaleidoscope of sunlight rippling on the golden surface of the river. My mind drifted to the hypnotic patterns, and my shoulders relaxed for the first time that morning. A stubborn breeze brushed the surface of the Rio de la Plata, curling ripples that melted into amber foam at the shore. Pungent scents of fall spiced the air. I loved watching the river, massive, peaceful, unapologetically stretching for miles. On a clear day you could even make out the Uruguayan coast. Letting the cool air fill my lungs, I stared at the fishing ships on the horizon, gray smudges on a perfect canvas.

"I don't believe it," a low familiar voice behind me said. I turned my head, shielding the glare off my eyes, and there *He* was again. Sebastián. My heart woke with a jolt of disbelief. But there he stood, just like I remembered him from my non-dream, deliciously glorious in jeans and a white linen shirt rolled up at the sleeves.

"Hi. What …are you doing here?" I said with a mix of thrill and apprehension. These coincidences were starting to get a bit weird.

"I work right over there." He nodded at a glass building. "And you? How's that ankle?"

"Sore," I said, my mind still reeling. "But nothing serious. I came to pick up something from my dad. He teaches bioethics at the university."

"And here I thought I had a stalker." He flashed a smile.

"Hey, I could say the same about you."

"I'm innocent, I promise." He lifted his hands in surrender. "I was on my way to get lunch. Want to come with?" He squinted through those endless eyelashes, and a warm sensation pooled in my belly. "It would be awesome to have a conversation with you that doesn't require me scooping you off the street first." He stifled a smile.

"Hey!"

A low chuckle rumbled from his chest. "So, what do you say?"

I debated for a moment. Then my conscience stepped up. No. I was injured. Besides, I needed to reflect on the morning and work on a plan to impress Madame. Biting my lip, I nodded at my ankle.

"I'm sorry, I can't. I need to get home and ice this."

"But you haven't eaten?"

"No, but—"

"I was heading to that place right over there, and what do you know? They have ice. It's five steps, and yes, *fine*." He rolled his eyes playfully. "Since you insist, I *will* carry you one more time."

"As if!" I shook my head. "Thanks, but I better get going."

"It's just lunch, Camila. Not a marriage proposal." He smiled smugly.

Weightless wings fluttered inside my chest at the way he said my name. It was only lunch. I would have the rest of the day to hatch my plan and wouldn't have to even think about food or eat one of Nata's carb-free meals. I glanced at the small restaurant, a quaint place with just a few tables overlooking the river, literally steps away. And I could take my painkillers now.

"Okay, something quick."

His answering smile made my insides swirl, and I pretended I wasn't breathing faster. It was so strange, the effect he had on me. The most puzzling part was I *wanted* to be there, with him. I craved how good and relaxed I felt in his presence. Safe. He helped me up and insisted I hold on to him so I wouldn't put any weight on my foot. He smelled divine, and the muscles in his arm were as hard as stone. Desire rippled through me as he pressed me against him, the heat of his body expanding to me. I let out a small gasp of surprise.

"This place is simple, but the food's good," he said. We made our way slowly while he held me with unnecessary care.

"So," I said. "You're an architect. You have an *actual* job. Saving girls in the middle of the night is just a hobby then?"

"Hard to believe, I know." He opened the door with one hand and held it while helping me in.

The restaurant was an understated, tranquil spot. I couldn't imagine a more perfect place. He signaled to the hostess, indicating we would take a small table outside overlooking the water. After pulling out my chair and arranging another one so I could rest my foot, he sat across from me. I told him to choose the food and surprise me. When the hostess approached, he ordered a salad and a pizza to share without even looking at the menu. I smiled. I was used to Marcos eating three times as much as I did, never wanting to share a morsel. A guy willing to share his food scored points in my book. Jesus, what points? What *book?*

We waited for the food in comfortable silence, and I gazed at the water behind him to distract myself from staring at his face. On the river surface, the sun shimmered in a blanket of sparks. A warm breeze whirled my hair, and suddenly it was as if the heaviness from the morning had left with it. I smiled inwardly at Papá's magic theory.

The waitress was back with our drinks and food. When I pulled out my painkillers, Sebastián poured mineral water in my glass.

"So how are you feeling this morning?" he said in that low, seductive voice that did naughty things to my insides. "I mean, aside from your ankle. You must've not slept much."

I let out a long, defeated sigh. "I didn't. I just can't go out like my friends do. I always pay for the sleep I lose. And last night. What a nightmare." I looked down at my lap.

"It's over. You're fine." He reached over for my hand and gently squeezed it. A chemical frenzy sparked and traveled up my arm. I looked up at him. Did he feel it too?

"I should've gotten a cab at the door." I frowned, eager to explain that I wasn't a complete idiot. "But there were still a bunch of people trying to go in, and I just wanted to go to bed. It was stupid to leave on my own."

The muscles in his jaw tensed, and he let go of my hand. "The doorman should've taken care of the cab instead of flirting with the girls at the entrance. I'll have a word with him." His tone was harsh. *A word with him*? "I'm glad I was able to help." I looked back up at him and was once again stricken by the pale color of his eyes. I wondered how the women in his office managed to get anything done.

"I'm glad too." I picked up my fork and slowly started on my food. "What were the odds? I mean, that you'd be at the Roxy last night?"

"I'm one of the owners."

I swallowed one big bite. "One of the owners? Of the Roxy?" Holy shit.

"I actually don't go there much. I'm just an investor and my partners manage it, but both are away this week and I had to take care of some business."

"How did you find me in the street?"

"I was leaving and I saw you head out. I figured your friends were outside, but when I got to the door, you were already turning the corner, alone." He shook his head. "I thought, what the hell." He darted me a fiery look that sent a heat wave through my body. He was so goddamn sexy. I stared down at my plate, desperate to grip the whirlwind of sensations inside me. Jesus, what was happening?

The waitress interrupted us to refill our drinks and told Sebastián how glad she was to see him again. Before she left, she gave him a longing look. He seemed unaffected. I watched her leave, swaying her hips as she turned.

"So how is it? Owning a place like the Roxy?"

"I'm only a silent partner. I want to know about *you*." He smiled playfully and bit into his pizza.

"What do you want to know?"

"You mentioned work. What do you do?"

"I'm a dancer?" *Why did that come out as a question?* I blamed those eyes.

"Right. The shoe. How could I forget." He chuckled. "Where do you dance?"

"Um, at the Colón Theater. I'm part of the permanent ballet company."

"That's impressive." He frowned, assessing me with curiosity. "You must be an incredible dancer."

Incredible! "And that is so hard to believe?" I suppressed a smile.

"I didn't mean it that way." He smiled shyly and it was adorable. "I've heard it's almost impossible to get into the Colón."

I nodded. The fact that he showed such appreciation for what I did made my heart expand. I grinned like an idiot. "I'm lucky. My life revolves around dancing, every day, all day. I love it. Right now, I don't do much else."

"I'm very impressed."

"Your turn. Tell me more about you."

He looked away for a second, then sipped his drink. Our eyes met, and a fleeting spark of hesitation flashed through the pale background of his. Then it was gone.

"Like I said, I'm an architect. My partner and I own that studio back there."

"You own the studio. That's impressive too. Though I can't say I'm surprised. You strike me as smart and probably extremely talented."

"Thanks." He smiled. "You're a more interesting topic, though. Tell me more about being a dancer."

I told him about *Giselle* and answered his questions as we ate. He absorbed every word I said and seemed genuinely interested. When we were done, he glanced at his watch. My heart fell. Right, I was supposed to be in a hurry.

"Thanks for lunch, Sebastián." I loved the sound of his name. "I should get going." Reaching for my bag, I peeked at my watch to realize we had been sitting there for over an hour.

"I really enjoyed your company, Camila. We should do this again." He flashed me a dashing smile as he slid some bills under his glass. I could run back to rehearsal for that smile.

My ankle felt stiff when I stood, and I wanted to walk a bit to stretch it. The painkillers were doing their job beautifully, and the throbbing was receding. Slowly, we made our way in the direction of the taxi stop. Our hands accidentally brushed, and I flinched at the contact. It was like a sting of static, but in a strange, good...*really good* way. A group of teens passed us, nearly bumping into me, and as if it was the most natural thing in the world, he interlaced his fingers with mine and pulled me against him to let them by. *Zap. Double zap. Mute.* Every vital function inside me came to a halt. I looked up at him, stunned by the boldness of the gesture, but even more surprised at how much I liked it. His hand completely enveloped mine. He glanced at me from the corner of his eye, and a little comma curved up his mouth. Heat rose to my face, and I hoped he couldn't feel the sudden rise in my body temperature. I wished we could walk like that forever. It was so strange to feel chemistry with anyone other than Marcos. I liked it. He broke my reverie when he stopped and turned to me.

"I want to see you again," he said.

My heart leapt into a Latin dance. I leaned back on the railing bordering the walkway along the river. I looked up at him, dumbstruck. He was beautiful, but it was that aura of masculinity and confidence that sent my pulse racing.

A sudden breeze whirled about, and he gently brushed my hair off my face. My skin tingled at the contact. Then, holding my gaze, he slowly leaned closer, placing his hands on each side of the railing, locking me in between. Desire thundered through me. It was so fucking sexy, I thought I was going to dissolve. We were just inches apart, and the warmth from his body was electric, a magnet. His fresh, delicious scent saturated the air around me, blurring my thoughts under a mix of suede, soap, sunshine, and something bewitching that was just…him. I wanted to launch myself forward and kiss him, grab his shirt in my fists and crush him against me. What was this? For a few seconds, neither of us moved, we just looked at each other in silence, the tension building between us, sparking. I racked my brain for words, trapped in that strange, magnetic force between us.

"What is it about you, crazy girl?" he murmured so close our lips were almost touching. "I'm spellbound. I want…"

My heart was galloping. Could he hear it?

"Actually," he went on, leaning closer. "Right now, I just want to kiss you. Is that…okay?"

Damn. My eyes locked on his mouth, his lips slightly parted, full, sexy as fuck, and I wondered how they would taste…*God.* What the hell was happening to me?

"I…Okay," I whispered, rapt in his spell, and closed my eyes. His arms suddenly closed around my back, and before I could breathe, his mouth was on mine.

Holy mother shit.

Desire exploded inside me, and the taste of him immediately invaded me. Suddenly there was nothing else, just him. *Us.* He inhaled sharply, and I parted my lips to give his tongue access. Clenching his shirt, I pulled him closer, like I had imagined. And I couldn't get enough of him. Of *this.* It was like a dormant addiction that had been waiting to be triggered. I clung to that moment as if it were the only thing that mattered. The world spun as he kissed me hungrily, then gently, until, very slowly, our lips finally parted. I looked up at him in a daze. His beautiful eyes were hooded, a storm of churning ashes.

"*Damn*," he whispered.

"Damn."

He closed his eyes and leaned his forehead to mine, our breaths crashing. Then he squeezed me in his arms and gave me one last, gentle kiss.

"You better go," he said, his voice gruff. "Before I forget we're out in public and *really* kiss you."

Oh, man. That hadn't been a *real* kiss? I wanted one, then. I wanted him to kiss the hell out of me. I wanted to forget about everything else. Forget about a world where I was doomed to be in love with someone who would never love me back, forget about my shitty rehearsal that morning and how I had screwed it up. The only place I wanted to be was here. Now. With him. For the first time in a long while, I had opened the door to a tsunami of emotions I had never allowed myself to feel, and I didn't want to think. Why couldn't we just forget…for a few moments at least?

Our eyes were locked in a silent stare-off. Pale uncharted against hazel. A corner of his mouth pulled up, but he didn't move. I bit my lip, wishing I was more experienced at this seduction stuff.

"Well…good-bye, Sebastián," I said, because I didn't know what the hell else to say, and I didn't want him to think I was an easy catch he just bumped into.

"How are you getting home?"

I gestured to the cab stop and he narrowed his eyes.

"Hm. Come with me," he said, taking my hand. Then he stopped abruptly. "No. Actually…stay here."

"What?"

"Wait here a sec. I'll be right back. Don't leave." He pressed a small kiss to my lips and made me sit on a nearby bench. He jogged to his building, his lean, beautiful body moving swiftly, then disappeared through a side door. I didn't know what I was still doing there, and yet, I was immobile, entranced by all these new sensations he had provoked in me. Holy shit. Who was this guy? I had known him for a day, and he already had me sitting on a bench, waiting for him. Where had my usual frostiness toward guys gone? Maybe it was that unshakable self-confidence of his. It was sexy as fuck. I wondered what Nata would say about this…

Just then, a silver-gray BMW motorcycle roared to a stop beside me. Pulling up his visor, Sebastián grinned, a boy with a cool toy, and handed me a helmet. I gave him a horrified look and shook my head.

"I'm not getting on that."

He rolled his eyes. "Do we *have* to do this every time I offer you a ride? You tell me you won't come, then I convince you it's safe, then you say yes and end up all over me, kissing me and whatever."

"What?"

He gave me a devilish grin. "Seriously. I promise you'll be home in less than ten minutes. But…if you'd rather pay for a cab, it'll cost you an arm and a leg in this traffic, and you almost lost an ankle last night. In your profession, body parts are precious."

I couldn't keep a straight face and glanced back at the bike.

"My ballet instructor would have a stroke if she saw me on a motorcycle."

He winked. "I won't rat you out."

I debated. It did look fun. When I was younger, I used to love riding dirt bikes and snuck away with my brother and his friends. This bike was a fine piece of hardware too. It surely cost a fortune.

"So?" He sighed. "We have to work on your decision-making. It's a *tad* slow."

I snatched the helmet from his hand. "You better get me home fast and in one piece."

"Yes ma'am."

He dodged the rush hour traffic with amazing ease. I wrapped my arms around his back, pressing my face to his shirt, grinning like a dumbstruck fool. I hadn't felt this free in years…and those few, blazing moments were just what I needed right then. True to his word, he pulled over by my door in record time.

"Seven minutes. Impressive," I said, pulling off my helmet and shaking my hair loose as I slid off the bike. He was watching me with amusement. If I knew better, I would say he was checking me out. I handed him back the helmet. "Thanks. It's been an adventure."

He gave me a long look, apprehension flashing in his eyes. "Have dinner with me tomorrow," he said, his expression serious. "Chila in Puerto Madero? I'll pick you up from the theater. What time are you done?"

"Oh." *Chila.* My breath caught. An exclusive, top restaurant by the water. I had never been, but it was always featured in magazines. It was elegant, romantic—*No, no.* I didn't need any more distractions. "Um…I'm usually done by seven, but—"

He leaned over and took my face in his hand. "Seven it is, then." He pressed a swift kiss to my lips, then quickly turned. Pulling his helmet back on, he roared the engine and sped off.

"But…" I let my shoulders drop, exhaling as my fingers reached my lips. What the hell was happening? My heart was pounding like crazy. It was like skydiving without ever reaching the ground. Shit.

I was in trouble.

Chapter 6

I came home to an empty apartment, took a shower, and wrapped myself in ice packs before dozing off in front of the TV. I woke two hours later with a nearly frozen ankle. The pain had receded, and for the first time in a while, I felt rested. I decided to make a nice dinner for Nata and me. I enjoyed cooking and needed to occupy my mind with something relaxing. A new kind of anticipation pulsed in the back of my mind at the thought of seeing Sebastián the next day. Crap. How would I manage to concentrate on work knowing he would be waiting afterward? And what the hell was I going to wear to Chila? Shit, I couldn't ask Nata for a dress. Normally she would be stoked if I told her I met someone, but after my recent incident in class, I feared she would articulate what my conscience was already grilling me about: my full focus should be on the new role Federico had given me and not on hot guys on motorcycles and fancy restaurants. I was walking on thin ice at work. But there was something about Sebastián I couldn't turn away from.

I cursed at the contents of our nearly empty fridge. Grabbing my bag and keys, I headed to the little shop downstairs to get ingredients for my signature chicken curry.

While I waited for the chicken to cook, I stretched out on a lounge chair in our modest penthouse balcony, watching the lights of the city below. My chest was heavy with my fuckups from the morning's rehearsal. Today had been…disconcerting. Getting distracted was not something I had ever struggled with before. Dancing was what I did, the core of who I was. My whole universe had always revolved around ballet. I liked it that way, simple. And yet, despite the solidity of my convictions, I didn't regret meeting Sebastián. He had brought a breath of oxygen to the usual vacuum of ballet and the torturous, constant longing I felt for Marcos. He had been a welcome distraction. One I knew I couldn't afford at the moment, but somehow kept luring me back for more. I slid deeper into the chair and clutched my shirt up to my nose to inhale the last traces of his scent. A wave of something beautiful swam in my stomach.

A loud *squat* on my sneaker startled me back to the present. Shit. Literally. I scowled at the bird flying off. I was being ridiculous. I had known this guy for five minutes, and he was screwing with my focus at work? *Hell* no. Today had been a warning. Madame wouldn't put up with my crap. *Focus, Camila. Focus.* I stormed off to the kitchen to set the table while I mentally prepared for the next morning.

An hour later, Nata walked in with Marcos, and let her bag drop. "You're hands-down the best roommate ever," she said, eyeing the food on the counter. "This looks amazing. Thank you. I'll go shower real quick, I'm starving." Turning theatrically on her toes, she hurried to her room.

Marcos kissed me on the cheek. "I'm staying. You made enough?"

"I figured." I slapped his hand as he took a carrot stick. "Out of here."

He lifted me up with one arm as he snatched a handful of sliced celery with the other. I kicked my feet in the air.

"Dude, I'm holding a knife. Put me down, I mean it."

He kissed my neck, laughing. "Mmmm, you smell amazing. Like butter and coconut. Makes me want to take a bite, right here," he crooned, nibbling my neck. I jabbed my elbow at his stomach, stifling the chill that ran through my body whenever we were this close. Before sliding me down, he kissed me again just to annoy me. He then grabbed a beer out of the fridge, leapt over the back of the couch and reached for the TV remote to flip through the channels.

"What happened to you today? You weren't there at lunch, and Verónica said Vronsky kicked you out?" he asked without taking his eyes off the TV.

I gripped the knife as I sliced through an onion. *Verónica…*a dancer from the corps with slightly more tenure than me. A climber with a distorted idea of her own talent, fueled by her first soloist role as Myrta in *Giselle*. That made me her understudy, and it was enough to make her feel superior. To me, she was simply a viper, perpetually infused in the otherwise innocent scent of lilies. Since the casting announcement, Verónica had pinned me as a target to terminate. While I took it as a compliment, the image of her whispering venomous comments in Marcos's ear stung.

"You listen to that bitch now? I did *not* get kicked out. Madame was worried about my ankle." My tone was sharper than I had intended, which I immediately regretted. I looked up to find Marcos watching me. "Sorry," I said. "That wasn't meant for you. I just…I totally fucked up today."

He sprang from the couch with a graceful move. Taking the knife from my hand, he set it down and pulled me into a hug. I pressed my face against his chest. He smelled heavenly. Anguish clutched my heart.

"I'm sorry. Anything I can do?"

"Shit, Marcos. What if I blew my shot at the understudy?"

"Well…whatever is screwing with your concentration, you need to let it go."

I pulled away from him, my throat thickening. His eyes studied me for a moment.

"What really happened last night?" he said in a low voice.

"What do you mean?" I looked down, picking up invisible lint from his sleeve.

"Who's this guy that brought you home?"

I glanced up at him. Marcos never missed a beat. I said nothing.

"Shit, Camila. Stop fucking around. You need to be laser focused right now. Every girl in the corps is after that understudy role. You have it, and you are putting it at risk."

"Some ego booster you are."

"Is that what you want? For me to *boost your ego*? Sorry, babe. Not gonna happen. Are you going to tell me, or what? You're not mixed in any weird shit, are you?"

"Weird shit? *Me?*"

"You wouldn't be the first."

"Seriously. What the hell?"

"Just checking. I know you feel the pressure. But coke or any of that shit ain't worth it."

"Marcos! For fuck's sake, I'm not doing coke. Why in the hell would you come up with that? I got no sleep at all last night. I'm not like you guys. And I'm trying not to dwell on it, but that asshole assaulted me! Why are you being such a dick?" Tears of anger welled in my eyes.

Marcos sighed and pulled me back into his arms.

"I'll find him, Cami. I called Nico today and asked him for a list of the bands that played at the Roxy last night. If you know his name, it'll be easy. We'll let that fuckhead have it."

"No." I pulled away. "Look, I don't want you to do anything. Just...leave it."

"Why?" He scowled.

"Because you know Nata. She'll be all over this and have one of her Russians glued to me. I don't want that. Besides, the guy who helped me was one of the owners of the Roxy. He took care of that asshole."

Marcos frowned, deciding.

"Seriously, he had a huge bodyguard. And he knew the creep. It's done."

"A fucking bodyguard?" His frown deepened. "Who is this guy, Cams?"

"Someone who wanted to help, that's all. Just leave it, okay? Thanks for having my back. Today was...weird. Let's move on." I dried my eyes with my sleeve.

His jaw tensed in anger. "I shouldn't have let you leave alone last night. I'm responsible. I'm sorry, babe." He hugged me again, tighter, and suddenly it all washed through me at once. The night, the attack, the morning, Sebastián, and of course...Marcos and the amazing feeling of being in his arms. I closed my eyes, smothering the tears against his chest, letting him hug me.

A few silent moments passed, and I forced myself out of his arms. He wiped a stray tear with the pad of his thumb, watching me with concerned eyes.

"Listen," he said. "Vronsky knows you've got what it takes for this role, even if she's constantly on you. She may have her doubts, but she respects Federico's judgment. Stay focused and show her she has no reason to question it. Get a good night's sleep tonight. You need it. Now stop beating yourself up over this." He kissed my head and went back to the couch.

"Beating yourself up over what?" Nata walked in, pulling up her long, wet, copper hair into a messy knot.

I shrugged and kept my eyes on the chopping board. I could feel her eyeing both of us suspiciously.

"Is this about today?" she said, sliding onto a barstool. "I heard. I can stay after work tomorrow if you want. We'll use one of the empty studios and go through the variation for Myrta. There are a few versions on YouTube that are worth watching, and I've done it before, I'm sure I can remember." Working after hours with Nata would be golden. It would help me learn the variation much faster, and as a principal dancer, she could give me lots of inside tips on the acting part. But that meant canceling my date at Chila with Sebastián. Shit.

"Thanks, but tomorrow I can't. I have some stuff I need to do after work." I hustled around with the food, avoiding her eyes. She would know something was up just by looking at me. My conscience kicked me. *What the fuck, Camila?* I slammed the door on it and forced a smile. "Maybe another night, if you can swing it?"

"I may have time on Thursday. If anything changes tomorrow, text me. It would be better, I have more time."

"Let her cook. I'm starving," said Marcos with his eyes on the TV.

Nata threw a kitchen towel at his head. "Who said you could stay? And we don't want to watch soccer." She winked at me. Marcos turned up the volume, tucking the remote under his leg.

We ate in front of the TV in comfortable silence. After the rich meal and two of Papá's painkillers, the exhaustion of the day swallowed me. I iced my ankle again and snuggled up in a corner of the couch. When I opened my eyes, I was in my bed, though I didn't remember getting there. I rolled over and was immediately asleep.

The next morning, I got up well rested and ready to claim my spot in the company. Ignoring my conscience, I packed a quick outfit for my date with Sebastián: a pair of black skinny jeans, boots, and the nicest top I owned, a cashmere sweater Mamá had given me for my birthday. Anticipation sizzled through me. I left Mamá's laptop on the kitchen countertop for her secretary to pick up and tucked my last pair of good pointe shoes in my already stuffed bag. The persisting reminder that I was making a bad call gnawed at me. I stuck three energy bars in my bag and decided to skip lunch to work on the understudy variation. It wouldn't be the same as a session with Nata, but staying in all day would at least show Madame I was committed and that yesterday had been nothing but a small setback.

I told Nata I would walk to work. My ankle was much better, and I wanted to warm it up before class. But as I was leaving, she told me to wait. Locking the door behind us, she smiled.

Shit.

Chapter 7

Nata and I fell into the usual chatter as we walked, Alexei and one of Sergei's friends trailing somewhere behind. The faint, autumn sun kissed the mirrored façades of the buildings lining the streets. A chilled gust of wind brushed my neck, and I tightened my coat. My body tingled with energy. I smiled at an invisible point in the distance. *Yes.* I was excited to prove myself at work today, but that didn't exactly explain the fluttering wings in my stomach.

"What's with you?" Nata clutched my wrist as she looked both ways down the street. A car blazed by and we hurried across. "You are unusually happy."

"I'm determined to show Vronsky I'm worthy of the understudy part Federico gave me."

"Of course you are worthy. Stop torturing yourself about yesterday. Just stay focused. Myrta is a challenging role, but you've got what it takes."

"Thanks, Nata. You're always my rock." I nudged her as we walked side by side.

Dodging through a sea of bodies rushing to work, we followed our usual route to the theater, the two Russians flanking us closer now that the crowd had thickened. The other one, Viktor, lit a cigarette. I scrunched my nose.

"Seriously," I said, "it's seven in the morning."

He dismissed me with a nod.

"Viktor, I thought you were going to quit." Nata frowned. He smiled apologetically and took a long drag while bluntly checking out a girl in a tight dress walking past us. Nata shook her head.

"I won't go out for lunch today. I brought PowerBars," I said, holding the theater door open for her.

"I see…Anyone I know?"

"What do you mean?" I adjusted my bag on my shoulder to avoid her inquisitive gaze.

"Are you perhaps going on a lunch date with the mysterious guy from the other night?"

Shit! "I wish. I'm staying in to rehearse."

"Right."

"Really."

"Are you ever going to tell me who he is?" she said as we reached the top of the stairs. We sidestepped a girl stretching her leg upright and behind her head.

"Who?"

"The guy. Who is he?"

I felt shitty hiding things from my friend, but something told me to hold back for now, until I knew what this was. "Nothing to tell…I barely know him."

"Did you meet him at the Roxy?" *Gah! Relentless.*

"Um…I actually met him that morning, when I lost my pointe shoe on the street. He helped me out."

"Wait, what?" She paused as we reached the door to her studio. "You met him randomly in the morning, then he was at the Roxy on the same night?"

"Yes, but—"

"He's a stalker, Camila."

"Nata—"

"What are the odds? Why didn't you tell me this before?"

"It's not like that. The coincidence was *us* being at the Roxy last night. He works there."

"At the Roxy—"

"Yes, Nata. Not everything is a conspiracy. Now go, you're going to be late." I nodded at her studio where the dancers were taking their positions at the portable barres. She turned, and her eyes widened when she saw she would be the last person in, and without saying good-bye, she rushed to the back to get ready.

The day flew by. I worked with a new stager Federico had hired for *Giselle*, committing every ounce of my energy to learning everything he taught me. My ankle protested, and I iced it in between classes and rehearsals. I was doing well, and Madame acknowledged me with a slight nod, then left the studio to work with the principals.

The stager finally called it a night. I was exhausted and sore everywhere. When I glanced at the clock, I realized I only had fifteen minutes before Sebastián would arrive.

In the dressing room, I quickly showered and changed into my street clothes. Anticipation wrung my stomach, and I quickly shoved my dance clothes in my bag.

Unable to hide the dumbstruck grin on my face, I pushed through the theater doors to the street, scanning the passersby for ash-colored eyes, my pulse accelerating with every second.

Maybe he would kiss me again tonight. *Really* kiss me. I had been thinking of that kiss since yesterday. Every muscle south of my navel clenched at the thought of that sensual mouth on mine. I looked around impatiently.

The Colón Theater took up an entire square block. My eyes swept the street from corner to corner, bordering the length of the building. I frowned at my watch. Seven fifteen. Where was he? I pulled out my phone and tapped on the contact I had created the night before under his name.

Straight to voicemail. "Hey, it's me…Um, Camila? It's after seven and I'm at the theater door, but I don't see you…. Just…call me back if you get this." I hung up and let out a pent-up breath, looking around. Maybe he had gone to one of the side entrances. Idiot me! Of course! I hadn't told him which door to meet me at. With my heart pounding, I rushed to the east entrance. But he wasn't there either. People hurried past me, tightening their coats as the evening air quickly chilled. A blanket of darkening clouds stretched over the sky, swallowing the stars. I racked my brain. What had I missed?

Another ten minutes went by. I tried his phone again, and again it went straight to voicemail. I reviewed our conversation in my head, wondering if I had somehow misunderstood something. Another fifteen minutes. Lightning sliced the thick gray above, followed by a deafening roar of thunder. I looked around in despair…Where was he?

I stood, shivering and hugging myself, unable to leave. An invisible claw gripped my heart and squeezed it as a sobering thought materialized.

He wasn't late…He wasn't *coming*.

Jesus. What a goddamn fool. I had made myself an open target. I bet he could smell my inexperience a mile away. A guy like Sebastián surely had loads of chicks after him. He was probably out with one of them right now. Shitdammit. What an idiot, wooed by his eyes, his smile, those lips, Chila…and that stupid motorcycle. Tears of humiliation rushed to my eyes. *Fuck, fuck!* And for this I had turned down two hours of golden rehearsal time with Nata. What the hell was wrong with me? Madame was right. I had succumbed to bad judgment. I was an immature, stupid fool.

Above me, a churning storm threatened to swallow the city. I shivered from the icy rain that seeped into my bones. Nata had made last-minute plans to go out with Teo, so the Russians weren't around. I would either have to find a taxi or walk home alone. The traffic was stopped in every direction. Throwing my bag over my shoulder, I rushed across the street, dodging the still cars. My ankle complained. I reached into my pocket, popped in one of Papá's painkillers, and chewed it. It was bitter, but so was I.

A sudden curtain of rain caught up with me from behind, pelting my jacket like bullets. I vainly tried hiding under my collar, and as if mocking me, the rain doubled. I mentally flipped it off and looked up to the sky, my tears and desolation washing away under the glacial rain. In a way, I was better off. Now I could concentrate on what really mattered. The only things that should matter to me: Ballet. My career. New York.

"Again," Madame barked as I finished my Myrta variation the next morning. Panting, I quickly grabbed a towel to wipe the sweat off my face. As

I did, my eyes briefly met hers. Approval flashed in the deep emerald of her eyes, betraying her usual glacial expression. Hope whirled inside me with the force of a tornado. I took my place in the middle of the room, letting the exhilaration kick the fatigue off my muscles, and closed my eyes, waiting for the music.

I flew through the ballottés, pirouettes, and complex steps I had rehearsed tirelessly during lunch the day before. I had already memorized a good part of the variation, and even Madame couldn't hide her surprise.

"An improvement," she said sternly. "But you need to get your strength and endurance up to speed. This role is very physically demanding, more so than any of the others. Now, on the port de bras, keep your shoulders down and be mindful of Myrta's demeanor so it is reflected in every movement. She is royalty, but her heart is dark. She's vengeful."

I smirked inwardly at the irony. Myrta: the Ghost Queen of Revenge. She had sworn to kill every man who ever caused a girl to die for love. How fitting. It was surprisingly easy to pour my own feelings into the part. From my periphery, I caught Verónica's reptile gaze. With venom slowly filling her, she was waiting for me to falter again. I smiled. I was back on track.

As I left the theater, I pulled my phone out of my bag to call Nata and let her know I would skip the drinks planned for the night and go straight home. My pulse jumped as I looked at the screen showing a voice message from Sebastián. My first impulse was to delete it right away. But my slaughtered ego peeked out from the trenches.

"Hey...Camila. It's Sebastián. Look, I want to apologize for last night. Something unexpected came up, and I was tied up until late. I had no cell signal where I was. I just got your messages. Shit, I feel horrible. I'm really sorry."

That was it. My apology. But he hadn't asked for a rain check. No *"I want to see you, let's try again."* I gripped the phone so hard I was sure I would crush it.

"Screw you," I spat out loud. A guy walking in my direction widened his eyes and lifted his palms in surrender.

I took a cab home and spent the next half hour under a scalding shower. I dressed in sweatpants and was wrapping a towel on my head when the downstairs bell rang. I hurried to the intercom.

"Yeah?"

"From El Jagüel. I have a delivery for Miss Camila Navarro."

Oh! El Jagüel was Papá's favorite flower shop. One of those fancy places on Avenida Alvear where only the most affluent could afford to order flowers. Knowing Papá, he wanted to cheer me up after seeing me injured and a bit beaten down the other day. When I was in ballet school, he used to have a custom bouquet of white peonies and lilies delivered to the house if he knew I was having an especially rough week. I pressed the buzzer.

"Come up."

A boy barely scratching teen status showed up at my door with a massive bouquet of white lilies, the sweet fragrance instantly invading the hallway air. His small frame was buried under a beanie and a jacket at least three sizes too big. He grinned widely as he pulled out one of his earbuds.

"Sign here, please?"

I obliged and thanked him, unclipping the white envelope from the tissue as I closed the door behind me. The front of the crisp, white envelope showed my name in perfect calligraphy. I admired the delicate, half-open lilies, masterfully arranged, their perfume quickly infusing my apartment. They were simply magnificent.

Reaching into a far up cabinet, I pulled out the only vase we owned and filled it with fresh water. I undid the layers of pale gold tissue and set the flowers in the vase. Sliding onto a kitchen barstool, I pulled out the card from the envelope.

I'm sorry about last night.

It drove me insane that I couldn't get to you.

Love,

Sebastián

My heart was suddenly pounding. I read it again and again and again. The reason for not showing up wasn't because he had changed his mind about me. I was frustrated at how relieved that made me feel. I clenched my teeth and crushed the card in my fist. It didn't matter. I had almost screwed up things at work by letting this guy sneak into my life. Damn it. I didn't know who to be mad at. Him? Me? Life? For the first time ever, I had let a guy derail me from ballet. That scared the living crap out of me.

I sat there for a while, admiring the flowers. They were almost out of place in the simplicity of the apartment. The hard side of me wanted them out of there immediately. Every time I looked at them, I would think of *him*. Yet, the softer side of me couldn't bring myself to throw them in the trash. They were gorgeous.

I could keep them, tell Nata they had been a gift from my father…Man, I was getting shamelessly comfortable with lying to Nata. I buried my face in my hands. Then an idea hit me. I took one last, long look, then wrapped the flowers back in the tissue paper as best I could and grabbed my keys.

Wrapped in a plush, pink robe and matching slippers, Mrs. Garibaldi opened the door of apartment 14B. Her hair was neatly curled into rollers under a silk scarf.

"Camila, sweetheart, what a treat to see you." She smiled widely. "Come in, come in. I will put on the kettle."

"Oh, no, you're in your pajamas. I don't want to bother you. I just came to bring you these from Nata and me."

"Oh, my lord! Why would you silly girls do such a thing?"

"You know as well as I do that if it weren't for you, all our plants would be dead," I said, handing her the flowers. She let out a long chuckle that echoed through her smoke-battered lungs.

"I like doing that, and you don't need to thank me. Nobody's ever given me flowers from El Jagüel before. But darling"—she frowned—"these must have cost a fortune. I don't want you girls wasting your money on an old hen like me."

"It's nothing. We love that you're our neighbor. You enjoy them, Mrs. Garibaldi. Good night."

She hugged me hard and kissed my cheek again, her eyes moist with joy.

Satisfied with my deed, I texted Nata, letting her know I had given Mrs. Garibaldi flowers from the two of us. We always talked about doing something nice for her. She texted back a thumbs-up emoji. I sprinted back to the apartment, taking the stairs two at a time and giving my heart a good reason to race.

The next few days at work advanced with clockwork precision. The thrill from having my first soloist understudy made me feel like anything was possible if I put my head and body into it a hundred percent. On the outside, I was a machine. I skipped lunch and concentrated on what I needed to learn and nothing more.

But inside, my guts were in a constant knot. Sebastián had left a new sense of emptiness in me. I resented the fact that he had awakened things I didn't know how to control. He had called a few times, but I had let them all go to voicemail, deleting the messages without listening to them. I was being a coward, I knew. I was running. But, being alone was safer. Just the few memories I had of him were a major distraction. I didn't let myself daydream about Marcos either. I ran purely on the adrenaline of moving closer to my goal. Closer to New York. Ballet was back to being my master, and I was in control.

Madame was visibly pleased with my new determination. She once even used me as an example to show the corps what she expected for the new choreography since I had already learned it.

We finished rehearsing the first variation for the Wilis, and Madame dismissed us for the day. Federico had come to watch the corps, and he and the teachers sometimes went out to dinner after a long day of rehearsals. He stated he was pleased with our progress. We had been working hard and made Madame look good in front of her boss, so she was in good spirits.

I stretched at the barre by the window while the other dancers dispersed and left the studio. Sweat drenched my back as I caught my breath, coercing my burning muscles into submission. This was why I loved dancing. I had nothing left to give, the tension completely wrung out of my body. I used a towel to wipe the sweat off my face and was startled by Madame and Federico standing next to me. Straightening up, I tossed the towel back in my bag with an unsettling sense of anticipation.

"Camila." Federico smiled benevolently, a proud father. "That was a great rehearsal. Your technique is much more polished than before. You seem centered, stronger. Whatever you're doing differently, I hope you keep it up, because I have great plans for your future."

"Thank you. I…I've just been working hard." I glanced at Madame, and she gave a slight nod.

Federico took my hand in his and gave it a reassuring squeeze. He then kissed both Madame's cheeks. "I'll leave you both to it. Great job, Camila."

As he walked away, I reached down for my bag. Madame grabbed the strap and placed my bag back on the floor. Her statuesque, delicate figure stood just a foot away, and I suddenly felt small. I held my breath, trying to conceal how intimidated I always felt in her presence. Her deep green eyes studied me with determination, but there was something softer in them this time.

"Well done, Navarro. Honestly, I didn't think you could handle the understudy. But you have learned it quickly. You are working hard, and that doesn't go unnoticed here." She paused, frowning. "Federico thinks you may be ready to take on the role of Myrta as a soloist."

"Really?" My heart thundered.

She waved her hand dismissively. "I am still not convinced. For now, you will share the role with Verónica. We will decide later who will take it on First Cast."

I opened my mouth in astonishment. This was *huge*. Not only were they giving me a shot at a soloist part, I could also potentially dance in First Cast and perform on opening and closing nights! Holy shit.

"In my opinion, it is too fast," she went on. "This role is extremely demanding, unforgiving. Some of the best primas in the world, have danced Myrta. You will be compared to them. If you are not ready, it can ruin your career. But it is up to you." She studied my expression, and for the first time, hers softened infinitesimally. "You have my permission to prove me wrong, *devushka*."

I blinked, speechless, my heart threatening to rip my chest open for air. I knew she wasn't handing me anything I hadn't earned with sweat, but there were so many talented principals in the company. And praise from Madame was simply shocking. I could count her compliments to me over the last year on one hand.

"Thank you." I grinned, resisting a sudden impulse to crush that deceivingly fragile frame in a hug. "Thank you so much."

She was gone before I could defrost from the shock. I threw my things in my bag and dashed to the studio where Nata and Marcos were rehearsing. They had just finished and were walking to the door when I approached. Nata's face lit up when she saw me.

"What! Tell me. Now."

"Vronsky just told me I'll be Myrta!"

"Oh my God! Are you serious?" Nata's hand flew to her mouth.

"Yes! And they haven't decided who's on First Cast yet, so I have a shot at it too!"

"Cami, that is…I'm speechless. And so proud of you!" Nata pulled me into a death grip. We ignored our smelly bodies, clammy from a full day of rehearsals.

"That's awesome, babe." Marcos joined in the hug. "I knew you could swing it. What'd I tell you? *Laser focus*." He lifted me up by the waist and spun me around. "Let's go celebrate." He planted a kiss on my lips before sliding me to my feet. I was so happy that it didn't register right away. He looked at me for a moment, smiling with what looked like admiration. I stayed in his arms, blinking like a starry-eyed fool. He finally broke the embrace, kissed my forehead, and tossed his bag over his shoulder. "I'm gonna shower. I'll meet you back at your place. Let's go somewhere good, I'm starving," he shouted as he walked away.

I shook my head and glanced at Nata, who was eyeing me with a concerned expression.

"What?" I said, opening the door to the street. "He's always starving. We're going out, it's not like we have to feed him."

She pressed her lips into a thin line.

"What? *What*."

"I don't know. It's just...the two of you. Maybe you should lay some boundaries with him."

"What are you talking about? What boundaries? We're friends. That's it."

"Friends...So you're not in love with him? I imagined it?"

"What?" My face was a hot coal.

"Cami, I know how you feel about him. And believe me, I get why you are not together. But Marcos doesn't realize the effect he has on you. It's not right."

"Shit," I said. "You must think I'm pathetic. Does everyone else think that too?"

She shrugged "People think you two are in love with each other but too caught up in your own egos to admit it."

"What? Why do they think that?"

"Because of the chemistry between you two. It's pretty obvious."

"It is?"

"The good news is that as far as appearances go, you come out all right. Egocentric is much better than pathetic."

"I'm not in love with him." I clutched my bag strap as we waited for Alexei at the theater entrance. "Whatever you *think* you see. We're good friends, but that's all. Besides, Marcos's only love is dancing. You know that. There's no room for anything or anyone else. He's way more obsessive than you or me. If I was really into him, I would be a wreck."

"Camila, sweetie. It's me," she said, tilting her head, her eyes searching mine.

"Okay." I sighed. "You got me. What do you want me to say? I'm not an idiot. I know it's a dead end." I leaned on a street sign and looked down at my feet.

"Cami," she said, rubbing my shoulder. "Marcos is not the guy for you. He's always got a swarm of babes throwing themselves at him. I know in many ways dating a dancer is easier. But you deserve someone different than Marcos. Someone that gives you a break from all this." She gestured at the theater. A fleeting thought of Sebastián flashed in my mind.

"I know," I muttered. "I would like that too. But what if it never comes? Sometimes I tell myself I don't need anything else. That ballet fills every space for me, and this friendship he and I have is enough. No demands, no fights. But whenever I see him with someone else, it gets to me. I can't help it."

"You need to get out and meet people. Go out on dates. What about that guy you met a while back? Have you seen him again?"

"No. That didn't go anywhere."

Alexei pulled over with Viktor, and we slid into the back seat. Rehearsals the next day would start later than usual, so Nata insisted it was the perfect night to go out. She called Marcos and told him we would meet him later at one of the bars. We mixed drinks at our apartment and had a blast trying on outfits in her closet. She dressed me in her new killer stilettos, skinny jeans, and a black silk tank top.

We met some of the other dancers at a trendy pizza restaurant downtown. Marcos joined us later at a bar nearby. The place was packed with people our age. Tobacco and perfume saturated the air, and the decibel level was unreal. More girls from the corps joined us. I had been spending a lot of time with them in the past week rehearsing for the dance of Myrta and the Wilis: damsels who had died of a broken heart.

The bar had a live band, and the music was fun and lively. We had more drinks and danced together to a string of popular songs. I felt relaxed and happy for the first time in weeks.

A couple of hours went by and after all those drinks, I was tipsy. The stilettos didn't help. I joined Nata and Marcos at a VIP area with low, half-moon-shaped couches. It felt good to be off my feet. When I stood, the room spun, and I had to lean on Marcos for support. Shit. He grabbed Nata and me by the hand and tugged us back to the dance floor where we joined the others.

Teo showed up and took Nata away. I went to the bar to get a water and saw them tangled up in a corner, dancing and making out. I ignored the growing emptiness in my chest.

Marcos appeared from behind and snaked his arms around my waist, pressing his body against mine in a slow dance. It didn't feel strange to have Marcos so close to me. I was used to it. When we partnered together in class, he handled me like clay, so his hands were familiar to my body. It wasn't a sexual thing, but as we slow danced, the familiar pull between us returned. He brought me closer, and I hesitated before circling my arms around his neck.

"What's wrong, babe? You're acting weird. Dance with me. Mmm...you smell good." His lips brushed my neck, and I shivered.

"Easy, there, playboy." I chuckled. "You have to see me in the morning, remember?"

"Not *tomorrow* morning." A mix of mint and alcohol laced his warm breath, sending another shiver through my whole body. *God.*

"Marcos..."

"Hmm."

"Marcos, come on, stop. We have a good thing between us, don't we? Don't screw it up because you're drunk and horny." I searched his eyes, but his mouth kept going back to my neck. "I'm talking to you." I pressed my palms against his chest and moved him away.

"What?" he groaned, finally meeting my eyes. "We're having a great time. Whatever this is, don't do it."

"You're slurring, you know."

"Oops." He smiled and pulled me back into his arms. I let him envelope me and surrendered to the temporary comfort of being pressed against him. Closing my eyes, I hugged him back, pretending for a moment that he was mine. I put my head on his shoulder, and he kissed my forehead. Our bodies swayed to the music, and Marcos squeezed me tighter. I felt him harden. *Oh, man.*

"You smell so good, Cami."

I squeezed my eyes tighter. Dammit. Why did this have to feel so great? I could just…let things play out. But deep down I knew Marcos was unreachable. He *wasn't* mine. This wasn't going to turn out the way I wanted. It would hurt. Damn it, I was pedaling backward. I broke away.

"Time for me to go."

"What? No, not yet," he said sulkily.

"It's late, I want to go home."

"Fine. We can go." He sighed, unwrapping himself from me. "You're such a buzzkill sometimes."

"Stay. I'll get a ride with one of the girls." I forced a smile. I needed to keep things normal. "There are lots of babes here looking for a cute ass like yours." I held his face, squeezing his cheeks together, and planted a kiss on his chin.

"No dway," he said through fish lips, then pulled my hand away. "I'm taking you home. I'm beat too. Let me get my coat."

We made our way to the door, saying good-bye to the others, then took a cab to my apartment. Marcos walked me to the foyer, taking my hand as I searched for the keys. When I turned to say good-bye to him, a black BMW parked farther across the street started the engine. The driver was hidden behind tinted windows. My heart kicked my chest. Could that be...? Oblivious, Marcos tugged on my hand.

"Can I stay? I'm a bit smashed."

From across the street, the BMW engine roared once. Then the tires screeched and the car darted away. I watched it disappear, then looked back at a sleepy Marcos.

"Sure."

"Cams, come here. You've got to see this," Marcos yelled from the living room where he was watching a rerun of *So You Think You Can Dance* while I changed into my pj's. "It's that chick Nata was telling you about. She's good."

Yawning, I moved his jacket and bag to the other couch. Marcos was almost as messy as I was. I sat beside him, and we watched the show in silence. When the commercial break came, he turned and wrapped his legs around my waist. His arms circled my neck, pulling me against him.

"Make out with me," he whispered, tracing wet kisses along my jaw. Fuck. How was I supposed to resist this? My stomach swam.

"Marcos...No." I pulled his hands away. "What's up with you tonight?"

"I want to make out with you. You look super-hot in these little pj's. It doesn't have to be complicated."

I cocked an eyebrow. "What happened to *friend-zoning*?"

"Free pass for a night?" He grinned.

My heart raced, pounding. *Yes! Yes! Say yes!* I shook my head no.

"Shit." He scowled and it was comical. "I'm permanently friend-zoned? I'm not sure I dig that."

"Well, it is what it is," I murmured.

"I can be your best friend with benefits." He raised his eyebrows suggestively.

Oh, man. That was a very, very tempting proposition. The devil had it for me, dammit. He kissed the palm of my hand, sensually, while his eyes burned into mine. In a trance, I watched him. He was a seduction master and I was his puppet. A shiver spread up my arm and down my back. Damn. I was so lonely, and the thought of sleeping curled up against his bare chest lured me in. Desire spread under my skin. His mouth moved slowly to my wrist, pulling me to him until our faces were close. He then took my jaw in his hand and kissed me on the mouth, so gently I had to close my eyes so I wouldn't melt in his hand. *Marcos*. He trailed kisses along my jaw while his other hand moved to the back of my head. I exhaled, lost. My God, was I letting this happen? He smelled divine. Heat radiated from him, and I exhaled, letting his stubble prickle the tips of my fingers when I touched him.

His phone's ringing startled us. I opened my eyes, the spell broken as our lips parted, and he reached back for the phone. He looked at the screen and smiled, then silenced it and tossed it back onto the couch. It was still facing up, so I could see the name clearly. Carla, one of the principals. I had seen her with Marcos a couple of times before, but it was a while ago, so I had figured it was over.

"Who was that?"

"Nobody," he said, interlacing his fingers with mine. "Where were we?"

Carla's name lit the screen again, this time in a text message. Two. Three. Then another call. Boy, she was persistent. Marcos growled and snatched the phone again.

"What's up?" He listened for a moment, smiled, and shook his head. "I can't right now." He paused, then laughed out loud. "Okay, then. Later." He hung up.

"Was that Carla?"

"Yeah." He reached for my hand.

"Are you two…dating?"

"Nah, not really. Nothing serious."

I looked down.

"Hey," he whispered, holding my chin and searching my eyes. "It's nothing."

The old knife in my chest sank a little deeper. Was I so desperate to have him close that I had almost let this happen? Fuck hormones.

"I'm tired, Marcos," I said, detangling from him.

"What? No. You're leaving?"

"Yup. I'm leaving your horny ass to go to bed. Good night." I turned away and blew him a kiss. My chest felt as if it was made out of lead. But I told myself that if I could walk away from Marcos, I could do anything. My life was finally on track, dammit. *I* was in control.

From my bed, I heard him fuss around in the living room. The clink of glass...Was he having another drink? His bare feet padded on the wood floor, approaching. I pretended to be asleep, feeling him standing at my bedroom door. My breathing was shallow, and I fought to keep it steady. I knew that if he came on to me again, it would be hard as hell to walk away a third time in one night.

In the darkness, I waited until complete silence filled the apartment.

Chapter 8

When I woke the next morning, Nata and Marcos had already left. The note on the counter made me smile.

My horny ass and I are leaving you to rest, Princess. Sorry about last night, I was a dick. I'll make it up to you.

X, M

Ugh. How could I *not* love him?

It was Saturday and I had no plans. It had been a full two weeks since my failed date with Sebastián, and his calls had finally stopped coming. Nata's romance with Teo was moving fast, and she was spending the weekend at his country house, so the forecast announced a quiet solo evening for me. I did my laundry, then an impromptu yoga class at the gym around the corner. My body was finally detangled and relaxed.

In just a few hours, I had managed to turn the apartment into a hurricane zone. My clothes were everywhere. Good that Nata was gone because she would have a fit. She was OCD-neat, and I was...well, much more *relaxed* about neatness. I slipped in bed at nine without feeling an ounce of guilt for not having plans.

Sunday, I sewed ribbons on my new pointe shoes and packed my bag for the next day. By early evening, I was done with errands, which left me alone with my thoughts—something I wanted to avoid. My personal life was at a negative, and the initial wave of excitement from my promotion was wearing off. In fact, I dreaded the next day's rehearsal. Working alongside Verónica so frequently was a drawback even I had underestimated. She was chronically bitchy, self-indulgent, and most of the time acted as if I weren't even in the room. Unfortunately, that also gave her the perfect edge to play Myrta, an air of superiority I lacked, and it made me anxious.

It was still early, but I was starving and didn't feel like cleaning up the apartment, so I decided to pay a visit to a nearby bookstore and get takeout. An evening with a book, sushi, and Freddo's dulce de leche granizado ice cream sounded perfect…and Nata wouldn't be home to carb-police me.

I showered and quickly dried my hair. As I stared into the mirror, I got a flashback of the BMW across the street from the night before. Had that been Sebastián? Sometimes it felt like I had imagined even meeting him. Unbidden, the memories flashed through my mind like a movie trailer, and the familiar weight of loneliness tugged.

I wandered the bookstore aisles, browsing the titles in the thriller section, making sure there was no romance involved. I settled on *The Girl with The Dragon Tattoo*, paid at the counter, and stepped into the crisp fall evening.

Outside, the night was wintry, the city lights hazy under the spell of an early fog. On the blocks back to my apartment, people passed me with their collars up and their chins down. The wind stirred a pile of dry leaves on the sidewalk. I zipped up my coat and hurried, resolving to go straight home and call for the takeout. As I turned the corner, the low hum of a car engine behind me grew closer. Even though the streets were alive with pedestrians, my mind immediately flashed back to the night of the Roxy, and my pulse jumped. Shit. Resisting the urge to turn around, I waited for the car to pass. But it lingered. *Go, you fucker.* My shoulders tensed and I quickened my steps. Seriously, what the hell? When had I become a stalker magnet? I was only a block away from home when the car behind me pulled over, matching my pace. Fuck. Adrenaline prickled my scalp. I forced my attention forward as I debated whether I should let whoever was in that car see me walk into my building. I was about to turn back toward the bookstore when the driver lowered his window. Shit.

"Hey," a low, familiar voice called.

That voice.

I whipped my head around and skidded to a halt. Sebastián half smiled from the driver seat. My heart lurched into my throat. What the f—

"Sorry, I didn't mean to scare you." He winced guiltily, and then that panty-melting smile stretched on his face.

I opened my mouth, then closed it. My heart hammered against my ribs. Shit. *Shit.* What the hell was he doing here? I set off in the direction of my apartment.

"Wait. Can we talk?" he said from the car, accelerating to catch up with me again.

I ignored him.

"Camila. Stop. I need to talk to you." His tone was suddenly low, commanding.

"I can't. I gotta run," I said, hurrying.

The tires screeched as he gunned the car forward, then slammed on the breaks and parked by my building a few steps ahead. He leapt out and faced me.

I stopped in my tracks. Bastard. Glorious as fucking ever. He looked delicious, his strong frame barely concealed under a navy blue sweater and faded jeans.

"Please, I need to talk to you," he said in a softer tone. "A minute of your time. That's all I'm asking for."

I forced myself to look away, fighting the immediate effect his presence was having on my body. Traitorous body.

"Get back in your car and disappear. I know you're good at that."

He lifted his hands in surrender. "Fine. I deserve that. Look, I don't like how I left things. I owe you an explanation."

I forced a smile. "Well, it's your lucky day. You're off the hook."

"You didn't return my calls. I left you messages. Did you get my flowers?"

I shrugged, looking down at my feet. "I gave them away."

"You did?"

"Yes. They were gorgeous. But I didn't want them in my apartment."

"So, you *did* like them." He repressed a smile, and it was contagious.

"Damn it, don't make me smile. I'm still mad at you." I crossed my arms over my chest and shook my head. God, why was he here, looking like that? I didn't need this now. We were standing by my building, and he glanced at the foyer.

"Can I come in?"

"No, my roommate is upstairs," I lied.

"Fine then. We can do this here." He ran both hands through his hair, letting out a long sigh. "I'm sorry I couldn't make our date. I was five miles offshore and had no signal. It was supposed to be a short trip, but then things went south. I had no way of getting to you. I'm so sorry."

"It's fine," I said, biting my lip.

"No, it isn't, and you deserve better." He took a cautious step toward me. "But I haven't stopped thinking about you."

What I thought was a very well-iced part inside me melted a tiny bit at those words. I tightened my arms around myself, not trusting my unscrupulous body, and leaned on the brick wall behind me, looking down at my Converse. They were much safer than his eyes.

He inched closer and his finger lifted my chin. I turned away and he let his hand drop.

"Are you still mad at me?" he said, his tone soft.

"I waited for you for almost an hour, and you didn't show up. It rained."

"Shit, I'm really sorry," he said, guilt leaking out with every word. "Let me make it up to you."

"No, really. It's okay," I said, still not looking at him. "I blew off rehearsing with a principal to go out with you that night. I let you string me along, away from what's important to me. And that's on me. I know better."

"I'm sorry. I didn't know all that."

I nodded, darting a swift look at him.

"Please, let me take you some place where we can talk and have dinner."

I looked up and searched his eyes. "You don't even know me. I'm just...another girl to you. Why are you even here?"

"You're not just another girl. I don't let people in easily, Camila, and I haven't stopped thinking about you."

I kept my eyes down so he wouldn't see the sudden turmoil those words caused in me. My instincts told me to flee. The heat radiating from him was electric, his presence strong, invasive. That magnetic force sparked between us, and I hugged myself tighter. Anything that could mess with my will this way surely wasn't good. His hand cradled my face, his fingers sending shivers down my neck, and I pressed myself back against the bricks.

"I'm so sorry," he said, closer. My skin tingled at the warmth from his hand. I closed my eyes, knowing our lips were inches apart. "The truth is… I know I shouldn't be here. I should let you be. I just… feel this strong impulse to protect you, from everything, from me. And yet, here I am, a fool, begging you for another chance, because I can't stop thinking about the way I felt when I kissed you." His voice was soft, tender, his sweet words brushing my mouth, and I felt the last of my breath leave my body. Then his lips met mine, softly, sensually, and as lethal as the first time. A whirl of emotions spun in my head while my body screamed for his touch. I let out a small gasp, and his fingers threaded in my hair, his mouth consuming mine, taking, giving, exploring. I gripped his sweater at the waist, holding on as hot, thick desire rippled through me. No, no, no. I couldn't do this. I couldn't let him in. He already had more power over me than I thought possible. Summoning all my strength, I tore myself away from him.

"I can't. I'm sorry, I just can't," I said, panting.

He exhaled, nodding in understanding. "Okay."

I needed to escape from this, from him. My skin still burned where he touched me, and my whole body ached for more. I looked down, still panting as I reached in my pocket for my keys.

Shit.

My keys.

I clenched my empty fist. A memory of placing them on the counter at the bookstore while I dug in my pockets for the bills flashed in my mind. Fuck, fuck, fuck. I tugged up my sleeve to glance at my watch.

"What's wrong?" Sebastián frowned.

I looked around, chewing on the inside of my cheek.

"Camila."

"I think I left my keys at the bookstore."

"I'll drive you."

"No." I shook my head and rushed to the intercom where I pressed the button to Mrs. Garibaldi's floor, since she kept a spare key to water our plants when we were gone. Nothing. I insisted, again and again. Where in the hell was she?

"Let me drive you," Sebastián said from behind. "It's almost eight. We may still catch them before they close."

I let out a defeated sigh and hung my head.

The second I got in the car, the engine roared and skidded into traffic. I gripped the seat as Sebastián deftly zigzagged his way through the few blocks to the bookstore. But when we pulled over by the store window, all the lights were off.

"Dammit."

"Sorry." He sighed. "Can I take you somewhere else?"

I scanned through my options. My parents' place was too far away. Marcos was out somewhere in La Imprenta, also far. Maybe Nata was on her way back...

"I'll try calling my roommate." I tapped her number, but it went straight to voicemail, which probably meant her phone was dead. I could call Alexei's phone—ugh, no.

I tried Mrs. Garibaldi's number again, and it rang for a long time. I was about to hang up when she finally picked up. She sounded tipsy and said she was having dinner with a friend and would be home in a couple of hours. That wasn't too bad. I could kill time in a café, and I wouldn't have to ask Alexei.

"Any luck?" Sebastián asked.

"My neighbor will be home soon, and she has a key to my apartment. I'll just wait for her over in that café. Thanks for driving me here." I reached for the door handle, but he gently caught my arm.

"Wait."

My pulse sprinted at the contact. I slowly turned my head, and those glorious eyes were waiting.

"Have you eaten?"

I chuckled. "Is that your favorite pickup line?"

He smiled smugly. "Have you?"

"Um, no, but—"

"Let me take you out, then. We can wait for your neighbor."

I opened my mouth to reject the offer, but he stopped me.

"I won't leave you to wait on your own. Please, let me take you to dinner. Make up for the date I owe you."

"You don't owe me anything."

"One dinner. Then I'll let you be if that's what you want."

Chapter 9

We pulled up by a quaint restaurant in Palermo Viejo overlooking a dimly lit park peppered with oaks. Sebastián killed the engine and looked up at the building.

"I come here sometimes. It's great, private. I know the couple who owns the place. You'll like them."

He opened my door and led me through an ornate iron gate enclosing a patio bathed in a soft, ivory glow. Inside, the building looked like it had once been a traditional Buenos Aires home. It was beautiful, only ten or fifteen tables in the main dining room. A woman in her late fifties greeted Sebastián with a warm embrace. A man about the same age rounded the bar and shook Sebastián's hand, affectionately patting his back.

"Sebastián, what a pleasure." His warm eyes immediately assessed me. "And with such delightful company. Welcome, miss."

Sebastián grinned. "Guillermo, Liliana, this is Camila."

The couple smiled and kissed my cheek. "Welcome," said Liliana, squeezing my hand.

"Thank you," I said, a bit taken back. Maybe he didn't bring many dates here.

Liliana guided us to a balcony with just one table overlooking the park. Tiny lights adorned the iron railing under a layer of jasmine foliage, the sweet perfume of the flowers infusing the air. It was private and damn, so romantic.

"It's beautiful here." I sighed in resignation, glancing at the park below. What was I doing here? I had promised myself I would stay away, and here I was, back at the start. But I couldn't help the way I felt with him. Free, cherished. And every time he touched me...my body was so aware of him. I opened the menu to distract myself.

"Yes. This is one of my favorite places. Removed from the reality of the outside world," he said.

I closed the menu again and set it on the table. "So…tell me about that. The 'outside world.' I don't really know anything about you. Tell me about your family."

"Jumping right into it, eh? My family…Well, you must have seen my last name on the card I gave you."

"So?"

"It doesn't ring a bell?"

I shook my head no, and he watched me with a puzzled expression.

"Well," he said, "Palacios is a…heavy name in certain circles. It can open a lot of doors because it's linked to many businesses, even politics, but unfortunately that also means lots of gossip."

"Sounds glamorous."

"Hm. More like…wearing. Constantly dodging the spotlight is a pain."

"So, you're like, famous?"

"Not by choice, or my own merit. My father's a well-known man in the business world. The umbrella of the public eye hovers over the family."

"Chased by the paparazzi—every dancer's dream."

He shook his head. "It is not as fun as you'd think."

"Why not?"

"The media loves to make stories up about my family and our businesses. It sells."

"What kind of businesses are you involved in?" I asked, breaking off a little piece of white bread and popping it into my mouth. Mmm, it was good. I couldn't remember the last time I'd had plain white bread.

"Personally, I'm dedicated to my studio. But I help my father occasionally at the docks in Puerto Madero."

I narrowed my eyes. "You're being a bit…evasive."

"I'm sorry." He smiled. "I don't mean to be, it's just habit. I don't like talking about my family. I'd rather keep things simple."

"I get it. You're a successful architect from a high-profile family with a questionable reputation. I'm a professional ballerina from a middle-class family with no such ties. We're not exactly in the same league."

He reached out for my hand, enveloping it in his, his expression serious. "No, Camila. You're a beautiful girl with a normal life. That's the way it should be."

"What does that even mean? And, I'm sorry, but my life is not exactly normal."

"It means you're free to do what you love, come and go as you please. You're free from the burden that comes with a name like mine."

"Everyone carries one kind of burden or another with them."

"Perhaps, but you're genuine, unaffected. That's why I like you."

Despite the guard I held up, I felt myself melt a little more at those words. He looked at me like I was his favorite person in the world, and it was…disarming. Liliana appeared with a bottle of Malbec. She and Sebastián talked briefly about the wine, and then she took our order. We toasted, and I took a sip, letting the rich, spice-laced Malbec warm my throat. I focused on my wine so I wouldn't look at him so much. It annoyed me that I found him so sexy—the soft, masterfully disheveled strands of raven hair that grazed his forehead, his striking eyes against olive skin, that five o'clock stubble, those full lips that tasted so incredibly good.

He wanted to know about my family, and I quickly ran through the basics, a bit self-conscious because, in comparison, we seemed so plain. Our worlds were almost opposite. He had unlimited access to things I only dreamed of. I wondered how it would feel to belong to a high-profile family and have the world be your playground, to be constantly at the center of the public eye.

A few minutes later, Liliana appeared again with our dinner, smiling warmly. Her curious hazel eyes assessed me with amusement, then she left silently.

"Okay, your turn," I said as I bit into my bife de chorizo, the Argentinean version of a rib eye steak. Mmm…it was mouthwatering. "What do you love most about your work?"

He thought for a moment, holding me under his intense gaze. Then a corner of his mouth turned up in a puzzled smile.

"What?" I said.

He shrugged. "Nothing. It's just…That's not a question I get often."

"Oh."

"Don't get me wrong. It's refreshing. People usually want to talk about business. Boring stuff. I like your question much better."

"Oh. Good then. So? What do you love about it?"

"I guess…it's what lies beneath the blueprints. I've always been amazed at how history is alive in every brick of a building." He glanced at the dimly lit neighborhood below. "Buildings always tell the story so much better than people can."

"Is that why you chose architecture?"

"That's part of it. I've always had a strong, creative impulse. Even as a kid, I liked turning things around and upside down, looking for new ways that make more sense."

"For example?"

"Hmm…I love how if you redirect natural light in the right way, it could make someone feel inspired and produce much more creative work."

"So, it's about having control?"

He chuckled. "Maybe. Though I would like to think of it as 'provoking inspiration.'"

"Okay. You like to inspire…to be influential."

"I do, but I also enjoy the challenging aspect of the job. There's a certain thrill that comes with innovation without compromising what's in the heart of the structure, adapting new technologies into the skeleton of an old building while keeping its soul intact. And the design has to be rooted in the soul."

"What if it's a brand-new house or building? What if there's no soul yet?"

He smiled like he was enjoying being challenged.

"Every structure, whether it's public or a private home, needs to reflect the heart of the people that inhabit it. That's where it starts, and it has to be present in every detail. I always study the people first, then think of the best possible design for them. That's what gets me out of bed every morning. Sorry," he said, "I'm rambling."

"No. It's interesting. You're so passionate about your work. Believe me, I get that."

His eyes blazed and I had to look away. He then reached for my hand again, and our fingers instinctively interlaced. I fought the feeling that infiltrated me, tugging me to him with the pull of that invisible magnet. He squeezed my hand gently, forcing me to make eye contact. A shiver ran through me.

"You haven't looked at me all night," he said.

"I...I'm sorry." I blushed furiously.

"No, Camila. I hate that I left you waiting that night. *I* am sorry." His thumb caressed my hand.

"Okay," I muttered, unsure what else to say. Our hands were still linked together, his warmth expanding up my arm and through the rest of me. *God.* I was on a roller coaster, the car slowly making its way up, rattling along the old tracks, preparing for the death drop.

A busboy approached and asked if he could clear. I looked at my half-eaten plate apologetically.

"It was delicious. I just can't eat any more."

Sebastián smiled. Our intimate moment dissipated and our fingers detangled. I stifled a yawn.

"Let's get you home."

We drove back to my place in comfortable silence. When we got to my building, he took my hand as we walked to the foyer. I looked down at our interlocked fingers, at the source of that overpowering warmth that threatened to swallow me. His hand was big, protective. Before I could do anything stupid, I pressed Mrs. Garibaldi's intercom, and she said she would be right down.

"Thank you for tonight," he said, his tone sincere. "I loved having dinner with you."

"I had a nice time too." I glanced up at him, and his gaze was ardent, waiting. He was so good-looking. In an earth-shattering way. I let my eyes devour him, memorize the beautiful lines of his face, his lips, his jaw, those broad shoulders that towered over me.

"I better go," he said, his voice low and sexy.

Unable to stop myself, I reached out and placed my hand on his chest, needing to touch him. He stilled, his breath catching as those beautiful pale eyes watched me. Shivers rolled through me, and those butterflies swarmed. His strong Adam's apple bobbed as he swallowed.

"Good-bye, crazy girl," he said, and his tone was hoarse. "I'm glad we met, even if you stole a piece of my heart." There was an undercurrent of sadness in those words, and it tugged at that place in my heart that wanted to know what was behind that strong, imposing façade.

"Sebastián." It came out as a plea. Way too eager for my own good. His presence was overwhelming, his warmth consuming.

He closed his eyes as if the way I said his name called at a place deep inside him. He let out a low, soft growl, and his hands clasped my face, his thumbs stroking my cheeks as his eyes opened and that intense gaze burned on mine. I held my breath, fighting the frenzy he was causing. Desire throbbed in my veins as the invisible tether I had felt that day at the river pulled us closer. He pressed a kiss to my forehead with a longing that mirrored my own. Unable to restrain the chaos inside me, I placed my hands over his, squeezing my fingers as my lips reached up to meet his. His mouth welcomed me, a desperate sound rumbling from his throat as his hands brought me closer. He pressed me against the brick wall, every part of him hard. My blood sang, pulsing with a need I had never felt before for anyone, not even Marcos. A need so voracious and raw that it scared me. I gripped his biceps, afraid my legs would give while his mouth devoured me.

The sound of keys in the foyer door broke the spell, and he pulled away, panting, his eyes wide with a mix of awe and shock. He traced my bottom lip with his thumb, catching his breath.

"Beautiful. Stunning," he said, his voice gruff. The hint of a smile curved up a corner of his mouth as he turned to Mrs. Garibaldi, who was watching us with a conspiratorial grin.

I stood, frozen and bereft as Sebastián exchanged a few pleasantries with my neighbor before turning back to me.

"You have my number...and all the power," he said with a shy smile. "Good night, princess. Take care of yourself, okay?" His tone was sincere, and that same longing from before settled in his expression. I smiled weakly at him, still caught in the tornado whirling inside me, the words strangled in my throat as I watched him walk back to his car and speed off into the midnight traffic, and away from me.

"Okay, let's run through the first variation again," Madame said. The corps girls quickly lined up and we waited for the music.

Outside the giant windows of the studio, weightless rain dusted the city. Flashbacks of my dinner with Sebastián a few nights ago taunted my concentration as I went through classes and rehearsals. I pushed them away.

I hadn't called him. I wanted to, more than I was willing to admit, but I was terrified of the way he made me feel. Keeping the possibility at a reachable distance gave me a sense of control and safety.

On the flip side, seeing Marcos with other girls salted the wound of being unwanted. Nata had been spending most of her free time with Teo lately, and even though I had my priorities where I wanted them, loneliness was starting to get to me. Both Nata and Marcos were able to handle a social life outside of ballet. Why couldn't I?

I was going out for a quick lunch when I caught a glimpse of Marcos and Carla tucked behind a column, making out. I paused, knowing they couldn't see me, and watched them in a masochistic trance. His hands traveled down her back, then grabbed her ass and lifted her so she hugged him with her legs. It was hot, indecent, and sensual as fuck. My heart constricted with pain. Fighting the knot in my throat, I ran outside for air. Hurt, loneliness, and that old anguish of feeling unwanted sliced through me. The ache in my throat swelled with the tears that wanted to break free. How long was I going to put myself through this? How many times? I pulled out my phone, clutching it hard. There was only one person that could take this pain away. My fingers flew across the screen as I tapped a new text message:

I want to see you.

Chapter 10

It was late afternoon, and Madame wasn't happy with the Wilis choreography. We had to stay late, and by the time we were done, the sky was dark. Outside, I shivered in the damp evening air. The sky had cleared, and scattered puddles of rain stained the sidewalk.

Beside me, Nata stood bundled inside a scarf and a long coat. I tightened my parka around me while we waited for Marcos. Alexei and Viktor fidgeted impatiently. After a brief exchange in Russian, Nata told them to give Marcos five more minutes. Alexei protested, and she waved him off in irritation. I was used to making out their conversations in Russian from their tones and gestures. After a day of back-to-back rehearsals, we were all irritable and short-tempered.

"What the hell is Marcos still doing in there?" Nata snapped.

I shrugged. "I saw him talking to Carla. I think she's the new catch."

"Dammit, Marcos. Alexei, Viktor, go get the car. We're out of here." She turned to me. "Do you have your keys? I left mine at home this morning."

"I think…" I fished in my bag, digging through a jumble of pointe shoes and ribbons and things. Bingo. As I whooshed them out, they slipped out of my hand and landed a couple of feet ahead. I bent forward in a mock arabesque, but the fatigue of the day kicked in, and I lost my balance and ended up on all fours on the wet sidewalk. "Fuckdammit."

Nata giggled. "What are you doing?"

I growled but froze when a pair of fine suede shoes the shade of tobacco stopped beside me.

Expensive shoes.

"Can I…help?" the familiar velvety voice said.

Shit. I snapped my head up and drew in a sharp breath. Sebastián's bright eyes watched me, amused. He leaned down, his mouth curved into that patented dignity-crushing smile.

"Here," he said, picking up and handing me the keys. He offered his hand and helped me up. The heat on my face could have smoldered an entire village.

"Thanks," I said, suddenly aware of my ruffled appearance. I normally didn't see anyone but dancers after work, and they were as sweaty and sticky as I was.

"Hi." His mouth repressed smug amusement.

"Hi." Shit. I had texted him earlier, but did he have to show up right then? I hadn't even changed. Discreetly, I lowered my chin to my shoulder and sniffed. How bad did I stink? I bet he was already questioning his decision to come. I was a total mess. In contrast, he was impeccably dressed in a white crisp shirt, a gray cashmere sweater, and a long wool overcoat. I adjusted my bag on my shoulder. He smiled again in that way that stopped my brain from performing basic functions.

A hand squeezed my shoulder from behind. Shoot. Nata. I had forgotten she was even there. I turned around, and she was frowning, her cerulean eyes puzzled.

"Cami, who's your friend?" Her tone was cautious, deceptively sweet. I stared at her blankly while my brain played catch-up.

"Yeah…Yes. Nata, this is…Sebastián. Sebastián, this is Nata." Crap. She looked annoyed. I hadn't really told her about Sebastián, and I knew she was shocked that a guy she had never met was stopping by my work at the end of the day.

She glanced at Sebastián, and her face suddenly tightened and paled, as if she had realized she was looking at something dangerous. He appraised her with the same intensity. Her eyes darted to his bodyguard standing a few steps behind. She inhaled sharply and looked back at Sebastián, letting the air out through flared nostrils. I frowned. What was her problem? And why was Sebastián looking at her like that? Not the reaction she usually got from guys…at all.

"How do you know each other?" she asked without unlocking her eyes from him.

Hmmm…Where to begin? I knew this would be a long conversation, and once I started, an avalanche of questions would follow. I gave an innocent shrug.

"We met the day I dropped Anna's shoe in the middle of the street. I told you, remember? Sebastián kind of…pulled me out of the traffic. He was also the one who helped me that night at the Roxy."

She frowned. "I see."

Sebastián intercepted. "I'm sorry to show up like this. I'm actually on my way to the airport, but I wanted to see you before I left."

"Oh. Um…where…where are you going?"

"Brazil. Short business trip. Can I give you a ride home?"

I rubbed the back of my neck. I was dog-tired, but I didn't want to stink up his car. Walking would give us more time together, and I could stretch my legs. The intense routine of arabesques for Myrta had my quads in knots, and walking would help.

"Do you mind if we walk?" I glanced over his shoulder, and the same bodyguard from the night at the Roxy nodded a brief greeting.

"Camila…" Nata said, but I handed her the keys, locking eyes with her.

"I'll explain later," I whispered.

"You're walking home with *him*?"

"I am. I'll see you in a few, okay?" I gave her a quick kiss on the cheek and turned away.

Sebastián took my hand and shot Nata a quick look. His lips were pressed into a straight line. The odd interaction between them made me shudder. When I turned my head around, Nata was watching us with her mouth slack, as if she wanted to protest, but the words failed her. A speechless Natascha. That was new.

"What was that between you two?" I said. "The way you were looking at Nata. It was weird." We stood at the light, waiting to cross.

Sebastián's eyes focused somewhere ahead. "She's very protective of you. I was intrigued, that's all. You look beautiful."

"Right. You're a good liar."

"No. You look beautiful." He looked down at me with a serious expression, making it hard to concentrate on anything else.

On the way home, the evening was alive, the streets flooded with pedestrians. He held my hand, walking awkwardly around people so he wouldn't have to let go. The familiar pull was there again. He kissed my hand and my insides fluttered. Somewhere behind us, his bodyguard kept a manageable distance.

"Does he go with you everywhere?"

He frowned. "Who?"

"The huge man that follows you around."

"Rafa. Yes." He chuckled. "Pretty much. I forget sometimes. But don't tell him I said that." He winked. "He'd be pissed."

"But you were alone the other night."

"I gave him the night off. I needed to find you," he said with a sly smile. We walked in silence for a couple of blocks. It was strange, new, thrilling. Suddenly he tugged on my hand and pulled me to the side of a building, away from people. He enveloped me in his arms, pressing us against the marble façade of a jewelry store. My pulse sprinted.

"Was it okay that I came? I didn't want you to change your mind. You made me wait."

I smiled shyly. "It's good for you. I get the feeling most people don't make you wait."

He smiled back, and before I could say anything else, his mouth closed on mine. His right hand was suddenly in my hair while his left pressed the small of my back against him. My mind screamed, *Jesus, you need a shower!* But the rest of me was hostage to the force that drew me to him. My blood ignited. How had I managed to stay away? I let my arms wrap around him and succumbed to the kiss, hoping my deodorant would be true to the 24-hour stink-block promises on the commercials. When he pulled away, we were both breathless.

"God, you're bewitching," he whispered against my lips. I blinked through the daze.

"I…I stink."

"What?" He wavered between smiling and frowning.

"I…You're all dressed up and clean, and I need a shower."

He threw his head back in laughter. "I don't care at all. It's kind of sexy, actually." The pad of his thumb caressed my mouth, and a shiver spread down my back and swirled between my legs. I looked up at those stunning eyes. My brain was in central crash mode. This beautiful man. A corner of his mouth curved down, a hint of suede and fresh soap teasing me as I breathed in. Shit. I felt like the rabbit facing the fox.

His arms tightened around my back, pressing me against him, and he kissed me again. I nearly expired. The heat radiating from his body threatened to dissolve what was left of my resolve. *Christ.* The roller coaster cart inched uphill, balancing at the drop-off. I closed my eyes, breathless.

"I like you, crazy girl. So much." He dipped his chin, and once again his mouth found mine. It was soft at first, then he crushed me against him as the kiss intensified. My insides clenched and I suddenly couldn't keep hold. So I let go, relinquishing all control, succumbing to the fall.

He devoured me, greedily, and blazing need spread through me like fire on dry brush. I surrendered to that expert mouth, my hands clenching his shirt. God, I didn't know what this was, or why I wanted this man in a way I didn't know was possible. I kissed him with abandon, lost in a turmoil of foreign sensations. My panties were wet. I pressed myself against his hard cock, and he squeezed me against him, fueling the desire pumping in my veins. His fingers stroked my back, sending tingles along my burning skin. He then withdrew gently and pressed his forehead to mine, our short breaths colliding.

"What are you doing to me, Camila? You are addictive. The closer I get to you, the more I want."

I blinked through the whiplash, fighting to recover my balance. He had articulated my own thoughts. My mind spun wildly, lost in the aftermath of a nuclear attack to my hormones.

"I think...I want more too."

"Does this mean you're giving us another chance?"

"Well...you left me intrigued about your tainted family reputation." I suppressed a smile.

"A thrill for danger. I'll have to keep a close eye on you." His hand snaked around my waist, and he brought me to him, claiming my mouth again. My legs wanted to give. He then let go, took my hand, and set off again, leaving me breathless.

We walked in silence. A thought barged into my head, and I frowned. "About that..."

"What?" He pulled me closer to let a group of teens pass us.

"The other night...Was it you parked across the street from my apartment?"

His expression tightened, then a small shrug. "I wanted to make sure you were okay."

I stopped mid-street. "At two in the morning?"

The light had changed, and he clasped my hand, tugging me across.

"One of my men saw you leave a bar and get in a cab with some guy. I was on my way home, not far from your apartment. I wanted to make sure you made it home safe."

This time I fully stopped. I let go of his hand and stared up at him. People walked past us, dodging us awkwardly.

"What's wrong?" His forehead creased.

"Do you have any idea how creepy that sounds? You had me *followed*?"

"I only kept a few tabs on you to make sure you were safe. Given that you were nearly killed the first time we met, and stalked by that shithead on the second, I was worried about you. I'm protective of whom I care about." His tone was firm, unapologetic. I didn't know if I was freaked out or turned on. Or both.

I shook my head. "That's…crazy."

"Your safety is very important to me." His hand circled the small of my back, bringing me closer. "Incidentally, the guy you took home with you. Is he someone you care about?"

"Who? Marcos? Uh, no. I mean, yes, I care. We're good friends and we work together, but that's all. He sleeps on our couch sometimes if he's too drunk to go home." I ignored the heat rising to my face.

"I see." His arm tightened around my waist and lifted me into an embrace. "I didn't mean to scare you. I just have this compelling urge to protect you."

"I don't need protection," I growled. "I'm a big girl."

He crushed me into a kiss, and the last of my armor dropped. His mouth was possessive and tender at the same time.

On the last few blocks, the conversation was lighter. He asked me about my day at the theater, and I blabbed about Madame being in a foul mood. People sidestepped us, mumbling curses at our slow pace. He seemed interested in every detail of my monotonous life. It was weird to talk ballet with someone who wasn't a dancer. Pretty much everyone I knew had a routine like mine.

At my building door, he cradled my face in his hands. "I came to see you tonight because I want to ask you out. On a real date."

My heart did a little pirouette. "Is it safe? I mean…will I need my own bodyguard to go out with you?"

He pulled me into his arms. "I'll keep you safe."

"Okay. Then, yes."

He watched me as if he were looking at something beautiful, even though I was sweaty, sticky, and had no makeup. Picking up a loose strand of my hair, he tucked it gently behind my ear. I leaned into his touch as the back of his hand caressed my cheek. He cupped my face, bringing me closer. Rolling to the tips of my toes, I brushed my lips against his. He covered my mouth with his. The kiss was soft and tender. I slipped my hands under his coat and clutched his shirt at the back. He smelled heavenly. Tasted forbidden. It was sinful, hot.

The guy from the third floor harrumphed behind us. Without taking his eyes off mine, Sebastián pressed me against him to let him by. My face was impossibly hot. The man closed the door behind him, shaking his head but smiling.

"I have to get going," he said. "My flight leaves soon. But I'll pick you up tomorrow night, and we can have dinner at my house?"

His house? Holy shit. "Okay."

He tipped his head down and gave me one last, slow, panty-scorching kiss.

Still tipsy, I stepped into the apartment and dropped my bag by the door. Nata stood behind the kitchen bar, her face tight as she tossed arugula in a bowl.

"Hey," I said.

"Whatever."

"Nata—"

"You've kept me totally in the dark! How long have you known him?" Her high pitch made me wince. She shot me a disapproving look, then went back to the salad. I slid onto a barstool across from her and leaned onto the counter.

"I'm sorry. You're right. What do you want to know?"

She placed both palms flat on the counter and looked up. "Camila, do you have any idea who that guy is?"

I frowned. "Do *you*?"

"Of course. And so does the rest of the city."

"What? What do you know about him?"

"Oh…where to start," she said in a sarcastic tone. "Let's see, he belongs to one of the biggest, most dangerous and corrupt families in the country. Yep. I think that covers it."

"Okay, well. He's not like that, okay? He's actually really nice, funny, and very charming."

"Well then, if he's charming, you should've led with that."

"What is your problem?"

"My problem? Are you out of your mind? You're in way over your head."

"Why?"

"That family is dangerous."

"Dangerous how?"

She let out a long sigh of irritation.

"Tell me."

She gave me a long look, assessing.

"Well?"

"My family's main imports go through the port of Buenos Aires, and Sebastián's family owns that monopoly. That's why I know them. Look, I stay out of all that, but I know enough to say that the farther you get from this guy, the better. The Palacios family is bad news."

"What the hell does that mean?"

She kept her eyes down, avoiding mine. Then she finally looked up, her face etched in concern. "They're high profile in very powerful circles. People call them the Kings of Midnight. They own all the docks in Puerto Madero. A lot of different businesses, too, it's a whole empire. Don Martín, Sebastián's father, controls everything. Nothing gets past him, or his right hand, Julián de la Viña. When it comes to imports, they call the shots, and if anyone refuses to play by their rules, they're out of business, for good, or they just…disappear."

"Come on."

"I'm serious. Find someone else, Cami. Anyone. Just…not him."

I took a gulp of water from an open bottle on the counter. Shit. I didn't want to know any more. "Let's drop it, okay?"

"Camila, just…be careful."

"Jesus, I only went out with him once."

"You already went out with him?"

"Yeah, the other night."

"Camila!"

I raised my palms. "It was just dinner. Then he brought me back here and said good night. Don't get excited."

"You have no idea what—"

"Nata. Please. I'm a big girl."

"Do your parents know?"

"No. It was one date."

"Why him?"

"Because...I like him."

She turned away and reached into a cabinet for plates. "Whatever," she said. "I just...I don't like this."

I rolled my eyes. "Look, seriously. I hardly know him. And before you flip out, I'm seeing him again tomorrow. He came by the theater tonight to ask me out." I busied myself with another long gulp of water.

She turned. "Another date?"

"Yes."

"I.... Shit." She sighed. "I still can't believe you didn't tell me any of this. Can I persuade you to reconsider? Meet one of Teo's friends?" She leaned casually on the counter, the brilliant negotiator she was.

"Let's drop this, really. Did you make enough for me?" I picked up a bag of sliced almonds from the counter and unzipped the seal.

Nata pulled the bowl away. "No almonds. All my costumes are almost finished. I really need to watch it till opening night."

"Stop it, you're a twig." I reached for her hand. "Hey, I want you to be okay with this. I'll take care of myself."

Her expression hardened. "I'll be watching him."

Friday rehearsal was painful. There appeared to be a lot of problem areas with Act I, which sent Madame's mood downhill. I snuck glances at the wall clock, wondering if the damned thing was broken.

When rehearsal was finally over, I bolted to the door, almost tripping over Verónica.

"Watch it!" she said, and I smiled. I took the stairs two at a time, then hailed a taxi as I rushed to the curb.

By nine in the evening, I was ready—and a nervous wreck. I browsed through my new *Pointe* magazine but couldn't sit still and kept turning pages without paying attention. *Jesus, calm down.*

I was all out of distractions when the downstairs doorbell finally rang. I sprinted. Pausing by the intercom, I chuckled at my lack of practice being on a date.

"Hey," Sebastián's low voice greeted me. Electricity traveled through me. *Damn.*

"I'll be down in a sec."

Chapter 11

He waited, leaning casually against the brick wall outside the foyer. Our eyes met through the glass door, and he gave me a little wave. I grinned like an idiot.

"Hello, beautiful," he said, and I couldn't remember how to breathe. His gaze locked on my mouth like he wanted to kiss me.

"Hi."

He tipped his head down, and our lips formed a slow, intimate kiss.

"I'm one lucky bastard." He held my face in his hands—something I was getting used to and it sent my pulse sprinting every time—brushing my hair back as he looked deep into my eyes. I lost myself in that uncharted color of his. He smiled, interlacing his fingers with mine and tugging me toward the street. "I can't wait to show you my house."

We walked, holding hands like two kids who had just became best friends. After a block or so, he stopped by a vintage, silver Alfa Romeo sports car and opened the passenger door.

"Very James Bond-ish," I said.

Inside, the car was sleek and elegant. A vintage piece of art. It suited him. Sebastián blazed in and out of traffic with ease. I worried we would get pulled over for speeding, but he seemed unconcerned. Goose bumps prickled my arm when his hand brushed mine as he reached out to switch gears.

At the light, I stole a glance at the defined lines of his profile and wondered what I had done right to have this glorious man interested in taking me out on a date. He caught me staring and flashed a smile.

"I have a confession to make," he said sternly, looking back at the road.

"Oh?"

"I'm very excited about this date. A bit nervous, even." He bit his lip to hold a smile. Mmm, his mouth was so sexy.

"Me too," I said. "But…why would you be nervous? Don't you do this all the time? Dates?"

"Hmm…Yes and no."

"Oh, come on. I doubt you have any problems meeting women."

He rubbed the back of his head and shrugged. "I meet people, yes. But they're always the same. Outside of work commitments, I don't go out much. I find the whole dating thing just…well, boring, to be honest."

At least we have that in common.

"But there must've been someone special," I said. "Someone that stole your heart?"

His expression was suddenly somber. "A long time ago," he said. A pang of jealousy flicked my mind. Suddenly I wanted to know everything about this mystery woman. "You intrigue me," he said, distracting me.

"I do?"

"Yes. I haven't met anyone I connected with…well, like this." He shot me a glance, and I could swear I saw him blush. It was adorable, and unbelievably sexy.

We drove north through the neighborhoods that bordered the river: La Lucila, Martinez, Acassuso. The houses quickly became more affluent and spaced apart as we turned toward the river and down the hills of San Isidro. He stopped by an ornate iron gate and punched in a code. The gate opened slowly, giving way to a long, winding road that disappeared into a thick forest. A collage of greens unfolded endlessly in every direction. Jesus, the property was immense. The road ended in a circular driveway by a beautiful home of…French design? It was classic and beautiful. I swallowed, my mouth dry.

A man in his mid-seventies approached from the entrance. He greeted Sebastián politely but with a familiarity in his manner that was warm and endearing. His face was weathered and heavily creased, his silver hair peppered with black and neatly combed back. He opened my door and offered me a smile that reached his deep blue eyes, immediately making me feel welcome.

"Camila, this is Marcél," said Sebastián. "Marcél, meet Camila."

"Camila, it is my pleasure, *ma chérie,*" said Marcél with a charming French accent. "Everything is ready," he announced to Sebastián.

"Thank you."

Marcél nodded and disappeared through the front door.

Inside, the estate was simply stunning, a masterful adaptation of the classic style of the house into large, livable spaces with window walls and modern furnishings. The sweet scent of jasmine mixed with wood lingered in the air. I found it comforting. The smell of a home. On the other side of the massive windows stretched a long downhill of green treetops with an unobstructed view of the river. It was magnificent.

"Wow." I sighed.

"You like it?"

"Like it? This view is incredible. And so is your house. Did you design it?"

"No, I remodeled it," he said, glancing around.

"It's the most beautiful home I've ever seen. What's the style?"

"The house itself is French-Norman. It's been in my family for generations. Over the years, I changed some things around to make it more comfortable, more modern. Want a tour?"

"Yes."

As he showed me around, Sebastián explained the house had been built by his great-grandfather in the early 1900s. He spoke passionately about the architectural details. I followed around with wide eyes, taking it all in: wide-plank floors made of mahogany, soft arches dividing the rooms, ceiling beams and huge windows that allowed every space to be flooded with light. Every room radiated a similar feeling of treasured history but had been adapted organically to incorporate the comfort of modern life.

Upstairs, he guided me down a hallway that led to several different rooms: a library with hundreds of books and plush leather couches, a gym with a treadmill and an ample section with neatly aligned weights, ropes, and bands, and then his office—wow. This room was a sanctuary framed by floor-to-ceiling windows overviewing the east side of the property. The view was mesmerizing. In the center, a large architect's desk held an unfinished sketch of a building. I grazed my fingers over the edge of the desk, afraid to disrupt the perfect harmony in the room. The space was immaculate. Everything was organized with methodical care. Not a paper out of place. He *worked* here? Where was the mail, the piles?

I absorbed every detail, spellbound, fascinated that he was letting me into the most private corners of his world. As we moved to the end of the hallway, he opened a door to an empty room. The walls were completely bare, painted in an off-white. To the east, and following the design of the house, a wall of glass showcased the forest outside. The view was stunning, an unobstructed panorama of the river, now a mirror to the golds and silvers left by the descending sun. I ambled to the middle of the room, keeping my eyes on the river.

"This is fantastic."

"It is," he said from behind me. "This is my favorite room in the whole house, and yet, I can't bring myself to decide what to do with it."

"This is where I would want to exist. Right here," I said, sitting on the floor without taking my eyes off the pink sky. "There's something magical about this room."

"That's funny," he said, standing next to me. "That's exactly how I feel about it." He looked down at me for a silent moment, then extended his hand. "Come."

In the dining room downstairs, a rustic table big enough for twelve people was elegantly set for two. Glass sliding doors opened to the forest that extended downhill all the way to the river, the foliage glistening in a mosaic of gold and greens. As the evening faded into twilight, the glinting lights of tiny sailboats awakened in the distance. I stood by the glass, dazed by the view, so perfect it almost seemed fake.

Sebastián took my hand in his and kissed it. "You're very quiet."

"I'm a bit…speechless. It's so beautiful."

"Indeed," he responded, but when I looked up, his eyes were on me. My heart did a triple ballotté and landed flawlessly back in my chest.

"Come. Marcél made a nice dinner for us. I think he was happy to cook for someone other than me." He led me to the table and pulled out my chair.

"You don't have people over often? This is such a big house."

"No. Just Julián, sometimes."

"Julián?" I remembered Nata saying that name and vaguely wondered if it was the same person.

"He's almost family and also my partner at the studio. He's a good friend. I don't bring women here, except Mercedes, Julián's sister. But she doesn't count as a 'guest,' I suppose."

"I would've thought you had parties all the time. It's the perfect house for that."

"No, I told you. I'm a very private person."

"I must be special, then."

"You are." He picked up a bottle of sauvignon blanc from an iced bucket and poured it into the crystal glasses. "To second chances."

"To second chances." I took a sip. Mmm, the wine was exquisite. "So, I want to know more about your family. What about your parents? Do you have any brothers or sisters?"

"My mother died of lung cancer when I was still in college."

"Oh, I'm so sorry."

"Yeah. It was quick, though. Sadly, by the time they discovered it, there wasn't much they could do. I have a brother, Alejandro, but he lives abroad. My partner, Julián, and his sister, Mercedes, are like siblings to me, though we are not actually related. Then there are a few aunts and uncles, but most of them live outside Buenos Aires."

"And your dad? Does he live close by?"

"No, he lives in an estancia just outside Buenos Aires. He's still very active and the head of most of the family businesses, but he now has more people involved and manages them remotely from outside the city."

I let his words linger, trying to imagine a life with almost no family. I loved growing up with three siblings. Life at home had never been lonely.

"What about Marcél? Does he live with you?"

"Yes. He's like family. I've actually known Marcél for a long time." He let out a heavy sigh and took off the lid of a large platter in the center of the table: steaks, roasted potatoes, and sautéed green beans. He served a generous portion on my plate. It looked delicious, but if I kept eating like this every night, I would soon be in trouble. He continued, oblivious, "It's quite a story."

"I love stories," I said, taking a bite of filet mignon. It was heavenly. I vowed to stop at half of my plate and skip lunch tomorrow.

"I met Marcél when I was a kid. At the time, my father was taking over as head of customs in the Puerto Madero docks. I was seven or eight, and he liked bringing me along with him. He hoped the atmosphere would become familiar to me and the business, second nature. I was mostly bored and used to kill time wandering through the docks.

"One morning, while my father was doing rounds at the warehouses, I chased after a dog, not realizing how far away I was getting. When I turned to go back, there were four men walking in my direction. I recognized one of them, but I don't think they knew who I was. The alleys between the warehouses are shady. Not a place for a kid. They were drinking, cussing, and smashing bottles against the walls. I was almost at the other side, so I kept going."

"You weren't scared?"

He shrugged. "No. One of the many traits of being a Palacios, I guess. People stay clear. Nobody ever bothered me."

I sighed inwardly. It was hard to imagine a young child who wouldn't be afraid in that situation. Whatever his last name was.

"Anyway, when they were just a few steps away, one of the men called me over. He was missing teeth, kept grinning. His eyes were pitch black. I remember he made me think of a crow. I was about to run when another man appeared from the side, blocking them. That was the first time I saw Marcél.

He was small, wiry. But he still yelled at them, threatening to turn them in to the boss. They laughed. Marcél told me to get out of there. I didn't want to just leave him, but I saw the fear in his eyes and ran to find my father." Sebastián's expression darkened.

"What happened?"

"They beat him to a pulp. We found him on the ground, half dead. My father had brought some of his men with him. They carried him back to the docks, and we waited till the ambulance came. Marcél kept rambling that he had no money. He begged my father to let him die in peace."

"God, poor guy."

"My father visited him at the hospital every day and told him he would never forget what he had done for me. Papá insisted he come live with us and work for him. Marcél had no family, so he agreed. I liked having him around. He was smart, worldly, and knew more about people than anyone I had ever met. Plus, he's an amazing cook. When my father moved away, Marcél stayed with me and became as close as family. I'm lucky I still have him."

I looked at my half-eaten plate, realizing I had eaten more than I intended. His was almost intact. "I'm sorry your food got cold."

He looked up and smiled, then worked on his dinner while I answered a few questions about my life at the theater.

We finished the last of the wine, and as his glass met his lips, his eyes pierced mine with that intensity that teased my heart rate. "I'm glad you came. I wanted this second chance with you." He held my gaze for a long moment, then got up and took my hand. What now? "Come. I want to show you something."

He led me to a terrace, an oasis under an iron pergola covered by a blanket of white, climbing roses. The deep perfume of the pale buds mingled with the evening breeze. In the horizon, the night sky stretched over the river like black velvet dusted with glimmering stars. The air smelled of freshly cut grass. A slice of silver moon watched us from afar. The view was sensational.

Sebastián snaked his arm around my waist to bring me close. Strange sensations unfurled inside me, urgent, impatient. I trembled when his breath brushed my lips.

"I can't stop thinking about you. You're so different from other women I've met. I'm glad you fell into my life, crazy girl," he whispered against my mouth. The sensation was inebriating. I closed my eyes.

"I'm happy I fell into your life too. Now stop talking and kiss me."

Soft laughter teased my lips, then our mouths melded. The night spun around us. I wrapped shaky arms around his waist, and his hands tangled in my hair, bringing me closer. His tongue played with mine, awakening my desire. I felt myself melt in his hands. When he broke away, we were both breathing hard. His pale eyes searched mine with what looked like astonishment.

"How do you do that?" he whispered.

"How do I do what?"

He shook his head, then took my hands and kissed them. I liked that he kissed my hands so often. It was romantic, endearing. He then turned me around, hugging me from behind as we admired the view. A full body shiver ran through me. "Let's go back inside. You're cold," he said, kissing my hair.

In the great room, a soft piano melody drifted in the air.

"Dance with me." He led me to an open space by an enormous fireplace where a fire crackled fiercely. His arms enveloped me, pressing me to him, while his body moved sensually with mine. It was sexy. Not like dancing with Marcos or any of the other dancers. This was different. *Hot.* He squeezed me tighter and I felt him harden. Thick, raw desire pulsed in my blood.

"I love having you here, to learn about your world. You're my sunshine," he murmured, threading his fingers in my hair. His eyes blazed into mine. My heart raced. God, I wanted him.

A soft throat clearing interrupted us from behind. Blushing fiercely, I snapped my head around. His bodyguard—um, Rafa, was it?—stood a few feet behind. Without letting go of me, Sebastián looked over my shoulder.

"Sorry to interrupt," Rafa said. "We have a situation."

Sebastián gave him a nod.

"Don't move." He kissed my forehead and released me before heading to the terrace where Rafa waited. I dropped onto the couch, catching my breath, my head and my heart spinning. After a couple of minutes, he was back and holding out his hand to help me up.

"I'm really sorry. There's something I need to do right now. Rain check?"

Oh. My heart plummeted. "Sure. Is everything okay?"

"Yes. Just…business." He sighed. "Julián is in New York this week, and I told him I would step in if something came up." His tone was calm, laced with regret.

"Okay." Dammit!

"I'll take you home."

"Oh…No, just call me a cab. It's fine."

He frowned. "Nothing's more important to me right now than making sure you get home safe."

I smiled.

Outside, Rafa and another guy waited by the black BMW. Rafa got into the driver's seat while the other bodyguard opened the back door for us. Sebastián sat by my side and took my hand.

"Camila, this is Tano, and you know Rafa already."

Rafa nodded from the rearview mirror. The other guy, Tano—slang for *the Italian*—turned his head and smiled. Frayed chestnut bangs brushed his forehead over intense brown eyes.

"Nice to meet you." He winked, then faced the front.

Sebastián kissed my knuckles. "Sorry, Cami. Can I make this up to you tomorrow?"

"It's okay. And yes, you can."

We rode back in comfortable silence. We were about to pull over by my apartment when both Rafa and Tano visibly tensed. Rafa glanced at Sebastián through the rearview mirror. Sebastián's jaw locked.

"Dammit," he whispered through clenched teeth.

"What's wrong?" I searched the street outside. Nothing seemed out of the ordinary. The night was quiet. Only a familiar gray car parked a few steps away.

"Nothing," said Sebastián. "Just a complication." He glanced up at Rafa. "She'll come with us."

Rafa nodded and switched gears, then with a screech of the tires, did a U-turn in front of the silver car. As he did, I caught a quick glance of Alexei sitting on the passenger side. I stuck my tongue at him, knowing he couldn't see me through the tinted window. Sebastián's grip on my hand tightened.

"Do you know them?"

I shrugged. "Yeah. Well, sort of. They're friends of Nata's brother. Her family is über-protective. Those guys are always hovering around. Why are we leaving?"

"How well do you know Natascha?"

"She's my best friend…and also my roommate. Why?"

Sebastián closed his eyes, his nostrils flaring.

"Fuck."

Chapter 12

"Sebastián, what's wrong?" I asked. Nata knew of Sebastián, but did he know who she was? Tano turned around and looked from Sebastián to me, then faced the front again.

Sebastián glanced out the window.

"Hey," I whispered, reaching for his hand. "What's going on?"

He gave me a stern look. "Russians are not good company, Camila."

"What? What are you talking about? Nata is my best friend. Those other guys are her brother's friends. They're bit weird, but they're cool." I searched his eyes, but his expression didn't ease.

"What did Natascha say yesterday after she saw you with me?"

Shit. I pursed my lips.

"Tell me." He frowned.

I looked down at my lap and shrugged. "She just said to be careful. You know...because of your family. She recognized you, I guess."

"Anything else?"

"No. What's this about?"

He let a few seconds pass, then kissed the back of my wrist. "Nothing you should worry about. Our families have some common business interests, and sometimes there can be animosity, but I'm not involved in any of it. Neither should you."

I nodded, unconvinced, but I wanted to get off the subject. He was right. Whatever went on between the two families was not my business.

Rafa parked by an unmarked building, the brick façade painted flat black. Two men in sharp, dark suits stood on each side of a double door. To the left, a line of people dressed for a night out waited to get in. A handful of photographers hovered, snapping pictures at the lucky ones who made it in. Rafa and Tano got out first and let us out of the car. As we approached, the photographers recognized Sebastián and began firing photos of the two of us. Sebastián clasped my hand and we hurried through, ignoring their interrogation about his mystery date. I had never had a stranger wanting to take my photo before, and I felt like a movie star. I grinned under a shower of flashes as we rushed to the entrance, flanked by Rafa and Tano. My pulse was flying. Was it always like this for him? How fun! But he seemed oblivious. The two bouncers opened the doors in unison and exchanged a brief nod with Sebastián.

"Good evening, Sebastián. Good to see you, sir."

Sebastián gave them a curt nod and ushered me through the door. Inside, Billy Idol's "Hot in the City" pulsed through the walls. Two couples handed their coats to a valet at a dedicated area close by. The men were dressed in expensive suits, and I recognized one of the women, a supermodel.

"Sebastián, that is Savannah, the model. She's gorgeous and wearing an Inés Fernandez dress. Lucky girl…"

Sebastián glanced at her, then leaned down to speak into my ear.

"I would choose you over her every day for the rest of my life."

I smiled at him, but my stomach twisted into a knot. I was way out of my league here.

The music grew louder as Sebastián led me down a long hallway lit by concealed lights from underneath a glass floor. We followed it to an open area of what I knew was one of Buenos Aires's most exclusive nightclubs. Holy shit. I was in Amsterdam. I had only heard about it, but I immediately recognized the features: Barbie waitresses in the trademark minuscule leather dresses and four-inch heels. All brunette, scarlet lipstick, long hair, and perfect curves. I looked down at my jeans and fitted sweater. Thank God I had given my Converse the night off and wore boots. Still, I knew I didn't fit in.

"Sebastián, I'm not dressed to be here," I shouted through the music.

He pulled me into his arms. "You're perfect," he said into my ear. His mouth found mine, and a shiver ran up my back. He withdrew slightly and pressed a brief kiss on my lips, taking my hand.

We took a side hallway to a private area with an elevator. Rafa and Tano got in after us, turning to face the door.

"This is just a meeting. It won't take long. Some new clients for the studio. Julián usually takes care of the entertaining." He smirked. "Not really my thing."

The elevator doors opened to a VIP area. I held my breath, taking it all in. An illuminated bar curved along the entire back of the room, and a thick glass wall isolated the area from the club below. The atmosphere here was relaxed, even more exclusive. I scanned the room where no more than thirty people lounged on plush couches, having drinks. A velvety female voice crooned a sensual melody that filled the air. In the dim light of the room, I recognized two top supermodels and a popular, hotter-than-hell polo player. I bit my lip and smiled, knowing Nata and Marcos would flip out when I told them I had been here. Principals were all about the show of being seen in the right places.

A girl about my age in that jaw-dropping leather uniform approached. She smiled broadly at Sebastián, showcasing her perfect teeth.

"Sebastián, what a pleasure. It's been a while, sir. Welcome." Her eyes quickly assessed me from head to toe, then returned to Sebastián, seizing every second to devour him.

Sebastián smiled curtly and asked her to give us a minute. She nodded and sashayed away. Tano's eyes were trained on her ass, his lips curving in a smug smile.

Sebastián pulled me to him so he could speak into my ear. *Goose bumps everywhere.*

"I'll be right back, baby. Tano will stay with you. Have a drink."

"Um, that's okay. I can wait for you over there." I gestured to a small lounge area by the glass wall with a few low tables hugged by couches. "Don't need babysitting." I smiled sweetly.

"I won't leave you alone. It would be rude. Besides, I'm responsible for delivering you back to your house in one piece." He kissed my forehead.

"Sebastián, I'm a big girl."

He brought me close until our lips were touching. "*My* girl tonight. No arguing." He pressed a chaste kiss on my lips and winked. With a slight nod at Tano, he left for the bar with Rafa at his side. *My girl*, the words bewitched me.

I looked up at Tano. Even though I was five eight, he towered over me by a good head. He gestured to the lounge area where people relaxed on couches and had drinks. I found a good spot by the glass wall overlooking the club. Tano shrugged off his leather jacket. An intricate tattoo of a dragon covered the length of each arm from under his fitted, black T-shirt.

Gesturing to Miss Barbie Legs, he ordered a vodka tonic for me, and a mineral water for him. He then sat on a couch across from me, surveying the crowd. His eyes paused on Sebastián and Rafa at the bar. He, too, probably wished he didn't have to babysit me. He smiled when he caught me yawning.

"Sorry we're keeping you up. Won't take long," he said over the music.

"It's okay. I'll be right back. I need to use the restroom." I stood, and he was instantly on his feet.

"Oh, no, no. Just point the way. You don't need to—"

"I like my job. I want to keep it."

I raised my palms in defeat.

When we came back, my drink was waiting. I took a sip and coughed. It was *stiff*.

"Something wrong?" Tano asked.

"Um, no. Super strong drink."

He reached for my glass. "I'll get you another one. Same?"

"Actually, just water, but—"

"Stay put," he said, and left abruptly. The waitress appeared and asked if I needed a refill. I explained Tano had gone to the bar already, but when I glanced, he wasn't there.

Through the window wall, I watched the crowd underneath. Then a steady string of camera flashes startled me. I turned to find a young reporter behind me.

"You're with Sebastián Palacios, right?" he said, firing a few more shots of me.

"Um...yes."

"I saw him kissing you." He smiled. "You his girlfriend?" *Click, click, click.*

"What?"

"You're so young," he said, finally lowering the camera. "You're not intimidated by the Palacioses? I mean, after what happened to his last girlfriend, Carolina?"

"I'm sorry, I—"

Tano gripped the man by the collar. "Get the fuck out."

The guy scurried away and quickly disappeared.

"What'd he say to you?" Tano's intense brown eyes locked with mine.

"Oh." I blinked. "Um, nothing. Something about... Carolina? Who's she?"

Tano's jaw clenched. "No one. Sebastián's ex. The press loves making up shit about that."

"About what?"

"Mmh," he growled, looking away. "The kind of bullshit the press feeds on, those fuckers are like flies. Don't mind'em." He unscrewed the bottle cap and handed the water to me. I forced a smile as he plopped down on a couch beside me.

"Thanks for the drink," I said to lighten the mood. "The waitress came right after you left, but you weren't at the bar."

"Oh," he said, and his expression stilled for a quick second. "Bathroom."

I nodded and sipped on the water while my brain went back to the reporter, racing to decipher his words. Who was Carolina? And what in the hell had happened to her? I would have to find out somehow. Maybe Nata would know? Dammit. I took a long swig of water. What was I doing here? Maybe Nata was right, and this whole date thing with Sebastián had been a mistake. I had let my neglected hormones and Marcos's rejection override my common sense. But Sebastián...I wanted to know everything about him. I craved the way he made me feel, the way he looked at me, touched me. And all this... I looked around and couldn't help the giddy sense of glamour I felt sitting among Buenos Aires's elite, even if it was accidental and short-lived. I relaxed into the seat and finished my drink, letting my mind and my paranoia drift.

Sebastián and Rafa returned a few minutes later. Rafa and Tano left to station themselves at a group of couches in the periphery. The lighting was hazy, making the secluded sitting areas even more private. All around us, couples sat having drinks, chatting, some making out.

Sebastián wrapped his hands around my waist and slid me onto his lap.

"You are light as a feather." His lips found my neck and kissed it, sending shivers down to my toes. I circled my arms around his neck. My heart raced at the close contact with his. "You smell so good," he said, burying his face in my neck and kissing me in a slow, sensual tempo.

It was sexy as fuck.

"Do you have to work tomorrow?" he asked.

"Mmmm. Yes."

His fingers caressed my hair at the nape while his lips peppered me with weightless kisses. "God, Camila. I can't get enough of you. I can't stop thinking about all the things I want to do to you." His mouth continued its torturous assault on my neck. It was heavenly. The reporter's words circled in my mind, but I shut them out and closed my eyes, giving in to the sensation.

"Sebastián..."

"Do you think about me? Tell me," he whispered against my neck.

"Yes," I breathed. His mouth slowly moved to my jaw where it trailed open-mouth kisses. I felt them everywhere.

"Tell me," he repeated without breaking contact. *Damn*. His arm pressing me against his granite chest, his mouth, his amazing scent. It was all lethal.

"I…" I let out a shallow breath. He pulled away enough to look into my eyes. The corners of his mouth curved up in a playful smile.

"Are you shy?" He took my face in his hand, and I bit my lip. His thumb pulled gently to release it. "Tell me." His eyes were hooded.

"I…" I looked away, and he held my chin to coerce me into meeting his eyes.

"Am I being too forward? I'm sorry."

"It's not that. I just…" I shook my head.

"What?" he said, his mouth so close, our breaths mixing.

I looked down to avoid his eyes. "I've always been busy dancing. I…I haven't…" Shit. I looked up, and he was watching me with a deep frown. Then his eyes widened fractionally.

"You've never…*been* with anyone? Babe, you are a virgin?" He cocked his head to the side as if I had suddenly grown another head.

"No, no. Well, not technically. I'm not… I'm not very experienced," I said. Shit. Why was it so hard to talk about this? I kept my eyes down. Wrapping my fingers around his wrist, I released his hold on my chin. I felt his eyes burning on me, but I met them straight on. His expression was etched in disbelief. To hell with it. Here goes nothing.

"I always felt self-conscious and kind of…I don't know…turned off when things got…heated with someone, so I always stopped before we got to that part."

He frowned. "But how? I saw how half the men here looked at you when we walked in. You must have guys all over you."

I blushed. "No. My life is ballet. I don't really let people in. But I've never felt the way I feel when I'm with you." I held his gaze, bracing for whatever came next. Guys were usually freaked out by inexperienced girls. He shook his head and sighed heavily.

"Holy fuck," he said. "I think I just fell in love."

Relief washed through me. "You're not disappointed then?"

His answering smile was smoldering. "Hands down, the best part of the night."

"Yeah? Why?"

"Because." He kissed me softly. "That makes you the most beautiful, most perfect woman in the planet. And it makes me a very lucky bastard." He squeezed his arms around me. I closed my eyes, basking in the safety of being in his arms and, as my body relaxed, I couldn't repress a yawn.

"Let me take you home," he said. "You need to rest."

"But I'm so happy right here."

"If you stay here another minute, I may not let you go."

I groaned softly. "I do need to be up early. Madame's been on my case lately. I guess I am a bit...distracted."

"I don't want to be a bad influence. Besides, I'd rather have you all to myself when we have more time, and less of an audience." His eyes moved to Rafa and Tano, who were keeping vigil a few feet behind.

While we waited for the elevator, a couple joined us. The man was much older, his white hair stiffly combed back, his frame wide and imposing under a dark suit. The woman was very skinny, her eyes glued to the ground, her long, brown hair draping down her shoulders and covering most of her face. She squirmed beside him, her movements sheepish even though she was dressed in a very tight, red dress that only enhanced her wiry frame. We stepped in the elevator before them, and as I turned around, the man took the woman's arm and tugged her in. The gesture was brief but aggressive. I caught Sebastián glowering at him, then his eyes moved to the girl.

Nobody spoke on the ride down, and when the doors finally opened, the man's phone rang. He looked around, then barked something to the woman in what I was pretty sure was Russian and stepped away. She walked out of the elevator with her head still down and stood submissively by the door. As we exited, she briefly looked up, and I was shock-stricken because she wasn't a woman, but a girl barely of legal age.

Sebastián told Rafa and Tano to get the car and meet us at the door. His eyes followed the Russian man leave the girl and step into the men's room. As soon as the man was out of view, Sebastián turned to the girl, and leaning down to meet her eyes, he spoke to her softly in Russian.

Second shocker, Sebastián spoke Russian?

The girl stepped back in alarm, her eyes wide, frantically searching in the direction where the man had left. Sebastián spoke again in the same gentle tone but sounding more insistent. The girl shook her head and started crying. He pressed on with a soft, gentle command, and she finally looked up at him. With pleading eyes, she spoke quickly in broken phrases and he listened intently, his features hardening as the girl talked. Then he clasped her shoulder and said something appeasing and what sounded like instructions. Darting a look at the hallway and then focusing back on the girl, he reinforced his last words, squeezing her shoulder gently. She nodded and Sebastián took my hand.

"Let's go," he said.

"What was that about?" I said, hurrying beside him toward the entrance. He walked in long strides, his jaw set. I tugged on his hand. "Sebastián…"

He growled.

"Tell me."

"Trafficking."

"That girl?" I turned my head as we walked, but the girl was out of sight. I had heard stories about people being kidnapped, and I shuddered at the possible implications.

"Yes," he said through clenched teeth.

We stopped at the door to wait for Rafa. Sebastián's whole body radiated tension.

"What did she say to you?"

He didn't answer, just shook his head in irritation.

"Please tell me. Who was she? What did she want?"

Nothing.

"I'm worried," I said. "She looked desperate."

"She was," he finally said with another long, frustrated sigh. He shook his head, his lips pressed into a straight line as he ran a hand through his raven hair.

"What did she say?"

He looked at me for a long moment. "She said they brought them in a cargo ship from Russia. Nineteen of them, including her sister, who's only thirteen."

"Jesus. What... for?"

His eyes were etched in concern, reflecting an internal debate.

"What will happen to them?"

"Believe me, you don't want to know."

"What?" I blurted.

"Prostitution," he said bitterly. "They're docked two miles offshore. She said they bring men aboard."

I closed my eyes, biting back a sudden wave of nausea. "Jesus," I whispered.

"Yeah. Fucking sons of bitches," he growled.

"Did she ask you for help? *Can* you help her?"

The BMW pulled over by the curb, and Sebastián opened the door, wrapping his arm protectively around me.

"Can you do anything for her?" I said as we hurried into the car.

"First, I have to find out who they are. These are usually large organizations with very complicated alliances." He met Rafa's eyes in the rearview mirror.

"Call Cardenas and Castro. See who's out in the midnight docks this week."

Rafa nodded.

"Will you be able to help?" I said, reaching out to hold his hand. "Should we call the police?"

He frowned. "No. The police are most likely aware and turning a blind eye. And Camila, there's no 'we' in this."

I pressed my lips. He was right. What the hell could I possibly do against Russian traffickers? "Then what?"

"I'll deal with it."

"You'll *deal* with it?"

"Yes. I gave her my word."

"But how? How can you help her?" I insisted.

He tilted his head and gave me a sympathetic smile.

"The less you know, the better."

I swallowed hard. "This seems dangerous. You won't... put yourself at risk, will you?" As I said it, I realized how stupid and naïve that sounded.

He squeezed my hand. "We'll try the civilized way first."

"What does that mean?"

He nodded at the street behind me. "Come on. We're here."

Outside my apartment, the street was deserted. No signs of Alexei or the silver car, or anyone else. Sebastián walked me to the foyer and enveloped me in his arms.

"I'll call you tomorrow," he said, kissing my temple. "Get some rest."

"I won't be able to stop thinking about that girl. She looked even younger than me."

"I know. I'll do everything in my power to help her and the others." His eyes were crystal blue, burning with determination, and I knew in that moment that he would keep his promise. A sudden wave of emotion slammed through me, and I clasped the front of his shirt, pulling him to me and crushing his mouth to mine. He responded with the same intensity, wrapping his arms tighter around me. When we broke away, we were panting. His eyes bore into mine. Taking my face in his hands, he kissed my mouth softly, then my eyelids, my nose, and my forehead. It was intimate and loving.

"In you go," he said softly. "I don't think I can restrain myself much longer."

I went in and watched him go, overwhelmed by the events of the night, the image of the girl in the red dress imprinted in my mind.

Up in my apartment, Marcos was passed out on the couch. He looked so peaceful, innocent even. *A wolf in a sheep's suit.* I covered him with a blanket.

Finally in bed, I stared out through the window at the distant stars, unable to sleep. My head was a whirlwind of questions about Sebastián. The attraction I felt for him was stronger than anything I had ever experienced. There was the physical aspect, yes. But there was something more, darker, that pulled me harder. In many ways he was still an enigma. While the shadow of his family's reputation lurked closely, all I had seen so far was a guy who showed up when things went badly for me, and for a desperate Russian girl who was somewhere in the dark, praying he wouldn't forget her.

Chapter 13

Something shook me awake.

"Hey, sleeping beauty. Wake up."

I squinted at the source of the shaking, Nata, and closed my eyes again.

"Cams, come on. I need to talk to you."

"Please stop shaking me." I pulled myself up without opening my eyes.

"Here. Have some coffee." She shoved a mug under my nose, the warm aroma rising. I took it, blinking off the cloudiness.

"What time is it?"

"It's seven, and I need to talk to you about two things," she said in a businesslike tone as she sat on the corner of the bed. "First, your date with the mobster. I want to hear everything." She eyed me for a second and smiled at my answering scowl. "But maybe that can wait until you are awake."

"Please tell me reason two is a big one, because otherwise you'll end up with a bruise." I rubbed my eye.

"Sheesh, drink your coffee."

"What is it, Nata? I want to sleep, and I only have a few minutes left."

"Okay, so remember that friend of my parents? Vladimir, the big mogul that lives in Barrio Parque? The one who owns the polo team." Her voice climbed to that high pitch she used when she was excited. I winced.

"Yeah, okay. So?" I vaguely remembered him. He was a big name within upper society. I only knew of him because my brother had a few friends who were professional polo players.

"Well, he's throwing a huge party this weekend and had scheduled Russian acrobats to perform. Anyway, something went wrong, and the Russians can't make it, so he asked me if I could bring a partner and perform a tango number."

"Sounds great, Nata. I'm thrilled for you. Can I go back to sleep, now?" Sliding the cup onto the nightstand, I sank back onto the pillow.

"No." She scooted closer. "I can't do it because Teo is flying me to Brazil for the weekend to meet his parents. Oh my god, I've got so much to tell you."

"I didn't realize you guys were that serious. Moving fast, don't you think?"

"I guess, but he's the real thing, you know? I think I'm in love with him."

I looked up and her eyes were swimming in excitement. Fully awake, I sat up and pulled her into a hug. Even if it was all too soon, it was great to see her like this. "I'm happy for you. I really am."

"What I wanted to tell you," she said, breaking away, "is that you and Marcos can do the number instead. Vladimir will pay you two thousand dollars each for the performance. It's a really good gig. You will meet lots of influential people. It will be great exposure for your career."

"Are you serious? Two *thousand* dollars? And you're turning it down? Are you nuts?" Nata didn't need the money, but it was an amazing opportunity. I couldn't believe she was passing it up. For a *guy*?

"Tell me you'll do it," she said. "Marcos already said yes. He really needs the money. The owner of his apartment sold the place, so he needs to move out. Oh, and about that, he asked me if he could stay here until *Giselle* is over. I told him I would talk to you."

I shrugged, rubbing my eyes. "That's fine, I don't mind."

"Are you sure? You come first. I don't want to make things difficult for you. He can find something else."

"It's okay. Besides, he's here half the time anyway. It almost feels weird when he's not around."

"What about Vladimir?"

"Yeah, sure. I still think you're crazy to pass it up."

She clapped her hands. "Let's go tell Marcos." She pulled me off the bed. I reluctantly went along, knowing she wouldn't let up until she got exactly what she wanted.

Marcos blinked sleepily. "She'll do it? That's awesome. Did you ask her about me staying here?"

"I'm standing right here, you dork. And yes, she asked me." I tossed a pillow at his face and plopped next to him.

"And? Can I stay?" He looked at me with pleading puppy eyes.

"No girls." I squinted. "And you do the dishes. Actually, I kind of like the idea of having a male slave." I winked at Nata and she laughed.

"I can do that." He yawned.

We had breakfast, then Marcos left to collect the rest of his things from his apartment. Even though it was Saturday, I had agreed to meet the stager at the theater for a couple of hours to work on some steps I was not too confident about. Before I left, Nata and I went to her closet in search of something I could wear for the tango performance. There was a small pile of black dresses and skirts covering her bed.

I frowned. "What are those for?"

"I've already put some options together for you. This is a big deal. You have to look absolutely stunning." She turned to the closet and browsed through the clothes. I sat on a corner of the bed, watching her walk back and forth with tops and dresses. I desperately wanted to tell her about last night, about the Russian girl, but that would lead to a thousand questions about Sebastián.

"I'm kind of nervous," I said, to get my mind off the subject. "Do you think we can put something together this quickly?"

Nata paused, her arms full of clothes, then gave me a big smile. "Of course you can. You always underestimate how great you are. It's a tango. I think you can probably do a modified variation of the Piazzolla tribute we did last season. Marcos has a few ideas already. Now tell me everything about your date with the gangster." Placing the clothes on the bed, she sat next to me, setting a pair of black tango shoes on her lap. They were gorgeous, black satin with tiny, black rhinestones around the ankles.

"Don't call him that and please don't make me wear those. I've never worn heels that high. I'm not you. I'll fall on my face."

"Fine. Wear the velvet ones, they're not as high. You sure? These are so much cuter." She held up the shoes like I was nuts to turn them down.

I grabbed the velvet shoes from the bed and smiled. "These are perfect. The date went great at first, then it turned… bizarre."

"Why? Where'd he take you?"

"His house for dinner. Then Amsterdam." I grinned.

"What? Seriously? You went to his *house*? And Amsterdam?"

"Yup. The VIP lounge."

"Damn. How was it?"

"His house is unbelievable. Huge, gorgeous. Amsterdam was intimidatingly fancy but super cool…" An image of the Russian girl barged in my mind and I pushed it away, focusing on the photographer's questions instead.

"What is it?"

"Nothing…It's just…the weirdest thing happened last night. Sebastián was at the bar meeting with someone, and this photographer showed up from nowhere and started taking photos of me, asking me if I wasn't intimidated by the Palacios family. And then he said something like 'aren't you freaked out after what happened to his last girlfriend?' I don't know. It was weird," I said, shrugging it off.

"Carolina." Nata's eyes widened. "That's right. How could I forget? My God."

"What?"

"Yeah. That happened long before we started doing business with Sebastián's family. Sergei may know. It was in the papers."

"What… happened?"

She shook her head. "I don't know, really. Sebastián was dating this girl, she was from a high-profile family too. They had…business in common, I think, but one day she was gone. Like *gone*. Disappeared. People said Don Martín had a hand in it."

"A *hand*?"

"Yeah, well…it's tabloid gossip, but it was never resolved. The cops just dropped it." She took my hand. "Look, Cami. I *want* to be happy for you. I do.

And if it was anyone else, I'd be bouncing off the walls. It's just…that family. What are your parents going to say? I mean, have you thought about that? Your dad's going to flip out when you tell him you're dating Don Corleone's son."

"Cut it out." I pulled my hand away. "It's not like that. Sebastián is not like that. His thing is architecture. He has his own studio with a partner. And I don't think he's that involved in the family business." Jesus, I didn't even buy into that. No matter how much I wanted to. Maybe his focus was architecture, but he sure as hell was involved in bigger things. But then, there was that other side of him, the side that kept knocking me to my feet. I sat up on the bed with my legs crossed. "I know it's too soon, but when I'm with him…I forget about everything else. It's like he somehow fills a space dancing never has, you know?"

"Yeah. I know exactly what you mean." She sighed in a defeated tone. "I feel the same way about Teo. Just be careful. At least till you know what you're dealing with."

I nodded, wishing things were different. For the first time, I was genuinely interested in somebody, and he came with a questionable amount of baggage. My thoughts drifted to my date with Sebastián, curled in his lap at Amsterdam, then the girl and her pleading eyes. A mix of doom and excitement filled me. Gangster or not, I knew already what kind of guy he was.

The kind you fell hard for.

Chapter 14

Early on Saturday, I hurried to the theater, unable to hold in the thrill about the upcoming performance at Vladimir's estate. Dancers waited a lifetime for an opportunity like this. Everyone that was anyone in the arts would be there. I breathed in and out, trying to rid my body of the panic simmering in my gut.

For my tango outfit, Nata loaned me a snug, black skirt open to the hip on one side, a matching slim, black top, and fishnet panty hose.

Marcos and I had only a few days to come up with a killer choreography and nail it. He had already figured out what he wanted to do, so I wasn't too worried. Marcos was an astounding dancer, plus we had been partnering more often during rehearsals and were used to dancing together. If everything went according to plan, we would kill it.

I squinted at the bright sun as I stepped out after my session with the choreographer. The sky was clear; an unusually warm breeze teased the last leaves left by the winter. My phone buzzed in my pocket, and Sebastián's name lit the screen.

"Hey," I said.

"How's my girl?"

"Good. Just finished a rehearsal."

"Do you have plans today?"

"Well…I was thinking of going to see my parents, but I haven't called them yet."

"Would you consider an alternative?"

I grinned. "I might."

Outside my foyer, Sebastián welcomed me in his arms. As if by instinct, his mouth claimed mine. Holy smokes. Those kisses did naughty things to my insides.

"Do you have any idea how sexy you are?" he said in a low, sexy voice. A wave of heat rushed to my face.

"Okay, I don't think jeans and a leather jacket qualify as sexy."

He brushed my hair back with his fingers, snaking his other arm around my waist. "Simple things are perfect the way they are. They don't ask for attention. To me, you are perfect."

Invisible wings lifted my heart out of my chest.

"Where are we going?"

There's a polo match in an estancia nearby. A friend of mine is putting together a team, and I'm thinking of sponsoring them. I want to check out the horses first, make sure his team doesn't suck." He laughed softly.

Hmm. Polo and Sebastián. A heady combination. "I'd love that."

He took my hand and led me to the Alfa Romeo. Rafa nodded from the black BMW parked a few steps behind. I waved him a hello.

"Why is Rafa not riding with us?"

"I wanted to have you alone. Sometimes we drive separately."

"Where's Tano?" Through the mirror, I looked back at the BMW.

"I don't need two people tailing me all day. Tano's usually around at night." He pulled into traffic. "Rafa takes care of a lot of things for the studio, so he's with me full-time."

"Oh." I nodded. I wondered what it was like to have someone with you all the time. It would drive me crazy.

"You tired?" He took my hand and interlaced our fingers, sending goose bumps up my arm.

"Yeah, it's been a long week at work."

"Before I forget, I have something to ask you. I'm working on a redesign of a hundred-year-old estancia. It's pretty amazing. The client's also a personal friend. Vladimir Koviesky, maybe you've heard of him."

My eyebrows shot up in surprise, but I didn't interrupt him. He focused on the road ahead.

"Anyway, he's throwing a big party at his house on Saturday. I wasn't going to go, but if you came with me, then it would be fun. His parties are some of the best I've been to." He glanced at me with a lopsided smile. "Come?" His eyes went briefly back to the road before meeting mine with amused curiosity. "What?"

"Well…" I grinned. "I'm actually performing at that party."

"What? You are?" he said, clearly taken back.

"Yeah, it was just a coincidence. I was going to tell you. Vladimir is also a friend of Nata's family. He asked Nata to perform a tango number at the party, but she's leaving town for the weekend so she asked me to do it instead. That's why I'm so tired. My partner and I have less than a week to learn the choreography and nail it." I squeezed his hand. "You have to go to the party so you can see me dance! And…we can hang out afterwards."

"That's quite an honor, babe. I know Vladimir, and the performers at his parties are unbelievable. They come from all over the world. But of course, I'm sure he knows how good you are." He smiled sweetly.

"I'm *very* nervous about it." I turned to him and frowned. "Hey, how come you have a Russian friend? Didn't you say, 'Russians are not good company'?" I drew quotation marks in the air.

"I was referring to *those* Russians. Vladimir is an exceptional person and a great businessman. He's a good friend."

"I'm glad you can make the distinction, because that's how I feel about Nata."

He ran a quick hand through his hair. "That family's different."

"Why?"

"Because." He sighed. "They have their hands on a lot of things."

"She said the same about your family."

His jaw tensed, and I immediately regretted bringing the Russians into the conversation. I had been dying to ask him about his ex, Carolina, and now I'd blown it. He remained silent for a few long seconds. I wanted to hit rewind and start over. As if he could read my thought, he reached for my hand and kissed it. "Let's not talk about this. I want today to be about you and me. We're here."

He pulled into a dirt road lined by eucalyptus trees on both sides. At the end, a couple dozen cars were parked around a field where polo players were hitting balls to warm up the horses. The afternoon was cool, the sky clean, and the spicy scent of fresh hay saturated the air. Sebastián wrapped his arm around my waist and pulled me to him, kissing my head as I lowered my sunglasses.

We leaned over the fence, watching the scrimmage. I hadn't been to a polo match since my brother, Javi, lived at home. My girlfriends and I used to go watch him play. It was a big social scene back then, and it didn't look like it had changed much.

The horses were stunning. Beautiful and majestic, they sprinted past, their glistening, sculpted muscles flexing as they abruptly changed directions to match the players' reflexes.

"I didn't know you were into horses. They are incredible." I nodded at the animals.

"Yes. It's a hobby. I enjoy it quite a bit."

"Do you play?"

"I used to. Now it's hard to find the time."

"But you're sponsoring this team?"

"Yes. Jake's a good friend, and he knows what he's doing. You like polo?"

I nodded. "My brother played. I forgot how much fun it was to watch."

"You don't go to games anymore?"

"Javi lives in Italy now, so no. It's still strange that my siblings are all in Europe, Sabrina in London, Sofi in Spain. I'm the only one that stayed here."

He wrapped his arms around me from behind. "We can come anytime. I like that you're here." He kissed my neck and I shivered.

When the scrimmage ended, Sebastián introduced me to a few friends, and by the third name, I could no longer keep track. I vaguely recognized some of the players. A group of them came to greet Sebastián, and I stepped away to watch the horses.

"What a surprise to see you here." I turned around at the deep voice that went with a familiar face. Milo, a friend from the past, approached, his tanned muscular body dressed in the usual polo gear.

"Milo!" I grinned as he pulled me into his arms. My brother had introduced us a few years back, and we had gone out on a few dates, but it didn't last. Milo had a busy social life and thought my schedule at the theater was insane. I didn't blame him. "It's been a while. How are you?" He smelled of leather, horses, and sweat. I freaking loved that smell.

"I'm great." He kissed my cheek and pulled back to fully look at me. Deep brown eyes met mine, and his face broke into his trademark winning smile. "What are you doing here?"

"I'm with a friend. Oh my god, it's been forever. You're playing professionally?"

"I am. I'm hoping to join this new team. You? Still dancing crazy hours?"

"Yes. What can I say, I'm hooked for life."

"And you're damn good at it. Sweetheart, you look beautiful, as always." His callused hand stroked my cheek. I blushed and gave him a small smile.

"Thank you. You look good too. But you already know that." I winked.

He laughed, shaking his head and flicking strands of golden hair off his forehead. "Why did I fall for the only girl that's not smitten by a polo player?"

"I'm still a sucker for horses, but you boys 'play' way too much for someone like me. I have a fragile heart." I sighed.

Milo laughed out loud, then held my face in his hands and kissed my forehead. "You're damn adorable. How's Javi, by the way? I haven't seen him in ages."

"He's good, I think. Doesn't call as much as he should."

Sebastián startled me, wrapping his arm protectively around my waist. He then extended his free hand to shake Milo's.

"Good to see you, man. You looked good out there."

Milo's eyes locked on Sebastián's hand at my waist. He looked back at him and finally shook his waiting hand. "Thanks. Jake put together a great team." His eyes went from Sebastián's to mine. "Small world. Are you two…together?"

I opened my mouth, realizing I didn't quite know how to answer that.

"Yes." Sebastián glanced down at me. Tipping his head down, he gave me a soft kiss on the lips. I blushed furiously.

Milo nodded. "I gotta go. It was good to see you, babe. Don't be a stranger and tell Javi I said hi." He leaned over and kissed my cheek, and as he did, Sebastián's grip on me tightened. Milo threw his jacket over his shoulder and shook Sebastián's hand again. "Thanks for your support with the team, man. You won't regret it." He gave him a smug smile and walked away. Sebastián's eyes stayed trained on Milo's back as he left, his jaw set.

"Hey," I whispered, reaching up to stroke his face. "Ready to go?"

"You know Milo?" His eyes searched mine under a frown.

"Oh, um…yes. He's friends with Javi, my brother."

"He seemed very affectionate," he said sternly.

"We went out on a couple of dates. But polo players are not my thing."

"And why is that?"

"Because they love to party, and they're very chauvinistic, and they have a super busy social agenda. That's not me. Oh, and they also love women. Lots of them." I smirked.

"I see." He wrapped his arms around my back and pressed me to him. "And what *is* your thing, Camila? I want to know." His breath teased my lips, and my insides swirled.

"Right now, you," I said against his mouth.

He buried my mouth in a deep kiss. My legs weakened and I clenched my hands on his shirt, clinging for my life. *Holy shit.* When he pulled back, those intense eyes were hooded.

"Come home with me."

The Alfa Romeo blazed through the dirt road, blocking the field behind under a cloud of dust. Rafa followed somewhere behind as we rode in silence to his house. I took a deep breath and summoned my inner will.

"Sebastián, there's something I've been meaning to ask you."

"Sure." He frowned.

"Who's…Carolina?"

His frown deepened, but he kept his eyes ahead and tightened his grip on the wheel. I chewed on my lip. Was this a good idea?

"A reporter…at the club last night," I said. "He asked me if I wasn't worried after what happened to Carolina."

"Those fuckers," he growled. His phone rang through the car speakers, startling me. Sebastián ignored it and sped up as we merged onto the Panamericana freeway. I clutched my seat and looked away from him, wishing I hadn't chosen that time to bring up his ex-girlfriend. But at the same time, I wanted to know. The phone rang a few more times and he pressed a button on the steering wheel.

"Yes," he said in an irritated tone.

"Sir, Cardenas is around tonight. Then there's a gap until next week," a mature male voice announced. Sebastián scowled at the panel in the center console like it was all its fault.

"Fine," he said. "I'll call him with instructions."

"Sir, there's… a problem, though," the man said. "Cardenas knows these people, and he doesn't want to go near'em. He was adamant. It took some convincing, but he finally agreed… on one condition."

"What condition?" Sebastián barked.

"That you or Julián will be there."

A long pause went by.

"Sir?" the voice said.

"Julián's in Germany. Tell Cardenas to send his coordinates to Rafa. I'll meet him aboard tonight."

"Understood," the voice said before disconnecting.

The air was tense, and Sebastián got lost in his thoughts. I remembered the name Cardenas had been mentioned the night before, when Sebastián gave instructions to Rafa after the incident with the girl.

"I'm afraid to ask," I said.

"Don't."

"Is this about the girl?"

Sebastián kept his eyes on the road. "I thought you weren't going to ask."

"I changed my mind. You're meeting someone tonight aboard a ship, and this person doesn't want to get involved unless you're there. I don't like it. You'll put yourself at risk."

"There's no other way," he said curtly.

"Jesus, Sebastián. I thought your thing was *architecture*."

"It is."

"Are you sure?" I said sardonically.

"Yes. But it's in my power to help these girls, so I'm not going to turn my back on them. You really don't need to worry about me."

"Too late."

"You'll have to trust me." He turned to look at me, then back at the road, and silence once again filled the air in the car. With a knot in my throat, I turned away and stared at the blazing scenery. Would life always be like this with him?

A few minutes later, we pulled over by my building.

"I'll need another rain check," he said. "I'm sorry we have to postpone tonight."

"I don't give a damn about tonight."

"Hey…" he said softly. "I'll be fine."

"Tell me where you're going."

"No." His tone was firm. His eyes said arguing was pointless.

"Dammit, Sebastián." I let out a long sigh of indignation.

"Camila," he said, containing his frustration. "This is the way things are. I won't put you at risk, and answering your questions would mean doing just that."

"Fine. At least answer my question about Carolina."

He dropped his head back against the seat. "Christ, I wish you would ignore the shit you hear about me."

"Then give me your version."

A silent pause went by. "Carolina was…is my ex-girlfriend."

Was? "Did…something…happen to her?"

"No. She's just gone, okay?"

"Gone…how?"

The seconds slowly passed. Nothing. I reached for my bag and he clasped my forearm.

"You can't believe the things people say about my family. Especially the press."

"That's hard when your last name is everywhere and you won't tell me anything," I snapped.

"What do you want from me?"

"I want you to trust me. I want in. We can't have a relationship if you keep me out."

He exhaled, his expression conflicted. "I'm not used to 'sharing.' My life is extremely private. It has to be."

"And I understand that. I do." I sighed. "I'll make a deal with you. If you're open with me, if you trust me, then I'll ignore all the things I hear or read about you. And I promise I won't share anything you say to me with anyone."

He debated for a moment. "Sounds fair. But there have to be boundaries. When it comes to certain things, the less you ask, the better. It's safer that way."

"Is Carolina outside the boundaries?"

"No," he said, his tone softer. "If I were you, I would probably be asking too." He stared through the window at the distant traffic, his thoughts lost in memories. "Carolina was someone I cared about, very much. A long time ago. But things between us didn't work out."

"Why not?"

"Because she couldn't fully come to terms with who I was...am, where I come from. She wanted some dream version of our relationship."

"How so?"

"She expected me to leave everything behind and move to Europe with her."

"She wanted you to leave your family? Your home? Why?"

"We were young, still in college, and things with my father's business were unstable at the time. Our relationship with the new government was not solid yet, so we constantly had to watch our back. Then one of my father's enemies tried kidnapping me. The whole thing was a joke, and he obviously failed, but after that, things changed. Carolina was afraid. All the time. It was fine at first, the parties, the glamour, but then things changed. *She* changed. She became paranoid and after a few months, mentally fragile."

"That must have been hard. I'm so sorry."

He shook his head. "Being with me was bad for her. *I* was bad for her. 'Toxic' was the word her parents used." His jaw tensed.

"What happened after?"

"She left. She moved to Europe with her family. I had to promise her I wouldn't contact her and nobody would ever know where she was, where she went. So, Camila, you can't ever speak of Carolina to anyone. Ever."

"Of course." I nodded, my mind still reeling that he was sharing something so private with me. My heart ached for that early version of him, young and brokenhearted. I wanted to clutch my arms around him.

"My last name can be a curse," he said.

"I don't care what your last name is." I stretched my hand out to squeeze his. "I care about you."

He looked down at me in that fierce way that messed with my breathing. "You may regret that later."

"Hey. Don't ever say that."

"Come here." His hand gave mine a tug, and he pulled me onto his lap. I sat sideways with my arms around his neck. "I don't like leaving you. Especially with guys like Milo around. I saw the way he was looking at you."

"I'm worried about your *life*, and you're worried about Milo?" I chuckled humorlessly. "You're really something," I said, brushing strands of hair off his forehead. "I told you, I don't like polo players and I don't know what spell you put on me, but the only guy I'm interested in is you."

His mouth seized mine and I tangled my fingers in his hair, pressing him against me. Lust pooled between my legs. His tongue invaded my mouth, exploring, claiming. Shit, why did he have to leave now? Would it be awfully wrong to have wild sex in a car in public? We were all tongues, heavy breaths, and hands everywhere. I squirmed against his cock, and a soft groan rumbled deep in his throat. He pulled his head back, and we were both panting.

"Fucking torture. Damn, Camila. Just thinking about you makes me hard."

I blushed and looked away. He held up my chin, forcing me to look at him.

"I'm sorry to be so blunt," he said. "But I want you to know the effect you have on me. I've never met someone like you. I know we hardly know each other, but I'm crazy about you."

"I'm crazy about you, too, Sebastián. Please, please take care of yourself," I said, unable to restrain the tears that spilled. "When will you be back?"

"Hey," he murmured. "I'll be fine." He wiped my cheeks with his thumbs. "I'll call you tomorrow night, after this is over." He kissed my forehead. "I may have to fly straight to Bariloche for a meeting, but I'll be back on Wednesday. And look, I'll have Rafa and a few others. You don't have to worry about me, Cami."

I swallowed hard, desperately wanting to believe that. The pad of my thumb traced his lips and he kissed it. God, I wanted that mouth on me, everywhere. I blushed at the thought.

"When I come back"—he kissed me softly—"you and me."

"You and me," I breathed.

Chapter 15

I was up most of the night, tossing and turning, praying Sebastián was safe. It was torture not to be able to call him. In the morning, I called my parents and made plans to join them at their rowing club. Since I joined the company, I hadn't seen much of Mamá and Papá. I missed them, and it seemed like a good distraction while I waited to hear from Sebastián.

I hurried through Estación Retiro, the main train station, a gargantuan marvel of French stylings and a steel frame made in Liverpool. Papá had told me it was once considered the most beautiful in the world and truly representative of Buenos Aires's European roots.

I found an empty seat and rode the train to the Buenos Aires Rowing Club, a traditional landmark located in the Tigre neighborhood, twenty miles north of downtown.

A relaxing sanctuary away from the dense air and noise of the city, the club's island on the Río de la Plata was a welcome change of scenery. There, I could lie under the peaceful dance of the wind and the willows and bring myself to a Zen state of mind that would last me for days. The Rowing Club island had always been a place where I connected with the real me and could see my life with clarity.

The train lumbered sleepily along the river, waddling on the tattered tracks. I sank into my seat, letting my eyelids drop and the exhaustion settle, and surrendered to the rocking motion.

The train stopped with a jolt, and I startled awake. Tigre station was the end of the line. Through the window I saw my mother at the club's landing by the shore. She was sitting on a bench under the shade of a weeping willow, her statuesque figure elegant even from a distance. Slipping my backpack across my shoulder, I waited for the doors to slide open, then jogged toward the landing.

Seeing my mother always felt like coming home after a long trip. That comforting feeling of stepping into your bedroom to find everything exactly the way you had left it. I greeted her with a tight hug, lingering a bit longer than usual, the familiar scent of roses from her L'Occitane perfume soothing me.

"Sweetheart, I'm so glad you're here."

"It's good to see you, Mamá."

She pulled away and studied me. "You've lost weight, and you look exhausted."

I rolled my eyes. "Mamá."

"Don't overdo it, Cami. It's no joke."

"Where's Papá?"

She raised an eyebrow. From the time I put on my first ballet shoes, she had warned me about the eating disorders that haunted ballerinas.

I sighed. "We've just been working longer and harder, that's all."

Her hazel eyes watched me with a mix of concern and understanding.

"Your father is in the club, choosing the boat."

"I'll go catch up with him." I kissed her cheek, then hurried across the street.

I pushed open the doors to the Tudor-style building that housed the Buenos Aires Rowing Club, a two-hundred-year-old beacon majestically erected across the river landing. Black and white portraits of crew races lined mahogany-paneled walls, interrupted by cabinets showcasing trophies from different eras. Perpetually polished, the checkered floors glowed under the slanted sun that filtered through the iron-framed windows. I had always found the atmosphere mesmerizing. A ghostly, mystical feel drifted through the hallways as I hurried toward the courtyard on the other side. I welcomed the familiar string of memories that paraded through my mind: Papá holding my hand when I was five, the two of us wandering the halls. He would point at the images while he told me about famous athletes, now fading ghosts forever memorialized in snapshots of greatness. His eyes would glint as he told the stories, which had always been my favorite part. Being a member here was a privilege that had been granted to my great-grandfather by a wealthy patient after he had saved the man's life. The membership was closed to newcomers for decades, even to this day, and could only be inherited from a previous generation.

"You must always stay a member of the club, Camila," Papá would say. "It's Abuelo Armando's legacy."

So, I had. Despite my demanding schedule, the ritual of rowing with Papá on the weekends was a cherished part of my life.

On the other side of the patio, Papá waited in the small office assigned to check out boats. Even from a distance, his frame looked a little less erect, and a faint, silver glint kissed his hair. I greeted him with a hug, basking in the comfort that I always felt in his presence.

"Cami," he said with bright eyes. "You're right on time. We have a good selection today."

"Good," I said, nodding. Picking the right boat was a key part of our routine.

"How's that ankle?" He signed the log and handed the attendant his driver's license.

"Oh, fine. Almost back to normal."

"Things going well at the theater?"

"I guess. I don't know, really." I shrugged. "I feel a lot of pressure to do well on this soloist role. The others are breathing down my neck. It weighs on me."

"Hmm," he said as he finished filling out the log. "One of the many prices of rising to the top. But you're a professional now, honey. You know what you're doing. Trust your instincts."

"Thanks, Papá. You have more confidence in me than I do, sometimes."

Papá squeezed my shoulder, and we strolled back to the landing, where Mamá waited, reading a magazine. Behind us, Paco, my favorite boatman, wheeled the boat along the rusted tracks that led to the riverbed. He always had a "new" joke I'd heard at least twenty times over the years, but I laughed anyway. I liked Paco because there was nothing you could do to sour his mood. He found happiness in the smallest things.

At the landing, Paco slid the boat onto the water. I carefully stepped in and scooted to one of the two wheeled seats at the oars. Papá took the other while Mamá sat facing us, arranging the steering ropes over her shoulders. Even without knowing anything about my mother's glory days as a prima, you would still recognize her as a dancer. Everything she did was graceful, even the way she sat, crossing her legs to the side, her feet softly bent, yet perfectly aligned. I admired her in silence, wondering if anyone would ever see me the way I saw her.

Papá and I flexed in unison, our skin glistening under the sun as we rowed the wooden shell through the copper Delta while Mamá steered, dozing off often and shifting our course.

"Inés, please. Stay awake and keep your eyes forward. You need to point the boat to the island." He gestured with his head. He winced at the sweat dripping down his temples. "Can you see it? Or do I need to take the steering too?"

Mamá adjusted her hat, dismissing him with a quick flick of the hand as he continued his mumbling. It was sweet and comforting to see them interact in the same way after so many years.

We veered into the heart of the forest, the river channels spreading out like veins. Over the canals, the willow branches intertwined in a dense canopy of greens, their protruding roots clawing the mud at the river ledge. Distant roars from motorboats faded behind us, swallowed by the deep silence of the forest and replaced by the chants of birds above us and the soft buzz of curious dragonflies circling about. We followed the familiar route, the river lapping rhythmically against the boat, with the soothing pace of the oars cutting through the patterns of filtered sunlight playing on the golden surface of the river. From the islands lining the canals, modest houses on stilts watched us pass. The stilts were an architectural necessity to endure the frequent high tides brought by summer storms. Hydrangeas grew wild in the Delta, splashes of purple and blue bursting like fireworks for miles. Papá and I rowed in silence as we had done for so many years.

At the club's private island, Mrs. Flores greeted us with a welcoming smile. A table covered with an array of tapas waited. She and Mr. Flores lived on the island, cooking for visiting members who were eager for a day away from the city. I checked my phone incessantly but there were no calls or texts from Sebastián. My anxiety rocketed, and out on this island I felt a million miles away from him.

"I can't wait for opening night. *Giselle* has always been one of my favorites," Mamá said without opening her eyes. We were lying on lounge chairs by the water after a scrumptious lunch. My chest tightened a fraction. Mamá had danced the part of Giselle many times in her time. I bet she could still get on a stage today and run through all the variations. But she had never played the role of Myrta, so my personal quest to make her proud piled onto the weight I already carried on my shoulders. Mamá stretched her feet, turning them at the ankles. "How are rehearsals coming along?"

"Fine. Vronsky's pushing us to the brink. That woman's ruthless."

"Is your ankle still bothering you?"

"Hmm...It was fine till this week. It hurts at night because I've been rehearsing through lunch every day. Oh, which reminds me"—I sat up on the chair—"I didn't tell you. Marcos and I are performing a tango this weekend at that guy's house...Koviesky. The mogul with the polo team? Javi knows him."

Mamá lifted her hat. "Vladimir Koviesky?" Her eyebrows shot up. "How did that happen?"

"Nata was invited to perform, but she turned it down to go to Brazil with her new guy."

"She turned it down? For a *boy*? That's absurd!"

"Exactly what I said. She's nuts. But she really likes him. I think this one's a keeper."

"Koviesky's party will be great exposure for you. Marcos is the perfect partner. You're doing a tango?"

156

"Yes, Marcos put together the whole thing. It's challenging, but if we pull it off, it'll be amazing."

Mamá smiled, but it was a mix of pride and sadness. She knew how I felt about Marcos. "I'm thrilled for you. And...I'm sure there will be lots of single men at this party."

"Mamá, I'll be working. Besides...I've sort of...met someone already." I reluctantly glanced at her.

Her face lit up. "Tell me everything," she said. "A dancer?"

Papá lumbered over and plopped on the lounge chair beside me. "Everything about what? Who's a dancer?"

"Cami has a boyfriend."

"Mamá!"

"Who's he?" Papá frowned. He was the epitome of the protective father, not big on distractions from my career.

"He's not my boyfriend. But...I do like him...A lot." I avoided their eyes and played with the end of my long ponytail.

"Is he a dancer?" Papá prompted now.

"No, Papá. It's *not* Marcos, if that's what you're asking."

"Hm. Who, then?"

"We met by chance on my way to work. Then...we ran into each other the day I came to see you for lunch." I looked up at him. "His building is by your office."

Papá pressed his mouth into a grim line. "Is it, now. What does he do?"

"He's an architect."

Papá thought for a moment, his frown deepening as he shook his head. "The only architects by my office are Palacios and De la Viña."

Why was I the *only* person in this planet who hadn't heard Sebastián's name before? I nodded. "Yup. He's one of them."

Papá's face blanched. "Camila...No. Are you serious?"

"I haven't even told you which one of the two he is. You're already disapproving? I'm shocked."

"Either one of those last names would be something I'd want you to stay clear of."

"Why? He's a nice guy. I like him." Suddenly I was four years old again.

"Which one is he," he spat out, both a question and an accusation.

"Palacios. Sebastián Palacios."

"No. *No*." He growled.

"Papá, I'm not a child."

"Then don't act like one. Do you know who the Palacioses are? It's not a joke. How in the hell did you end up mixed with someone like that?"

"Like what? Papá, I like him. And for the first time, I may have a chance to be happy with someone instead of looking through a glass wall at Marcos while he makes out with the entire cast. There, have I humiliated myself enough for you?" I looked away, swallowing through the thickness in my throat. Mamá's hand covered mine and squeezed it.

Papá groaned. "I'm not happy about this, Camila. It's a detour and a bad idea."

"Why? Why does everything in my life have to be so carefully planned? Every single thing I do has to have a purpose. There's got to be more than dancing all the time. Maybe it's not so bad if I have fun for a change. I'm young."

He let out a breath through flared nostrils. "Think about what you're trying to build for yourself. What you're working so hard to accomplish. What do you think the company will say when they find out one of their rising ballerinas is dating a *gangster*?"

"Papá!"

"Camila, those people are *criminals*!" He slammed his fist on the chair so hard Mamá and I jumped in unison.

I rubbed my forehead and clenched my teeth. "I don't even know why we are having this conversation. I'm an adult. And I've only seen him a few times."

"Read the papers. Go online and Google them for Christ's sake. They don't only control the docks. They have their hands in casinos, oil companies, waste management, refineries, wine, you name it. All money laundering. Don Martín himself has been under investigation more times than anyone can count. He's got politicians in his pockets, so no one can touch them. It's scandalous how deep the corruption goes. I don't want you associated with that. Do not jeopardize your career over some punk you just met." He turned to Mamá. "Are you hearing this?"

I pulled up my feet and hugged my legs, holding in the tears. Why in the hell did I think telling Papá about Sebastián would be a good idea? Deep inside I already knew he wouldn't approve. Did I subconsciously want to get this out of the way? I quickly wiped a stray tear off my cheek.

"Camila." Papá reached for my hand. His tone was softer, but I kept my eyes down, pressing my chin to my knees. "This is your life. Your future. But you dance at the most prestigious company in the country. That means that from now on, you *have* to consider every step you take. You're so close to what you've always worked so hard to achieve. Don't put it at risk."

"Esteban," Mamá said, finally interrupting her long silence. Papá looked up and met her eyes. Amazing the speech that woman could deliver with just one word. Mamá understood my career path better than anyone. But she also knew well the things she had turned away for the sake of dancing. Like me, ballet had been her master, owner of her young years and her free time. From the time they were both young, Papá had been at her side through all of it. Ballet had always come first. It wasn't until after her career had peaked that she finally stepped out of the ballet world to have a family. She could've kept going, but it was what she wanted, I knew that in my heart. But like me, Papá felt we somehow had to make her feel like her decision to give it all up had been worth it. That *we* were worth it.

I knew Mamá probably wasn't thrilled with my choice in Sebastián, but she often insisted I should bring balance to my life. She also always had my back when it came to Papá.

Sulking, Papá sank back in his chair, his gaze lost somewhere in the horizon. I hated arguing with him. We had always been close, but I had inherited his stubbornness, and when we didn't see eye to eye, it wasn't pretty.

A silent half hour went by. I checked my phone for the millionth time, but there were no messages from Sebastián. Anxiety unfurled in my gut.

"Did you get any sleep last night?" I muttered. "You look tired."

He half smiled, and I knew the storm had passed for the moment. He closed his eyes, and I guessed he hadn't slept at all. Part of me felt guilty for making last-minute plans to come rowing, but I also knew he enjoyed our time together as much as I did.

Mamá shifted in her chair, her face hidden under her hat. "Esteban, why didn't your patient just call the ambulance?"

"He's old. He was just scared." Yawning, he leaned back in the chair, his eyelids growing heavy as Mamá began talking about their upcoming trip to Europe.

Staring at my phone screen, I listened to their conversation absentmindedly, hoping they had change their minds about Sebastián once they met him. All this negative press on him weighed in my mind, but I had promised him I wouldn't buy into it. I wanted to trust him, though the rational part of me needed to know more.

Later in my apartment, I paced around like a caged animal. It was nearly eleven at night, and my damn phone was quieter than ever. I folded laundry and did the dishes, but my mind was racing through the options as my anxiety peaked. What if something had gone wrong? What if he was hurt? My phone vibrated in my pocket, and I jumped, almost dropping it as I yanked it out.

"Thank God," I said without hiding my desperation. "Are you okay?"

"I am," Sebastián said. "It's over."

"And the girls?"

"Safe." His tone was low, exhausted. "Cami, I can't talk now. I need to board the plane, but I'll call you in the morning?"

"Yes, of course. I'm so glad you're safe. The last twenty-four hours have been torture."

"I know, I'm sorry. I miss you."

"I miss you too."

The line went dead, and I closed my eyes, plopping back in my bed. He was safe, and apparently so were the girls. How in the hell had he pulled off something like that? The Palacios name became bigger and harder to avoid with every passing second. Sebastián had done something that a regular person wouldn't have been able to do at all, and not only that, he had succeeded. Rescuing trafficked girls surely required contacts with important people, dangerous people. The thought lingered and the red flags telling me to flee flared in the back of my mind. Would I constantly worry about him? Would I be in danger too?

I vowed to do research on the Palacios family, but for the moment, my mind surrendered to Morpheus, and I let exhaustion win.

Chapter 16

On Monday, I met Marcos at lunch to go over the choreography he had already come up with in his head. I was once again blown away by his talent. Marcos would make a great artistic director someday.

The upcoming performance for Vladimir Koviesky was a welcome distraction. Marcos taught me the steps and we rehearsed them. Tango routines are difficult because you have to keep your eyes locked on the other dancer's and can't check yourself in the mirror. Marcos led with unbelievable ease and passion. His movements were strong and decisive. The choreography he had created was full of dramatic sexual tension between two hotheaded lovers. We tangled our bodies together, entranced by the sensuality of the music. To make it more cutting-edge, Marcos added a few acrobatic moves that required strength and control. After rehearsing a few times, I was breathing hard and my muscles burned.

We ran through it one more time and ended on the last step with me bent backward over Marcos's arm and him hovering over me. Our faces were an inch apart, his short breaths kissing my lips, warm and sweet. I looked down at his mouth, the curve of his lips, almost too full, which, to me, made them so much sexier. He inched closer, and for a moment, time stopped. Then he pulled back and grinned, still holding me in his arms. "You're a helluva dancer. We're going to kick ass."

I smiled and squeezed his shoulder. He seemed so happy it was contagious. Excitement twisted into the familiar knot in my stomach. The number was phenomenal and was sure to impress the highly demanding audience. I hugged Marcos good-bye, picked up my bag, and ran back to my studio to rehearse Act II for *Giselle*.

By the time Madame dismissed us for the day, I felt completely drained and sore everywhere. All I could think of was sinking into the tub, then wrapping myself with ice packs in front of the TV. I checked my phone, and there was a text from Sebastián. My heart hiccupped.

Sebastián: I miss u. How was your day? I'm tired of babysitting these people. Much rather be with you.

Me: Just finished. I wish u were back. I had a long day with no breaks. Need to ice my ankle now. Call you later? Miss u. X

Sebastián: Are u hurt?

Me: No, just watching it. I'll call you when I get home.

No mention of the girls or the rescue. My mind raced through the scenarios. How had he done it? Was he safe or was someone after him? Would he tell me if that were the case? I growled inwardly.

Marcos, Nata, and I shared a cab to the apartment. He browsed through our takeout menus while Nata and I went to our respective bathrooms to shower. When I stepped out, wrapping my hair in a towel, Marcos had covered the countertop with boxes of Chinese food.

"Oh my God...You are a god." I hugged his neck and gave him a quick peck on the cheek. "You're totally sucking up and I love it." I poked his ribs.

A devilish smile played on his lips. He handed me plates, and we immediately started on our food.

Nata emerged from her room a few minutes later. She opened her mouth in astonishment, then closed it and exhaled through flared nostrils. "Marcos, you are the devil! But I kind of love you right now. I'm famished." She sighed.

We ate in front of the TV with our ankles and knees wrapped in ice packs. Now that Marcos lived with us, there was hardly any room left in the freezer for anything else. It was perfect for us three. Marcos and Nata rehearsed together almost every day. Their schedules were pretty much identical, so it was more than convenient when it came to sharing rides and meals. The only downside was that, when it came to neatness, Nata was screwed big time. She was obsessive, and Marcos and I were...basically pigs. She constantly nagged us. But for the most part, we all took care of each other. It really felt like a family.

We finished eating, and I left to my room to call Sebastián.

"There you are. I was wondering what happened to you." His voice was low and soft. He sounded tired, but I could hear him smile.

"Sorry it took this long to call you. I'm dog-tired and didn't eat much today, so I was starving. How are you? I'm dying to know about the girls."

"Cami, I'm sorry, but this falls behind one of those boundaries I mentioned."

"Oh, come on!"

"I can't. I'm sorry."

"That's not fair," I said like a petulant child.

"It's better this way."

"Are they safe? All of them? At least tell me that."

"They are. Hey, I miss you." His voice was low and raspy, laced with longing and anticipation.

"Don't change the subject. Are *you* safe? How do you know these people won't come after you?"

"Nobody will come after me. When can I see you?"

Despite my frustration, something beautiful fluttered in my chest. I let out a heavy sigh and my throat tightened. "I'm so busy this week I won't be able to see you until the party. I'm sorry." Tears rushed to my eyes. Seriously, I was *crying* now? I was so exhausted, everything seemed much more dramatic.

He groaned. "Okay, we can catch up after the party. I have an urgent trip to London and I need to leave on Sunday, but my flight isn't until later in the afternoon."

"Oh, when will you be back?"

"Tuesday. You sound tired, babe. Get some sleep," he whispered.

I yawned as we said good-bye and was immediately asleep.

The next two days were surreal. I couldn't tell when they started or ended. It was all a steady string of choreographies without much in between. Marcos and I worked on our variations for *Giselle* during the day and used lunch breaks and stayed after hours to rehearse the tango. My body complained, but I pushed harder. In the evenings, I wrapped myself in ice packs till I was numb. Marcos did the same, and it was good to share the excruciating routine with someone. We pulled each other forward.

Bundled up on the sofa, we shared a blanket as we phased out in front of the TV, our feet tangled together. Marcos smiled from his end of the couch, eyelids heavy with the fatigue of the day, and I knew he was content. He had started looking at me differently after we began working on the tango together. He even spoke to me with the same professional respect he used only with the principals. This is what it must be like for a prima, and it was every bit as amazing as I had imagined. It was like a dream, and I didn't want to wake up.

Seeing me work with Marcos during lunch fueled Verónica's venomous rivalry. She wanted to know what was up, and why Marcos, the most sought-after and respected principal in the company, would throw away his precious breaks rehearsing with a lower-rank dancer like me.

Late one evening, I pushed the door to the dressing room and paused when I heard Verónica's voice hissing. She couldn't see me from where I was, and I stayed put when she mentioned my name as she spoke to a group of girls from the corps.

"She doesn't come up to scratch! I was shocked they even gave her the understudy. Obviously, a push from her mom. I heard she had a thing with Federico back then. It's sad how corrupt it all is. And now she's even using the studios after hours to work on another choreography with Marcos. Vronsky should just put her foot down with Federico and replace her."

I took a step forward and leaned against the lockers, watching the change on the girls' faces when they saw me. Verónica whipped her head around and smirked.

"Oh, speak of the devil," she said.

"So much free time, Verónica. I'm flattered, but it's a little sad that I'm your best subject."

She narrowed her eyes and turned around, letting her towel drop to the floor. She was skinnier. Her pale, skeletal body looked unhealthy and fragile. She slipped into a scarlet thong, the long, satin Victoria's Secret tag sticking out, almost larger than the garment itself. Even her underwear suited her.

Nata poked her head in to let me know Alexei was outside. Verónica's eyes darted to us from the mirror. She envied Nata, and the fact that I had been chosen to be Nata's roommate only made Verónica more bitter. I winked at her on my way out.

The next day was the big day. The tango was finally ready. Marcos had compiled several variations together. There was love, hate, jealousy, and redemption all in one dance. The number was a piece of art.

"It's incredible." Nata shook her head after we finished rehearsing it for her. "Camila, I don't think I would have been able to dance that as well as you."

"Right." I rolled my eyes.

"No, I mean it. You two are…perfect partners. The fire…the chemistry on stage is electric, and that's crucial for a tango performance. Shit, now I wish I could go!"

"Well…" I grinned. "You have better plans. Don't forget to call me. And Nata, thank you so much for this opportunity. You're the best."

"You're the ones doing me a favor. Vladimir's not easy to turn down!"

We hugged and she left to her rehearsal. She was flying to Brazil in a few hours, so I wouldn't see her again till Sunday night.

That evening Marcos and I ate spaghetti in front of the TV and fell asleep on the couch over a pile of our clothes mixed together. I woke up an hour later, turned the TV off, and covered Marcos with a blanket. I was getting used to sharing my space with him. It was nice having him here, and I knew I would miss him when he eventually moved out.

Dressed in my performance clothes, I blinked at the tango dancer that watched me back from the mirror with a surprised expression. I hardly recognized myself. I looked slick, sexy. Nata's clothes fit me like a glove. My hair was tightly wrapped in a French twist, my makeup clean but dramatic: pale complexion and bright red lips, fake eyelashes and black eyeliner accentuating my eyes. I totally looked the part.

Marcos was insanely good-looking in a black suit and tango hat. He had a silk scarf around his neck the way tango dancers wear, and a long overcoat hanging from his shoulders. I smiled and gave a tug on his scarf.

"You won't be alone for long tonight looking like this," I said. "Remember, no girls here. You'll have to find one with her own place." I winked.

He gave me a smug grin. "Damn, Cams. You look incredible." He wrapped his arm around my waist and pulled me against him. "You're so fucking hot in these sexy clothes. Maybe I'll come home with *you*."

I met those hazel eyes, and a gust of mixed emotions whirled in my stomach.

"Nah, then it'll be me again in the morning. Here. For you." I tucked a red rose in the front pocket of his coat. "Have fun tonight."

He watched me secure the rose, glancing back at me with smiling eyes. An uncomfortable silent second went by.

"You're very special," he whispered so close that if I tilted my chin up, our lips would meet.

I swallowed the boulder in my throat and smiled. "Let's go."

A long line of imported cars filled the driveway to Vladimir's house. When our cab reached the end, two valets opened the doors in perfect synchronization. We stepped out, and Marcos wrapped his arm around my waist as he addressed one of them.

"Good evening. We're here to perform. We were told to ask for Misha."

The valet flashed a quick smile. "Of course, right this way. Mr. Misha will be with you in just a second." He spoke into a wireless microphone on his collar, then excused himself to tend to the next car.

A tall, slender man in a smart suit appeared behind us.

"Good evening. I'm Misha, Mr. Vladimir's personal assistant. He has asked me to show you to the room where you will perform. If you will follow me, please."

Misha led us through several rooms, all equally magnificent in size and separated by ornate archways. Vladimir's home was spectacular, the way I imagined royalty. Enormous, white flower arrangements dressed every table among fine crystal and silver. The party was in full swing as guests poured in through the entrance in a steady flow.

We followed Misha through the main hall. High ceilings, crystal chandeliers, and polished marble floors adorned the colossal room. French doors opened to the outside, where a famous waltz echoed from an orchestra in the distance. Mesmerized, I paused to admire the view. In the garden, hundreds of tiny lights glinted from inside the trees, bathing the party with a soft glow. It was breathtaking. A playground for the rich.

Misha opened the door to a mahogany-paneled room with plush couches, silk red curtains, and an ornate chandelier that matched the opulent decorative style of the house. He gestured to a table stocked with drinks, platters with caviar, cheese, and all sorts of elaborate, miniature delicacies.

"There are refreshments specially prepared for you. Please help yourselves. Through those curtains, you will find the room where you will perform. Please, feel free to get acquainted. If you would like anything else, or if I can be of any further assistance, you may ring the bell by the door. Mr. Vladimir is delighted with your presence and wishes for you to feel welcome." He nodded politely.

Marcos handed him a drive with the music for our number and gave him a few directions. Misha nodded and excused himself, disappearing through the door.

Marcos and I looked at each other and grinned.

"Fuck, Cams. Look at all this. It's incredible." He looked like a kid locked in Disneyland, his eyes wide and bright as he scanned the room. Marcos had never been around money. As the oldest of five brothers raised by a single mother, he grew up with finances always being tight.

I followed him to the room where we would perform. Countless chairs surrounded the spacious stage raised three feet off the floor to provide an intimate setting between performers and audience.

We rehearsed a few moves on the stage to get used to the dimensions, then left to get ready.

A million invisible ants crawled under my skin while I peeked from behind the heavy, velvet curtains separating us from the main room. More guests than I could count already filled the chairs.

"Marcos, there must be over two hundred people in there!" My stomach twisted in knots. Marcos hugged me from behind and kissed my neck softly. I immediately relaxed.

"We dance at the Colón, remember? A *lot* more people watch us perform there."

"I know, but with all the lights on my face, I don't see them. This is different. Look, they'll be right *there*. That's way too close." I grimaced.

His warm breath brushed my neck softly as we watched the guests fill the chairs. After a few moments, he unwrapped his arms and took my hand.

"Let's fucking do this." He grinned. His eyes were bright with confidence.

Misha stepped in to let us know everything was ready. Vladimir would be making the introduction.

Once all the lights were out, we traveled silently across the room. It was completely dark except for a dimly lit path marking the way. We took our places in the center of the stage and waited for Vladimir's introduction. Marcos's confident arms held me in place. My heart pounded with anticipation.

A single spotlight sliced the darkness from above, focusing only on Marcos and me. We held our position, his arm around my waist and his free hand holding mine up in a typical tango pose. Our eyes were locked on each other's, our blood surging with excitement. A deep voice with a Russian accent interrupted the low humming of the crowd.

"Ladies and gentlemen, it is my pleasure and honor to introduce Camila Navarro and Marcos Sánz, two of the most remarkable soloists in the permanent ballet company of the Colón Theater. Camila and Marcos will present a tango performance that they have created exclusively for us tonight. Let us give them a proper welcome."

The crowd responded with a warm, enthusiastic applause. I took a deep breath and smiled to hide my nerves, keeping my eyes on Marcos's.

The soft melody of a violin drifted in the air, interlaced with the unmistakable nostalgic sound of a bandoneón. The audience grew completely silent. You could slice the air with a knife.

"*Merde*, babe," Marcos whispered.

"*Merde*," I mouthed with my eyes on his.

As soon as we took the first step, my nerves vanished. Marcos's movements were strong, decisive, dominant. He marked his territory without hesitation, his eyes never leaving mine. My body was liquid around his, our legs intertwining in quick, agile hooks. I followed his every move with flawless synchronization as my character debated whether or not to surrender to her passionate lover, a man she knew was no good, but she couldn't resist. I snaked one leg around Marcos's waist, and he spun me around as if I weighed nothing.

Warm air brushed my face. I landed on one foot, arching my body backward as he pressed me tightly against him. I turned my head away, and he gripped my chin, seductively coercing me back to him. He held my gaze for a frozen moment, his sweet breath blending with mine. I arched my back and closed my eyes as his lips traced a path down my throat to my chest, then back. I could feel *everything*, each of my nerve endings amplified. His warm, panting breaths sent shivers up my back, fire brushing where his lips touched my skin. He moved slowly, sensually, savoring the proximity of our pumping hearts.

I tilted my head sideways, exposing my neck, pretending to surrender to his hungry lips, then pushed him away abruptly, my eyes defiant. His arm tightened around my waist, commanding, possessive. His mouth curled up in a wicked smile, our faces an inch apart. I stared into his blazing eyes, and in that moment, we were the only people in the room.

We continued the banter between our characters, the tension building, the temperature in the air rising. Two young lovers ruled by nothing but raw passion, pouring their hearts into a dance.

We ended on the last note with my body bent backward over Marcos's arm, our lips almost touching as we held each other's gaze in one last minute of tension. What would it be? Would my character surrender to her lover's spell? The moment was suspended in the air, the room completely silent, frozen in anticipation. Then Marcos suddenly closed the gap between us and kissed me hard on the mouth, pouring the need and tension from the dance into the kiss. My character surrendered to him, not because she wanted to, but because it was the only thing she could do if she ever wanted to breathe again. *I* surrendered because I was lost in the moment, and even though Marcos and I were not together, it was the right ending to such a perfect, passion-filled performance.

The room exploded into applause. The audience went crazy, cheering, whistling. Marcos didn't let go and deepened the kiss. *Holy crap.* I molded into his arms, completely surrendered, letting him own that moment, letting him own *me*. People rose to their feet yelling, "Bravo!" Whistling louder.

I finally broke the kiss, and Marcos smiled at me with genuine joy. A rain of white flowers peppered the stage. Marcos held my hand up as we took a bow. He blew a kiss in the general direction of the crowd, then winked at me. I never wanted this moment to end. I was floating away from everything. This is why I danced. All the uncertainty, the physical pain, the constant fight. It was worth it. All of it. Marcos kissed me on the cheek, and we bowed once more before running offstage, our pulse racing with excitement.

In the back room, Marcos hugged me again, so tight I could hardly breath. We were panting, our hearts drumming against each other's chests. It was the most incredible feeling, so different from the theater performances. This was much more intimate, so much more alive. You could really feel the energy in the room.

Soft knuckles knocked on the door before Misha walked in carrying a huge bouquet of white roses. "For the queen of the evening." He bowed. "Mr. Vladimir would like to thank you personally. He was quite taken with your performance. Magnificent job, if I may say so." He smiled as he held the door open for a tall, heavyset man with a thick beard and rosy cheeks. He was handsomely dressed in a tuxedo, and I immediately recognized Vladimir from the pictures I had seen in magazines.

"You were fantastic!" he said in a thick Russian accent, taking both my hands to press a gentle kiss to my knuckles. His eyes were moist. "Camila, you are a true gem." He then turned to Marcos and shook his hand enthusiastically. "Marcos, I have heard great things about you, but I have to say I am completely astounded." He looked back and forth between Marcos and me. "I can't wait to see you both in *Giselle*. I look forward to opening night. Please join the party as my guests of honor. Help yourselves to whatever you want." He smiled broadly, then thanked us again before leaving the room.

Misha approached us holding two envelopes. "Your compensation. Mr. Vladimir has added a bonus as a token of his gratitude and hopes you find it suitable. He hopes you enjoy the party. Please let me know if I can get you anything else." He handed us our payment, then walked out.

Marcos looked into his envelope, quickly counting the money. "Jesus fucking Christ. There are *four thousand dollars* in here. This is insane."

"What? Are you serious?" I eyed the thick pad of bills. I couldn't breathe. Four grand in *one hour*. "Wow," I muttered.

Marcos pulled me into his arms. "You were amazing. I had the best time. I'll talk to Vronsky. I want more solos with you. You're the most talented dance partner I've ever had. And I've had lots," he said, looking into my eyes. The sincerity in his voice was disarming. I blinked through the daze.

"Thank you. You're pretty amazing too." I looked down, but he gently tilted my chin up, prompting me to look at him.

"Something changed in the last few days. For me." His eyes bore into mine. "I feel...a strong connection to you. I care about you."

"I care about you too. Your friendship means a lot to me."

"I don't know...if I like our friends arrangement anymore." His hand cupped my face.

"Don't say those things."

"Why? We could see where this takes us."

I pulled my chin away. "No. Marcos, you're with Carla. And I'm dating...someone else."

"You are?" He frowned.

"Yeah. It's recent."

"Who is he?" He let go of my face, his tone hardening.

"No one you know. I'm not one of your playthings. And I don't like you saying stuff like that when you're with someone else."

"Carla and I are not in a relationship right now."

"Well, *I* am."

"Who's the lucky guy?"

"I told you, no one you know."

He watched me for a silent moment, then let out a sigh and nodded. "I want you to be happy, Cams."

"Yeah, I know." I half smiled, glad that Sebastián was in my life. The old me, the one who suffered through all of Marcos's emotional whiplashes, would've been devastated that Marcos hadn't even put up a fight. "Go on," I said. "Go have fun."

"Yeah." He picked up his coat. "Maybe I'll go find a rich blonde and get laid. I've earned it."

"And there he is again. My old friend."

He chuckled, throwing his coat over his shoulder. As soon as he left the room, I plopped into an armchair, closing my eyes and letting the adrenaline from the performance wash through me. What a roller coaster. A trail of images from the past few days paraded in my mind: Marcos leading me, holding me firmly as he explained the emotions that went with each step. Eating our lunches together, propped against the empty studio wall, exhausted and drenched in sweat. I had spent so much time with him. Then the kiss tonight, and his words after. Was he just horny? Or was it possible his feelings for me had changed? Why now? I sighed. No, in a few days, things would go back to normal. And it didn't matter, anyways. I wanted to be with Sebastián.

I sank deeper into the plush seat, fatigue settling in. The night had been a dream. Who knew performing in such an intimate setting could be this fulfilling?

My bliss was interrupted by a firm knocking at the door. I stood and opened it, smiling at the sight of Sebastián, then my smile instantly faded. His jaw was clenched, his eyes blazing. Shit. The kiss?

"You're here," I said, looking to somehow break the tension in his expression. He walked past me into the room, running both hands through his hair. Shit. *Shit.*

"What the fuck, Camila."

"If this is about the kiss on stage, it was a performance. Nothing else."

His eyes narrowed. "This is the guy you've been spending every free minute with?" His tone was controlled, withholding a storm. I took a hesitant step toward him.

"Marcos and I are friends, dance partners. Nothing more."

"Good to know." He sneered. "You let all your dance partners kiss you that way?"

"My relationship with him is not romantic. We were just in the moment and that's...Marcos," I said, failing to sound convincing even to myself. Squeezing the back of my neck, I looked down. "Listen—"

"No. You listen."

I flinched.

"I'm not a goddamn fool," he said. "The chemistry between you and that guy is bold. I saw the way he looked at you, the way he handled you, the way he fucking kissed you. He wants you."

"I want *you*."

"This is not a game to me, Camila."

"It's not a game to me either. There's nothing but friendship and work between Marcos and me. It was just a kiss after an...intense dance. That's all. It didn't mean anything, I swear."

He turned to face the window, his hands interlaced behind his head. Under his controlled demeanor, his body radiated tension. Dammit. Just when things were starting to get good between us. The sudden thought of losing Sebastián tightened my chest. I walked to him and hugged him from behind. He didn't move, so it felt awkward.

"We're dancers. Like...actors. Please don't be mad. I'm with *you*. There's nobody else." I moved around to face him and circled my arms around his neck. "I'm sorry about the kiss. I get it. I would feel the same way if the tables were turned. But you have to trust me."

He looked at me, his expression unreadable.

"Look," I said. "You won't like what I'm about to say, but I don't want to keep things from you, especially after this. Marcos... is staying at my apartment at the moment, but he'll move out at the end of the month."

His features hardened a fraction. "Wow," he said in a low, controlled tone. "This just keeps getting better and better."

"That's all there is. I just wanted you to know. Don't let this come between us," I said, carefully placing my palm on his chest. "I haven't seen you for so long. I've missed you." He didn't move; he just pinned me under his icy glare. "You're overreacting," I said.

His eyes narrowed fractionally. "If you haven't figured it out already, I don't like to share."

"What are you, four?"

"Fuck. This is not a fucking joke. I told you my personal life is extremely private. I don't easily let people in either. I thought we had something here."

"We do."

"I want him gone. Out of your apartment. Tonight."

"You're joking."

"Do I look like I'm joking?"

"You expect me to kick my friend out? *Tonight?*"

"That, back there. That's not a friendship."

"That's crazy. I'm not going to do that because of a stupid kiss that was part of a performance. Give me a fucking break. Besides, it's Nata's apartment."

"You're not going back to that apartment if that guy is living there," he snarled.

"You can't order me around. I'm not one of your bodyguards."

"He wants to get in your pants, Camila," he snapped. "Are you that fucking naïve that you don't see that?"

"This conversation's over." I turned around, but he snatched my arm.

"He wants you."

"Let go."

He immediately did, and I hastily slipped into my coat, avoiding his eyes. A knot swelled in my throat. This was the price I had to pay to be with him? Kick Marcos out in the middle of the night? It was so insanely ridiculous.

"That guy," he said, pointing at the door where Marcos had left, "wants you, and the fact that you minimize it concerns me."

I looked at him defiantly. "I'm not minimizing anything. Marcos is just a flirt, and even if you're right, the feeling is not mutual. If we're together, you have to trust me."

"After what I saw back there, I don't fucking know what to trust."

I reached for my bag and threw the rest of my things in it. Way to put an end to a dreamy night, *asshole.*

"I'll take you home." His tone was stern, commanding, slicing me. I squeezed my eyes tight and clenched my teeth.

"No."

Without turning, I stormed out, slamming the door. The hell if I was going to let some egomaniac order me around. I practically ran outside, wiping the mascara off my eyes as I rushed through the guests toward the entrance. At the main foyer, I stumbled into Vladimir. He held my arms, searching my eyes.

"*Krasivaya devushka.* You are shaking. Are you all right? Did somebody upset you, darling?" He frowned, his plump cheeks turning a deep crimson.

"Oh, no, of course not." I forced a smile. "It's been a very long week. I just need to go home. Thank you for the invitation and for your generosity. It's been such a pleasure to dance here tonight."

His expression softened. "The pleasure was all mine. I'm sorry you must leave so soon. Please allow Misha to drive you home." His eyes were warm, and I had to swallow the knot in my throat so I wouldn't bawl in front of him.

"That won't be necess—"

"I insist. It's the least I can do. Thank you again, darling. You were truly magnificent," he said, kissing my knuckles.

Misha appeared from nowhere and offered me a hand in an old-fashioned manner. The small gesture rushed new tears to my eyes. I placed my hand on his, and he walked me to a limousine. Through the tinted window, I glanced up at the house. Sebastián stood next to Vladimir, looking in my direction. Knowing he couldn't see me through the tinted window, I let the tears spill. This was not the way I had imagined the night to end.

Closing my apartment door behind me, I kicked off my shoes and dodged a pile of clothes as I charged to the kitchen cabinet for the booze. I gulped down a long swig of warm vodka straight from the bottle, letting it burn my throat. Closing my eyes, I leaned back on the fridge, wondering how tonight's dream, an evening I had been waiting for so many days, had turned so sour.

I lumbered to my room and stripped off my clothes, letting them drop to the floor. I dug in my drawer for shorts and my David Bowie long-sleeve shirt, a comforting memory from a trip to England with my brother, Javi. It had been my first concert, and I really wanted to get a shirt, but they were forty euros and we were poor backpackers. We had been saving for months for the tickets. But Javi said I needed to remember that concert, so he pulled out the last wad of banknotes from his pocket and bought me the shirt.

I pulled the pins out of my hair, shaking my head brusquely to relieve my scalp from the tight hairdo. In the mirror, the beautiful woman from a few hours ago was replaced by a pathetic ho with smudged mascara under her pink, puffy eyes.

I curled in a corner of the couch, ignoring the mess Marcos and I had made over the last few days, and stared blankly at the TV, surfing through the channels for nothing. My mind kept going back to Sebastián storming into the room and turning my dreamy night into shit. Damn him. Fresh tears burned my eyes and I let them spill.

The sound of the knob turning in the front door startled me. I wiped my eyes with my sleeve. Shit, who was it? My heart pumped hard in alert. Nata wouldn't be back till Sunday, and Marcos was surely heavy into partying with some expensive blonde. I pushed back into the couch, holding my breath.

Marcos laughed as he stumbled in, tugging an exotic blonde creature by the hand. His scarf hung loose over his half-buttoned shirt, and she was wearing his hat. On impossibly high pumps, she unsteadily followed him in. Her dress was so small, half her boobs spilled out like toothpaste.

I sighed heavily. "Dude, I said no girls here. Take it somewhere else."

"Oh, shit. I didn't think you'd be here. Sorry, babe. This is Sonia—"

"Cynthia," she corrected in a high-pitched squeak.

"Sorry, sweetheart." He chuckled, flashing her a smile before turning back to me. "I just wanted to get out of this suit and I—Hey…" He frowned. "What's wrong?" He rounded the couch and sat beside me, his eyes creased with worry. Or at least I hoped it was worry, because I hated pity.

"Nothing. Shitty night." I wiped my nose. "Go on, get out of here. I'm fine."

He stayed there, watching me.

"Go have fun, you earned it, remember?" I said, faking a smile, though I didn't want him to go. Flashy Boobs tapped an impatient shoe behind us.

Marcos stood and without looking away from me, handed her the wrap she had tossed on the couch.

"I'll call you tomorrow S—Cynthia. I forgot there's something I need to do tonight."

She narrowed her eyes and snagged the wrap off his hand. "You're an asshole. Don't even bother calling me. Like, *ever*." She stormed off, slamming the door behind her.

Marcos ignored her and moved closer. He sat and wrapped his arms around me. "What is it? You were so happy when I left you back there."

I cried on his shoulder, like a kid, but it felt good to cry. In that moment, all the love for Marcos that I had buried so deep inside me broke through the layers of packed dirt. I didn't understand anything anymore. If Marcos and I weren't meant to be together, why was he the only constant in my life? Always there, hug ready. Now he had turned down a well-deserved lay.

"Tell me what happened and let's get shit-faced. I think we have vodka." He pulled me up by the hand and tugged me to the kitchen.

"I'm way ahead of you. The bottle's on the table."

There weren't any clean glasses left, so he poured straight vodka into coffee mugs. I told him about Sebastián, about the fight.

"Shit. I'm sorry. The kiss, I know. But shit, it felt *right*. It was the right ending, too, you know? And it felt so good to be there with you."

I smiled weakly. "It did."

"Cams," he said, wiping a tear with the pad of his finger. "Those things I told you tonight...I meant them."

What the fuck. "Marcos...I don't think I can take an ounce more of anything tonight."

"Fuck, it's my fault. It's just...you looked so hot in that tight tango skirt. And you know me." He gave me a lopsided smile. "I can be a Neanderthal sometimes. I'm sorry."

"Look, your friendship is important to me. I won't let Sebastián set the boundaries, but I'm not one of your girls either. For fuck's sake, you were with someone else ten minutes ago!"

"Fine. Fine," he said, raising his palms in apology. "I agree. It's just...fuck. Sorry I ruined your night with your man."

"You didn't. He was being an ass."

"But you like him."

"Yeah. But it may have just turned into the shortest relationship in the history of relationships." I took a long swig of vodka, welcoming the burning sensation as it traveled through me.

"Come on, don't be so dramatic. I gotta say...I'd be fucking pissed if you were my girl and some asshole kissed you like that. Would've beaten the shit out of him. Plus, you can't really blame him, I mean...most dudes find this totally threatening." He winked, gesturing at himself. "Ah, he'll get over it. Fucking cheers, babe. We were fucking amazing. Nobody can take that away from us. Come on. Let's get hammered and watch shit TV, just you and me."

"Thanks for being here. I don't know how, but you always make me feel better. How do chicks resist that shit, huh?"

"They *don't* resist it. They dig it. That's why I'm here listening to your sorry ass. I'll have more Sonias lined up by tomorrow." He grinned.

"It was Cynthia, you arrogant dick. Give me the remote."

Chapter 17

I winced at the bleaching morning sunlight that invaded the living room. Through the open balcony door, a breeze ballooned the weightless, white curtains. What time was it? Inside my head, a mallet pounded my skull with painful persistence. I rubbed my eyes through the strands of hair plastered to my cheek. I tested my aching limbs, half-numb after a restless night on the couch, and it wasn't till then that I realized I wasn't alone.

On the opposite end of the couch, Marcos lay unconscious, his chest rising and falling with the peaceful rhythm of his breathing. Our legs were still intertwined, his feet resting against my shoulder. Through the fogginess, the pounding in my head became louder. *Thump, thump.* Shit, *I must not drink again. I must not drink again.* I let my eyelids drop. The last thing I remembered was watching *The Terminator* with Marcos, doing tequila shots whenever a commercial came—which I could swear was every three minutes. Everything after that was black. I secretly prayed I hadn't done anything stupid like have sex with Marcos, not that he would hold it against me.

I detangled from him as carefully as I could and stood. The room spun, immediately sending me back onto the couch. I sat with my head in my hands. *Thump, thump.* A new pain, an arrow, stabbed my head at the nape. Shit, I was still drunk. *I must not drink again. Ever.* I rose again, slowly, gripping the back of the couch for balance. Marcos stirred but didn't open his eyes. He looked innocent, younger, his endless eyelashes perfectly fanned over his cheeks. That angel face, I thought, the face of the devil, and I smiled, because he had turned down a fun night to stay here, with me. That's what friends do, and Marcos was loyal.

An uninvited image of the fight with Sebastián barged into my mind with another stab to my skull. Regret churned in my gut, but I knew I had made the right decision by holding my ground. Sebastián didn't understand how things were with Marcos. Our time had already passed, I could've explained that to him. We could've had a mature conversation about it—but no, he had to go all thermonuclear like a jealous teen. *Yeah, like a gangster*, Nata's voice whispered in my head.

I stumbled to the kitchen and poured a glass of orange juice and downed it in a long swig. The pain in my head echoed. I browsed through the cabinets for something for the hangover and popped two Aleve. On the counter, my phone showed a stream of texts from Nata asking about last night, the tango, Vladimir's house. I sent her a quick response.

Amazing. It was just amazing. I'll tell u everything when u get back.

She had also sent some photos of her and Teo on a white-sand beach. Selfies of the two of them against the sunset, heads together as they laughed and tried sipping from the same straw in a caipirinha.

One of us was happy.

My brain pulsed against my skull. Carefully, I lay back on the couch next to Marcos, pulling a blanket over us. Within minutes the fatigue from the night settled, and I drifted away.

Soft knocks on my front door woke me. I blinked through the fogginess, at Marcos, but he was sound asleep, clutching the blanket now tightly wrapped around him.

The knocking on the door returned, louder, more persistent.

Shit. What time was it?

I stood without waking Marcos, rubbing the sleep off my eyes, and stumbled to the door.

"Coming, coming."

I unlocked, opened a few inches, and froze. Sebastián stood there, rubbing the back of his neck.

"Doesn't look like you had a better night than I did." He half smiled. Fuck. *Fuck!*

"What are you doing here?" Panic rose to my face. Marcos was on the couch behind me. I leaned against the open door, blocking the view.

"May I come in?" he said in a soft tone.

"No," I blurted. His eyebrows raised in surprise. "The place is a mess. Just...give me a second. I'll meet you downstairs." I shut the door in his face and leaned back on it, biting my lip hard, my heart pumping against my ribs. Marcos stirred, oblivious, snoring softly.

I scrambled around for a quick outfit. A T-shirt and yoga pants. I checked myself in the mirror. No. I needed something sexier so Sebastián would regret the fight. I changed into a tight tank top with a scooped neck and very short shorts. *There. Swim in regret.*

Outside the foyer, Sebastián waited, straddling the BMW motorcycle. A tousled, raven mess fell over his forehead. He was dressed in faded jeans and a white T-shirt that accentuated his biceps and looked like a modern Brando. Damn him. Damn his good looks. This would all be so much easier if he were just...*fugly*. I gripped the keys inside my pocket and unlocked the door. He looked intently at me, and it felt like a kick on my chest.

"What do you want?" I said in a raspy voice. He frowned, a sulky teen. I pressed my lips, protesting my own body's reaction as much as his presence.

He dismounted and ran a hand through his hair, letting out a heavy sigh.

"I'm sorry. I really am. He had...his hands all over you. It made me crazy." He closed his eyes for a brief moment, shaking his head as if the thought pained him. "When I saw the connection you had with him, I almost lost it. I wanted to jump on that stage and kick his ass."

I scowled at him, and he shook his head again.

"It caught me off guard," he said. "I'm good at keeping my emotions in check, but since I met you, my control's been tested in more than one way."

I leaned on the wall, crossing my arms and staring down at my sneakers.

"Say something. Hit me, be mad, yell, whatever. But don't give up on us. Don't give up yet." His voice was low, a soft plea. And I wasn't above pride;

having a strong, powerful man like Sebastián begging at my door was sexy as fuck. I shrugged.

"I don't know what to say. Marcos has always been there for me. Through all the hard stuff I went through this year. His friendship means a lot to me, and you don't turn your back on the people that matter because it makes someone else uncomfortable." I didn't look at him. I didn't want his reaction to make me hold back. I needed him to know I wasn't backing down.

He lifted my chin, searching my eyes. "I'm sorry. I didn't expect you to be that close with someone else. To be honest, I want to be the one you connect with that way. The only one. I know that's selfish, but it's how I feel about you. Last night, when I saw how happy you were dancing with him, it drove me insane because I want to be the one that makes you feel that way. I couldn't stand the thought of someone else—"

"There is no one else. What I feel for you is *different*. Bigger. Marcos and I...we spend a lot of time together, but it's never been like it is when I'm with you. Don't you get it? It would be easier to date him, and yet, here I am."

He pulled me into his arms and wrapped me tightly. I squeezed my eyes shut, holding on to my guard. I was standing on thin ice again. I knew that. I took a long breath and his glorious scent invaded me. *Shit, not the scent.* His arms tightened around me.

"Crazy girl, what are you doing to me?" He pulled away and leaned his forehead against mine. "I want to be with you." His hand caressed my face. "I'm sorry I've fucked things up. I want you. I want you in my life."

I brushed a loose strand of hair away from his eyes, and he took my face in his hands, bringing me to him and covering my mouth with his. He tasted heavenly, of desperation, anguish, and need. Tears welled in my eyes, and I broke away to catch my breath. He wiped the moisture off with his thumbs, pain etching his face.

"Please baby, don't cry," he said. "I'm sorry." He leaned down and nuzzled my nose, then kissed me again and again, as if trying to erase the sadness. I gripped his shirt at the chest and shook my head.

"I just…"

"What is it?" He stroked my cheekbone. "Tell me."

"I don't know how to do this."

"Do what?"

"This. You and me. It's so…intense. I feel like I'm on a roller coaster. You overwhelm me with attention, you take me to places I've never been, you dazzle me with your world of VIP places and people. And you're sweet. You treat me like I'm special, beautiful, I love that. But on the other side of it, there's this constant danger that surrounds you… I'm trying to adjust. To you, to this world you exist in, to what people say about your family." I wiped the tears that spilled. "And I didn't care about any of it. I really didn't. But then you storm in on such a special, amazing night for me, and you act like I'm something you bought. And I think…I think maybe I'm just stupid and naïve, and maybe I should listen to everyone's warnings and—"

He pulled me into his arms and pressed me against his chest. "Shh. It's all right."

"No, it's not. I'm a simple girl. This is not simple."

"I know." He kissed my head. "Please don't cry." He pulled back gently, his forehead creased with worry. "I know I come with a lot of baggage. I behaved like an asshole yesterday. But we have something good…I don't want to lose it. I don't want to lose *you*."

I swallowed a sob.

"You are a breath of fresh air, Camila. You make me feel that among everything that's fucked up in the world, there's hope. And I haven't felt like that… maybe ever."

I bit my bottom lip.

"I missed your perfect mouth. You looked so beautiful last night. I just wanted to take you home with me," he said in a soft tone, wrapping me tighter against him.

"I wanted that too," I muttered.

"Let me make it up to you. Let's get out of here and spend the day in Colonia."

I frowned. Colonia is in Uruguay, a whole different *country*. It's just across the river but still a good hour and a half away even on the fastest ferry.

"What about your trip to London?"

"I cancelled it. This was more important."

I nodded, and he searched my eyes. "So Colonia…"

"That's…romantic, but by the time we take the ferry, it will be late."

"I wasn't thinking about taking the ferry. My partner, Julián, has a small jet in Jorge Newbery. I already made arrangements."

"You made arrangements. So you assumed I would say yes? That's presumptuous."

"You can say no. But if you do—"

"If I do, what? You'll just accept it and you'll go?"

"I'll accept it, yes, I'll go. With a broken heart," he said with a lopsided smile, bringing his hand to his chest. I nodded, focusing on my sneakers to escape those eyes. Bastard. He took my hands and wrapped my arms around his waist.

"Come on. Let's start again. One more time."

In my apartment, I quickly changed into a summer dress and a denim jacket while Sebastián waited downstairs—no need to give him a visual of Marcos lying on the couch in his boxers. I left a note saying I would be late, and kissed him on the forehead while he slept. He looked edible, sandy blonde hair ruffled up.

At the local airport, Rafa waited by a small private jet. He nodded curtly.

"Camila."

"Hi, Rafa." I smiled.

The pilot shook Sebastián's hand. After they exchanged a brief greeting, we took our seats and he closed the latch. Anticipation pooled in my stomach. Inside the main cabin, everything was cream leather and light wood. It smelled of luxury. The engines roared to life and I squeezed Sebastián's hand. Within minutes the aircraft charged along the runway and took off into the midday sky. Down below, the Rio de la Plata stretched into a canvas of caramel and gold. Sebastián smiled down at me, serene, content.

My head was a tangle of contradicting thoughts. I knew I was walking into unknown territory with him. But at the same time, I didn't want to let go. Something told me that underneath that possessive shell was an amazing man with a big heart, and I wanted to get to know that man. The stubborn side of me wanted to know where it would lead.

Less than an hour later, we landed in a small airport in Colonia. At the end of the short runway, a driver waited in a black Land Rover SUV. He welcomed us, and Sebastián gave him directions to a restaurant by the water. We cruised through the cobble stone streets of Colonia while the historic town dozed under the afternoon sun. It had always been one of my favorite places to visit. Nostalgic, romantic, it was completely unaffected by time or progress. In the streets, the air was dead quiet, announcing it was time for the siestas. An autumn breeze stirred the neat piles of dry leaves bordering the curbs. A dog's barking echoed in the distance like a cough.

In the heart of the town, the picturesque colonial houses stood side by side in a collage of terra-cottas and golds. Street lanterns from a previous century lined the sidewalks. Grandfather oaks on both sides of the narrow streets interlaced their foliage overhead, shaking to the wind like tapping rain.

The small restaurant sat by the old lighthouse. It was magical, just a handful of tables arranged on the sidewalk. An old man with creased, leathery skin greeted Sebastián with a firm handshake, patting his back enthusiastically.

"*Bienvenido*, Sebastián. It's been a while. Good to see you around these parts. Where's that old crab Marcél this time?" His eyes paused on me. "And who is this beautiful creature?"

"It's good to see you, Roberto." Sebastián grinned. "Marcél is at home today, keeping the boat afloat. This is my girlfriend, Camila."

Girlfriend? I blushed scarlet as Roberto assessed me with an approving smile.

"Wonderful to meet you, gorgeous. First girlfriend this one brings around, and by the looks of you, it was well worth the wait." He winked. He handed us a one-page menu before walking away, then returned shortly after with a basket of homemade bread and a pitcher of sangría.

"On the house." He smiled warmly.

We had a long lunch by the water, and in many ways, this was like a first date, a new start. Sebastián asked me a million questions about ballet, about my family and life at the theater, deftly avoiding Marcos. He seemed genuinely interested in every detail of my monotonous life.

When we were finished, the driver dropped us off at a small bike shop. We rented a Vespa and set off to explore the streets of the small town. The day was warm, the air saturated with the aroma of fresh baked bread from the bakeries rounding the main square. I squeezed my arms around Sebastián's waist and pressed my face to his back, taking it all in. He smelled of fresh laundry and that musky scent I was now addicted to. The breeze lashed my hair around, and I grinned, free.

"Can we stop at that bakery?" I shouted through the buzz of the engine. He lowered the speed and pulled over by the little shop.

A heavyset man smiled benevolently as he unlocked the door to let us in.

"Oh my God, they have vanilla cupcakes. Look." I pointed, biting my lip in resignation.

Sebastián raised an inquisitive eyebrow. "I've never seen you this excited about food."

"A good vanilla cupcake is not *just* food. You'll see."

Armed with two vanilla cupcakes, we sat side by side on the curb. I forgot about the world as I savored every morsel of the most delicious of treats. The frosting was still soft, and as I slowly licked it, it melted against my tongue. Sebastián wiped a crumb off my chin with his thumb, smiling appreciatively.

"If I'd known this is all it took to make you eat..."

I smiled, liking the tip of my finger.

"So...you introduced me to Roberto as your girlfriend."

He turned his head to look at me, and a corner of his mouth pulled up. "Was that too presumptuous?"

I shrugged, looking down at my sneakers. "No...I liked it." I glanced up at him and his eyes narrowed slightly.

"It was presumptuous. I should have asked you first...Camila, do you want to be my girlfriend?" His expression was serious. A flash of apprehension crossed his eyes and it was...oh, so endearing. My heart melted a little more. I leaned closer, swimming in the intensity of those pale eyes. They were now a mix of silver and blue. Closing the distance, I kissed him. His lips were soft, warm and...damn, they tasted like vanilla and sugar. I reached one hand up and threaded my fingers in his hair, bringing him closer. His arm wrapped around my back, his mouth matching the intensity of mine.

"You play dirty," I said once our lips finally separated. He arched an inquisitive eyebrow. "You taste like vanilla frosting. Right now, you could ask me for anything, and I would say yes."

"Anything, eh?" He grinned playfully. Taking my hand, he stood and pulled me up with him, then tugged on my arm so I was pressed against his body. His arms wrapped around my back. "I know I can be a fucking pill. My world is very different from yours, and at times it can be daunting. But since I met you, I've started thinking of what I really want. And I want you in my life,

Camila. I know it's selfish, you have so much more to offer me than I can offer you. But I've never felt this way about anyone. Only you."

My heart was thumping. A swarm of feelings I didn't know or fully understand whirled forcefully inside me. I could have said those exact words to him. How could he think I was the one who could offer more? I blinked, holding his gaze, words failing me. Then I clasped his face in my hands, bringing his mouth to mine, and poured all my feelings into the kiss.

We mounted the bike and headed toward the beach. Along the streets, people emerged from their siestas and sat on midget chairs outside their front doors, sipping on shared mates and watching the afternoon sun slowly retreat behind the trees.

We parked the Vespa by an old shack on the beach and walked along the shore. Sebastián wrapped his arm around me and kissed my hair.

"I'm glad you came." He dipped his head down and kissed me, sending a shiver through me. Oh, man, that taste of vanilla frosting. A whirl of dark desire swam inside me.

We sat on the sand, a few yards from the shore where it wasn't so windy. Over the horizon, the sun stretched lazily, painting the sky with ochre and gold. An old Sinatra song drifted in the air from a party somewhere nearby. Sebastián slipped off his shoes, reached for my feet, and pulled them onto his lap. I stilled.

"What's wrong?" he said.

I grimaced. My feet were a part of my body I felt self-conscious about: battered, not pretty and soft the way the feet of a girl my age were supposed to be. Most people that weren't dancers shuddered at the sight.

"Have you ever seen a dancer's feet before?"

He didn't laugh or make a joke of it. "May I?"

"Okay…but I warned you."

He took off my shoes one at a time, then caressed my feet slowly. His hands were warm, gentle. Holding my breath, I watched him as he peeled off my socks, but he didn't flinch at the sight of the blisters. Then, with diligent care, he kissed my feet one at a time. I nearly expired.

"You're beautiful." He looked up and our eyes met. His fingers massaged my feet gently, sending delicious tingles everywhere. His thumbs moved up and down in small circles, and I got lost in the heavenly sensation, the direct skin-to-skin contact sending sweet vibrations between my legs. When he was finished, he pulled off his sweater and stretched it on the sand so I could lie on top of it. Propping his weight on one elbow, he slid down beside me, watching me with hooded eyes.

"Thank you, that felt great," I murmured. "My poor feet had no rest this week."

He smiled and gave a soft kiss to my lips, but his eyes held an unknown emotion. Apprehension? He cradled my face in his hand.

"Are we good?" he murmured.

I wanted to drown in the depths of the ice-clear blue of those eyes. He tilted his head, waiting. This was it. I was here. *We* were here. Standing at the precipice. Should I jump with him? Again? I wanted to jump. I let out a short breath.

"Yes. We're good. Now come here." I snaked my arm around his neck, bringing him closer.

He chuckled and rolled on top of me, holding his weight on his elbows. Desire darkened in his eyes. They were liquid, stunning. Our mouths were close, almost touching. His breath brushed my lips, and my stomach spun.

"Sebastián…" My chest heaved up and down, welcoming the inebriating feeling of his whole body on mine. The heat radiating from him was blazing. He hardened and my breathing hitched. *God.*

Taking my wrists in one hand, he gently pulled my arms over my head. He dipped his head and our mouths brushed. His breath was warm, sweet, and I wanted to kiss him, hard. He ran his tongue along my bottom lip, sending a heat wave through my skin. *Holy shit.* Forgotten sensations quivered between my legs, and I took a sharp breath.

192

He kissed me, softly at first, then it slowly deepened. I was spinning, lost in a vacuum where it was just the two of us, tangled. Glancing up through half-open eyes, I pushed my hips against his hard-on, watching his beguiled reaction at my inexperienced attempts to seduce him.

He intertwined his legs with mine and shifted his hips, pressing against me. A warm sensation pooled in my stomach. Our bodies wanted to meld together, the kiss climbed. His fingers raked up my legs, skimming under the light fabric of my dress. My skin was on fire. His hand moved to my backside, his thumbs grazing the edge of my panties. I moaned into his mouth and he pressed harder against me, letting his weight smother me. I mumbled his name, welcoming the sensations while my whole body screamed for more. I panted into his mouth. I wanted all of him.

We kissed until my lips were swollen, desire burning through my veins as his hips rocked against me, following the tempo of his tongue. Trembling and drunk, my heart pounded against his chest.

He groaned, breathing hard against my mouth. "Fuck, Camila." His voice was husky, his tone gruff as his words teased me into the challenge of breaking his control. Figures in the distance caught my eye: a couple walking away, their hands interlaced.

"I want you," I said. "But not here. Someone may see us."

"I'm not worried about appearances, babe."

"Still…"

"Okay, but I don't want to stop. Please."

Wrapping my legs around his waist, I kissed him forcefully, adjusting my body under him so he was pressing against all the right places again. Hard denim rubbed the soft silk of my underwear as he resumed the slow, rocking motion, grinding against me, spinning me into delirium. A primal need bottled up inside me screamed. I dug my nails into his back, and a low growl escaped from deep in his throat. It was sexy, addictive, hot. My hands moved to his head, clenching fistfuls of his hair as I pressed myself harder against him. We moved together, his jeans scraping against my thighs. It was heaven, hell, torture, sheer need. It scared me how much I wanted this, *needed* this. *God, don't stop.*

"Camila," he said through broken breaths, lifting his head slightly, "open your eyes. Look at me." It was almost impossible to keep my eyes open and not completely surrender to the divine sensations, but I did as he asked. He looked into my eyes and continued the torturing motion, teasing me in and out of delirium. I parted my lips, panting, and he caught every breath. It was total surrender, erotic, even though we were still dressed. From a distance, we were just a couple, fully dressed and making out on a deserted beach. But my panties were soaked, and every time he pushed against me, the feeling between my legs intensified, the need coiling and ready to snap. His sweet, torturous rocking accelerated, driving me to the edge of something that promised to be beautiful.

"*Mine*," he whispered against my mouth, pressing his hard-on against my clit. A heat wave exploded inside me. I arched my head back and squeezed my eyes, gasping for air as his mouth ravaged my neck. I moaned, pressing myself to him as I rode the sensation. Letting out a sharp breath against my neck, he interlaced his fingers with mine and pushed one last time, harder. My body trembled in spasms as sheer pleasure filled me. I closed my eyes and floated, weightless, in the most beautiful state of half-consciousness.

We lay in silence as our hearts and breathing recovered their normal pace. I couldn't move a muscle. I had never felt so completely sated in my entire life. It was as if a giant vacuum had sucked every last trace of stress in me, and it was absolutely divine.

"You are incredible," he whispered, rolling to his side and caressing my temple. *Seriously*, how was he getting this backward?

"Mmmm," I moaned. "That was…" Our eyes met and I and couldn't finish the thought.

"What?"

"I've never felt anything that intense before. And we didn't even…" I blushed. "Well, *you* didn't…I mean, that was all for me."

Smiling sweetly, he brushed loose strands of hair off my face. "My beautiful crazy girl, so goddamn sexy. I'm just a lucky bastard who got another chance."

The last of the afternoon sun quickly faded into a sea of orange and indigo. I shivered and Sebastián bundled me in his sweater. In the distance, tiny white lights glimmered from a beach party while Bono sang, "I've got you under my skin." We walked toward the music, a bride and her groom dancing barefoot to the melody among a few dozen guests. The setup was simple but so romantic: white-dressed tables scattered over the soft sand under the dim light of paper lanterns. Sebastián interlaced his fingers with mine. "One dance before we go?"

"Here?"

"Here is perfect. Away from everything and everyone. Just you and me." He pressed his palm against the small of my back, and we swayed to the spell of the song. The evening wind whipped my hair, and he tangled it in his hand. He was a skillful dancer, and I wondered where he had learned. Surely a private instructor. In families like his, where parties were a regular component of the social routine, dancing well was expected.

We moved to the music, the heat of his body enveloping mine, sheltering me from the world. I wanted to stay on that side of the river, with him, away from expectations and unreachable dreams and family complications. I pressed my face to his chest, to his heart. Across the massive length of the river, the lights of Buenos Aires sparkled, a callback to the world.

The apartment was dark when I walked in. A note from Marcos was tucked under an apple. It made me smile.

I'll be back late—chill, a brunette this time.

Hope you had a good day. X, M.

I did a few loads of laundry, showered, and cleaned the apartment, erasing all traces of the tornado Marcos and I had left. I was folding clothes in front of the TV when Nata walked in.

"Hey." She smiled, dropping her bags by the door.

"Hey. How was Brazil?"

"Incredible." She threw her coat on a chair and plopped next to me on the couch.

"Yeah? Are you engaged yet?"

"Hell, no."

"Oh, come on. You can't tell me you haven't already planned your wedding in your head and the eighty-four redheaded babies you guys will have together."

She laughed, blushing a bit. "Okay maybe, but we are not quite there yet."

"What do your parents say? And Sergei?" I asked as I folded the last of my underwear.

"Oh, they love Teo, even Sergei. They hit it right off." She pulled her shoes off and stretched her long legs onto the coffee table.

"Really? That's a first. Insanely protective Sergei hitting it off with someone?"

She rolled her eyes. "Yes. Turns out Teo's family did business with ours a few years back. Papá knew his dad. Small world, whatever. And it doesn't hurt that Teo is über-protective of me too. Sergei likes that." She shrugged.

"Well, you deserve a good guy."

She nodded, watching me with apprehension. "So…" she said. "I talked to Marcos on my way back from the airport."

Shit.

"He said you and your…*boyfriend* got into a fight last night? He's your boyfriend, Cami?"

I rolled my eyes. "Nata."

"*Nata* what? You guys are getting serious then?"

To busy myself, I picked up a pile of socks from the laundry basket and started matching them.

"Are you?" she pressed.

"Yeah. We are. And…it would be awesome if you got onboard and stopped making me feel like shit about it. I already have my dad on my back."

"Good, he should be."

"No. It's *not* good, all right?" I said, tossing the socks aside. "I'm finally interested in someone other than Marcos. You of all people know what that means to me. It's like…*finally*! And it's somebody who feels the same way about me." I let out a frustrated sigh.

"Cams—"

"No. I know you've got this preconceived idea about who Sebastián is and what he does, but I'm telling you, it's not like that. He's a decent guy who cares about me. Period. So please, lay off." I stood and headed to the kitchen for a drink, a bit surprised at my outburst. Opening the fridge, I crouched behind the door, reaching for a can of Diet Coke, blocking her laser eyes from me.

"Look," she said from behind. "I want to be supportive. It *is* a huge deal that you are so into someone, and I don't mean to be a drag about it. But it worries me that out of all the guys you could be interested in, you picked *this* one. He's coming on strong, and I don't want you to get sucked into something that'll be hard to get out of if you decide it's not what you want, you know?"

"You're wrong about him." I turned, standing.

"I hope I am, but…I doubt it."

"All right. Let's just…leave it alone." I opened the drink and headed back to the couch. She followed and sat beside me, reaching for my hand, her cerulean blue eyes searching mine.

"Just promise me you'll be careful."

"I'll be careful."

We finished folding my laundry in silence. I hated this new, dense air between us. I tossed a pair of socks, and they hit her on the forehead. She looked up and smiled, and the weirdness lifted.

"Tell me about Brazil."

She replayed every detail about her weekend. I could hear the wedding bells in the background, Nata sounded so happy. A pang of sadness flicked my heart. Things between Sebastián's world and mine didn't align nearly as easily. There was still so much we needed to learn about each other. I wanted to get to know *him*, away from all the rest. But that ghostly side of his world lingered, hovering closely.

Chapter 18

The next morning, I engaged every one of my cells into the choreography for Queen Myrta. I wasn't progressing as quickly as I wanted to, and Madame hadn't been lying when she said it took so much physical work, but I could literally feel my body get stronger. Rising to the demands of the variation became my new reason to get out of bed in the morning.

Today's rehearsal was particularly challenging, and I was glad for the distraction so I wouldn't agonize over the next three hours until I saw Sebastián for lunch. Madame eyed me warily, nodding as she walked by.

During my break, I sat against the back wall, drying the sweat off my neck as I downed a bottle of water. Nata slid next to me and pulled out a bottle with a deep green liquid in it.

I made a face. "What the hell is that."

"A vitamin boost. You should try it. Kale, spinach, celery, and—"

"Okay, okay, gross, I don't need to know any more."

"You're doing well, Cams. You almost have that new variation down." She downed her concoction in one gulp and pulled out a water, took a few sips, then tightened the ribbons on her pointe shoes.

"My ankle's killing me. I see stars whenever I put my whole weight onto it. I'm glad Vronsky didn't say anything."

She nodded in understanding. Dancing through injuries was just another part of our routine. Nata let out a sigh while stretching her neck to both sides. "Wanna have lunch at the vegan stand after this?"

"I can't. I need to run a couple of errands."

"Vronsky's back," she murmured, then stood and left without turning.

At the lunch break, I quickly changed into the jeans and top I brought for my date with Sebastián, and bolted downstairs.

He was waiting against the BMW, Rafa reading a newspaper at the wheel. In faded jeans, a white linen shirt rolled at the sleeves, and aviators, Sebastián looked like a model from a Ralph Lauren ad. When he saw me, he lowered his glasses and smiled. A sudden breeze messed his hair, and I half expected a stampede of women elbowing their way to get a number and stand in line for that smile. *Damn,* he was all mine.

He pulled me into his arms, tipping his head down to kiss me.

"I've been thinking of you all morning." He trailed kisses on my jaw while his arms pressed me against him, sending shivers up my back. I gripped his biceps and pushed away.

"Let's go," I said. Turning, I opened the back door and slipped across the seat. He followed with an amused expression.

"In a hurry?" He chuckled.

"I only have a little over an hour."

"Where do you want to go?"

"Away from here. How about somewhere near your studio?"

"Great. I can show you off, and there're a lot of good places around there."

The Palacios y De la Viña studio in Puerto Madero was an expansive building of exposed brick bearing the nostalgia of the Buenos Aires docks in the 1900s. Inside, the work spaces were airy and surprisingly modern. Everything about the recycled loft had been designed with flawless efficiency. Bright midday sun filtered in from shrewdly spaced skylights, giving the spacious suites a clean, bright feel. Facing the river, oversized windows lined the ground floor. Inside, glass-walled offices bordered an open lounge area with plush, stylish couches, a pool table, and an espresso and draft beer bar. The rich smell of coffee lingered in the air. From a high corner, a giant screen featured Kelly Slater in one of those surfing documentaries in white-sand beaches. It looked like an awesome place to work.

Sebastián showed me around and introduced me to some of the staff. They greeted me with warm smiles, watching us with amused curiosity. Most of the employees were in their early to mid-thirties, the majority of them men. A tall, young woman in a gray pencil skirt and immaculate makeup approached Sebastián and smiled broadly as she handed him a manila folder.

"Romina, this is my girlfriend, Camila." Sebastián smiled back, wrapping his hand around my waist. A wave of heat rose to my face.

Romina greeted me warmly, introducing herself as the studio manager. I also met a few of the architects, but there were no signs of Sebastián's partner, Julián. When I asked about him, Sebastián said he was due back from Germany the next day.

Sebastián's own office was an immense, glass-walled sanctuary with a stunning corner view of the golden river. Holy shit. Unbidden, that feeling that I was in way over my head returned.

He locked the door and touched a switch next to it. The glass walls instantly darkened into gray fog. A sly smile played on his lips as he sauntered towards me. My heart pumped hard.

"I missed you. After yesterday, I can't seem to focus on anything else." He took my hands, turned me around, and hugged me from behind, squeezing me tight while he trailed kisses along my neck. His erection pressed my backside and my whole body shivered. He pinned me against a massive architect's drawing table facing the window. I closed my eyes, letting the delicious thrill travel through me. Warm moisture pooled between my legs, wetting my panties. Jesus, how much longer could I resist him?

"One day I will take you here, bent over my drawings," he whispered in my ear. His breath was hot. I gasped and he squeezed me tighter, kissing my neck sensually. My heart hammered against my ribs. "Do you know how sexy you are? What you do to me?"

His hands caressed my breasts, and my nipples immediately hardened. I relaxed in his arms, savoring the sensation. I was breathing hard and wondered idly if anyone in this office knew what we were up to.

"Answer me," he said against my neck. The heat radiating from him blinded me. I couldn't focus on anything except the incredible feeling of that hard body pressed against mine. "Camila," he growled in my ear.

"N-no...I don't...know..."

"Let me show you." His hand slid into my yoga pants, and his thumb skimmed me gently over my panties. I gasped, my blood soaring as the urge between my legs intensified. I closed my eyes. The feeling was divine. I shivered and his arm tightened around me, holding me in place while his intrepid fingers slipped into my underwear. *God.* It was so hard to restrain all the sounds that wanted to come out of me.

"*Fuck.* You are so wet, baby," he whispered while his fingers stroked me back and forth. His voice was husky, making my skin sizzle. He slipped a finger inside me, and I bit my lip hard, my breaths coming out in shallow spasms. I blushed everywhere. This was...so forbidden, *naughty*, and hot as fuck. His finger moved around and around, raising me to a holy place. He held me tighter and slipped another finger in. I arched my back, stifling a moan. *Jesus.* His fingers moved faster, and I squeezed my eyes while I ground against his hand. A sweet, overwhelming sensation invaded me.

"That's right, baby. Feel me. Feel me inside you." His burning breath on my neck, the torturing assault of those skilled fingers, his sweet, dirty words in my ear. It was suddenly too much, and I exploded in a blinding orgasm. *God.* His arm tightened around my waist as my legs melted like hot butter.

Turning me around, he lifted me, and I straddled him while he claimed my mouth. I moaned when his hard cock pressed between my legs. I was spent but I wanted more, so much more. We had made plans for a date on Thursday, but I didn't think I could wait till then to have more of this.

"I don't know if I can wait until Thursday," he said against my mouth, articulating my thought.

So, our first time would be on his desk. Not the most romantic first, but my hormones didn't give a crap. On the desk it is.

His cell phone startled me when it vibrated in his shirt pocket. He ignored it at first, and it eventually stopped. Then it started again.

I growled against his mouth, "Get it."

He reluctantly pulled away and frowned when he looked at the screen, then picked up.

"Yes?" he said without hiding his exasperation. "Alejandro, I've been trying to reach you all morning." He lifted up is index, letting me know he needed a minute. I detangled from him. In a way, I was relieved. My self-restraint was apparently on vacation, and an office building in the middle of the day was hardly the place to explore my sexuality.

"You said you would be here for this," he snarled. "Julián is still in Germany, and the studio is swamped." He listened and sighed, following me with his eyes as I sat on a couch by the window, watching the bobbing sailboats in the distance. "Fine," he barked, ending the call. "Sorry about that, Cami. It was my brother and I needed to talk to him."

"No worries."

He pushed a button on his intercom, and Romina appeared a second later with a tray of sushi rolls and seaweed salad. My stomach growled in appreciation.

"I figured this would be better, since you're pressed for time. Hope it's okay?"

"It's perfect. Thank you."

The minutes flew by and it was time for me to go. Sebastián made a quick call, and within seconds Rafa appeared in the BMW and drove us back to the theater. It was the end of lunch break, and a few dancers were hurrying back to the door as we stepped out of the car. I quickly kissed Sebastián good-bye, but he pulled me into his arms and kissed me deeply. A familiar stab of longing sank in my chest, and my whole body complained when I pulled away. Up to that point, I had absolutely underestimated the power of hormones. He looked at me with wary eyes before wrapping his arms around me for one last kiss.

"I want you to meet my family," he said.

My heart took off. Shit. What? The Sopranos? "Um…I don't know. It's a bit too soon."

"It's not too soon. I want them to meet you. And I want to meet your family too."

At that, my heart rate tripled. I shifted in his arms so he wouldn't notice the change in my pulse.

"What is it?" he said.

"What?"

"Earlier you practically flew in the car, and now you can't wait for me to leave. What's going on?" He frowned. "Are you embarrassed of me?"

"What? No! It's nothing like that."

"Then what?"

"It's…I don't know. My parents…"

"They don't approve," he murmured.

I glanced away.

"I can't say I'm surprised," he said, "or that I blame them."

"They'll come around. They have to. We just need to give them some time."

He nodded, scanning the streets behind me.

"Look, I want you to meet my family, Camila. You're important to me," he said in a stern tone.

"What if they don't approve either? The circles you and I move in are so different." I looked down and he lifted my chin.

"I don't need anyone's approval. I want you in my life. Come on, say yes."

"Are you sure?"

"Yes. I'm sure." He caressed my temple. "Sooner or later you'll have to meet them. Julián and Mercedes are a good place to start. She's having a party for Julián's and her birthday Friday night. Most of my family will come into town for it. We'll have fun."

"Mercedes?"

"Julián's twin sister. They're like siblings to me."

Fuck. The dark ghost of Sebastián's family was closing in on me. My plan to keep that part of his life separate was quickly evaporating.

"Um...okay." I looked at my watch. "My rehearsal starts in less than ten minutes. Can we talk about this later?"

"Okay, but first say yes."

"Yes, okay, yes. If you think it's a good idea, I'll meet them. And if I survive, you can meet my parents. Now I've got to go." I gave him one last chaste kiss, and he let out a throaty laugh.

As he broke the embrace, he looked over my shoulder and tensed. Rafa leapt out of the car and rushed past Sebastián to stand behind me.

"What?" I frowned. Sebastián's jaw was set. His arm wrapped around my waist and pressed me against him.

"Don't those fuckers have anything else to do than hover around?"

My frown deepened as I turned. Sebastián loosened his grip but didn't let go, holding me protectively in his arms. Relief washed through me when I saw it was just Alexei and one of Sergei's friends standing by the theater entrance. Recognition etched their faces when they both saw me. Their bodies instinctively straightened, and they set off toward us, their hands closed into fists at their sides.

"It's just Alexei," I said, quickly freeing myself from his arms. "They're always here. They wait for Nata." I nodded a hello at Alexei, but his face looked like he was about to have a coronary. He regarded me with a mix of rage and confusion. *Jesus, chill.* He approached cautiously, his friend flanking him. Rafa stepped to the side, blocking us. Then he reached for something in his belt. Clutching the object, he lowered it to his side.

A gun.

Holy fuck. Sebastián gripped my waist and tugged me behind him.

Rafa stood immobile, a tiger about to pounce, shielding us from Alexei. I wrestled out of Sebastián's arms, my eyes glued to Rafa's gun.

"Sebastián, what the hell? What's Rafa doing with a gun?"

"He's my bodyguard," he said in an even tone.

Of course, stupid. But I hadn't seen it before. Even the night at the Roxy.

"Look," I said, pushing away. "I know these guys. I need to go."

"Camila," he said. "Just stay put."

"No, this is nuts. Listen, I—We'll talk about this later, I'm going to be late."

Alexei took another step forward, then stopped when he spotted the gun in Rafa's hand. He looked up at me, the veins bulging in his already reddened forehead. His eyes narrowed and his nostrils flared. His hand moved to his belt where his own gun was concealed under the leather jacket. Fuck. Him too? Did he always carry it? No wonder he never took off that goddamned leather jacket.

"Hands still," warned Rafa.

Alexei's jaw tensed. "This is not open territory," he said in a low, thick Russian growl. "This is Zchestakova territory."

"Really? Since when?" Sebastián said calmly.

"Miss Zchestakova dances here. *Our* territory."

The other guy took a step forward, but Alexei raised his thick hand, blocking him. Rafa tightened his grip on his gun.

"Miss Navarro dances here too. So fuck off and get lost before my finger slips," spat Rafa.

What the hell. We were in broad daylight. This was insane. In all directions, people rushed past us, oblivious to the gun in Rafa's hand. It was like a scene from *Goodfellas*.

"You first." A slow, chilling smile spread on Alexei's face, but it didn't reach his sunken, dark eyes.

"Okay, listen. I need to go in." I gripped Sebastián's arm. "Get in your car and go. I'll be fine." I clutched Rafa's arm and his bicep immediately tensed. He frowned at my hand. "Rafa, go, please. It's okay."

"I'll walk you to the door," Sebastián said.

I let out a heavy sigh. This was testosterone central. Nobody here was going to take a step back.

"Alexei," I said, as calmly as I could manage. "Would you *please* mind stepping back so I can get to work? You know what it's like when we're late. Please? Then everyone can go back to what they were doing." I smiled, even though inside I was shaking. What the fuck did I think I was doing? I guess in my mind I was more afraid to face Madame.

Alexei let a silent moment pass, then slowly took a few steps back, his eyes never leaving Rafa.

"Thank you." I turned to Sebastián and pressed a quick kiss on his mouth. His jaw remained locked. "Please go. I'll be late and that will cause me problems."

"I'll wait here till you go in."

"Fine." I bolted to the door. Before going in, I waved at Sebastián, gesturing for him to go car. He and Rafa reluctantly got back into the BMW. Alexei glared at me with a *What the fuck?* look on his face. Letting out the breath I was holding, I turned and rushed up the stairs.

Panting, I pushed past the dancers lingering at the door and scanned the studio for Nata. She was warming up at a portable barre across the room. She frowned when she saw me charging toward her.

"What the fuck?" I said. "Does Alexei always carry a gun?"

She studied my face for a moment. "What do you mean?"

"I mean a *gun*. Like…a *real* one. Does he always carry it? Is that why he never takes off that smelly leather jacket? Because he's hiding a freaking *gun*?"

"Shhh. Lower your voice." Nata's expression didn't change as she stretched a leg up, pressing it against her ear.

"*So?*" I hissed.

"It's just for protection."

"But he always has it on him?"

"Yes." She looked at me skeptically.

The assistant entered the studio and announced Madame would be delayed a few minutes, but we should begin with the warm-ups. I didn't move, fighting the storm in my head. Nata watched me with a careful expression.

"I can't believe I never noticed before," I said. "I hate guns, they make me nervous. Besides, it's the middle of the day for fuck's sake."

She frowned. "You saw Alexei pull out his gun? Just now?" Her tone was suddenly alert.

Shit.

"What happened?"

"Nothing, I...I had lunch with Sebastián," I said, unable to tell her any more lies. Her eyebrows shot up in surprise.

"Oh, your...*errands*. Right."

"*This* is why I didn't tell you. Nothing happened. Sebastián just dropped me off here. That's all, but Alexei and that other skinny guy were like wild dogs, ready to let loose when they saw him."

"He can't come here, Camila. You'll cause me problems," she said. "Shit, when Sergei finds out—"

"He just dropped me off. Jesus. Will you all just chill?" I hurried into my pointe shoes and tightened the ribbons. She picked up a towel to dry her face, sighing heavily. For a moment, it felt as if she were a complete stranger. "Don't you feel uncomfortable?" I said. "Having all these people around you carrying guns?"

She scanned the room filling up with dancers at the portable barres, then looked into my eyes. "My family does business with a lot of people. Not often, but a few times, things got out of hand. Sergei is just careful. *Especially* around the Palacios family."

"Why especially?"

"My family's business is imports. The Palacioses own the docks. Do the math, Cami," she said in an impatient tone. "That's how I know of them, and who they are. But you don't want to hear any of that, so what's the point?"

She left to take her spot, and I watched her, speechless and feeling like a complete idiot. I knew I lived in my own ballet bubble, but *this*...I was a suddenly a spectator in my own life. My best friend and the guy I was dating were surrounded by people who carried guns for protection. Surely that wasn't the way it was for most people. What the fuck.

I hurried to my usual barre next to Nata's, my head spinning.

"Save a few undivulged facts, my family and I are the same people you've always known," Nata whispered from beside me. "I can't speak for your boyfriend, but *we* are not thugs."

I scowled. "Stop it. And I didn't say that."

"But you're wondering. You're not sure what to think, right?"

I didn't respond and focused on my raised left leg, keeping it balanced as I stood en pointe. A slow, blazing pain expanded through my ankle. I squeezed my eyes shut and focused on the pain to block Nata.

"Russia is not like here, Cami," she continued in a lower voice. "Here, a lot of people don't like us just because we are Russian." I glanced at her and she cocked an eyebrow. "And there isn't much we can do about that."

The ambient noise suddenly ceased when Madame entered the class. People focused on their movements, and she began her walk-through. I switched feet so she wouldn't see the pain in my expression. She ignored me as she passed and started her lecturing.

Glancing over at my best friend, it was as if I was looking at her for the first time. An oppressive heaviness filled me. I had never even imagined things for her in Buenos Aires could be difficult just for being a foreigner. I had always assumed she had it easy because she was a natural-born dancer. *Russia is not like here, Cami.* I let her words sink in while we followed the class in silence. Madame's voice became background noise as we rehearsed the familiar movements in unison, like oiled machines. "*And up and down and one and two. Pa, pa, pa. Carla, straighter. Like this, not like this, girl.*"

I stared forward, at nothing. My head was filled with images of the Russians and what it must be like to have to constantly watch your back; the skepticism, the unwanted attention, and the usual stereotypes of criminal activities that were associated with them. I had heard things before, but I usually dismissed them as stupidity or ignorance. I never really thought about how that might affect their life as a family. Nata always looked so collected. Suddenly, some of those things I had always considered peculiar about her fell into place. The little knife she always carried, her mania about safety. That was the world she knew. She never complained, and even though it was a very real part of her life, she hadn't dragged or burdened me with the hassle of it all. She just accepted me as the oblivious spaz that I was. To her, I was just her friend. I smiled at her even though her back was to me. And in that moment, I loved her a little more.

Chapter 19

Tonight was *it*. Thursday night. The night I was having sex with Sebastián. *Sex, sex, sex, sex.* Finally!

I pushed away the uneasy current that buzzed through me. We hadn't talked since the quarrel with Alexei at the theater the day before, and I needed to talk to Sebastián about the gun issue. I didn't want them anywhere near me. I eased my mind, vowing to bring it up tonight, before we went any further.

Crisp evening air slapped my overheated cheeks when I pushed open the theater doors. I was panting as much from running down the stairs as from the knot in my gut.

"Evening, Camila."

I snapped my head around at the hoarse grumble. Alexei was leaning on the wall in his trademark weathered, brown, leather jacket. My eyes went straight to his beltline but if he had his gun, it was concealed.

"Hi, Alexei. Nata was right behind me. She should be out in a sec."

He nodded. "You ride back wit' us?"

"No."

A flash of realization crossed those sullen raven eyes, and his expression darkened. "You be careful," he muttered.

I searched the street and spotted the black BMW a few steps ahead. My heart karate kicked my sternum. I vowed to find us a new meeting spot but grinned when Sebastián stepped out, opening his arms in welcome.

I jogged over and leapt into his arms, wrapping my legs around his waist, not caring that Alexei was watching. Sebastián squeezed me hard and my stomach whirled.

"Mmm, I've missed you." he said, lowering his mouth to mine. He kissed me tenderly. "Ready?" As he slid me down, he glanced over my shoulder and winked at Alexei. I shook my head and thanked Rafa who had opened the back door for me. I kept my eyes down to avoid glancing at his belt.

Sebastián rounded the car and sat beside me in the back. He interlaced our fingers and kissed my wrist. "Did you have a good day? Are you tired?"

"Um, a little. I need a shower."

"I have a big tub." He winked, making my face burn. "Do you need to get anything?"

"Uhm, no. I have a change of clothes in my bag."

"Perfect." He glanced up at the rearview mirror. "Straight home."

I stretched in my chair after dinner while Sebastián refilled our wineglasses. I had showered, changed into clean clothes, and was absolutely replete with Marcél's sinful cannelloni.

"I'm glad I don't have a Marcél," I said. "I'd be rolling out the door."

"Yes, he's amazing. Puts my Italian relatives to shame."

I glanced through the windows to the forest outside, the treetops brushing the sky in their waltz with the wind.

"Everything okay?" he said, gently squeezing my hand in his. "You were very quiet on the way home. Are you tired?"

"A little. But it's not that." I looked down at our interlaced hands.

"What is it? Are the Russians giving you trouble? They better not be, or I'll—"

"No, no." I shook my head. "They're not giving me trouble, and please don't talk like that about them. Nata is my friend, and you don't really know what it's like to have to watch your back just because you weren't born here."

"I know plenty about having to watch my back. But what's the matter, then?"

"It's about…the guns."

"What guns?"

"The *guns*. The guns in general. Until the other day, I had no idea everyone around me—Rafa, Alexei, and the others—all carry guns. I'm very uncomfortable around them."

"I can't speak for your...friends, but *we* only use guns for protection. In fact, I don't like them either. Most of the time I don't even carry one myself, even though Rafa insists on it. But when you belong to a family like mine, unfortunately, that also means you have to protect yourself. Babe..." He lifted my chin, searching my eyes. "It's okay. I would never let anyone hurt you."

"I know..."

"No, I need you to understand that," he said in a soft, concerned tone. "Your safety is very important to me. And if that means we need armed bodyguards around us all the time, that's what we do. This is not something we can negotiate on, okay? I need you to be okay with it."

I took a deep breath. This was one of those red flags, a pretty damn neon one. One of those things people ask after a disaster: *Didn't you see the signs?* So, what now?

"There're no guns around the house," he said. "I have one, but it's locked away. Only my bodyguards carry them, and they're concealed most of the time."

"But what happened the other day...it was in broad daylight. What the hell, Sebastián?"

He ran a hand through his hair. "Things with the Russians have been tight lately. They do business with my father, and there have been problems. We'll just have to make sure we keep things separate and more civil. Rafa was only being protective."

"Does this have anything to do with the Russian girls?"

"Christ, Camila. No. You need to let that go. The tension with the Zchestakovas has to do with the way they handle their business at the docks."

"Why didn't you tell me that before? That there are problems between your family and theirs and you're tied to them through your business?"

"Because it's not *my* business. It's my father's, and I'm not directly involved. I don't want my father's business dealings to come between us. Look, I know things are probably tense for you and your friend, but let's just keep things separate, okay? I personally don't have anything against them, and they better not be giving you crap about being with me."

He waited for my response. I just shook my head no.

"All right," he said. "Let's just put this behind us. I'll make sure Rafa tones it down around them." He squeezed my hand. "Are we okay?"

I nodded. He pulled me to him and kissed me softly.

"Come," he said, taking my hand and leading me to the living room. He threw in a few logs into the fireplace, and soon after, a full fire crackled to life. Sliding next to me on the couch, he reached down and gently took my Converse off.

I tensed. "What are you doing?"

"Giving you a foot massage. I remember you enjoying it the last time."

I smiled and he scooted back, bringing my feet onto his lap as we lay back facing each other on opposite ends of the couch, my legs in between his. He began massaging my feet gently, careful to avoid the tapes concealing my blisters. I took a deep breath and closed my eyes, letting the tension slowly leave my body.

"You said you have Italian relatives," I said without opening my eyes. The sensation rising from my feet to the rest of me was heavenly. "But Palacios sounds…Spanish."

"My mother was Italian. The Ricci family. Most of them are still there."

"Sicily?" I stifled a smile.

"Cute. No. My family is actually from the north. My mother was from Bologna."

"Tell me about them. Mmmm. That feels *so* good."

"My father met her on one of his business trips to Italy. They were young, and he was being groomed to take over my grandfather's businesses at the docks. My mother's family was simple and very conservative, so the idea of her dating a foreigner was out of the question. But my father, being who he is, knew what he wanted. And he wanted my mother. They were in love, and he convinced her he would change their minds.

214

"And did he?"

"For thirty days and thirty nights, my father sat outside the Ricci home, holding a bouquet of white roses. He would leave it at their door, then get a new one the next day and wait for her to come out and accept them, accept him."

"Oh my God. I'm dying, what happened?"

"My mother's brothers beat him up a few times. They called the cops, everything they could think of to get rid of him. He was thrown in jail a few times, but as soon as he was out, he was right there again, outside her window, waiting with a new bouquet of white roses."

I shook my head. "And this is your *father* we're talking about. The man everyone tells me is the King of the Argentinean docks. Tough, ruthless."

"The very same."

"So, she came out one day...obviously."

"She did. Her parents came around and finally gave their blessing. Though my father had to promise to bring her back for every Christmas and let her spend the summers with the family if she wanted."

"That is so romantic."

He lifted my feet and pressed a soft kiss on each one. "I am glad you're here," he said softly. "Dance with me." He stood, reached for my hand, and tugged gently. "You and me."

The house was quiet. I wondered if his men were lurking somewhere close by.

"Where is everyone?"

"I gave my staff the night off," he said. His eyes darkened with a carnal promise.

A soft, velvety female voice crooned from somewhere in the air. He took my hand, then enclosed me in his arms. My body trembled as his hands stroked my skin, awakening the pent-up desire inside me. His thumbs caressed the soft fabric of my shirt over my ribs, grazing my breasts, and I wanted to melt. Was it possible to want someone this much? He tipped his head down, and those clear eyes met mine, dark desire burning in the pale background. And there it was again, the pull, a seamless bond between us. It didn't matter who he was, or who I was. It was just us. He held my gaze in silence. I had never known you could say so much without speaking a single word. Our bodies swayed to the soft melody of the song, a sexy ballad of love and surrender. His thumb traced my bottom lip, and his eyes focused on my mouth. My heart beat faster. Hot desire pulsed in my blood as he inched closer, sending goose bumps down my back, pressing soft kisses on my jaw, then my mouth. Lust coursed through me. Rolling to my toes, I curled my arms around his neck. He lifted me and, in one move, lowered me down to the plush rug with him. He climbed over me, sliding his leg between mine. I moaned into his mouth, desire pooling between my legs. His fingers skimmed my shirt up, grazing my stomach, tracing a path of fire on my skin. I pressed myself to him and, hooking my fingers on the hem of his shirt, I pulled it over his head. He unbuttoned my shirt with painfully slow movements, savoring the contact with my blazing skin. Then his mouth followed the path of his fingers, trailing kisses down my chest and around the lace of my bra. His hand unhooked the clasp at the front before sliding it with my shirt down my arms. His gaze trailed down my bare torso, then he looked up at me.

"God, I want you. You are so beautiful." He kissed the corners of my mouth, then my neck, teasing me with his tongue as he traveled down to my breasts. He cupped one and closed his lips around my nipple, his tongue tracing torturing circles, then he moved to the other, kissing, gracing his teeth against my skin. *Christ*, I was on fire. I felt exposed, but everything about him was sensual, confident. His free hand slipped under the band of my jeans and unbuttoned them. I lifted my hips to help him pull them down and, as he did, his fingers covered the length of my legs, caressing every inch. Adjusting his body between my legs, he pushed his hard-on against me. I inhaled sharply, arching my back. I had never wanted anything so badly. His fingertips brushed the inside of my thigh, trailing up, teasing my desire. His hand moved between my legs, then stopped before sliding back down. I clasped his wrist and moved his hand back into place, grinding my hips against it to let him know what I wanted. Smiling against my mouth, he caressed me through the soft silk of my panties. My whole body trembled when his thumb slipped under the fabric, slowly stroking the moisture back and forth over my clit. My muscles clenched, and I pushed harder against him.

"Sebastián…"

A sea of sensation flooded me, aching for a release. I rocked my hips against his finger, mirroring his pace. His mouth covered mine, and he slipped two fingers inside me. I gasped and he continued his torturing assault, sliding his fingers back and forth, sending me over the edge while he ravaged my mouth. A heavenly feeling invaded me. The heat expanded, my body quivering with pleasure, lost. I moaned. His hand pressed hard against me and I exploded in a spiraling orgasm.

I smiled as my body trembled in aftershocks. Collapsing at his side, I sighed, spent. His fingers caressed my stomach while my heart stuttered to its normal pace. I sneaked a peek at his profile. Damn. How did I get so lucky?

"Sebastián, that was—"

"Just a preview." His eyes darkened. "Now I want you in my bed." *Oh my.* Picking me up in his arms, he carried me to his bedroom. I rested my head on his shoulder and kissed his neck, high on the ecstasy of being in his arms with nothing between our bare skin.

He carefully lowered me down to the bed. I watched him take off his jeans, admiring that perfect body. As a dancer I was used to being around sculpted men. Hell, Marcos was practically Photoshopped, but Sebastián…Anticipation sang in my veins. This half-naked god was about to make love to me. Finally.

He crawled onto the bed, propping himself on his elbows, his body over mine.

"I love the way you smell, the way you sound when I'm kissing you, the way you move. I'm one lucky bastard." He grinned, his lips teasing me as he spoke, his nose brushing mine.

"Shhh," I whispered against his mouth. "Stop talking."

He kissed me hard. His hands caressed my waist, wrapping around my back and squeezing me tight. Slowly, his fingers traveled down and slipped into my panties, caressing my backside. Hooking his thumbs on the lace, he pulled my underwear down. I ran my nails along his back, and he shivered. Tucking my hands under the band of his boxers, I eased them down with clumsy hands. He kicked them off and pressed his body against mine. He was hard, hungry, *big,* the contact of his bare skin on mine blazing. He kissed my neck, running his tongue along my collarbone to the soft indentation in the middle. His mouth moved down slowly, his lips tracing every inch of my skin. He kissed my breasts one at a time, following the path to my stomach. My skin was on fire. I moaned and closed my fists in his hair, pulling hard. He groaned as his mouth trailed down, his tongue torturing me, sending shivers down my back, my insides quivering with want.

Where is he going...is he—Oh. My. God.

I felt his tongue between my legs, and I thought I was going to combust. Part of me was embarrassed, I had never felt so exposed, but the pleasure was blinding. His hands slid to my thighs, pulling my legs farther apart as he continued with the sweet assault. My body moved in sync with his mouth, rocking slowly, lost in the delicious sensation. I pulled his hair harder and pushed him against me as everything inside me began to quicken, dark pleasure building. He let out a soft groan, and it rippled through me. I climbed higher, higher. My broken breaths filled the room. I cried out loud as a tidal wave slammed into me, spiraling me into an unconscious bliss. He quickly eased up and kissed me hard on the mouth while my body melted into surrender. I tasted my own saltiness in his mouth, and despite what I would have imagined, it made the moment so intimate, hotter. Propping up on one elbow, he looked into my eyes, our breaths colliding.

"Fuck, Camila. You taste so sweet. My girl...Baby, if this hurts, you have to tell me, and I'll stop, okay?"

I nodded, panting. I couldn't imagine pain bad enough to make me want to complain, much less stop. *Yeah, please don't stop.* He reached for something in the nightstand drawer. Gripping the condom between his teeth, he ripped the foil open. It was sexy as fuck.

"Wait," I breathed. He frowned.

"I'm on the pill, and…you don't need to worry about STDs because…well, you know why. You?"

"I get tested every few months, and I haven't been with anyone since the last time. Why are you on the pill?"

"It helps with my cycles," I said. Was I really discussing my cycles with a guy?

A winning grin stretched his lips as he let the foil packet drop from his mouth. He claimed my mouth hungrily, his tongue dancing with mine. He eased into me, slowly, and I let out a sharp breath. *Fuck.* My body tensed and he pulled his head back.

"You okay?"

"Yes, yes. Please…don't stop."

He inched in slowly, filling me completely. A burning sensation stung as he pressed deeper. Then he began moving with a sweet, rocking motion, slow and gentle. I squeezed my legs around his waist and matched his pace, ignoring the discomfort, tracing my fingers on his back and up his neck to his hair.

"God, you feel incredible," he mumbled, the words drowning in my mouth. I grabbed a fistful of his hair and tugged. He moaned against my neck and started moving faster. *Oh, man.* It was heavenly. I phased in and out of consciousness while his mouth ravaged me, our fingers interlaced as we melded our bodies.

"Fuck, Camila." He slammed harder, deeper, and I couldn't hold the torrent of sensation that exploded inside me. I cried out loud, lost. My body convulsed as we found our release together, and I free-fell in a sky peppered with stars. Sebastián collapsed on top of me, our hearts banging against each other's chests. He nuzzled my neck, burying his face in my hair.

"Holy shit, Camila." His soft breath tickled my neck, and he pulled his head up to look into my eyes. "I never knew…What I just felt…You are amazing." His eyes burned with awe and...veneration? He pressed a soft kiss to my lips.

"I didn't do anything." I smiled, breathless. "It was all you. Did you forget I'm a rookie at this?"

He kissed the tip of my nose, my chin, and my lips. "Baby, you can do the same things with a million different people, and it would never be like this."

"A *million*, huh? And here I had you pinned as the selective type."

He rolled to his back and let out a throaty laugh. "No, not a million."

"Close?" I raised an inquisitive eyebrow.

He turned and caressed my cheek, brushing my hair off my face. "You're the most beautiful, unexpected thing that's ever happened to me." The sincerity in his eyes was disarming. "I would do anything for you. I want you to always remember that."

I squinted in the morning sun and stirred, tangled in the soft sheets of Sebastián's glorious bed. I stretched out my hand beside me and found an empty space where his body should have been.

His fingertips brushed my back from behind, sending chills up my neck. He leaned down to plant a kiss on my bare shoulder. "Good morning, gorgeous," he said softly.

I turned to see his pale eyes assessing me with amusement. He looked fresh and impossibly beautiful in a plain, gray T-shirt and faded, light blue jeans. Wet strands of raven hair fell artfully around his face. *I'm a lucky girl.*

"Hmmm, you look pretty gorgeous yourself." I grinned.

"How do you feel?"

"I feel...amazing," I whispered. A blush rose to my cheeks, and a crooked smile curved his lips. It sent my pulse racing.

"Last night was incredible, baby. It's late, I think I wore you out. Are you sure you're all right?" He caressed my back rhythmically, tracing invisible patterns.

"Yes, a bit sore, but…" I smiled. "I'm better than all right."

He breathed a smile on my shoulder. "I guess I'll just have to spend the rest of the day pampering you."

My stomach interrupted our intimate moment with a growl.

"Hungry?" he chuckled.

"Famished." I wrapped my arms around his neck and pulled him back to bed, forgetting all about my stomach and everything else.

Chapter 20

I packed the last of my clothes into my bag. I was showered, dressed in clean clothes, and absolutely starving. Who knew sex could make you this hungry? I blushed. The memory of Sebastián's hands exploring me made my skin tingle all over again. I had finally crossed the line of making love for real and ripped the almost-virgin label off my forehead.

A flick in the back of my mind snapped me out of my bliss. This was *real*. Things with Sebastián were moving along quickly. No more fooling around. This was where I had to stop being the lust-smitten girl and take control. It was time to know more about him and face the black cloud that was his family.

I pulled my jeans up and winced at the burn between my legs. Smiling inwardly, I followed the scent of fresh coffee to the kitchen.

"Hi, beautiful." A smug smile played on Sebastián's lips. I leaned over to kiss him, and he held my jaw in his hand, pulling my mouth to his. *Oh, my.* He glanced over my shoulder. "There's someone I want you to meet."

I whipped around, blushing furiously. *Oh.* A six-foot-four Adonis in a black cleric suit greeted me with a full smile that showed perfect teeth. His deep cobalt eyes assessed me curiously.

"Camila, this is Father Juan Pablo."

"Oh...Hi. Nice to meet you, um...Father?" Shit. Why had I said that as a question? Father Juan Pablo's smile widened. He was probably well aware of the effect he had on women. Erasing the distance between us, he leaned down to kiss my cheek.

"Nice to meet you, Camila. At last." He was charming and had the easy familiarity of someone who is good with people. My brain stalled. Maybe it was the contradiction between Father Juan Pablo's stunning looks and his attire that had me at odds. It seemed paradoxical that God would keep such a treasure for Himself. Unless...Yup, God is a woman.

"Nice to meet you too," I said.

"JP is a good friend. I'm helping him with his program to bring soccer uniforms to underprivileged schools to support education. It's been a great way to get kids to show up for class."

Father JP nodded. "Couldn't have done it without Sebas's help. This project would've failed without his contribution. Really, Sebas, I don't think I can thank you enough."

"No need, man. You know I enjoy doing it."

Father JP looked at me. "He's humble. This project is as much his as it is mine."

I turned to Sebastián. "What a cool thing to do. Soccer for books. I love it."

"Yes," he said, "and it's been successful beyond our expectations. JP here knows what he's doing." Sebastián's phone buzzed from the kitchen bar. He frowned at the screen. "I need to take this. It'll take just a sec. Don't leave without the check, JP."

"Don't worry, I won't."

Sebastián stepped away to take the call, leaving me alone with Father JP. I took a sip of coffee, a little uneasy under his confident gaze.

"Sebastián looks happy," he said. "I suspect it has a lot to do with you. I'm glad we've finally met."

"Me too. I haven't met many of Sebastián's friends. How long have you known him?"

"Ah, since we were kids. We went to school together, played rugby in the same club for a few years. He's like a brother to me." He smiled warmly.

I played with my spoon. Suddenly, I wanted to grill this man with a million questions about Sebastián.

"Something's bothering you. What is it?" His tone was soft. I looked up at him in surprise. That was pretty direct. He seemed to be able to see right through me. I bet people confessed their darkest truths to this man. He had the face of an angel.

"I just...I don't know. I'm wondering...I keep getting warnings from people around me about the Palacios family. Do you think I should be...worried? I mean, are they really as bad as people say?"

Father JP tilted his head to the side and pressed his lips. *Shit.* Shit, shit, shit. Me and my goddamn mouth.

"Why are you asking me that?" he said.

Good point. I looked down at my hands and shrugged. "You're a close friend of Sebastián's and...a priest. I care about him. It's tough to think objectively, you know?"

"Camila, Sebastián is a fine man. He has a big heart, but you must know that by now. He really cares about you too. As far as his family goes, I assume you've decided you can deal with it, or you wouldn't be here."

"I didn't know anything about his family until I met him."

"Oh?"

"I'm a ballet dancer. He and I don't move in the same circles." I smirked. "Not even remotely. My friends are all dancers too. Our world is the theater. It's somewhat disconnected from the outside." I bit my lip. This sounded a lot like a confession.

He rubbed his chin. "I see. Sebastián said you were unaffected by all of it. I guess I didn't realize to what extent."

"Tell me. What are they like?"

"Camila," he said, "take your time. Get to know each other. You will find your answers."

"Oh, come on, Father." I smiled as sweetly as I could manage. "Be my insider here. I know you priests keep golden information behind that suit."

Father JP chuckled, shaking his head. "You're quite the negotiator."

"You better believe it. Come on, tell me. Tell me about the Palacioses."

"What do you want to know?"

"Sebastián's father. People say he's powerful, dangerous, even. Sebastián seems...I don't know, kind of upset whenever he talks about him. What's he really like?"

He let out a heavy sigh. "Don Martín loves Sebastián more than anything, but he also has a firm grip on him. Sebastián has tried to break away from the family businesses several times, but Don Martín always manages to lure him back in. He's smart about it too. Doesn't confront him. But ever since Sebas's mother died, Don Martín relies heavily on him. It's hard for Sebas to completely turn his back on things. If you are willing to accept that, then you will be all right. No matter what Sebastián thinks, the Palacioses are a package deal. That's the truth."

"A family is always a package deal as far as I'm concerned."

"I agree. But the relationship with his father is an ongoing struggle for Sebastián. Constant negotiations that don't always end the way he wants. His love is architecture. It's been that way since he was a kid."

"I guess I don't really get it then. I do what I love and there is no compromise there."

His full smile took me off guard. "Then you may be just what he needs."

"Just what who needs?" Sebastián stepped in and pulled me into his arms from behind, kissing my neck.

"Camila, here," Father JP answered. "She's the real thing, man. You're lucky I'm off the market." He winked at me and I blushed beet red. "Now about that check?"

"I'll leave you two to it." I kissed Sebastián's cheek. "I need to call Nata, I don't want her to worry." He nodded and I gave a small wave at Father What-a-Waste.

I fished my phone out of my bag to call Nata and cringed. My screen was filled with five missed calls and a string of text messages from Nata. Shit. I had completely forgotten to take my phone off silent mode after work. I tapped on her name, bracing for the storm.

"Jesus, Camila. What the hell? You don't call me all night? I left you a thousand messages. I've been worried sick."

"I'm sorry. My phone was on silent. I'm fine."

"Shit, really." Her tone softened. Despite her outbursts, she could never stay mad at me. "You're out with that guy...You expect me not to worry?"

I rolled my eyes. "His name is *Sebastián*. And yes, I expect you to stop worrying. I'm *fine*."

"Camila, look. We have to talk. There's just...stuff you need to know about them."

"Nata, enough, okay? I appreciate your concern, but this is a bit much. I'm not asking you to support all my choices. Just accept this, please. Sebastián is important. I don't get why you're so determined to convince me I shouldn't be with him. Or, I do, but that ship has sailed." My heart pumped hard. Nata had always been my cheerleader. A long silence went by, and I wondered if the call had dropped.

"Look." She sighed. "There's a lot you need to know, not just about him, but also...about me and my family."

PART 2

KINGDOMS

Chapter 21

"Christ, Nata. There's *more*?" I said, pacing around Sebastián's massive bedroom with the phone pressed to my ear. "I mean, who are you? All of a sudden I feel like I don't know you."

"Let's talk when you come home. You on your way?"

"No. I won't be home till tonight, or tomorrow. Sebastián invited me to his cousin's birthday party."

"You're going to Julián de la Viña's house?"

"You know him too?" Seriously.

"*Everyone* knows him. Does the last name De la Viña really not even ring a bell?"

"No!"

"Will Don Martín be there too?"

"You know Sebastián's father?"

Nata sighed in exasperation. "Look. Let's talk when you get home. Will you please do me a favor and keep your phone with you tonight?"

"Nata—"

"Shush. Shut up and listen. I will explain all this later, I promise. I'm just asking you to trust me for now. Keep your phone with you, and if you need anything, *anything*, you call me, or Sergei. We'll stay close."

"Nata, I really don't need you to go into panic mode. Sebastián would never let anything happen to me."

"Just promise. Please."

"Okay, okay. I promise. And you promise to chill."

"Everything okay?" Sebastián leaned on the door frame.

I nodded, slipping my phone in my pocket. "Let's go have lunch. Somewhere by the river?"

After a long lunch overlooking the water, Sebastián went into his office to make some calls while I soaked in the egg-shaped tub in his guest bathroom. When I came out, there was a dress on the bed. I approached and immediately recognized the design. It was the Inés Fernandez that the model was wearing at Amsterdam the other night. Holy shit. How? I grazed my fingers over the soft velvet. It was gorgeous and surely cost a fortune.

I did my makeup and changed into the dress. It was black with a very low back, and a perfect match for Nata's stilettos. This was so much nicer than the gown I'd brought. Feeling ecstatic, I looked at myself in the mirror, but the knot in my stomach hadn't eased. The thought of the party and meeting Sebastián's family pulsed in my mind like a ticking bomb.

A nostalgic tango melody traveled down the hallway. I followed it to the great room, then stilled at the sight of Sebastián strumming chords on an acoustic guitar. *Holy mother of all hotties.* I held my breath. He was lost in the music, his low voice humming the melody. I waited till the song ended, and took an unsteady step into his line of sight. His eyes widened, he blinked, then shook his head.

"Wow." A sly grin stretched on his lips. He stood and held my hand up, making me twirl so he could get a full view. "This dress is a weapon. I won't let you out of my sight. You look exquisite." He kissed my neck while his hand traveled down my bare back, sending chills up my arms.

"You don't look bad yourself," I said. He was dressed in soft, gray linen shirt and black slacks. "Thank you for the dress, but—"

"What?" He pulled me to him, and I nuzzled his body wash-kissed skin.

"It's too much. I'm not sure... how I feel about accepting it."

"Please don't overthink it," he whispered, kissing the path from my ear to my shoulder. "I remembered how much you liked it, and I thought it would make you happy. That's all. Though it will be very hard to keep my hands off of you when you're wearing so little."

I bit my lip and smiled. "Then don't."

Chapter 22

Julián's house was only a few minutes away from Sebastián's. The property was massive, and when we passed the gate that separated this kingdom from the outside world, my stomach clenched.

At the end of a long, cobblestone driveway, two valets opened the car doors and greeted us. The young valet on my side offered me his hand to help me out. A slight blush rose to his face when our eyes met. His fingers held mine a second too long, then let go quickly when a firm hand clasped his shoulder.

"I've got it, man," Sebastián said in a frosty tone. The guy blanched, recognizing who it was, and hurried to get the next car. Sebastián kissed my shoulder, wrapping a protective arm around my waist. "I'm going to have my hands full I see."

"Possessive, are we?"

"Very." He kissed my temple softly.

We followed the arriving guests through the main entrance, guarded by security guards who nodded at Sebastián as we passed.

Julián's home was nothing short of stunning. Like Sebastián's, it was an architect's dream, but this house had an ultramodern, minimalist design. Every detail of the estate and its surroundings had been carefully drawn with the clean, elegant sophistication of someone with taste and money. Lots of money. The one-story home wrapped around a rectangular infinity pool, its mirrorlike surface glimmering under a blanket of floating candles. A forest of mature willows peppered the property, a thousand white lights twinkling from within the branches as far as the eyes could see. The atmosphere was dreamy. I felt like Cinderella at the ball.

In the garden, the party was already in full swing, framed by a bar on each end. Waiters in crisp uniforms mingled with the guests, balancing trays of champagne flutes and mini delicacies. It was like a scene in one of those Beverly Hills parties you see in movies, loaded with everything imaginable, and holy shit, one of Buenos Aires's top indie bands was playing on a nearby stage. I squeezed Sebastián's hand, slowly letting out the breath I had been holding as I stared wide-eyed at Buenos Aires's elite, dressed in what I guessed were nothing less than Valentinos and Diors. I reassured myself that if you didn't know I was a middle-class girl with borrowed shoes and a dress that cost twice my salary, maybe you would think I fit in too. Maybe.

Sebastián's thumb stroked my back rhythmically as we sipped perfectly chilled Cristal. I shifted my weight from one foot to the other.

"You're nervous. You have no reason to be," he said, leaning down to kiss my bare shoulder.

"I don't belong here," I said, glancing at the guests.

He held my chin and gently turned it so I would look at him.

"Don't ever say that," he said, serious. "You are a queen, Camila. These people are just posers." I looked at him skeptically and he smiled, then pressed a soft kiss on my lips. "I don't think I like this dress anymore. I can't wait to take it off," he murmured. A shiver traveled up my bare back.

"You bought it for me," I said coyly. "But you don't like it?"

"No." His eyes darkened.

I shrugged nonchalantly and took a sip of my drink. "I don't have any clean clothes, so I'll have to walk around your house naked."

"Hmmm. I don't object. Let's say hi to Julián and get out of here," he whispered in my ear, tracing open-mouth kisses on my neck. I nearly expired. That perfect mouth...*Jesus*. But I knew this was important to him. And I was eager to prove to Papá and Nata that the gossip around Sebastián was nothing but that. We could be a normal couple at a normal party. I summoned all my self-control.

"Sebas," I breathed, "we are here. Let's meet your family."

He groaned against my neck.

We joined the party and Sebastián introduced me to his cousins, Gonzalo and Rami. They smiled easily and confidently. Each kissed my cheek and pulled Sebastián into a man hug. They engaged in casual chatter while I rested my head on Sebastián's shoulder and listened absentmindedly. Rami ran a quick hand through his hair (a family trait?), and a gold Rolex slid down from under his cuff.

A few other cousins and uncles stopped to greet us, all dressed impeccably, the trademark Etiqueta Negra and Ralph Lauren logos embroidered on their shirt chests. I felt their eyes assessing me while they spoke with Sebastián about their family and kids. They were all very affectionate toward him. But something in their eyes made me uneasy. I couldn't say exactly, but each time I met a new member of the Palacios family felt like stepping into one of those airport scanners. Damn my paranoia. Damn Nata.

My glass was never empty. I lost count after the second refill, and soon the overall glamour, conversations about yachts, houses in Punta del Este, and vacations in Gstaad, all spun in my head. I figured I had probably drank the equivalent to my salary. Every few seconds a new person stopped by to greet Sebastián and his *new girl*. I felt like a purse Chihuahua. I couldn't remember anyone's name and wondered how on earth you could know that many people and keep track of them in your head.

Massimo, a tall polo player with russet skin and a crooked nose, greeted Sebastián with the usual man hug.

"Massimo, this is my girlfriend, Camila," Sebastián said.

Massimo kissed me on both cheeks. "Finally, a girl worth the wait, no doubt."

I blushed and his grin grew wider. The beat of the music picked up, and Massimo stepped closer, pulling me into a sexy dance, brushing his body against mine.

"Hey. Easy," Sebastián said, stepping between us and pulling me away. "Keep your paws off my girl."

"Ah." Massimo chuckled, shaking his head. "He's worried that you'll find me more charming, which undoubtedly, you will." He winked.

Sebastián shook his head.

"It was a pleasure, Camila." Massimo gave a friendly punch to Sebastián's shoulder, then blew me a kiss before joining a group of girls dancing beside him.

With so much alcohol flowing in my veins, the fatigue from the week settled in. I was beginning to wonder if we would ever meet Julián or his twin sister. By now, a good hundred guests were spread around the garden, dancing, laughing, clinking flutes constantly refilled with Cristal. From where we stood, the house looked like an oasis of massive windows and light, overlooking its own private paradise. I rubbed my arms, wishing I was back at Sebastián's house, in his bed. My gaze stopped at a figure on the other side of the pool. He nodded at Sebastián and I immediately knew it was Julián. He set off in our direction and a slow chill traveled down my back.

Shit. This was it.

Julián de la Viña was almost as tall as Sebastián and, if I hadn't found him terrifying, I would've thought he was extremely good-looking. Just like Sebastián, his most defining feature was his stunning eyes. Julián's reminded me of a cougar. They were shrewd and of an intense emerald green, blazing against his olive skin. Strands of auburn hair brushed his forehead. His jawline was sharp, square, masculine. He was in great shape, the outline of his broad shoulders and defined biceps undisguised under his pale blue shirt. His presence was striking. He was the epitome of confidence.

"Sebas, good to see you." He pulled Sebastián into a hug, patting his shoulder. Then he turned to me and suddenly I couldn't remember how to breathe. "Good to finally meet you, Camila. I'm Julián. Sebas has spoken a lot about you."

The words were right, but his tone was chilled, laced with contempt. What the hell was his problem? I felt like the prey and he was the predator debating whether or not I was worth eating.

I tilted up my chin and gave him a polite smile. "Nice to meet you too. And happy birthday."

"Thanks." He nodded before turning to look at Sebastián pointedly. "Your father's been asking about you. He wants to discuss some strategies for the situation at the docks." Something about the exchange made me feel uneasy.

"Shit," Sebastián muttered, taking a long sip of his drink. He surveyed the crowd, then gave a slight nod at someone in the distance. I followed his gaze to a middle-aged man heading in our direction. It took me a moment to realize I was looking at Don Martín Palacios as he approached flanked by two oversized men in black suits.

How I had envisioned Don Martín fell short against the live version. He strode with the confidence of a man who owns everything that surrounds him. He was tall, somewhat thick, his shoulders wide and muscular. His raven hair was dusted with white and neatly combed back. Don Martín's creased skin was kissed by a dark tan, his eyes, a deep hazel. He wore a crisp white shirt open at the collar and gray slacks. As he got closer, he appraised me from head to toe, and an amused smile twisted up his mouth.

"An angel has paid us a visit," he said, slightly bowing his head to me. "And my son is the lucky one at her side."

"Papá, it's good to see you," said Sebastián. "I want you to meet Camila."

Don Martín awarded me his full attention. My pulse sprinted as he gently took my hand and pressed a soft kiss to my knuckles. I felt like when I was on stage, those few first seconds when everything is overwhelming.

"Exquisite," he said, matching Sebastián's words from earlier. "I am delighted to meet you, darling."

I straightened my shoulders and smiled. "It's nice to meet you, too, Mr. Palacios."

"Please, *princesa*. Call me Don Martín." He gave my hand a soft squeeze before letting go and shifting his attention to Sebastián. "It's been too long since you last visited me." Don Martín wrapped his son in a tight embrace, then broke away and held him at arm's length. "You look well." He turned to Julián and gave him an affectionate pat on his arm. "You too. I miss having you both closer. As you know, we have pressing business to discuss." Addressing Sebastián, he said, "You've caused quite a commotion."

"Papá, it's Julián and Mercedes's party," Sebastián said, kissing my temple. "Can it wait?"

Don Martín smiled and gave him a nod, then looked up at Julián. "And, as usual, it's a fine party. Your sister's skills are unmatched. Happy birthday. I will see you and Sebastián before I leave."

"Of course," Julián said. He glanced at me, absorbing my reaction to Sebastián's father's presence.

"May I have this dance, darling girl?" Don Martín once again took my hand in his, and I flinched.

"Oh, um…"

When I looked up, Sebastián gave me a wink.

Nearby, the band played "Georgia on My Mind." Don Martín led me to an area by the pool, a few steps away, where people were dancing. He raised my hand, placing his other one on my waist. His fingers grazed my bare skin, making me regret my choice of dress.

"You're a magnificent dancer," he said. "But of course, you're a professional, so I'm not surprised. I hear you are part of the Colón's permanent company. Quite an accomplishment."

"Thank you. You're an excellent dancer as well."

He took in everything around us, smiling benevolently. "My son is quite taken by you. It's good to see him so happy. He's always been the one who takes care of everyone else. I like seeing him smile."

"I care about Sebastián too. Very much."

"I can see that. You're passionate. It's in your eyes. Sebastián sees it as well, I can tell. His mother was like that. I've never loved another woman the way I loved Silvana." He let out a faint sigh. Then his expression sharpened. "But passion can be a dangerous thing if it's not well directed."

"What makes you believe my passion isn't well directed? I'm passionate about my work, and so far, my career is going well."

He chuckled. "A fair point, dear girl." He let a moment pass before his expression grew serious. "I was referring to my son. But while we're on the subject, may I be candid with you?" His low, raspy voice betrayed the darkness in his tone.

"Please."

"You see…" He paused for a moment, as if to find the right words. "I have built an empire from the ground up. It's my entire life's dedication, and it will all belong to Sebastián one day. Maybe to you too," he said more lightly, but his eyes told me he didn't miss a beat. "But as a part of this family, Sebastián has a great deal of responsibility. Difficult choices at times." He scanned the crowd over my shoulder before looking back at me. I realized he did this often. "I'm wondering, Camila, if you're willing to accept that? The challenges that will come your way?"

I did my best to appear unfazed, though inside I was shivering. We had only met a minute ago and I already smelled fire. Sirens blasted inside my skull. *Get the fuck away from all this.*

"Don Martín," I said in a steady voice. "Sebastián and I have only just met. My main aspiration is to become the best dancer I possibly can. What Sebastián decides to do with his future is his own decision."

Don Martín's knowing smile widened. "Of course, I'm getting ahead of myself as usual. I hope I didn't offend you, sweet girl. I'm just very protective of my sons. If you're important to Sebastián, then I must also be protective of you. I can't promise it will always be easy, but being a part of this family also brings many benefits. I want you to keep that in mind."

Was he negotiating with me? My heart raced, and I was relieved when Sebastián appeared at my side. "Papá, you're monopolizing my girlfriend."

Don Martín let out a throaty laugh. "Ah. I should be so lucky." He clasped a thick hand on Sebastián's nape. His smile for his son was dashing. "It brings me joy to see you happy, son. Don't forget to come see me before you leave tonight."

"I'll stop by before we leave."

"She's one in a million," Don Martín said warmly at the two of us. "It was a pleasure to meet you, Camila. Don't be a stranger." He winked, then walked away shadowed by his bodyguards.

In that moment I knew exactly what Father JP had meant when he said Don Martín was smart about the way he lured Sebastián in. In his smooth, charming manner, he had clearly let me know he wanted me in his corner.

I rested my face on Sebastián's shoulder. My head spun.

"Don't let him intimidate you."

"Hmm. Too late."

"He has a big heart, once you get to know him." His lips brushed my temple. "Do you want to get going?"

"Yeah."

"Come." Interlacing our hands, he led me in the direction of the house.

"You're not leaving already, are you?" a smooth voice called from behind us.

No, no, no. What now?

Sebastián turned around and his expression instantly lightened.

"There you are. I've been looking for you. You look striking, sweetheart. Happy birthday." He let go of my hand to embrace a five-foot-ten supermodel in his arms, kissing her cheek.

Sweetheart? Jealousy flashed through me.

"Camila, this is Mercedes, Julián's twin sister," said Sebastián. He wore my favorite smile as he gazed at the ridiculously hot Barbie with a familiarity that made me clench my teeth.

"It's a pleasure," she said with a half smile. "Sebas has been blabbing nonstop about you." She glanced up at him with soft eyes. I narrowed mine. Funny how he barely talked about her and *completely forgot to mention she was ridiculously hot.*

"She's gorgeous, Sebas," she said, giving me a onceover. "You weren't exaggerating. And a ballerina at the Colón. How peculiar." She turned to me. "Are you enjoying the party?"

"Yes, thank you," I said. *Peculiar?*

While she chatted with Sebastián, my attention fell hostage to her imposing appearance. She was tall, gorgeous, and impeccably dressed in a silk gown that went down to her feet. Her features highly resembled Julián's but were flawlessly drawn in sophisticated, soft lines. Silky layers of auburn hair cascaded halfway down her bare back. With eyelashes that went on forever, her green eyes bore the same feline features as Julián's, contrasting sharply with the same olive skin tone they all shared. She had a statuesque nose and full, high cheekbones. I hated her.

"Listen to me, rambling on and on," she said, shaking her head and smiling brightly at Sebastián. "It's a party, Sebas. Don't look so serious." Leaning closer, she pinched his chin. "He loves you," she crooned. I assumed she meant Don Martín and, for a moment, I felt as if I was intruding in a personal conversation. The familiarity between them set my teeth on edge. I wanted to strangle her.

Sebastián's shoulders relaxed and he nodded in agreement. Jealousy flicked my ear. Mercedes seemed to have an immediate effect on him. They obviously had a deep connection. I racked my brain, trying to remember what Sebastián had said about her. Were they childhood friends? How close? I couldn't remember, but I hoped they were close enough to make any romance between them inappropriate.

"Happy birthday, Mechi. Great party, as usual," he said, stroking her cheek affectionately.

She looked back at him, enamored.

"Oh," he said, spotting someone in the crowd. "I need to talk to Martín Cassas before we leave." He turned to me. "I'll be back in a sec, babe." Before I could respond, he was gone.

"Great party. Thanks for having me." I smiled at Mercedes as I nervously swirled the champagne in my glass.

"Yes, I'm happy with the turnout," she said, looking around at the guests. "Must be a nice change of scenery. For you, I mean."

"Pardon?"

"This party. The guests, the champagne, that *dress*." She shrugged, hurrying the last of her drink. "I imagine you're quite out of your element here. He bought you that dress, didn't he? It's an Inés Fernandez. I know her work. Well, enjoy it. And then go right back to whatever suburb you came from." She looked down at me, suddenly a foot taller.

My brain stuttered and I blinked.

"He's *mine*, darling." She sneered.

"Wh—"

"Look, I get it," she said, rolling her eyes. "He's just having a bit of fun. Another one of his ways to cross Don Martín, but that's all this is, you understand? I'm doing you a favor, you know." Her serpent glare pinned me to my spot.

My jaw dropped. This fucking party, the alcohol, this venomous bitch! I wanted to vomit.

"Excuse me," I said, and set off toward the house.

I heard her chuckle behind me. Everything around me spun wildly, and I thought I was going to faint. I hurried through the guests. Their lively chatter now struck me as a sinister mock, reminding me I was an intruder. Finally inside the house, I leaned against a column, closed my eyes, and breathed deeply to force down the bile that rose to my throat.

"Cami, are you all right?" Sebastián gently clasped my shoulder from behind.

"Can we go?"

"Sure. Everything okay? You're pale."

"I'm just tired."

"I'll get your coat."

Arguing voices burst from the foyer. Sebastián frowned.

"Stay here." He took a step in the direction of the main entrance, but I clutched his arm.

"Where are you going?"

"Please wait here. Promise me." His eyes focused on something behind me. He gave a nod, and in an instant, Rafa appeared by my side. "Stay with her," Sebastián ordered.

"Let me see what's going on first," Rafa said in a strained tone.

"No. Stay with her." He turned and stalked to the foyer. Rafa cursed under his breath. I stumbled off after Sebastián, but Rafa's massive hand clasped my arm.

"Stay here."

"Then *you* go with him," I pleaded.

Rafa's attention turned to the main foyer. The voices grew louder, and I looked up at him with desperation. He hesitated for a moment, then let go of my arm and took off. I gave him two seconds, then followed, everything around me spinning.

As soon as the foyer came into view, I was suddenly sober. An army of about a dozen men crowded the main entrance. I immediately recognized the two Russians. I didn't know their names but remembered them from times when Nata and I had gone out with Sergei. They looked drunk, arguing loudly in broken English at the giant shadows of Julián's bodyguards. Instant panic that Nata, Sergei, or even Alexei might be amongst them seized me. Two more men, each with a date, appeared at the door behind them, protesting in Russian, but there were no signs of my friend or her brother. What was this? More men in suits, all armed to the teeth, gathered at the door, surrounding the intruders. My insides twisted into a knot.

I stopped at a massive wall separating the foyer from the main room, a few feet behind Rafa. Sebastián saw me and shot Rafa a murderous glare. Realizing I was standing behind him, Rafa shook his head in frustration.

"Dammit, Camila," Rafa said, shielding me behind his large frame.

"Sorry," I whispered.

Julián stepped in from the periphery. His men tensed, their guns pointed at the intruders, while others searched them, though they seemed to be unarmed. They struggled, yelling threats in Russian, and the commotion grew louder.

"What the hell is this?" Julián barked.

"We want to speak to Don Martín Palacios," one of the Russians growled. The others struggled behind him, restrained by the bodyguards. Their dates smiled and seemed unconcerned, bored even.

"Throw this garbage out. I don't want them upsetting my guests," said Julián with detestation. "You assholes have no boundaries. This is my fucking *house*. Zchestakova sent you? Is this his way of *asking* for business now? Give him a message from me. Tell him his imports are fucked now. For good."

The two Russians in front wrestled under the bodyguards' grips. One of them spat at Julián, and a massive guy backhanded him hard, smashing his knuckles into his nose. A furious stream of red gushed down the Russian's chin and onto his shirt. Jesus. I looked away.

"Get them the fuck out and search the property," Julián said.

Sebastián turned to me and took my hand. "Show's over. Let's go." He rushed me back into the main living room. I stumbled, almost tripping on my heels. "Stay here with Rafa. I need to speak to Julián, then we can go."

I frowned.

"I mean it, Camila. Stay with Rafa."

"Fine." I let out a petulant sigh and plopped on an oversized sofa. Would this night ever end? I rested my head, staring through the glass wall. Outside, the party was alive, the guests oblivious to the intrusion. After a few minutes, I stood up and Rafa mirrored me.

"I'm just going to use the bathroom. Be back in a minute."

"I'll come with you." Rafa quickly surveyed the room.

"We really have to work this out. I've been going to the bathroom all by myself since I was three."

He shrugged. "Just doing my job."

"As you wish."

His phone buzzed in his pocket, and he pulled it out, pressing it to his ear. He listened for a brief moment and said a curt yes before hanging up.

"Sebastián needs me for a minute," he said. "Will you please just wait for me here when you're back? Won't be long."

"Sure."

As soon as he left, I beelined to the bathroom and stumbled into a young waiter in a crisp white coat.

"Sorry, I—"

"Miss, I was told to give you this." He handed me a small, white, sealed envelope and turned away before I could say anything. I frowned and quickly opened it, pulling out a thick paper card. My blood froze when I recognized Nata's handwriting.

Meet me outside in the back of the west wing by the slate fountain. Bring Sebastián and no one else. Please.

Chapter 23

The west wing, where the hell was the west wing? Dammit, Nata. I hurried down a long hallway leading to what I assumed was the right way. My head swam in alcohol and disbelief. At the end of the hall, a wood-framed glass door was ajar. I pushed through it to a small, private garden.

Sergei Zchestakova tensed when he saw me, immediately putting out his cigarette.

"Where's Palacios?" he said in his thick Russian accent.

"Where's Nata?"

"Not here. She just wrote the note." He slipped another cigarette between his lips and lit it. Betrayal punched my gut. *She's in on this?*

"Oh."

"Only way." He shrugged. "I needed to bring him out here. Where is he?"

I whipped my head around to make sure nobody had followed, then closed the door behind me.

"For fuck's sake, Sergei. This house is a fortress, and Julián's men are all over the property. Looking for you, probably. What the hell are you doing here?"

"Shhh. Shhh," he admonished. "Quiet down. I really need to speak to Don Martín, but your boyfriend will do also." He nodded dismissively.

"Absolutely not. This is crazy. You have to get out now, you hear me?"

He took a long drag from his cigarette and didn't answer.

"Look, whatever it is you want, I can't help you. Please, you have to go."

"Not before I speak to one of them," he said.

Behind me, the door burst open. Sergei's mouth twisted in a sly smile.

"Palacios, good timing." Sergei blew out smoke through his nose.

"What the fuck?" snarled Sebastián, gripping my arm and pulling me behind him. "Zchestakova. I should've known. What do you want?"

"I came to talk to your father. Or to you." He shrugged.

Sebastián let out a humorless chuckle. "You've got balls, I'll give you that. All that circus upfront was so you could slither in?" He shook his head in disbelief.

"I'm a desperate man, Palacios." Sergei flicked his cigarette, then threw it on the gravel and let it burn there.

"You're a stupid man," Sebastián corrected. "You know what'll happen when they find you here. Julián's not known for his patience, or his compassion." He smirked.

"He can't freeze all our shipments," Sergei spat out. "If he doesn't release at least one of them soon, he puts us out of business. Your father doesn't want that. I need to speak with him, not Julián."

"My father will not speak to you," Sebastián said. "This is not how he does business. You broke in. Mocked his men. He will not listen to you."

"Then you help us," Sergei said.

"That's not my turf. Even if I wanted to help you, I couldn't."

"Of course it's your *turf*. You're a Palacios. Camila," he said, glancing over, "talk to him. This affects you too. If we're forced to leave Buenos Aires, Natascha's career here is over. Don't you care? We have ten days before we lose everything."

Dread filled me at the thought of Nata being punished because of some business quarrel. But Sergei could be bluffing. I didn't know what to believe anymore.

"Sergei, you have to leave. Now," I said. "We can talk about this tomorrow, somewhere else. Please."

"There's no out for me now. But I knew that, coming here." He looked at Sebastián. "My family needs those shipments. Or we won't survive." Anger flashed through his glassy eyes. "*Now* is the perfect time to let us in with big shipments. The docks are chaos after the Russian girls were taken from Ivanov's ship."

Russian girls? I darted a look at Sebastián. He held my gaze and shook his head fractionally. *Don't.*

"We've got things under control," said Sebastián.

"Like hell you do," Sergei spat out. "Ivanov is like a rabid dog, searching all the boarding houses in the city for those girls. Now is the time to move. He's distracted. With him out of the way, we can push in our biggest cargo."

I darted another anxious look at Sebastián, but his eyes were focused on Sergei. Sebastián's expression was serious. Something Sergei had said was new information. I hadn't mentioned anything about the girls to Nata or anyone, but it was obviously spreading fast. Shit, would it come back to Sebastián? My head hurt.

Rafa charged in and instantly drew out his gun, aiming it at Sergei. "Step back, asshole."

"Whoa. Is that really necessary?" I snapped, turning to Sebastián. "He's not armed." I darted an inquisitive glance at Sergei, and he looked away. "Sergei and Natascha are like family to me. There's got to be another way. Please, please help him get out of here."

"Julián's men are everywhere," Rafa said to Sebastián. "He'll never make it out. Your father's men will tear each other to pieces for his head."

"Dammit, Sergei. Your sister needs you to take care of your family," I said. "You can't do that if you're hurt."

"I'm not afraid of them," Sergei said, looking at Sebastián. "Without your help, my family is as good as dead."

I clutched Sebastián's arm. "Please. Help him."

Sebastián ran a hand through his hair. "Fuck, Sergei. You're starting to be a real pain in my ass." He let out an exasperated sigh as he nodded to Rafa. "Take him out to the fourth garage. Take the Maserati, hide him. Tell the men at the door I sent you home to get documents for my father to sign. Then let him loose at the nearest bus stop." His tone was firm, measured with the confidence of a man who is used to giving orders. In that moment, there was no doubt he was Don Martín's son.

"Sergei, go." I pulled Sergei into an embrace so I could talk into his ear. He stiffened and didn't hug me back. "I'll do what I can to help. Now go.

Please. For Nata." I pulled away, and he looked at me with skeptical eyes. Then he followed Rafa to the garage a few yards away.

Sebastián shook his head. Growling, he took my hand. "Let's go."

In the hallway, Mercedes intercepted us as she came out of the bathroom. All my muscles tensed. *You've got to be fucking kidding me. What now?*

"Sebas," she said, ignoring me. "I need your help to get Julián out of there." She gestured to a closed door beside her. "The cake is ready."

"Sorry, Mechi. We're on our way out."

"No, you can't!" she said, shaking her head and placing her hands on his chest. She looked up at him and smiled widely. *Poisonous snake.*

Sebastián relaxed a fraction.

"Please." She pouted. "Julián's been in there with your dad for ages. Can you please do it? For *me*? It's my birthday, too, and I don't want to blow out candles alone. All you have to do is slip in there and tell Julián he's needed in the pool area." She tilted her head to the side.

Sebastián let out a defeated sigh. He turned around and kissed my forehead. "I'll be right back, babe." When he saw the disappointment in my face, he whispered, "I won't be long." Then his expression changed, and he cursed under his breath. "Actually, my father needs to talk to me…and Rafa is gone. Do you want me to have someone drive you home?"

"It's fine. I'll wait. Excuse me, I have to use the bathroom." I glanced behind him at Mercedes, who shrugged with a winning sneer. "Something's made me feel sick."

I shut the bathroom door and slumped against it. The white marble room spun wildly around me, and my pulse raced. Dammit. This evening had turned into a nightmare. Suddenly, all the things that seemed beautiful when we first arrived, now whirled in my head. Mercedes, this party, all these fucking people. All those *guns*. And Sergei, here, using me to get to Sebastián.

Nata. My best friend. She had used me too.

I rushed to the toilet and emptied the contents of my stomach, heaving painfully. Tears burned down my cheeks like acid. *Dammit, Nata.*

I splashed my face with cold water and, as I looked up in the mirror, my mind was suddenly clear: I didn't care about any of it. I didn't want to be part of this fucked-up family.

I wanted out.

I quickly dried my face and stormed out of the bathroom. I searched my purse for my phone. I would call an Uber and wait outside by the gate. I would be gone by the time Sebastián came out.

"Cami." Startling me, Milo grabbed my arm from behind.

"Milo. Wh-what are you doing here?"

"On my way out, actually."

"Oh. Can you give me a lift?" I said.

"Sure…" He frowned. "Aren't you here with Palacios?"

"Yes. No. I mean…" I shook my head. "He's busy. I was about to call an Uber."

"Okay. Wait here, I'll get my coat."

I plopped down in a hallway armchair to wait for Milo. I rested my head back, closing my eyes. Arguing male voices burst from a room a few steps away. Sebastián…There was silence, then another outburst. I stood and silently stepped closer. The voices became more discernible, and I stilled, sure that one of them was Sebastián's. He was arguing with…*Don Martín*? I pressed myself to the wall, pretending to look for something in my purse.

"You made this mess. You undo it," Don Martín was saying.

"With all due respect, they were trafficking girls on our waters. What the hell did you expect me to do?"

"There are codes for these things. Do I need to remind you how things work?"

"Those girls were being raped every *hour*," Sebastián growled. "We couldn't leave them there, waiting for our 'codes.'"

"Dammit, Sebastián. You know damn well Ivanov won't stop until he finds who's behind his ship's ambush. And he won't give a fuck about our codes either. If Julián doesn't release the cargoes, Zchestakova will become more desperate to save his business. He'll capitalize on Ivanov being distracted to make up for the lost profits. Who knows what he'll try next."

"I assure you it won't come to that, Papá."

"I don't want these vultures near us. They're savages. I'm too old for these games. Talk to Julián. You two resolve this…mess. If this comes anywhere near us, we'll be facing a war." Don Martín's husky tone had turned hoarse, strained. Even through a brick wall, it still managed to send a chill down my back.

"Papá," Sebastián said in a calm tone, "this won't come near you. I'll make sure of it."

"I'm leaving to Italy tomorrow to see your brother. I'll need you to keep an eye on the new car shipments that are coming in. It's a large midnight load, and I don't trust anyone else. All the paperwork is ready."

"Julián's a better man for that."

"I want *you* to do it."

"The studio is busy and I need to be there full-time. I'll help if Julián needs me, but you need to talk to Alejandro about moving back here."

"I need you by my side, goddamnit. You're a Palacios. Stop fucking around!" A slam against wood made me jump, and I immediately stepped away. Sitting down onto the same armchair, I put my head in my hands. Shit. I needed to run—I knew that much. But I couldn't. Not tonight. There he was, facing the storm after helping those girls, facing his father who kept sucking him into the business, and I was jumping ship. Guilt filled me. I didn't know if we could be together, but I couldn't leave him now. Not like this.

Milo appeared, holding his coat. "Ready?"

"Actually, I'll wait. Sebastián won't be long after all."

He watched me for a moment, then squatted down beside me and took my hand. "What are you doing with this guy? How did you end up mixed with these people? This is not you."

I bit my lip hard, holding back the tears. "I'm okay. Thanks for offering me a ride."

He nodded, concern etched in his eyes, then kissed my cheek. "Take care, Cami." He stood, threw his jacket over his shoulder, and calmly walked away, turning once before disappearing down the hall.

When Sebastián stepped out of the room a couple of minutes later, his expression was strained.

"Sorry I kept you waiting," he muttered and held my hand to help me up. I followed him down to the entrance. There were no traces of the Russians or Julián's bodyguards. A couple approached Sebastián to say good-bye. He nodded politely and signaled to the valet to get the car.

Within seconds, the valet pulled over in the BMW. "Is your driver with you, sir?"

I tightened my fingers around Sebastián's hand and felt him flinch, so I immediately let go. His hand was swollen and blotched with pink around the knuckles. He let the valet know he would be driving himself and ushered me in the car. The knot in my gut eased a fraction. We were finally leaving this nightmare.

"What happened to your hand?" I said as Sebastián drove past the main gate and onto the road.

He stretched it out and scowled at the pain. "Nothing, it's nothing."

Sinking deeper into the seat, I let my eyelids drop. How in the hell had I ended up in the middle of all this? I wasn't even sure what all this was. What I did know was that I hated guns and I was suddenly surrounded by them. My best friend was keeping things from me, and that made my gut hurt. But she was also in more trouble than I could grasp, and ironically, I seemed to be her family's only hope. When the night had started, I was determined to prove to Nata and Papá that Sebastián and his family weren't gangsters. But they were. Don Martín, Julián, Mercedes. It was a thick weave of complex ties, and Sebastián was at the very center of it. I pressed my head to the cool glass. Mercedes had been right about one thing.

I didn't belong here.

Chapter 24

On the ride home, Sebastián was quiet, deep in his own thoughts. His eyes were lost in the road ahead, the moon kissing his perfect profile. He drove up the private road to his house. At the top of the driveway, Rafa and Tano were waiting inside a Maserati. Sebastián killed the engine and told them to go inside. They headed toward a sort of guesthouse a few yards behind the cavernous garage. I hadn't even seen Tano at the party. Had he been there too? There was so much I didn't know about Sebastián's world.

We watched the two men disappear. The night was still, and the silence of the black forest enveloped us. I shifted in my seat so I could face Sebastián.

"So…what's all this between Nata's family and yours?"

"Cami…" He sighed.

"Tell me."

He shook his head. "Sweetheart, no."

"Why?"

"Because…it's late. And because the less you know, the better."

"What happened to your hand?" I said, nodding at his swelling knuckles.

He looked down at his left hand and flexed it. "I had an argument with my father."

"You *hit* him?"

"No, I hit a beam." He frowned. "He presses all the right buttons sometimes."

"Sergei took a huge risk by coming to Julián's house. What's happening with their business? He seemed desperate. Is it true they have only ten days?"

"Camila, babe, this isn't something you and I will discuss."

"Why not?"

"Because it's just business. My father's business. I'm not involved."

"Then take me home."

"What, now?" He scowled. "You're not going back there tonight."

"It's my place."

"No. It's *their* place."

"If you're not going to talk to me, then I want to go home."

"That's out of the question." Pushing the door open, he stepped out and circled the car to get my door. He held it open, but I crossed my arms over my chest, pressing back into the seat. He sighed in exasperation. "Camila, please get out of the car. Let's not do this here."

I stepped out and he reached for my hand, but I pulled it away. He rolled his eyes, running both hands through his hair.

"Please," he said, "let's go inside. It's late."

"This is not how this works. We can't be together if you keep me in the dark."

He held my shoulders gently. "I don't want you involved in all this shit. Please let it go. Trust me."

"But, see, that's the thing. I'm already involved." I shook my head. "You're so contradictory. First, you want to keep me as far away from your family as possible. Then you want me to meet them. You draw me into this world of yours full of guns, and secrets, and in every way so different from mine. I ignored everyone's warnings and let it happen because…I wanted to know you better. But as soon as I get close, you push me away."

"Camila." He took my face in his hands, caressing my cheeks. "If anything happened to you because of me. Anything at all…"

I brushed a few disheveled strands off his forehead. Worry lines creased it. "You won't tell me about the Russian girls, and that worries me because what I'm sure are very dangerous people are now looking for you. Something Sergei said tonight interested you."

"Yes," he murmured. "We need to move fast. I'll take care of it."

I gave him a pointed look.

"Don't ask any more." He sighed.

"Tell me something. Tell me what's happening with Nata's family business."

"No." He shook his head. "Just…no."

"Sebastián." I coerced his eyes to meet mine.

"No." He frowned. "The only way you'll be safe is if you don't know anything."

"Dammit, I'm not a child!"

"For fuck's sake, it's two in the morning. Can we please just go inside?"

"I want to talk about this. I don't want to be in a relationship where you call all the shots and I...*obey*."

His face softened, and his mouth curved down in a sad smile. "Obey? You have so much power over me. Haven't you figured that out by now?"

"What?"

He gently took my waist and brought me to him, pressing his forehead to mine. Our broken breaths collided, and I closed my eyes to block the immediate effect he had on me.

"I don't belong here," I whispered, fighting the tightness in my throat. "Mercedes is right."

"Mercedes?" He pulled away. "What's she got to do with anything?"

"After you left, she said to me...she said I don't belong here, and that you're *hers*."

"What? Cami." He chuckled. "She was just messing with you. Mechi has a strange sense of humor."

"She was very convincing."

"I'll talk to her. Whatever she meant, we'll straighten it out. I want you two to be friends."

Right. "It's not even her. *I* feel I don't fit into your world."

"Yes, you do," he said, pulling me closer. "You fit in with me. His lips brushed mine. "You're my angel. To me, you're light. And through all the darkness around me, I see you, the most beautiful woman in the world. Please, please don't run."

The words winded me. His mouth met mine, consuming me. His fingers threaded through my hair at the nape and clenched it while his other hand wrapped around my waist and lifted me up. I straddled him as he pressed me against the car, his weight pinning me to the window. I shivered when my bare back met the cool glass. He pushed himself between my legs, and desire exploded inside me like the Brazilian Carnaval.

"You drive me crazy," he said against my mouth. "It was hard to control my thoughts…and my hands tonight. Speaking of hard…" He pressed his hard-on against me and kissed me voraciously. When we broke for air, I drew in a sharp breath.

"Sebastián…"

"Please," he whispered. "Stay."

God, I wanted him, but I needed to clear my head. I was quickly getting sucked into the dark Palacios web. But his soft, sensual lips molding to mine overrode my thoughts, flooding them with caresses, and love, and affection.

The tension from the night broke free inside me. I clutched his shirt at the back while his mouth ravaged my neck. *You're my angel.* The words swirled in my mind. He held me in place while he kissed me, more gently now. His hand slipped under my dress, and he stilled, then smiled against my mouth.

"Where's your underwear, babe?"

I blushed furiously. I had forgotten all about that, an impulse as I was getting dressed. Now it seemed stupid. "Um…I wanted to surprise you. I thought it would be…sexy."

"I'm very pleasantly surprised." He grinned, squeezing me into his arms. His mouth covered mine, devouring me once again while his cock rubbed against me through the fabric of his pants. I moaned and he exhaled against my mouth. "God, you're going to kill me."

I gasped, my hands clutching his hair, and I pulled hard as every muscle in his carved body hardened against mine. I arched my head back to give him better access to my neck. That glorious mouth…I wanted it everywhere. We were a tangle of hands, legs, and tongues. I was glad the house was asleep because I was sure we were putting on quite a show. My hand moved to his belt and the zipper, and I quickly undid them, pulling his pants down with his boxers. Before I could breathe, he was inside me, pounding, filling me completely as I held on to his biceps. I felt powerful, letting him possess me like this, knowing he was as lost to the force that pulled us together as I was. My blood was on fire, and I climbed, my muscles singing as they clenched in ecstasy. I moaned my release and we climaxed together. Spent, he held me against the cool glass.

"Let's go to bed," he said, his voice husky. I groaned, coming back to the now. He picked me up in his arms, and we headed inside.

Soft kisses trailing down my back woke me. I blinked through a fog of sleep, wrapped in the luxury of the softest Egyptian cotton.

Sebastián pressed a soft kiss on my bare shoulder and I turned around. He was sitting on the bed beside me, fully dressed and his hair was wet. I frowned.

"What time is it?"

"Early. I didn't want you to wake up alone and worry. I need to deliver some soccer uniforms to a new school. I'll be back soon."

"Oh…" I yawned and sat up on the bed. "You do that yourself?" I looked out the window. "It's still dark outside."

"My staff usually handles the deliveries. But I need to meet with someone today."

"Do you want me to come with you?"

"No, baby. Go back to sleep. It's just a quick run. You can come another time and meet the kids." He pressed another soft kiss on my lips. "I'll be back in a couple of hours."

I slipped back under the covers but lay wide awake as an avalanche of thoughts flooded my head. Through the massive window, I watched the moon cast shadows on the forest outside. The willows swayed to the early morning wind. I thought of Sergei and what might have happened to him after he left with Rafa. The desperation in his purple-rimmed eyes haunted me. What would happen when I went back to my apartment? Not *my* apartment. Sebastián was right, it was *theirs*. Nata had gone behind my back to help Sergei with his plan. My chest tightened at the thought. I would've helped them if she had just asked.

I tossed and turned until the sun finally rose to a decent enough hour to go on the hunt for coffee.

Keys turned in the front door. Sebastián walked in, followed by Rafa and Tano. I sipped Marcél's heavenly coffee at the breakfast bar.

"Good morning," Sebastián said, wrapping his arms around me from behind and giving me a sensual kiss. I blushed, knowing we had an audience. He turned to his bodyguards. "We'll stay around here today. You two can take it easy."

"I'll take the car back to Julián's and have Tano drive me back." Rafa then nodded at me. "Morning, Camila."

Tano winked a hello and followed Rafa.

"What do you want to do today?" Sebastián poured himself a cup of coffee.

I looked silently at him until our eyes met.

"What?"

"I want to talk about what happened at the party."

He growled. "Camila."

"No, don't *Camila* me." I shook my head. "I meant it when I said this won't work if you keep me in the dark. I'm in the middle of all this now. I *need* to know."

Letting out a heavy sigh, he slid onto a barstool, then picked up his coffee. "Okay, I'm not promising anything. What do you want to know?"

"First, I want to know about the Russian girls."

"Out of the question. And you understand you can't even mention that topic to anyone. Especially not to Nata and Sergei."

"Of course I understand that. But those people are after you."

"I'll be fine. We were careful. And you and I can't talk about this either. You never know who's listening."

"Sebastián—"

"Next question."

"Fine. Sergei took a huge risk by coming to the party. What's going on between them and your family?"

Sebastián rubbed the fatigue off his eyes. "Most of the Zchestakovas' business are imports that enter the country through our ports. The relationship between them and my family has always been strained, to say the least, because they can't be trusted. They're always trying to slip in contraband, avoid the customs fees."

"Contraband?"

He shrugged. "Yeah. Electronics, alcohol, cosmetics, you name it. They've done it all. But that's not what last night was about. We deal with contraband on a regular basis."

"Then what?"

Anger crossed his face and he looked away, taking a sip of coffee. "Last month, one of Sergei's morons shot Julián's best customs agent and six others when they embargoed a shipment the Zchestakovas were bringing in through Mendoza. Six hundred kilos of ephedrine smuggled inside fertilizer pallets."

"What?"

He nodded. "Till then we had managed to keep things civil. The Zchestakovas have always stayed away from drugs. I don't know what triggered the change. They must've been desperate, who the fuck cares."

"That can't be. I mean, I know the Zchestakovas. I admit, they're odd, but they would never…" I shook my head, searching for words. They had shot six people? *Drugs*? No. Nata's family couldn't be involved with any of that. I knew my friend. Or did I…"What happened to Julián's man and the others?"

"Most of the crew were shot dead, and Julián's man was badly injured. They beat him up good, though, put two bullets in his shoulder, and left him there like a dog, among a half dozen corpses." Anger blazed in his pale eyes.

"*Christ*. That just sounds insane. What happened after?"

"Julián shut down the borders to them, indefinitely. All their cargoes are on hold at the docks for inspection." He took my hand and interlaced our fingers. "Look, whatever you hear or learn about my family, there's one thing you need to know. First, we take care of our own. No matter what. Second, we don't go near drugs. Ever. We are vehemently against them. My father's been accused of a lot of things, but he's always protected his family. And he's never dealt with drugs."

I nodded, trying to process. "What about the guns?"

"We use them for our own protection. We have to. But we don't move them in or out."

I sighed. I was in way over my head... I felt like one of those hostages in Netflix's *Money Heist*, the one who fell in love with one of the robbers. Would I end up like her and join the guys with the guns? "So, what happens now?"

"I don't know. The Russians are screwed. Julián's pissed, and I don't blame him. The guy they shot, José, was Julián's right arm. With him out of commission, Julián's been at the docks almost full-time. He doesn't trust anyone else. It's affecting the studio."

"How?"

"Julián personally manages the business end of our most important accounts. I handle the main designs, and even with the help we've got, my plate's more than full."

"So what's gonna happen then? It seems like this isn't good for anyone. Especially Nata's family. Is it true they'll have to leave? Can they survive without any imports?"

"I imagine it would be hard. But that's not your concern."

"She's my best friend. Look, I'm not condoning the drugs, or the shootings—Jesus, I still can't believe that. There's got to be an explanation, and there's got to be a way to work this out. Is there anything you can do?"

"Me? No. They fucking made this personal when they went after José. He's like family. Plus now he's got permanent hearing loss in one ear. Fuck them."

I racked my brain for words.

"Look, babe. Just stay out of this," he said.

"Stay out of it? What do you think is going to happen when I go back to my apartment?"

"You don't have to go back. You can stay here."

My eyebrows shot up in astonishment. Sebastián reached for my hand and tugged me into his arms. "Come here. It's going to be okay."

"How, exactly?" I closed my eyes. What a goddamn nightmare.

"I want you to be safe. I can drive you to work in the mornings. Stay here. In fact, you can just move in with me."

I pulled away so I could look at him. "You're not serious."

"I am."

I searched his face for a trace of…what, humor? But he looked sincere.

"I can't, Sebastián."

"Why?"

"Because I already have a place to live."

"It's not safe for you to be there. Those fuckers are unpredictable. They'll use you to get to us again."

I was about to say Nata would never do that. But she already had. She'd written the note, baiting me to Sebastián. "Don't call them fuckers," I murmured. "They're my friends." I looked up at him, trying to decide what to do. "I think I'll stay at my parents' for now."

He threw his head back. "For fuck's sake. Stay with me. I'll make sure you get to work on time every day. Will you please stop arguing with me?"

"Let's just see what happens. I have no clothes here anyway. I need to go back home."

"I'll come with you."

"No, let me do this alone."

"I'll wait downstairs if you want, but I'm not sending you there unprotected."

"Sebastián—"

"Camila."

"Fine." I rolled my eyes. "I'll go get my things. Let's get this over with."

Chapter 25

When I walked into my apartment, Nata and Sergei were sitting on the edge of the couch. Nata stood, her face etched with fatigue from what I knew had been a long night of worrying. My eyes met hers, and her expression fell. I clutched the strap of my bag and swallowed the lump in my throat. Sebastián was waiting downstairs. I needed to be quick if I didn't want him to come storming in.

"Camila…" Nata said, her tone laced with guilt.

"I came to get a few things." I looked away and set off for my room, but she intercepted me.

"Wait. We need to talk."

"Now you want to talk?"

"Please," she said.

"I don't want any part of it. Whatever it is."

"I'm sorry about the note last night but—"

"Yeah, that was a bit ironic because you were the first one to tell me not to get involved with Sebastián's family. And I don't want to get involved, but you two dragged me right to the middle. And you didn't even ask. You baited me."

"Bah," Sergei said. "Don't be so dramatic. Nata was only helping me."

I gave him a dirty look and turned back to Nata, shaking my head in frustration as she slowly lowered herself onto the couch. Dropping my bag at my feet, I sat on the only other armchair we owned.

"I'm sorry," Nata said. "I am. I know there's no excuse for any of this. You have every right to be angry. But you were the only way we could get Sebastián alone."

"I am angry. You went behind my back. I would've helped you if you had just asked."

"You're right," Nata said. "I'm sorry, I'm a hypocrite. And after everything I've said to you against Sebastián and his family, I was afraid you'd say no. I couldn't blame you if you had. But we're desperate." Her hand reached for mine and I flinched.

"You're like my sister, Nata."

She withdrew her hand and rubbed the fatigue from her eyes. "I'm sorry."

"Drop it, already," Sergei said. "I made her do it." He paced by the balcony door like a caged tiger, then he suddenly stopped, shaking his head in irritation. "Last night you said you'd help us. You *have* to talk to them." His sunken blue eyes glinted in the morning sun. He winced, scowling at the glare like a vampire breaking out of a coffin.

"I only just met Julián last night, and it was pretty clear he didn't want to be BFFs with me."

"Talk to Sebastián, then," Sergei said. "As Don Martín's son, he has all the power."

"He's really not involved in his father's business."

"Ha!" he said. "Don't be naïve. Camila, you're our only hope. You have to do this."

"Hey." I frowned. "I don't *have* to do anything. You're the ones shooting people and dealing drugs. This is your mess, not mine."

Sergei's eyes narrowed. A warning. "We don't smuggle drugs."

"No? Where did the ephedrine in fertilizer tanks come from?"

"Another clan. A guy named García conned us. Everyone knows the Palacios family doesn't deal with drugs. We're not that stupid."

"Cami," Nata said, "we wouldn't risk our business with the Palacioses. You have to believe us."

I let my head drop against the backrest. "I don't know what to believe."

"Us. What we are telling you. We're like your family, Camila." Nata's hand reached for my arm. "I'm so sorry we've put you in this position. It's not fair to ask any of this of you. But we're desperate. If they don't release those shipments soon, my family's business will collapse. We'll be left with nothing. I'll have to"—her voice broke—"go back to Russia." I turned to her just as her hand quickly wiped her eyes. My insides twisted in a knot. I had never seen Nata cry before.

"I don't know why you think Sebastián will listen to me," I said with resignation. "He didn't want to discuss any of this. He says the less I know, the better."

"And he's right." Nata nodded with regret in her eyes. "Sergei tells me only the most important things for that same reason."

"Natascha," Sergei snapped and blurted something in Russian. "We *need* this."

She gave him a defiant glare and he groaned in irritation.

I scowled at him. "Julián is pissed because your people shot his crew. All except one were murdered. What the fuck. Or that wasn't you guys either?"

"That was not us, I told you. Enough!"

I turned to Nata. "Is this why you've always been so vague about your family? Is Sebastián right when he says you guys are...dangerous?"

Nata shook her head. "It's not that simple."

"I can't believe how naïve I've been." I let out a humorless chuckle. "I thought Sergei was part of some gang. But this is like real mafia shit."

"It's not like that," Nata said. "First of all, that wasn't us. We're not murderers. Sergei's telling you the truth. Second of all, things in Russia work differently, and we're very exposed here. We need protection. The world my family and Sebastián's family exist in has a different set of rules than the rest. It's...complicated."

"Jesus, Nata. Drugs? Guns? Who are you guys?"

She closed her eyes and shook her head. "I told you my family doesn't go near drugs. Julián knows it was García, even if he doesn't admit it. His people are dead and that cargo was linked to us. Someone has to pay."

"Sebastián said your guys try to push contraband regularly."

Sergei rolled his eyes. "Oh, please. Spare me. They count on the contraband. That's how they make most of their money. Undeclared imports, cargoes in transit that vanish. They call them midnight shipments because they come in late at night. No paperwork. If the seller doesn't pay Don Martín's fees, the cargoes are embargoed at the docks. Indefinitely. Like they did with ours. The Palacioses control everything."

"Camila," Nata said, "my family wants to make things right. Sergei won't let anything like that happen again." She looked up at him, and his jaw tensed.

"I shouldn't have trusted Dimitri. He was the one who helped García, then sold us out with De La Viña. But he isn't part of our business anymore, or *any* business." He mumbled the last part under his breath. "I'll personally handle the shipments from now on. That's what I wanted to tell Don Martín."

I pressed my forehead to my knees. This was way too much to process. Nothing was black and white. Everyone seemed to have an angle.

"Look," said Nata, "let's just all take a step back. Camila and I've got a very busy week coming up. We need to focus on that." She placed her hand on my shoulder. Her eyes were red rimmed with fatigue, and I wondered if she had slept at all. "I'm sorry about all this, Camila. If you can do anything to help us, then that's more than we can expect. I know it's really for us to resolve. And most likely, Sebastián won't like the idea of you being in the middle."

"Yeah. He wants me to move in with him. He doesn't think I'm safe here."

She exchanged a look with Sergei, then turned to me. "Nobody here will ever hurt you. You need to know that. Do you believe me?"

A silent moment passed, and I nodded.

"I mean it. Jesus, you are my sister. You think I would let anyone hurt you?" She sighed. "What do you want to do?"

"I'm not ready to move in with him. We've only just met. And even if that's what I wanted, I wouldn't do it now. Not like this."

"Good." She gave my hand an affectionate squeeze. "I know this whole situation sucks. But you're sort of in it now, and I need you."

"What can I do?"

"All we need is for you to explain our side to Sebastián and let him know Sergei's commitment to handle things personally. He needs to know we don't go near drugs. That's our only hope they'll let us back in. And I promise we will not ask anything else of you. You have my word. Sergei"—she looked at her brother who had resumed his pacing—"maybe you and the guys should stay away from here for a few days. Give Camila some air to come and go without causing her problems with Sebastián. He needs to know he can trust us. After all, this really does not concern her. You have to show him you won't involve her again."

Sergei's jaw tensed, but after a moment, he nodded.

Nata turned to me. "I'm meeting Marcos and the others for dinner at Piola in an hour." She smiled weakly. "Come with us?"

I ran my hand through my hair. Was I already picking up Sebastián's habits? "Sebastián's waiting downstairs. I made plans to have dinner with him."

"Okay." She nodded. "It's going to be all right. Thanks for listening to our side. I needed you to hear all this from me."

Downstairs, I bumped into Marcos when I stepped out of the elevator. He had been staying with Carla for a few days, so I hadn't seen him much outside of work. He wrapped one arm around my waist and spun me around. I gasped, holding on to his biceps as I searched the foyer. On the other side of the glass Sebastián stood, facing away with his phone to his ear. Panic gripped my chest and I quickly wiggled out of Marcos's arms.

"What are you doing here?" I said.

"Came to get a few things. Hmm…" he said, leaning close again. "Why do you smell like dude perfume?" He pulled back and squinted. "Ralph Lauren?"

"Marcos." I pushed him back, my heart pounding and my eyes trained on Sebastián's back. Marcos turned his head at the foyer, then faced me.

"What's up?" He chuckled. "Why are you so feisty?"

"Sebastián's waiting outside, and I really don't need any more confrontations."

He gave a sulky nod, then squeezed my hand. "Come to dinner with us."

"I can't," I said. "I'll catch up with you later, okay?" I kissed his cheek and rushed to the foyer.

I pushed through the door and Sebastián turned, ending his call. He glanced at the elevator closing behind me and scowled. "Everything okay?"

"Yes." I said, nodding.

"Was that Marcos?"

"Yes, he's staying at Carla's and was just picking up a few things. Wanna go?"

"You don't have a bag." He frowned. "You're not spending the night with me?"

"I have an early day tomorrow. I'd rather be here tonight."

"Was Sergei in the apartment?"

"Yes, both he and Nata were there. We talked. I'll tell you everything, but can we go out to dinner? I know it's early, but I'm starving."

I curled up against Sebastián in the plush, white couches of Bistro Sur at the Faena Hotel. Unusual and too extravagant for my taste, it reminded me of a setting from the movie *Moulin Rouge*. Sebastián had to briefly meet with one of the owners about an architectural project beforehand, so this saved him a step. It had been a long day for both of us.

"I'm so tired." I yawned. "And I ate too much."

"You hardly ate half of your meal."

"It was still too much."

He pressed a soft kiss on my lips. "I don't want you to be away tonight. I'll miss you."

"This is easier and we're both tired. I'll see you later this week, and we have the weekend."

"Camila," he said, running his fingers through the length of my hair. "I know it's soon, but I meant it when I said I want you to move in with me." He brushed the pad of his thumb across my mouth, and I kissed it.

"It's way too soon. Besides, when we're ready to do that, I want it to be *our* decision. I don't want to move in with you because we're forced into it."

"We're not being forced into it. It's what I want. The situation with the Zchestakovas just expedited it."

I shook my head. "Not like this. I need time."

He pulled me onto his lap. "Will you at least think about it?" His mouth hovered over mine. I closed my eyes and kissed him.

"I don't want to rush into this, Sebas."

"Okay, okay," he said, nuzzling my nose. "I'll wait. Though, you should know, patience is not my best quality."

"You think?" I smiled ruefully, sliding back onto my seat. "Sebas..." I weighed my words. "I know you've already answered a lot of my questions today, and that means so much to me, because it means you trust me, and you're finally letting me in. I don't want to abuse that, but I want to talk to you about Nata and Sergei."

"Jesus, what now?" he said as he gestured at the waiter for the bill.

"Nata swore they have nothing to do with the drugs. It was a guy named García."

"Huh, so they say."

"I believe her," I said sternly. "You know it wouldn't make sense for them to put at risk the relationship they rely on the most."

"Whatever the case, I'm not involved in all that. I told you, Julián handles their business."

"Maybe you could talk to Julián, then?"

"No. Why do we keep coming back to this? Let it go."

I reached for his hand. "Please. I promise I'll stay out of it from now on. Just do this one thing for me. Please."

Ire flashed across his eyes. "What the fuck? Why are you getting involved in Sergei's shit? It doesn't concern you. This is why I didn't want to even talk about it. I knew they would try to use you to get to us."

"They are not using me. They're desperate. And Nata is my friend. I can't stand seeing her so hopeless. This isn't her fault."

He leaned his head back against the seat and looked away, cursing under his breath. "I don't know what you expect me to do."

I coerced him to meet my eyes. "Julián will listen to you. I've seen how every one of those men responds to you. Rafa, Tano, your father's men, even Julián. Their body language changes when you walk in the room. They respect you."

He picked up his keys and took my hand as he stood. "I'll see what I can do, but I'm not promising anything." I stood on my toes and curled my arms tightly around his neck until our mouths met, then kissed him hard, taking him by surprise. His arms wrapped around my back and he gave into the kiss. When we pulled away, we were breathless, and his expression was unsettled, his eyes boring into mine. "You sure know how to put me at your feet," he breathed. "Let's go before you ask me for my car keys."

Chapter 26

In the week that followed, Nata and I did our best to get back into our old routine of being dancers and roommates. It was a bit awkward at first, but I think we both needed to keep that part of our friendship intact.

Opening night was only days away and my nerves were frayed, and not just because of my first performance as a soloist. Introducing my parents to Sebastián throbbed in the back of my mind. I knew Mamá wouldn't be a problem, but Papá...

It was tech week and that meant rehearsals 24/7, so I only saw Sebastián a few times for lunch. We didn't discuss Nata's family further, but I trusted he would handle things. My head was one hundred percent into the rehearsals.

Sergei kept his promise to stay away, and though I suspected he was close by, he didn't let himself or any of the other Russians be seen. Neither he nor Nata brought up the outcome to my conversation with Sebastián. We all waited, silently hoping.

On opening night, the Colón Theater glowed with the timeless charm that made its name famous. With the eclecticism typical of the twentieth century, gold trim and burgundy velvet adorned every inch of its interior. Romantic touches of the Italian Renaissance blended harmoniously with the solidity of German architecture and the pompous exorbitance of the French. Inside the salons, floor-to-ceiling mirrors perpetuated the shimmering gleam of colossal crystal chandeliers.

In the grand foyer, the atmosphere was magical. The air buzzed with vibrant energy. People poured into the main hall in tuxedoes and silky, long gowns. Waiters scurried in and out of the crowd while balancing trays filled with champagne flutes. Anticipation grew as glasses clinked, and when the last call was announced, people hurried to finish their drinks.

Backstage, the main dressing room looked like it had been thrashed by a tornado. As I rushed to my section, I tiptoed around pointe shoes, leg warmers, tights, and all sorts of garments covering the floor. I loved this part of my world and took mental snapshots as I passed. Dancers sat in different positions, sewing ribbons on their shoes, putting on makeup, or stretching wherever they could find open space. Others walked around in various stages of undress, the hard boxes of their satin shoes clacking on the floor.

As soloists, Nata and I were given our own rooms, which provided privacy to get mentally ready. I finished my makeup to the calming sound of the soft classical piece funneling from my portable speaker. The anxiety and fatigue from the past weeks weighed heavily on me. Here I was, getting ready for the most important role I had ever gotten, and I couldn't shake off that tonight, after the show, the moment I had been dreading would be waiting. Sebastián would meet my parents.

"Hey." Marcos flashed a smile from the door, startling me. He looked stunning dressed as Prince Albrecht.

I smiled back, immediately comforted by his presence.

"Your first solo." He bowed deeply and kissed my hand. "You ready?"

"As ready as I'm ever going to be."

"You look incredible," he whispered. His eyes were warm, glinting with what I thought was admiration, and…something else. Something sensual. I pretended to check my mascara. "You're blushing," he said. "You look stunning."

Our eyes met in the mirror for a moment, and that familiar warmth that invaded me so many times in the past when we were alone, filled me once again. I shook it off and smirked at him.

"Smart. Sucking up so you can still crash at my place when you're drunk or Carla kicks your ass out."

He chuckled, a magic sound. He then took a step toward me, and his smile vanished. Taking my hand, he pulled me up and wrapped his arms around my waist.

I stopped breathing.

"I mean it," he whispered so close I could almost taste the mint he was playing with between his teeth. "You're beautiful, Cami, and one helluva dancer. That boyfriend of yours better be a fucking prince to you. Or else."

I stared deep into those caramel eyes, and the warmth swam in my stomach. I knew in that moment I would never be immune to Marcos being this close. Our mouths were inches apart and I shivered.

"Let's do this, babe. It'll be fun." With a swift kiss on the lips, he took my hand in his, and we hurried to our places in the wings.

Dressed in my villager costume, I shifted my weight between my feet, waiting for the curtain to go up. Behind me, a girl from the corps finished hooking the back of my corset. My first role was a small one, one of Giselle's friends in the harvest scene. I jogged in place to stay warm and took a few cleansing breaths. A few feet away, the other villagers clustered around the box of rosin, tapping their feet on the white powder.

"Places, places, please!" the stage manager said.

Marcos hugged me from behind. "*Merde*," he said to my ear, kissing my neck and sending a shiver.

I grinned and stepped onto the stage on cue with the music.

The performance unfolded like a dream. I knew exactly how the audience was feeling. I knew the entire theater was caught under the spell of Nata dancing the romantic *Peasant Pas* with liquid-like movements. Where once was air became a vacuum from the audience holding their breath as the innocent spirit of Giselle slowly came alive with every piqué and pirouette.

Marcos was breathtaking as Albrecht. He was the ultimate prince on stage. As if he were suspended in air, he made his leaps appear completely weightless, landing with the utmost precision. He and Nata performed as if every variation had been created exclusively for them. She melted into his movements with flawless grace, like only Nata could. But then, Marcos had the gift to make any partner look stunning. I watched them, mesmerized, as they traveled across the stage with effortless moves that we all knew were anything but. The characters of Giselle and Albrecht required not only the skills of extraordinary dancers, but experienced actors as well. Nata was still considered young for the role, but her talent had proven to be exceptional.

The story circled around Albrecht, a young duke who fell in love with a village girl, Giselle, the moment he laid eyes on her. Engaged to be married to a duchess and not thinking about the future, Albrecht disguised himself as a villager, escaping the castle to meet Giselle secretly. Immediately charmed by Albrecht, Giselle fell helplessly in love. Their romance continued until Hilarion—a villager also seeking Giselle's love—discovered Albrecht's ruse and exposed him in front of Giselle and the duchess.

Heartbroken and betrayed, Giselle ran off, then stumbled over a sword and plunged it willingly into her heart. Despite Albrecht's attempts to revive her with desperate kisses, Giselle's body lay lifeless on the ground.

Later that night, Albrecht wandered sadly to Giselle's grave, not knowing Hilarion was there as well. He saw Hilarion dancing by her grave, possessed, and remembered the legend of the Wilis, the spirits of girls who perished for love. According to the legend, the Wilis lured young men to their death by forcing them to dance to exhaustion. Soon, Hilarion collapsed, exhausted, and fell into the lake, drowning. Hungry for another soul, the Wilis sought out Albrecht and brought him before their queen, Myrta. Despite his pleading, Myrta was pitiless and commanded the Wilis to engage Albrecht in a deadly dance. Giselle could not bear to let this happen, and even though she could not disobey her queen, she danced with Albrecht so gently and lovingly, he was able to continue till dawn, when the spirit of the Wilis vanished.

Exhausted, Albrecht finally collapsed, and Giselle had just enough time to revive him with tender kisses as she, too, was compelled to fade. Albrecht survived through the strength of Giselle's love for him and once again carried her lifeless body in his arms, back to her grave. As the sun began to rise through the trees, Giselle disappeared forever.

I dove into my role as Queen Myrta and got lost in the enchanted story. I became the music with my sisters, dancing in perfect unison around me as the Wilis.

The anguish in Marcos's face at the loss of Giselle was heart wrenching. I had to hold the tears back, overwhelmed to be on stage with some of the best dancers in the country. They were my family, and we had all worked so hard for this moment. Back at the wing, I panted to recover my breath, wondering what I had done to deserve being here.

We leapt into the final steps of the ballet with our bodies dripping in sweat and our faces glowing. The orchestra ended the last note, and the curtains closed on a heartbroken Albrecht. The audience exploded into deafening applause.

The applause continued for several minutes as the dancers walked in from the wings to take their bows in groups. I caught a quick glimpse of Verónica standing with the corps as a Wili. She shot me an icy glare, a good indication that my performance had been a good one.

I ran from my wing and took a bow, letting the sound of the applause and cheers soak through me. To me, this was the moment when it all came together: the work, the pain, the glory.

Marcos held Nata's hand up as they bowed in unison under a steady stream of whistles and flowers that quickly covered the stage. The crowd cheered louder, and my heart pounded hard against my chest. Somebody handed Nata a huge bouquet of deep-red roses. She nodded her head graciously, thanking the crowd. She then signaled to the maestro, who walked on stage to take a bow himself.

When the curtains finally closed, I hugged Nata and Marcos as we congratulated each other. The energy backstage was electric. Everybody was exhausted but beaming with excitement.

Back in my dressing room, I hurried out of my costume, rushing through the mandatory steps to leave all the pieces ready for the next performance. After a quick shower, I dressed myself in a silky top and black pants. My feet complained when I slipped them into my flats.

Outside the stage entrance, an enthusiastic crowd of the dancers' closest family and friends waited eagerly. I scanned the familiar faces until I found Sebastián. Holy shit. He looked stunning in a tuxedo, holding a gigantic bouquet of tea-colored roses.

This godly man was waiting for *me*.

He cut through the crowd and captured my waist with his free arm, pressing me against his chest. Ignoring my throbbing feet, I rolled to my toes to kiss him. Desire surged through me.

"You were incredible, baby." His warm lips brushed mine. "I am in awe of you." He took my hand and placed it on his chest, over his heart. "Feel," he whispered. His heart raced, pumping hard. Tears threatened, and I closed my eyes, pressing my face against his chest and breathing in the familiar scent of Ralph Lauren.

"Thank you," I murmured.

From a few steps behind us, Rafa nodded a greeting and I thought I saw a hint of pride in his expression. Sebastián kissed my head and pulled away to hand me the flowers.

"For you. *Exactly* twenty-five."

"Pardon?"

"My mother used to say twenty-five was my number. It's creative and adventurous but also caring. I thought that's you too. It could be *our* number." He smiled. "My mother was into astrology. Anyway, here you go."

"They are so beautiful. And my favorite. How did you know?"

He winked and tipped his head down to kiss me. It was soft, sensual, it made my pulse race. But our romantic moment was interrupted by a gentle hand on my back.

My mother.

"Sweetheart, what a fantastic performance." She kissed my cheek and tightened her arms around my waist, squeezing me hard. "I am so proud of you. You made me tear up."

Managing the flowers in one arm, I turned around to hug her, letting my own tears build. I knew this was as big of a moment for my mother as it was for me. She had always been my mentor, but more than anything else, she had been a mother. The best mother, always there with me, every step of the way since I was three years old, enduring auditions, triumphs, rejections. Papá had driven me to classes and waited, reading in the car while I worked restlessly in the studio. The appreciation I felt for my parents, and the emotional buildup of being part of such a big production were suddenly overpowering. I squeezed Mamá tighter and grinned at Papá, who patiently waited for his turn, over her shoulder.

"Cami, sweetie, don't cry. You'll ruin your beautiful makeup." She smiled, wiping a stray tear with her thumb. As a former prima, Mamá knew the letdown of emotions after a performance was always huge, and if I started crying now, there would be no stopping me. In what I figured was an attempt to swing my mood, she turned to Sebastián without bothering to hide her astonishment. "And this must be Sebastián." Mamá's pale blue eyes did an instant scan. I held my breath.

Sebastián gave her a slight nod and leaned down to gently kiss her cheek. "It's a pleasure to meet you, Inés. I've been eager to meet both of you."

Mamá smiled and managed a brief response. Papá's thick hand startled me as he squeezed my shoulder from behind. *Showtime.* I turned and hugged him.

"Be good," I whispered in his ear. He broke the embrace and smirked as he looked over at Sebastián.

"Esteban Navarro," Papá said curtly, extending his hand to shake Sebastián's with a firm grip. "We finally get to meet you." His eyes narrowed a fraction. *Crap. Here we go.*

"Sebastián Palacios. It's a pleasure, Esteban. You have an incredibly talented daughter. You must be very proud."

"I am." Papá's eyes softened as he gazed at me. I tilted my head and smiled at him. He had always been my rock, even during my teen years when my insecurity had skyrocketed. Now here I was...here *we* were, finally tasting some success.

My reverie was suddenly interrupted by an explosion of flashes as a small group of photographers closed in on us, shooting nonstop. Sebastián wrapped his arm protectively around me and shielded our faces while stepping back.

"Sebastián, here! Sebastián, is this your girlfriend?" one of them asked as he aimed the camera at the two of us and shot a string of stills. My parents moved aside, giving way to the intrusive photographers.

"How long have you been together?" another asked. "Are you exclusive?"

"Enough," said Sebastián. "Back off." He nodded at Rafa, who wedged his thick body between us and the photographers.

"Palacios and his ballerina. My boss is going to love it," a short, balding guy said as he fired one last photo.

"Get out of here. You people make me edgy," Rafa said, bumping him. The man quickly retreated and moved on to get shots of Nata and Marcos.

"I'm sorry, sweetheart." Sebastián kissed my forehead. "They're a pest. You'll get used to them, eventually."

I squeezed his hand, *It's okay*, and looked around for my parents. They were standing near Nata a few steps behind. Papá gave me a wary look, shaking his head.

At Piégari, my favorite Italian restaurant, tucked under the 9 de Julio Avenue bridge, a long table dressed in white linens and crystal had been set for the principal dancers and their families. Most of us preferred to wait to eat a big meal after a performance because we were nervous beforehand and had to hold our stomachs in while we danced.

A few of the families were sitting when Sebastián and I arrived. At one end of the table, Marcos and Carla sat next to my parents, who were directly across from the two empty spaces reserved for Sebastián and me. We sat and a waiter immediately filled our glasses with champagne. Marcos locked eyes with Sebastián, and that was that. I couldn't avoid it any longer.

"Marcos," I said, clearing my voice. "This is Sebastián. Sebastián—"

"I'm Marcos." He stretched out his arm across the table to shake Sebastián's hand. "Cami's tango partner." Marcos grinned sardonically.

"I'm Sebastián. Cami's boyfriend." Sebastián's gaze stayed locked on Marcos's in a silent warning. My eyes flew back and forth between them like a ping-pong match. I felt trapped in the middle of two tigers. Which would pounce first?

"Marcos," Mamá said, and I finally exhaled. "You were stunning." She looked at him with adoring eyes. "I remember Baryshnikov as Albrecht. I never thought anyone would ever come close, till tonight."

"Thank you, Inés." Marcos gave her his signature *I know I killed it* smile. My mother blushed slightly. I wanted to crawl under the table.

"What did you think of the Wilis' costumes, Mamá?" I said, gulping the last of my wine. "I heard they cost a fortune. Up close they're a work of art."

"Ah, yes," Mamá said. "Immaculate. A small shop in San Telmo, I heard. They do incredible work."

"Any chance you will partner with Camila anytime soon?" Papá sipped his champagne while addressing Marcos as if I wasn't even there. Beside me, Sebastián shifted in his seat.

"No, Papá," I said, "Marcos is *Nata's* partner. She's the prima, remember?"

"Right," Papá said, nodding. "But that could change, potentially?" He looked over at Marcos, who gave him a wicked grin. The bastard.

"That could indeed change." Marcos nodded back, avoiding my death glare. "In fact, Cami would be a better partner for me height-wise. And Nata partners well with Diego. I wouldn't be surprised to see Cami in more principal roles after tonight. She's doing incredibly well." He finally met my eyes and winked. I wanted to strangle him. Beside me, Sebastián radiated tension.

"I think Camila will be successful no matter who her partner is," said Sebastián, holding Marcos's gaze. "She's very talented." He then turned to me and caressed my cheek. "And passionate." He smiled and I blushed scarlet.

"She is," Marcos said. "Very passionate." He grinned. Sebastián glared at him in another warning.

Marcos was playing a dangerous game and having fun with it. I knew the drill, and in the past, I loved going along with it because it meant pretending that for a little while, Marcos and I were a couple. But things were different now, and I had to stop Marcos before this game became a runaway train.

"Cami," Marcos said, leaning back on his chair and sipping his champagne, "you're still thinking of auditioning for the Aurora part, aren't you?"

"Oh, Aurora!" Mamá cheered. "That was one of my favorites. Cami, you'll audition?"

"Mamá," I mumbled. "It's a long shot."

"It's a great opportunity," Papá said. "Marcos, you'll audition as well?"

"Absolutely," he said smugly before finishing his drink.

"Pass the wine, please," I said with a pointed look at Marcos that said cut it out. They were purposely making Sebastián feel like the outsider. Marcos suppressed a smile and filled my glass before turning his attention to Carla.

I vowed to keep the conversations between Marcos and my parents short through the night. Marcos had been one of my parents' favorite people since I joined the company. Mamá adored him. As a former prima, she was thrilled he was practically family, and I knew for a fact she rooted for us to be more than dance partners. Papá tried to stay neutral, but it was pretty obvious his wishes weren't too different from Mamá's.

The atmosphere at the restaurant lightened as the rest of the families arrived, taking their places along the long table. Nata and her family eventually came and sat on the opposite end of the table, no doubt to stay away from Sebastián.

Sergei sent a steady stream of sullen looks at Sebastián. He seemed agitated and kept downing and refilling his champagne. Rafa and Alexei kept vigil from their own tables in opposite corners. Though Sebastián and the Russians did their best to ignore each other, in the air I could feel an impending storm building.

Mamá sent me a few empathetic looks while Sebastián engaged my father in a conversation about Papá's upcoming hospice project. Sebastián asked a million questions and seemed genuinely interested, which I hoped would help change Papá's mind about him.

"It's truly a great project," Papá said. "It took almost ten years just to get it off the ground."

"I'm glad it's finally in place," Sebastián said, "and that you've put together such a qualified team to work basically pro bono. That's amazing."

"Yes, well, I wish the city mayor thought the same. He has a shifting agenda these days. There's talk that after the elections he might shut the whole thing down if the budget doesn't add up," Papá said, his features hardening.

"The mayor…" Sebastián said, lowering his voice. "You mean, Padilla?"

"The very same." Papá nodded, finishing his drink.

"Hm. I collaborate in a few of his social programs. I can try talking to him," Sebastián said. "A hospice should be at the top of the list, not one of the first things to cut."

Papá's eyes swept the room uneasily. "I appreciate it. But I'd rather handle things without outside interferences."

"Esteban," Sebastián said, "with all due respect, most items in the political agendas are handled with outside help. Especially if there are conflicting interests at stake. I'm not guaranteeing anything, but I can try to open the dialogue with Padilla."

"Thank you. But the answer is still no," said Papá in a stern tone.

"As you wish," said Sebastián calmly. He then excused himself and headed to the restroom.

I waited until he was far enough that he couldn't hear me say: "Papá! That was rude. He was offering you his help."

"And I don't want it. I thought I made that clear. What are you doing with this guy? I don't understand you, really. And I don't want my project to go forward just because now we have access to politicians."

Mamá squeezed his arm to rein him in while Marcos pretended to be busy in conversation with Carla, though I knew he wasn't missing a beat.

"Christ. How can you be so stubborn, Papá? This involves a lot of people. People you care about. You know better than anyone that if that mayor decides to close the hospice down, all those patients will be left bereft. Sebastián can help you."

"No." Papá glowered, his deep brown eyes darkening with the same passion and determination that made him an outstanding doctor. "The day I accept a Palacios's help is the day I turn my back on the hope that things will eventually come for those who choose the right path."

"Papá, that's insulting. You don't even know him."

"Neither do you," he barked, his disapproving expression deepening. I pushed my chair back, looking around in frustration. Papá had such blinders on that sometimes he couldn't see anything but two feet ahead of him. His ideals about the way the world worked were also his demise in times like this. Augh, what was the point in arguing with him?

Marcos topped everyone's glass, smiling widely to break the tension.

"You guys are moving fast here." He signaled to the waiter for another bottle of champagne. "We'll need reinforcements," he said in a conspiratorial tone. "Federico's about to give his speech."

Papá relaxed his shoulders a bit and chuckled. Trust Marcos to swing Papá's mood in an instant. I was grateful for the distraction, but still boiling inside. From across the table, Mamá gave me an empathetic look.

Federico stood and asked for everyone's attention as Sebastián reappeared beside me.

"I'm so sorry," I whispered.

"About?"

"My parents, Marcos. They're just—"

"Don't worry about it," he said, kissing my temple.

"Everyone here tonight deserves a grand celebration," Federico began. "My most talented dancers, you are the best in the country, and you all know it doesn't come without the exceptional hard work and dedication you all commit, day after day…" In my mind, his words faded as the argument with Papá resurfaced. What if he never came around and refused to accept Sebastián? I had never imagined being in a family that was divided. A heavy sense of dread filled me, and I sank back into my seat. Federico wrapped up, raising his glass for a final toast, and everyone clinked their champagne flutes. I felt as if I were watching them through a thick glass.

Madame skipped her speech, as usual, and simply toasted to a triumphant production.

Dinner came and I focused mainly on my food. I was famished and wanted to eat and go to bed, but after a few bites, I lost my appetite. The tension always upset my stomach. Nata looked at me from across the table. She gave me a small smile and raised her glass. I reciprocated, wishing the circumstances were different and we were sitting on the same side of the table. I loved dinners with Nata's family. Her parents had a great sense of humor and enjoyed making me laugh with their half-Spanish, half-Russian jokes while I tried to expand my scant foreign vocabulary. Even Sergei would tell jokes, and everyone downed impossible amounts of alcohol without seeming affected. But tonight, we were not a family. In fact, we looked like enemies in a battlefield, guarded in opposite trenches.

Sitting beside me and across from Marcos, Diego was neutral territory, a buffer. His light sense of humor rerouted Papá's grilling of Sebastián about the Palacios family and their businesses.

Desserts and espressos followed as the night stretched into the late hours, and then the time came for final toasts. I set off to leave when Sergei stood from his seat on the opposite end, raising his champagne flute almost theatrically. "For Natascha and her magnificent role as the beautiful Giselle, a true princess fighting against the bureaucratic oppression of the rich and influential." He turned as he said it, his eyes narrowing on Sebastián.

I felt the blood drain from my face. Sebastián's jaw locked as he slowly shook his head. I cursed under my breath, but Sebastián gently squeezed my knee. I put my hand over his. *Sorry.*

"What was that about?" Papá murmured, frowning.

"I'm not sure." I looked away and hurriedly drank the last of my espresso. "It's getting late. Should we go?" I said to Sebastián, and he nodded.

Despite Sebastián's nonreaction, Sergei didn't let up and walked unsteadily to our end. Rafa and Alexei stood up in unison, ready for whatever came next. Sebastián gave a stern look at Rafa: *Don't.*

"So…Palaciossss," Sergei said, slurring. "What do you say you and I step outside and have a smoke?"

"I don't smoke."

Papá tensed in his seat, his eyes darting from Sergei to Sebastián, then me. I glowered at Sergei. What the hell was he up to?

"A drink, then," Sergei insisted.

"We're leaving," I said. "Another time."

"Nooo good," he said, sneering. "We have things to talk about, he and I." He pointed at Sebastián with his index finger. Rafa and Alexei simultaneously took a step forward, then turned to face each other, two alphas.

"We'll find another time to talk," Sebastián said calmly. "This is Camila's night. And your sister's."

"We talk *now*," he snarled.

The whole table quieted. From their end, Madame and Federico watched us with puzzled expressions. Shit.

"Stand up, Palacios. Business doesn't wait."

"Sergei!" Mr. Zchestakova stepped in from behind Sergei and clasped his son's shoulder. Shoving Sergei back, he barked a reprimand in Russian. Sergei shot a murderous glare at Sebastián, then stumbled as his father scolded him and ushered him to their side of the table. Nata gave me an apologetic look. She turned over to Sergei, and by the way her lips curled, I knew she was letting him have it.

"We'll be going," Papá said in a clipped tone as he stood. He shook Sebastián's hand, and they exchanged a brief good-bye. Sebastián's phone rang, and he said he would meet me at the door.

I escorted my parents to the exit where we waited for the maître d' to bring their coats.

"I don't like any of this, Camila," Papá protested.

"Papá. Nata's family does business with Sebastián's father. But Sebastián isn't involved. There's really nothing for you to worry about, okay?" I said, realizing how naïve I sounded.

"Sweetheart," Papá said, taking my hands in his, "I am *very* worried about you."

"Why?" I said stubbornly.

"Because there is no happy outcome from a relationship with a Palacios."

It was as if he had slapped me. I let go of his hands. "You don't know him."

"It doesn't matter. Don't you see? Everything that surrounds this guy is bad news. I don't want you involved with him," he said firmly. His eyes were dark, his tone serious.

"That's not your choice," I said, holding back a sudden rush of tears. "I care about him, Papá. It doesn't matter what anyone thinks. This is *my* life, and I'm happy with him. If you'd bother to know him, you would realize he's good, selfless, and considerate. He's *not* his family. And he treats me like I'm a...princess or something. Like he's lucky to be with me."

"He is!"

"It's late, and I'm tired." I kissed my mother quickly and she pulled me into her arms.

"Camila, sweetie," she said. "We care about you. You've worked so hard to get here. Just remember that, please."

"Good night."

"Okay, okay. It's enough, I know. But we're still your parents." She pulled away, searching my eyes. "We love you."

"I know." I wiped my cheeks. "Good-bye, Mamá, Papá. Thank you both for coming."

Papá enclosed me in his arms and squeezed me hard. "Please, please think about the choices you make. The way you've always done. You know how much we love you Camila. I'm so proud of you."

I nodded. "I love you too. Enjoy your trip to Europe. Tell Javi and the girls I love them."

Sebastián interlaced his fingers with mine as we walked outside to wait for the car. The tension of the night was suddenly overwhelming.

"I'm sorry, about all of it," I said. "I wish everyone would just mind their own business."

"I'm the one who should apologize. I told you, my family—"

"*My* family and *my* friends were the ones making a scene. It was embarrassing."

"Your parents were just being protective. I don't hold that against them. I have to say, though, if I hear the name Marcos one more time—"

"I know! I'm sorry about that too. Marcos is probably the only person my parents wouldn't object to because he's a dancer and that could actually *improve* my career." I sighed heavily. "It's exhausting."

"Yeah well, he wants you. *I* object to that."

"I'm so tired. Do you mind if I sleep at my place tonight? I'm completely out of laundry. I can come to your house in the morning after I do a couple of loads."

"Sure." He nodded, his expression grave as his gaze got lost somewhere in the distance. Cars passed by, splashing through the remainders of an earlier rain. I shivered in my coat and reached for his hand.

"Despite that crazy dinner," I said, "I'm glad you came to watch me dance. This was a big night, and you being there means so much to me."

He tugged on my hand and enveloped me. I slid my hands under his coat the way I loved doing, and pressed my face to him, relishing his warmth.

"I've missed you so much," I said, pressing my face to his chest. "I hated not being with you for so many days."

"I've missed you too." He squeezed me tighter. "Cami, I don't want to make things difficult for you," he said. "Your career is just starting."

"You're not making things difficult."

"You know that's not true. Thing is, I'm used to people reacting that way to me, and I don't care. But you...you have so much going for you."

"It's going to be okay," I said, looking up without letting go of him.

"Cami." He pulled away and searched my eyes. "Not one of the people who are closest to you approves of you being with me. I don't want to drag you to a place where people shut you out because you're with me." Fatigue etched his eyes and I wanted to kiss him. Instead, I gripped his coat at the chest.

"I won't let anyone tell me who I can or cannot be with. I told you that before." As I said it, my gaze went past Sebastián and stopped on Sergei walking out of the restaurant. He stood still, watching us, his eyes narrowed. I held his stare, but a second later, the BMW pulled into view. "I changed my mind," I said to Sebastián. "Let's go back to your house."

Chapter 27

Scorching heat enveloping my body woke me. Sebastián's arm was locked around my waist, his chest pressed against my back, and our legs tangled. The bleaching glare of a midmorning sun filled the spacious bedroom. A sudden rush of panic seized me. I was late for work. Wait, no. I relaxed, remembering I was off for the next few days. I grinned. I would finally get to spend time with Sebastián.

My head throbbed from the mix of wine and champagne the night before, and I decided Marcél's heavenly coffee would be my fix. I shifted carefully under Sebastián, but the arm around me tightened. Warm lips met my neck.

"Where do you think you're going?"

"You are too hot."

"You're not bad yourself." A soft chuckle tickled my hair.

I slapped his naked side playfully. "Get off. I need a shower. And coffee. *Strong* coffee."

"*Get off?*" he said against my neck. "Oh yes, my queen. At your service." In one move, he flipped me around, pinning me under him. His knees pushed my legs apart. I tried fighting him, then inhaled sharply as his hard-on pressed my clit. A sudden gust of desire whirled in my stomach as his mouth devoured mine hungrily, warm and wet. I wrapped my legs around his waist and squeezed him.

"Impatient, are we?" His breath was hot and his hips teased me with slow, erotic movements. I clenched my hands in his hair, and our eyes met.

"I always want more with you."

"Lucky me," he said against my mouth. His fingers traveled down my side, leaving goose bumps in their path. He cupped my breast, and my nipples immediately hardened. My body already knew him well, anticipating and responding to his every move. A growing ache writhed inside me, and I tightened my legs around him. God, I wanted him. I gently bit his bottom lip while digging my fingers into his glorious back. He lifted his head and smiled.

I was breathing hard, admiring him through half-open eyes. His fingers grazed my thighs and slid between my legs, working their magic as they glided in and out of me, torturing me. I clutched the sheets at my sides and squeezed my eyes shut.

"Sebastián...*please*."

"Please...what?" He panted. "*Tell me* what you want."

The sweet urge between my legs intensified. I moaned. "I want you inside me. *Now.*"

Groaning in my mouth, he moved his hands to hold mine, threading our fingers and thrust into me. I gasped as he filled me, my muscles clenching hungrily around him. It was deep, intense. I let him possess me, savoring every second. He moved slow, oh so slow, torturing and beautiful. My mind drifted and my body took charge, meeting him move for move.

"You...feel...so fucking good..." His chopped, erotic breaths blended with mine as our mouths collided. I could barely hold on. I tried to make a mental effort not to come just yet, but after having spent so much time apart the last week, my body wasn't up for debating.

His pace accelerated and my head spun, my muscles quickening. *God.* He slammed into me once more, and I think I blacked out. All I remembered was floating, weightless.

He kissed the corners of my mouth, his lips following the contour of my jaw, nibbling softly.

"Good morning." He smiled against my mouth.

I chuckled. "You can wake me up like this whenever you want."

"You are a goddess," he whispered. "So sensual. And my bed was lonely without you."

"Hmhm..."

"Your Highness got what she wanted?"

"Hmmh..."

Soft laughter tickled my shoulder. "I'm famished. Let's eat. I need to get my strength back before I make up my mind to spend the day between your legs." He kissed me chastely and stepped off the bed, pulling me up with him. Then in one move, he threw me over his shoulder. I gasped and kicked my feet in the air, squealing.

"You can't…" I giggled. "Put me down!"

He laughed, carrying me into the gargantuan shower stall. As he opened the door, warm water began cascading from several shower heads. He slid me to the floor and kissed me hard, pinning my body against the cool marble wall. I shivered and buried myself in his arms. *God help me.*

Sebastián sat at the bar, intent on a newspaper. I smiled at the fact that he was reading an actual paper. There was something vintage and kind of sexy about it. I took a seat beside him, and Marcél placed a tray with coffee and fresh pastries on the counter. A warm smile creased his face.

"Marcél, good morning," I said. "You can't spoil me like this. My breakfast is usually a banana."

"*Ma chérie*, it's my pleasure. And after such a week, you need your strength."

"Thank you." I blushed, thinking of all the reasons why I needed my strength, which had nothing to do with dancing.

Sebastián kissed my cheek. "You're adorable when you blush." As he pulled away, he nodded at a page in the social section. "Looks like we made the papers." A center photo featured the two of us outside the theater the night before. He looked dreamy in his tuxedo. I looked…startled. The headline read: *Palacios and His Ballerina. She's Fearless!*

I glanced up at Sebastián and he was frowning.

"I told you, the media's a pest," he said. "Anything to print the Palacios name in the gossip section. We may have to do something."

"Do something?"

"Throw money at them." He sighed. "The only way to get those dogs off our backs."

"Are you serious?"

"Money is usually the only thing that's effective," he said sternly. "It's either that, or they broadcast every move. It's one thing if they're after me, but I don't want you involved in my father's crap."

I thought about that for a moment. I had been having fun with the attention, but what would Madame say when she saw my photo in the most popular newspaper in the city? And Federico? Would this be a problem at work? Reading my mind, Sebastián slid his hand behind my neck and kissed me softly.

"Don't worry about it. For the moment it's just a photo, and a little publicity never hurt anyone. I'll take care of it."

I nodded, unsure what to make of it. "So, what's up for today?"

"I figured we could take it easy, so you can rest?"

"I actually wouldn't mind that." I sighed, stretching my neck. "I'm tired and sore everywhere."

A wicked smile stretched across his face.

I rolled my eyes. "You know what I meant."

"Yes. I do." He winked, making my cheeks burn again. "Come here. I have something to tell you." He took my hand and interlaced our fingers. "Julián agreed to release one of the Russian cargoes. That's all he's willing to do for now, but it's the main one and a step forward."

"Really? Oh, Sebastián, thank you. Thank you so much." I squeezed my arms around his neck and kissed him with everything I had.

"I'm starting to look forward to the way you thank me," he murmured against my mouth.

I kissed him again and leaned back to look into his eyes. "That is such good news. Did it just happen?"

"Yesterday actually."

"Yesterday? So when we were having dinner, you already knew the cargoes would be released?"

"Of course I knew."

"Sergei made that scene...and you didn't budge."

"Sergei needs to learn to control his temper."

"Right, but wouldn't it have been easier to settle things right then?"

He shook his head. "No, the Zchestakovas need to know we are in charge, not them."

"I don't get it. Either way, I'm glad you convinced Julián. I was so worried about Nata. She looked stressed lately."

"The truth is," he said, brushing my hair back with his fingers, "having cargoes on hold isn't good for anyone. It's in our best interest to release them. Julián knows that. He doesn't want the Russians thinking they have leverage, so he's been stretching things out. But it's been long enough, and my father's tired of those cargoes taking up so much space. Besides, I owed Sergei one. The information he unintentionally gave me at Julián's party allowed me to keep the girls safe."

"I'm glad. I've been so worried about them. And Nata, she'll be so happy. I can't wait to tell her the good news." I slid back onto my seat, letting out a long breath. "Why don't we spend the day by the pool today? It's warm and I've missed the sun. My friends are meeting at a new bar tonight. We can go with them." I bit into a warm croissant and moaned. Mmmm...heavenly.

Sebastián frowned at my food orgasm.

"Sorry." I chuckled. "This is so good. And I'm famished."

"No. I'm thinking I need to go to Julián's tonight. The studio is starting a big project on Monday. We won the bid against some of the best architects in Buenos Aires, and I want to make sure I go through the final details with Julián before we break ground." He reached for my hand. "Why don't we just stay here tonight? After I'm done with Julián, I'll come home and we can order food in, watch a movie. Whatever you want."

"That sounds great, but I really want to see my friends tonight. Could we do the night in tomorrow? It's the first time we all go out together after *Giselle*. We've been doing nothing but work. I miss hanging out with them, and most are going away tomorrow till the break ends. I can come back here afterward, but I want to go."

"I haven't seen you much lately, either. All you do is dance, and when we are together, you're always exhausted. Stay here and rest, so we can have some normal time together."

"Since we met, I've spent every free minute I have with you. I haven't seen my friends outside the theater in ages. I'm not complaining, but I've made a lot of adjustments since you came into my life."

His jaw hardened. "I've adjusted too. I've been patient, flexible, even though it hasn't been easy on my end."

"I know you have, but I'm a *dancer* and my career's just starting. My life focus is performance after performance. I need some social balance once in a while. I don't want that to come between us."

"I know." He closed his eyes as if reining in his patience. "I'm trying to find the way. Look, I don't mind you seeing your friends. It's good to have that balance. But tonight, I want us to spend time together. I know it's selfish, but I want you with me as much as I can get you."

I placed my hands on his biceps, searching his eyes. "I'm right *here*."

"You are, and you aren't. Stay. We can…celebrate."

Crap. Seriously. I wasn't leaving the country, I just wanted to hang out with my friends for one night. I fought the urge to push away from him and tried another tactic.

"I'll come back here afterwards. We'll spend the rest of the night together." I pressed another soft kiss on his mouth. He didn't pull away but let out a sigh of resignation.

"What bar are they going to?"

"Isabel, in Palermo Hollywood. I heard it's really cool. I've been wanting to go for a while."

His jaw tensed. "I'd rather you didn't."

What the fuck. I pulled away. "Why?"

"Because it's a place I would like to take you to."

"Possessive much?"

His lips pressed into a straight line.

"Sebastián, what is this about?"

Anger and frustration flashed across his pale irises.

"What?" I said.

"I don't want Marcos's fucking hands all over you," he growled.

"What the hell is that supposed to mean?"

"You know exactly what it means."

"Is this about last night?"

"It's about all the fucking times he's around. About the way he greets you, the way he touches you, like he's somehow entitled. It's bad enough he's your dance partner. I don't want you hanging out with him at a bar. At *that* fucking bar."

I sighed. "Let's not do this. I'm not going out with Marcos. I'm going out with a group."

"Will *he* be there." It was a question but he made it sound like a statement.

"He's dating Carla. Are we really having this conversation again?"

"Answer my question. Will he be there?" His jaw didn't give, and jealousy blazed in his eyes. Fuck. I threw my hands up in defeat and stood, needing to put space between us. Adrenaline surged in my veins.

"Yes, *he* will be there, but he is dating *Carla,* and I'm with *you*, so stop this control freak shit and tell me you are okay with me seeing my friends, because that is a deal breaker for me, Sebastián."

"A *deal breaker*?" he said, louder, narrowing his eyes. "The fact that Marcos thinks he can put his fucking hands all over you is *my* deal breaker, babe."

"It's not what you think!"

"It is not what *you* think. For fuck's sake."

My heart was racing, I felt like a corralled rabbit. But I couldn't back down.

"Sebastián. You have to trust me."

He rubbed his forehead in frustration. "I do trust you. But Marcos has feelings for you. I can't say I blame him, but he needs to back the fuck off."

"He's a friend and a dance partner. Part of the package," I said, looking straight at him. Standing my ground felt good. "Besides…" I winced. "I haven't said anything more about Mercedes and the way she fucking hounds you. What about *that?*"

"*Hounds* me? Don't be ridiculous." He scowled. "Mercedes is like my sister."

"Yeah," I scoffed. "I don't think she sees you that way."

"What are you talking about?"

"The night of the party she damn made sure I knew you're *hers*."

"What?"

"Yup. She instructed me to go back to 'whatever little suburb I came from' because I didn't belong in *your* world."

He shook his head. "I'm sorry about that. She was out of line. Mercedes is very territorial with people outside the family. I've already talked to her about it. She felt bad you took whatever she said seriously."

"Right." I raised my palms. "Whatever. Look, I want to go out. You're welcome to come with me, but I'm going."

He pushed his barstool back. "Have it your way." He cursed under his breath and stormed out.

Staring at the open door, I dropped back on my seat, my heart racing as I clenched my teeth to fight the tears. Shit. Our issues went deeper than I had thought.

I took my cup to the sink, leaving his on the counter in a pathetic protest, then left to get my things.

In the bedroom, there were no signs of Sebastián, and I felt relieved. I shot a quick look at the empty bed where we had been so happy just moments ago. My throat tightened, and I couldn't stop the tears that spilled. I looked around for my clothes and found them on a chair, neatly folded in a pile. How could he be so infuriating and so sweet? My heart sank deeper. I threw them in my bag and called a cab. I was stalking down the hallway when I almost stumbled into Marcél. He stepped back.

"Camila, *ma chérie*, are you all right?"

I met his worried eyes and bit my quivering lip. "Yes, I'm fine. Will you please tell Sebastián I took a taxi home?"

"Of course. The taxi's already here. I was coming to let you know. But, if I may, I think Sebastián would prefer that Rafa takes you home. I can get him in just a moment. We can cancel the taxi."

I shook my head. "Thank you, but I'll take the taxi." I offered him a half smile and he nodded, placing a gentle hand on my shoulder.

"*Ma chérie*, be patient please. Sebastián can be stubborn. He's not used to compromising. But he cares about you, very much."

I swallowed through the ache in my throat and nodded, then quickly turned and rushed to the door.

Chapter 28

I unlocked the front door to my apartment and was immediately relieved to hear music coming from Nata's room.

"Nata? You home?"

"*Back here*," she sang.

In her bedroom, Nata walked back and forth between the closet and the bed, carrying hangers with clothes. She smiled when she saw me. I chuckled at the obscene amount of garments scattered all over her bed. This was my old friend.

"Are you moving?"

"No!" She scowled, horrified. "These are new."

"I thought you were worried about money."

"I am. Teo knows what's going on, and he insisted on taking me shopping to celebrate opening night. It's an excuse, I know. But honestly, it helped take my mind off things." Dropping the clothes on the bed, she pulled me into a hug. "It's good to see you. I worried after you didn't come home last night. I was so angry with Sergei. Look," she said, pulling away, "I got stuff for you too. An olive branch after everything we've put you through. Don't worry, I've paid for these myself."

"Nata, no. You don't have to buy me stuff."

"I know, but I wanted to, really. Don't be mad. I'm not trying to buy you or anything. It's just a way for me to thank you for interceding for us." She smiled affectionately. "Why don't you wear this tonight?" She signaled theatrically to a pair of skinny jeans and a coral silk top laid on her bed.

"Okay. What? I *love* these." I bit my lip in guilt and pulled her into a hug. "Ugh. Thank you. I hate all this other stuff that got between us. I'm still…coming to terms with all I've learned about your family. It's a shock. But I had no idea things were so tough for you guys here. I can be so clueless. I'm sorry if you felt you couldn't trust me."

"Hey." She held my shoulders, searching my eyes. "It's not your fault. Or mine." She shrugged. "We'll figure it out."

"Actually, there's no need. I couldn't wait to tell you and got distracted by all this. Sorry! Sebastián talked to Julián and got him to release one of the cargoes on hold. The main one, he said."

Her eyes widened. "Seriously?" She wrapped me into a death grip. "Oh God, that's great news. Thank you!"

"It was Sebastián, not me."

"Yeah, but he did it for you. Seriously, thank you."

"Let's try our new clothes on."

It felt good to be around Nata without Sergei and Sebastián, and my parents, and the Russians, and all the crap from the outside world. It all vanished, and we were back to being two girls getting ready for a night out.

I let her do my hair and makeup, knowing she would go all out. When she was done, she turned my chair to the mirror.

"Do you like it?" She smiled.

I blinked at my foxy reflection. She had traced my eyes with black kohl and smoky eye shadow, and my hair was up in a high ponytail that swirled at the end. She loaned me a pair of hoop earrings and a wide, silver cuff that hugged my wrist. My mood dipped at the thought that Sebastián wouldn't get to see me all done up. Nata noticed the change in my expression.

"You don't like it. I can try something different."

"No, It's not that." I frowned, looking down. "I…"

"Tell me."

"I just…I had a fight with Sebastián about Marcos," I said hesitantly. I wasn't sure I was ready to talk to Nata about my issues with Sebastián. I watched for any change in her patient expression, but her face was neutral.

"I see."

"We don't have to talk about it," I said. "It'll be all right."

She squeezed my hand. "No, I know this has put distance between us, but I want you to talk to me. The way we used to."

I nodded. I wanted that too.

"What's going on?" she said.

I shrugged. "He's jealous. He thinks Marcos is more than a friend."

"Marcos needs to keep his hands to himself."

"Whose side are you on?"

"Yours. But you know I'm right. You have to set boundaries. Honestly, I don't like that he plays with you the way he does. You used to have strong feelings for him. What, all that is like, gone now?"

"Yes, it's gone," I said. "I want to be with Sebastián. Not Marcos."

"Listen, you know I have your back, always. And it hasn't been easy getting used to the idea of you and Sebastián. But he has a point."

"You, defending Sebastián? *That*, I wasn't ready for."

"I'm not defending him. I just want you to open your eyes and protect yourself more when it comes to Marcos. Whether you want to admit it or not, he will always have an effect on you, and the only way to control that is by putting some physical boundaries between you two. Outside of work, he shouldn't manhandle you."

I was about to speak, but she raised a palm, and I closed my mouth.

"Just think about it. Come on. Let's get out of here."

It was past eleven when the taxi pulled into the crooked streets of Palermo Hollywood. Outside Isabel, Marcos stood with other dancers in conversation. The street was alive. People gathered and walked by, dressed for a night out. Music funneled out from the bars, mixing with laughter and friends greeting each other. It felt good to be out, free.

Wearing an indecently short dress, Daniela, a principal in the company, hugged the doorman at Isabel affectionately, which granted us a quick entrance of cutting the line.

Inside, the place was surreal, and I immediately understood why Sebastián wanted to come here together. The main area was a gargantuan living room with Art Decó sofas upholstered in green velvet. To the beat of the music, lights phased into different shades on a ceiling that, according to Dani, was inspired by the Whitney Museum of American Art in New York. A bar wrapped around one side and behind it, hundreds of liquor bottles filled floating shelves lit from underneath. I grinned at everything, thrilled to finally be out with my friends in such a cool place.

We took over an open area with crescent-shaped sofas, and everyone ordered appetizers and drinks. Marcos wedged himself between another dancer and me, wrapping a muscular arm around my shoulders while deep in discussion with Diego about a recent soccer game. Nata shot me a *See what I mean?* look and I rolled my eyes, shifting under Marcos's arm. He tightened his grip, flashing me a quick smile before going back to his conversation.

After a couple of drinks, I needed to find the restroom. When I pushed through the door, my head spun. The alcohol swimming in my head was enhanced by the endless effect of a mirror-paneled ceiling and walls. My mind kept going back to Sebastián and how much he would have liked the overall design of this place. Dread filled me at the thought of him with Julián instead of me.

I rejoined the group, and Marcos gripped my hand, then led me to the dance floor. I hadn't seen Carla all night and wondered if things were tense between them again. Their relationship was volatile, so the rest of us stayed clear. He pulled me into a slow dance and kissed my neck.

"Marcos."

"Hi, babe. It's been ages. I've fucking missed you." He smiled, his glassy eyes crinkling at the corners. "Give me some love." His arm snaked around my waist to bring me closer as he pressed soft kisses on my neck. Lemon and vodka laced his breath. Awesome.

"It's good to see you too."

His hands stroked my back as he swayed us to the music. Pressing me against him, he suddenly hardened. I tensed, but he squeezed me tighter. Shit. *Shit.*

"Marcos." I put my hands on his chest and pushed away.

"Sorry." He smiled, pulling me back to him.

I detangled from him and gestured to the bar. "Let's have a drink." I immediately regretted saying that. He didn't need more alcohol, but I needed out.

Marcos reluctantly followed. I slid onto a barstool and ordered a vodka tonic. The barman nodded and flashed me a flirty smile. Marcos shot him a dirty look, then turned to me. He gave my outfit the once-over and winked.

"You look hot tonight, sweetie."

"Where's Carla?" I said.

Marcos rubbed the back of his head as if the question had stabbed him there. "Who the fuck knows. We had a fight today. She's pissed." He sighed, scanning the crowd. "I think we need some space. Can I crash at your place tonight?"

"Sure, but why? What's going on?"

He raised his eyebrows, shaking his head in exasperation. "Fuck, I don't know. She wants more, I guess. They always want more. Why can't all girls be like you, Cams? You never ask anything of me."

"You and I aren't dating, that's why I don't want *more*. Stop being such a dick to Carla. I know she matters to you."

He eyed me for a moment. "Maybe she's not it. Maybe I'm better off with someone like you." His gaze stayed on me, challenging me. Fuck. *Fuck.*

"The only reason you're saying that is because you're scared of where things may go with her, which proves my point that you really do care. Maybe more than you're willing to admit." I sipped my drink and frowned. It was strong.

Marcos grabbed my hand, pulling me to him until I was pressed against his chest. Shit. *Boundaries would be good, Camila.*

"Marcos, I'm trying to talk to you."

"I'm done talking. Let's go back to dancing," he whispered in my ear. A few weeks ago I would've been thrilled. I liked dancing with him, and he was sexy and fun. But Sebastián's and Nata's words about Marcos's hands all over me sent guilt flashing through me. I grabbed his wrists from behind my back and pulled them away.

"Marcos, I can't. I'm dating Sebastián. We can't fool around like we used to."

He smiled. Then his hand reached behind my head and curled my long ponytail around his wrist, bringing my face to his. "You're my best friend. I don't ever want to lose that," he whispered. "But…"

I opened my mouth to argue, but an iron arm yanked me back by the waist, forcing Marcos's hand to unwrap painfully from my hair.

"Get your fucking hands off her." Sebastián's voice cut through the music, his tone charged with pulsing anger.

Marcos frowned. "What the fuck?" Then he recognized Sebastián, and his expression relaxed into a smirk of recognition. "Oh, yeah. The *boyfriend*."

"Damn right. And I'm just about to knock your fucking teeth out if you don't keep your hands off her." He stepped in front of me and right up to Marcos's face.

Marcos straightened and hissed, "Fuck off." His eyes blazed.

Shit. I knew Marcos wouldn't back down. He didn't take crap from anyone, much less if they provoked him. But even though Marcos was six feet tall, Sebastián still looked down at him.

"Stay the fuck away from her. I mean it." Sebastián gripped Marcos's shoulder forcefully. Marcos shoved his hand off without breaking eye contact.

Shit. *Shit*. I wedged myself between them, facing Sebastián. I looked over at the barman for help, but he glanced at Sebastián and smiled. *Asshole*. What the hell was this place? I turned to Sebastián.

"Sebastián, let it go," I said. "Please," I whispered.

He glared at Marcos. "That was your only warning." He then clutched my hand and tugged me toward the back.

We cut through the crowd and I stumbled to keep up. He stopped at a hallway at the very back and I yanked my hand away. I was so mad I wanted to punch him.

"Let's talk in there." He pushed through a closed door behind me. *What the fuck?*

"You can't just walk in there."

"Camila, stop pushing my limits. I want to talk to you somewhere quieter," he said, his nostrils flaring.

I stormed in without making eye contact. It was one of those VIP rooms reserved for private parties. Someone would walk in at any moment and kick us out. We would be on a banned list, and I would never be able to get in anywhere cool ever again. Asshole. I crossed my arms and pressed myself against the bar, close to the door and away from him.

"You know," I said, "for someone who's such a progressive negotiator, you're more in line with a caveman."

A muscle twitched in his jaw. Good. Now that he had ruined my night, he could brew in his own anger. I didn't give a shit. He ran both hands through his hair, looking around.

"What the fuck, Camila."

"What are you doing here? I thought you were busy," I said. Shit. *Shit.* I would never hear the end of this now.

"That's what you have to say? After what I walked into back there?"

"That wasn't what you think it was."

"I'm getting fucking tired of this argument. He was all over you. What the fuck?"

I looked away. Shit. "Someone's going to walk in here. I don't want to get kicked out."

"It's fine."

"No, it isn't. I want to go. I'm uncomfortable here."

"I own this place," he muttered through tight lips.

This time I looked straight at him. "You what? You *own* this place? As in, you own this whole bar?" Fuck. Of course he did. The design, the crowd, the asshole barman. It all added up. "Jesus, what else? What else do you own that I don't know about?"

Yup. I walked right into that one, and realized as soon as the words came out. With one move, his hands were on my ass, lifting me onto the bar as he pressed himself between my legs. He smothered my gasp with his mouth, claiming mine as his tongue thrust between my lips. I stilled, shocked, blazing with anger and...dammit, annoyingly, so fucking turned on. He bit my bottom lip, breathing heavily as he pushed his hard-on against me. Desire exploded inside me, and my anger morphed into lust. I clenched my fists in his hair. His hands cupped my breasts over the silky fabric of my top, and my nipples throbbed against his palms. I breathed hard on his neck. He tugged down my zipper and peeled off my jeans, tracing his fingers up my thighs. Moist heat pooled between my legs as his mouth devoured mine. He unzipped his jeans, then slipped two fingers under the lace of my panties and ripped them off with one tug. My breathing stuttered. He parted my legs wider, squeezing the inside of my thighs, then he laid me back onto the bar, and his hand traced the path from my neck to my stomach. I felt completely exposed, but I didn't care. I just wanted him to fuck me on top of that bar, feed the ravenous need I had for him. Somewhere in the back of my mind, a single bell chimed. *Slow down.* But his intoxicating scent, his hands, his mouth. They mixed together, blinding my senses, clouding my head.

His thumb stroked my clit. "You are so wet," he muttered. "You drive me insane." His voice was hoarse, sending goose bumps along my skin. He climbed over me as I watched him with hooded, spellbound eyes. He was so fucking sexy, all ruffled up, his hair a glorious mess. Lowering himself to me, he ravaged my mouth with his, then my neck. His tongue traced my collarbone, his lips devouring my blazing skin as I moaned. His mouth seized mine in a savage kiss while he spread my legs wider, his cock grinding against me. Then he thrust inside me and began moving, pumping hard, pushing me to the verge of climax. I yanked his hair harder, and a low groan sounded deep in his throat. Hot, broken breaths licked my neck as he slammed inside me, again and again.

"You. Are. *Mine.*" He pumped harder on the last word, and we came together, sweet breaths colliding against each other's mouths.

He hugged me tight through the aftershocks of our climax. We stayed like that for a second, or an eternity, I couldn't tell. He cupped my face, and his lips traced the line from my jaw to my mouth and kissed each corner. Our eyes met, and the dark rage from minutes ago was replaced by the deep stillness of a lake. I held his face in my hands, looking into his clear eyes. This man. *Dammit.* So possessive, dominant. Our worlds were incompatible in so many ways and yet, I couldn't let go.

"What am I going to do with you?" I whispered. He pressed a soft kiss on my mouth.

"You're going to stop fighting the fact that you belong with me, so your friend out there can live a long, happy life with someone else."

"You can't go around claiming me like I'm something you bought."

"He had your hair wrapped in his fucking hand," he muttered through his teeth. Pulling away, he turned to pick up his jeans before sliding them on. I sat up.

"Sebastián—"

"Look. I get that he's your dance partner. But outside of work he doesn't get to put his fucking hands on you."

"Okay, yes. But you have to let me take care of that part. I know…that's not what it looked like back there, but I promise you I will. Please trust me."

He pressed his lips into a straight line, and I reached up and ran my fingers over his stubble. His beautiful face relaxed a fraction, and he helped me off the bar. I picked up my jeans and lifted up my ripped panties.

"I have no underwear." I sighed. He gave me an innocent smile, and I shook my head, pulling my jeans on. "You're lucky I like you so much."

He came closer and circled his arms around my waist, bringing me to him, leaning his forehead to mine. "It may not make you lucky, but I love you," he said, his expression serious. I froze, the air leaving my lungs at once.

"What?"

"You heard me." Those clear blue eyes watched me with love and adoration. "I know it's soon and everything is moving fast, but I'm in love with you. There's no one else for me, Camila, that's why I'm so possessive about you. You're my sun, my hope. You make me want to be a better man. I want to be the man you deserve and give you everything. I want to lay the world at your feet."

I closed my eyes. God, this man. And I had fallen for him too. So hard I no longer knew which way was up.

"Sebastián..."

He kissed me deeply and the world spun. And I knew there was no one else for me either. I just wanted to be here, with him.

Chapter 29

"These look great," I said. "The kids are going to love them." I folded the last soccer shirt and placed it back into the box.

"This is the best part of this whole thing. You'll see," Sebastián said, sliding the box into the van Rafa and Tano were loading.

Excitement surged through me. In that moment, he wasn't the powerful entrepreneur, or the son of the Argentinean customs boss. He was simply someone who couldn't wait to put a smile on the faces of unprivileged kids.

Tano and Rafa got in the van, and Sebastián led me to a small Renault Clío parked behind it.

"Whose car is this?" I said, getting in.

"Mine. I keep something low profile for the visits to the schools. The other cars are too conspicuous. I would be an easy target."

"Target? For whom?"

"A van full of soccer uniforms, supplies, and food makes a very attractive bounty. No need to add a Beemer behind it. Especially in the areas where we take this project," he said, pulling into traffic behind Rafa.

"Oh." I shuddered inwardly. Was he a constant target? And by being with him, was I one too? I pushed the thought away. "So how many schools are we visiting?"

"Just one today. I like to stay and play a soccer game with the kids. I usually start the teams and coach them until we find someone full-time. This school has a new coach, and I can't wait to see how they've progressed."

"So, I get to watch you play?"

"Yup. Lucky you."

We drove north through San Fernando, Beccar, and Victoria, then turned west. As we left the freeway behind, the neighborhoods became more humble, rural. Tiny houses on dirt roads. Most had bars on the windows, their small yards barely a patch of dirt. Along the back of the modest lots, clotheslines crossed from one end to the other, the garments flapping in the midday breeze.

Chickens wandered loose here and there, and from behind a wire fence, a stray dog barked a protest when we passed by.

We turned into a narrow dirt road lined by houses on both sides. Sebastián parked outside a white building I assumed was the school. The air was warm and doused with the aroma of freshly cut grass and baked dirt. From across the street, a woman in a black dress waved as she hurried to us.

"Sebastián, finally. So good to see you, *mijo*. The kids been waitin' for you." In the midmorning sun, her deep black eyes shone like dimes. They were etched with shrewdness, the way I imagined a fortune-teller's. She then looked from Sebastián to me, regarding me with curiosity.

"Rosa, this is Camila, my girlfriend."

"Welcome, welcome." She hugged me, then smiled at Sebastián. "She's a princess."

"Yes, she is. My princess."

A stampede of school kids in white pinafores charged us and crowded around Sebastián, pushing through to wrap their arms around him however they could. They ranged from six years old to middle school age. The little ones got Sebastián's legs, while the bigger ones hugged him over the others. Sebastián stumbled, chuckling. The decibel level was unreal as the kids yelled greetings and questions over each other. Father Juan Pablo appeared from behind the kids, wearing a wide smile. I didn't remember ever seeing a happier bunch.

"Camila," Father JP yelled over the kids as he cut through to greet me, nodding toward Sebastián. "They love him here."

"I'd say."

Father JP led me to the van where Rafa and Tano were unloading the boxes and separating them in stacks.

"Good to see you, Father. The uniforms are in those boxes over there," said Rafa, signaling with his head. "Tano and I will bring the rest inside."

An older man with a crooked back and a labored pace approached from the school building. He shook his head, smiling at Sebastián who was still barricaded by the growing crowd of kids. Father JP introduced him to me as

Eduardo, the school principal. His white hair was neatly combed back, his face heavily creased with lines of wisdom.

"Camila, it's a pleasure. Welcome. The kids hurried their lunch today because they knew he was coming." He turned to watch Sebastián. "He's their guardian angel, you know. Gives these kids hope in people. God knows most of them here need it."

Principal Eduardo ordered the kids to scatter and return to the playground. They tugged on Sebastián's arms, pulling him along with them. We followed them to the school building, a humble structure of concrete and peeling paint. The classrooms bordered a courtyard of crooked tiles where boys and girls played games of basketball, jump rope, hopscotch, and elastic bands. Some rushed over to greet and hug Sebastián.

The back of the school was a large patch of grass that had been turned into a soccer field fenced with chicken wire. Father JP and Principal Eduardo divided the kids by age groups, directing them to stand in single lines. With the help of Rafa and Tano, they opened the boxes and handed each kid a soccer jersey embroidered with their team name; shorts, cleats, and a pair of matching socks. The kids hurried out of their pinafores and tried on the uniforms over their clothes.

I hadn't noticed until then that there were only boys in the lines. The girls were gathered in a single group farther behind.

"What about them? The girls?" I asked Father JP.

"The girls don't want to play soccer, so Sebastián brings them other things."

"Like what?"

"You name it. New clothes, jump ropes, art supplies, music, nail polish. Whatever they ask him for."

"Really?"

"Yeah, they've got him wrapped around their little fingers."

"This is so cool," I said, watching Sebastián help a little boy put on his shirt. Love tugged at my heart. This man. When they looked at him, most people saw a Palacios, a gangster. But underneath that name was a brave man with a big heart who used his privilege and his means to help others, innocent people with no hope. First the Russian girls, now these kids.

Father JP followed my gaze. "Wait till you see him play soccer with them. I don't know who's happier."

The girls charged us when Father JP opened a pink box. I helped him hand out all kinds of things, and within minutes the boxes were empty. Sebastián jogged to me. He had a little girl in a white dress strapped in his arms. She couldn't have been older than four. Her skin was the color of milk chocolate, her hair the shade of molasses and pulled up in a high ponytail.

"Cami, this is Luciana. Will you keep her company while I play a game with the boys?"

Luciana tightened her arms around Sebastián and tucked her head in the crook of his neck. "I want to stay with you."

"Luci, I need you to take care of my girlfriend for me, okay?" He kissed her hair. "Did I tell you Camila's a ballerina?"

She frowned, assessing me suspiciously. "She doesn't have a tutu."

"I do," I said. "At home. Maybe next time I can bring it with me. Would you like that?"

She nodded and loosened her grip on Sebastián's neck. "Do you have lipstick?"

I pulled my pink lip gloss out of my purse, and Luciana stretched out her arms to launch herself to me. Sebastián gave me a soft kiss on the lips, then ran back to the boys.

"He kissed you," Luciana said, pressing her little palms on my face. "That means he loves you."

We sat on a bench in the shade, and a group of teachers brought lemonade while Sebastián and Father JP divided the kids into teams.

"It's my favorite day of the month," one of the teachers said. A long auburn braid hung down her back. Her deeply tanned skin was weathered and traced with worry lines.

"It's everyone's favorite day of the month," an older one corrected. "Sebastián's their guardian angel." She echoed Principal Eduardo's words from earlier. She then turned to me. "How did you two meet?"

I told them about the day I dropped the ballet shoe on the street. It seemed so distant, like it belonged to someone else's life. So much had happened since then. It was strange to even think of my life before Sebastián. I watched him move with ease as he passed the ball to his younger teammates, dodging Father JP. This was a new side of him, and I loved it.

A half an hour later they stopped for a drink. Sebastián winked at me from among the children, then wiped his forehead and went back to the game.

Luciana shifted on my lap. "I'm tired. Can we go home?"

"It's okay," one of the women said. "I'll walk her. It's just across the street."

"No, I want Camila," Luciana said, wrapping her arms around my neck like she had done with Sebastián.

"I'd like to take her if that's okay," I said.

The woman nodded. "Her mother's name is Rosa."

"Oh, yeah. I just met her. Luciana, are you ready?"

She jumped off my lap. "I can dance too. I know how to stand on my tippy-toes. Look." She put her hands on her waist and rolled onto perfect pointe. I watched her with wide eyes.

"That's amazing. How do you do that?"

"I don't know." She shrugged.

"You have a gift." It had taken me more than five years before I could stand en pointe like that.

Luciana grabbed my hand and tugged me toward her house, a small square about the size of Sebastián's bathroom.

Inside, Rosa was bent over a steaming pot on a stove. There was a single bed to the side and a small dining table beside it. She turned around when Luciana squealed and ran into her arms.

"Mami, I have a new friend. She's a ballerina, but she doesn't have her tutu. Isn't she pretty?"

Rosa smiled benevolently. "Camila, thanks. You needn't bother."

"It's not a bother at all. She's very talented. Does she take ballet?" I felt foolish as soon as I said it. Dance was not likely at the top of their priority list.

"No, just around the house."

"Well, if it's okay, I could teach her a few things. Maybe next time Sebastián comes?"

"Sure. That's very nice of you."

Luciana clapped her hands and rolled onto her toes.

I shook my head in disbelief. "I'll arrange it with Sebastián."

"Thank you, thank you," she said, nodding.

"What size of shoe does she wear?"

"A size one, though we make do with whatever we 'ave in hand." She smiled sweetly at her daughter.

I hugged Luciana hard and promised to visit her soon. A little piece of my heart chipped off and stayed with her.

Chapter 30

"Mmm...this is heaven. I love your idea of staying in," I purred, stretching out by the edge of Sebastián's glorious swimming pool, a rectangle of crystalline water with an infinity drop-off. I curled my toes, basking in the energy of the morning sun. He rose from the water beside me, planting a sensual kiss on my neck, his cool lips sending goose bumps down my skin.

"Anything to get you in a bikini and have you all to myself."

"Oh." I chuckled, running my fingers through his dripping hair. "Ulterior motives. I see."

His lips sucked harder and I squirmed, giggling.

"Stop. You're going to give me a hickey."

"Just marking my territory."

I shoved his forehead, pushing him back into the water. He shook his head, splashing me.

"Sebastián!" I wrapped my arms over my head.

His soft laughter got closer, and he pressed another cold kiss to my shoulder.

"Come here," he said.

"No. It's cold."

He bit his lip to stifle a smile, and before I knew it, I was in the pool with him.

"Jesus, it's freezing!" I gripped him with my arms and legs. A deep chuckle rumbled from his throat, and as he brought me to him, his mouth found mine. Blazing heat inside me rushed to all the right places. He pressed my back against the cool tiles, and I kissed him hard.

"I'm lucky to have you," he said tenderly.

"Says the man who has everything."

"The only thing I really want...is you."

"And you have me." I pulled a strand of wet hair off his forehead. "I'm the lucky one. What you do for those kids, Sebas...it's so generous."

"Most of them have rough situations at home. I can only make them happy for a few moments of their day. But it gives them hope. At least they know they can choose something different. Sometimes all people need is a little help."

"I love you, you know?" I said, finally setting the words free while I traced the line of his jaw.

Relief and joy crossed his eyes. "I love you too."

"You have such a big heart. This thing with the uniforms. How did you get it started?"

"Actually, it's Julián who's the most involved. He runs several charity projects," he said, shaking the dripping water off his hair and onto my face. I laughed, then frowned when the words registered.

"Wait...Julián? Seriously?"

"Julián has a rough past. He spent some time in the streets when he was a kid. Long story. Now he leads like ten different charities." He brushed my wet cheek with the pad of his thumb.

"That seems totally out of character with the man I met the other day."

"Appearances can be deceiving."

"I'd say." He lowered his head under water while I racked my brain, trying to merge the two very different versions of Julián in my head. Sebastián rose and I kissed his wet lips. "I want to help however I can, which gives me an idea. Can we go back to Luciana's house a bit later? I'd like to bring her something."

"Sure. What?"

"You'll see. I just need to make a stop first."

Later in the afternoon, we drove down a small street in Martinez until I found the address I wanted. I hadn't been there in years.

I waited a few minutes at the door. The little house hadn't changed much. The front garden was meticulously manicured, just as I remembered it. Laura opened the door and gasped, immediately wrapping me in her arms. She had been my seamstress since I started ballet and had sewn every single costume I ever wore until I joined the company at the Colón. To me, she was family.

"Camila, darling. Look at you. All grown up, and skin and bones!"

"You always say that no matter what I weigh. This is my boyfriend, Sebastián."

He bent down to greet her with a kiss on the cheek. "It's a pleasure to meet you."

"A boyfriend! *Dios mío*, and he's so handsome. Camila, you really are all grown up. Come on inside."

"Are you going to tell me what we're doing here?" Sebastián whispered into my ear.

"You'll see."

"So. What exactly did you have in mind?" said Laura as she led us into the last room in the hallway. Just stepping into Laura's sewing room made my heart race. It was an enchanted space that smelled of cotton and the cedar blocks she hung between the fabrics to keep moths away. When I was young, I believed this was a place where dreams were made true. Laura would pull out her measuring tape and make all sorts of calculations I was sure were magic.

Sebastián followed me in, looking as mesmerized as I had always felt in here.

"This place is incredible," he said.

"Go ahead. Look around." Laura gestured with her hand, and he followed suit, disappearing into the hundreds of costumes hanging on bars throughout the room. She looked at me over her half-moon spectacles, her hands locked at her waist. Her now white-dusted hair was pulled into a neat bun. Laura was only five feet tall, but her tone and her demeanor made you stand up straight when she spoke, kind of like Madame. And nobody could sew like Laura. She was a gift to ballet.

"I need a tutu for a four-year-old girl. Something embroidered with rhinestones, or flowers. What do you think?"

Her eyes narrowed in thought. "I'm working on some costumes for the Nutcracker. They are along the lines of what you are describing. I'm sure I can add one more to the count." From several dozen sparkly white costumes neatly lined up on a freestanding hanger, she pulled out a white satin bodice with gathered layers of tulle at the skirt intricately embroidered with rhinestones and snowflakes. It was stunning. "I would let you take one now, but all the sizes I finished are much bigger. I could have it ready in about a week? Just the tutu?"

"Yes, just the tutu will do. Thank you, I know how busy you are. This should cover it and the delivery fee," I said, reaching for my purse and pulling out my checkbook. I let her know I would call her later with the address, and wrote her a check for a generous amount. When Laura saw it, she shook her head.

"Camila, no. That is way too much money."

"I will hear no more," I said, signing the check and sliding it on the table. "I'm barging in and imposing this on you."

"You are never an imposition. I'm so glad to see you. Sit down for a moment and tell me about life at the Colón. Must be so glamorous. And thank you for the tickets to *Giselle*, I can't wait to see you dance as Myrta." She moved some boxes from a chair so I could sit.

I glanced over at one of them. "Are those slippers?"

"Yes, we had to order them in advance to match them to the costumes." She opened the box and pulled out a white satin ballet slipper.

"Oh, Laura, they're gorgeous. You wouldn't have any extras? Maybe a size one?" I grazed the fabric with my fingers. It was delicately embroidered with silver rhinestones.

"Actually, we need to order more. They added some extra girls to the corps." She browsed through the boxes and pulled a small pair from the bottom. "Ah. Here. A size one. Take them. And these are on me, or I won't give them to you." She held them up in the air.

"Fine?" I rolled my eyes and she nodded, reaching for my hand.

"Now tell me some naughty gossip from life in the company."

An hour later, Sebastián parked the Clío by Rosa and Luciana's modest house. The afternoon sun cast angled shadows through the trees. A group of sparrows flew away from the front window when we approached. The neighborhood looked ghostly.

The front door swung open, and Luciana ran to us and wrapped her arms around my hips.

"Camila, Camila, did you bring your tutu?"

"I brought you something better. Let's go inside."

She reached up to Sebastián so he would pick her up. Wrapping her arms around his neck, she kissed his cheek. "You smell fancy."

Rosa appeared at the door and waved us inside. "What a surprise." Her smile reached her dark eyes, which had sunk a bit deeper than the last time I saw her. I imagined she was tired.

"I just have a little present for Luciana and wanted to bring it to her."

Luciana's eyes were trained on the box in my hands. Rosa greeted Sebastián and signaled for us to sit down at the small dining table.

"Is that box for me? Is that my present?" Luciana said.

"Yes," I said, opening the box. "These are ballet slippers. My mother bought me my first pair when I was a little younger than you. And look, they come with silk ribbons that your mother can sew on them."

Luciana immediately discarded her shoes and put on the slippers.

"Mami, look. They fit." She stood en pointe, and once again I was blown away at her natural ability.

"Camila, thank you. Thank you so much." Rosa squeezed my hand, her eyes moistening while Luciana danced around the house, leaping and holding her hands over her head.

"Look! I'm like you now, Camila."

I grinned and leaned over to Rosa. "You know, if you want, I could leave two tickets for you and Luciana at the Colón to see *Giselle* on Saturday. Would you like that? It would be an honor for me if you came to see me dance. They'll be under your name at the box office. Just pick them up at seven thirty, half hour before the show."

"You've found your angel, Sebastián," Rosa said. "God rewarded you for all the good you do for us." She turned to me. "We'll come. I promise. God knows this little one will never stop talkin' about it."

We stepped out onto the desolate street where we said good-bye to Rosa and Luciana. The sky bled crimson and purple that smudged with a graying horizon. Sebastián took my hand as we headed to the car. Tires screeched behind us, and a black SUV with tinted windows pulled over beside us. Sebastián stopped abruptly, squeezing my hand.

"What the fuck," he growled. Despite Rafa's apprehension, Sebastián had ordered his bodyguards to stay at home while we made this short trip, and for once, I wished they were with us. Two guys in black suits exited the car and stood on each side of us.

"Palacios," one said. "El Patrón wants to have a word."

"Have him call me, then."

"We're already here, sir." The other guy opened the door to the SUV, and the one who spoke gestured to the back seat.

"Camila, wait for me in the car," Sebastián said, the muscles in his jaw tensing as he handed me the keys. "Go on." The look in his eyes dismissed any argument, and I nodded, then hurried to the parked Clío a few yards away. The SUV didn't move. It just stood immobile with the men inside. Blood rushed in my ears as anxiety coiled in my stomach. Shit. What was this? Should I call the cops? I squeezed the back of my neck in thought, then pulled out my phone, and without lifting it into view, I dialed Sebastián's home line. Marcél answered promptly, and I urged him to get Rafa who cursed out loud when I explained what had happened. He said he would text me his direct number, and stressed I should lock myself in the car until he got there.

Five agonizing minutes passed. Now the street was completely dark. I fidgeted in my seat, vainly trying to see through the SUV's tinted windows. What was happening in there? *Rafa, please hurry.* A few more minutes passed, and Sebastián finally stepped out of the SUV. The second he was out, it skidded away, leaving a cloud of dust behind.

With clumsy fingers, I unlocked the doors. He slipped into the driver's seat and started the engine.

"I'm really sorry about that," he said in a clipped tone that was charged with tension. He glanced at the rearview mirror as Rafa pulled over beside us and exited the BMW, clutching his gun, the veins on his forehead bulging.

"What the fuck happened, Sebastián?"

"The Medina brothers."

"What did they want?"

"Let's talk at home. I want to get Camila out of here."

Rafa rushed back to his car and waited for us to pull forward so he could trail behind.

"What was that about? Are you okay?" I asked, my heart still galloping with fear.

"I'm fine. I'm sorry you had to witness that. Won't happen again. From now on, you'll be protected. Always."

"Who were those guys? Who's El Patrón?" Suddenly I needed to know everything about the dark aura around the Palacios name.

"Business partners of my father's," he said, glancing at the rearview mirror.

"What do they want with you?"

"Camila."

"This is scary shit. I was sweating bullets back there. I deserve to know."

He let out a heavy sigh. "My father doesn't like the Medinas. I've helped in the past, mediating with them. But last week I told them I was done. Things at the docks have been unstable since the incident with the girls, and they're...nervous."

"Okay, so?"

"They want my help again."

"Will you help them?"

"No."

"Why not?"

He groaned. "Because they're not good people. And they're volatile."

"And they'll accept that?"

"They'll have to."

"Sebastián…"

He reached for my hand. "I'll deal with it."

We rode the rest of the way in silence, and I thought of all the warnings Nata had given me about the Palacios family. Unease unfurled inside me. What if it wasn't possible for Sebastián to walk away from his father's businesses? Would I, too, eventually get tangled with Don Martín's affairs? As if Sebastián had heard my thought, he reached for my hand and squeezed it.

"I'll keep you safe. I promise."

Sebastián tossed the keys onto the kitchen counter and pulled me into his arms. "Are you all right? I'm so sorry, so sorry."

"It's okay."

"No, it isn't." He pulled away and paced toward the window, his hands raking his hair. "Fuck, this is my fault."

"How is this your fault?" I walked over to him and placed my hand on his bicep.

"I dragged you into my fucked-up world," he said, his gaze lost somewhere in the distant forest. "It was selfish. I had no right."

"Shh," I said. "I'm all right, I promise." I forced him to turn to me. "Don't say those things. I chose you as much as you chose me. But I am worried about you."

"There's nothing to worry about," he said, kissing my head. "I know how to take care of myself. And I meant it when I said I'll keep you safe. Always."

"I know." I closed my eyes and hugged him tightly.

"Let's stay here tonight. Maybe watch a movie and lie low?"

"Sure. Sounds great."

"I gave Marcél the night off. Let's order something."

I nodded.

"Don't be worried. Come here." He pulled me back into his arms and kissed me sensually. My insides quivered. Rafa appeared at the door and Sebastián detangled from my arms. "I'll be back in a minute."

I made myself a chamomile tea and sat at the kitchen bar. I stared at the cup, watching the steam rise while I reflected on what had happened. The front doorbell chimed twice. What now? Male voices approached, and a couple of seconds later, Julián walked in behind Sebastián. Fucking peachy.

I gave him a curt smile. "Hi."

"Camila," he said, nodding without approaching me. "Good to see you." Once again, the words were right, but the meaning was completely absent. I tried to imagine Julián as the philanthropist Sebastián said he was, but I couldn't.

"Likewise," I said. His eyes narrowed a fraction and I looked away. Why did I find him so intimidating?

Sebastián kissed my cheek. "Do you mind ordering something while Julián and I talk? Look through the menus in that drawer and choose whatever you like. I won't take long." He pulled out his wallet and took out a wad of cash, placing it on the counter. My eyes widened with horror, and I pushed it away.

"I've got this," I said. He gave me an admonishing look, but I smiled and turned to Julián. "Will you be joining us?"

He paused for a moment, and that familiar shiver I had felt in his presence crept through me.

"I have plans," he finally said. "But thanks."

Relief washed through me. They disappeared into Sebastián's office, and I pulled out a Chinese food menu and scanned through it, then ordered the food. The delivery would take a half hour, so I had time for a quick shower. As I turned into the hallway, I browsed through the emails on my phone and froze when I saw Federico's name. An urgent email from Federico summoned the whole cast for a meeting the following afternoon. I leaned back against the wall. Excitement bloomed in my chest, my pulse racing as I read the rest of the message. The tour to New York was back on. Holy shit. The theater had planned it over a year ago but had then canceled it due to lack of funding. In the message, Federico vaguely stated that an anonymous donor had made an extremely generous contribution to support the company's performances overseas. My heart pumped hard. New York was my big dream. I could finally share my mother's legacy of performing at Lincoln Center.

Julián's loud voice from Sebastián's office startled me. Knowing Marcél wasn't around, I stepped closer and quietly leaned on the thick mahogany door.

"Your father wants you at the docks until things settle down. Ivanov is becoming a problem, and that's enough in our hands. Don't fuck with the Medinas. This is not the time to make a statement, Sebastián."

"This is *exactly* the time to make a statement. I told you. I want out."

"What the fuck, man. What did this girl do to you?"

I held my breath. *This girl?* Me?

"Leave her out of it. I thought you of all people would get it. I don't want to end up like my father, surrounded by crooks and alone. She's what I want in my future. Not this." There was silence. I turned and pressed myself against the wall, processing, that last sentence circling inside my head. *She's what I want in my future. Not this.*

"The Medinas only want you as their mediator," Julián said in a calmer voice. "If you want to protect Camila, play along for now."

"They had the balls to show up today in broad daylight. How in the fuck did they know where I was? Less than a handful of people knew: Rafa, JP, Tano, and the school principal. All trustworthy."

"I don't know, but I'd say we have a problem now that they saw Camila."

"They *will not* get near her. Nobody will," Sebastián said in a guttural, chilling tone. Then the voices lowered, no longer discernible. I scurried away, my heart racing. Shit. No wonder Julián didn't like me. I was in the way. *I* was the reason why Sebastián had once and for all decided to sever his ties to the family business. Closing my eyes, I rubbed them hard. The last twenty-four hours had been more than sobering, a clear picture of what I was walking into. Why had I consistently ignored the signs? Perhaps that said more about me than it did about Sebastián. At first, all this gangster stuff seemed distant to me, a dramatic tale fabricated by the media, but as I learned more, each realization that I was stepping into dangerous territory became more solemn than the one before.

I was almost at the bedroom when the office door opened. I rushed inside and into the bathroom. Quickly stripping off my clothes, I slipped into the shower, my blood pulsing with a mix of adrenaline and anxiety.

Sebastián walked in a few seconds later, his body radiating tension. I wiped the fog off the glass and gestured for him to join me.

He undressed and stepped into the shower. His eyes were etched in anger. I caressed his face, and he relaxed slightly as I pulled him under the cascade of warm water. Wrapping my arms around his back, I pressed my face to his chest, kissing him there. His arms closed around me.

"I'm glad you're here," he said, kissing my head. "I'll always keep you safe. I promise. No matter what I have to do."

Chapter 31

I blinked at the late morning sun and turned to Sebastián, but found a note on his pillow. It was just three lines in his perfect handwriting:

I have an early meeting. Will be back soon.

Don't leave.

I love you. S

I rubbed my eyes, unease wreathing my mind. His argument with Julián the night before lingered in my head. I hadn't asked Sebastián about it. But the fact that Julián—and possibly Don Martín—saw me as a threat had me on edge.

Rolling off the bed, I lumbered to the shower. A knot in my stomach reminded me that in just a few hours, Federico would announce the casting for the performances of *Sleeping Beauty* on the international tour. The news of the tour had been sudden, and we were running against the clock. There was no time for auditions, so Federico had told the cast that the decisions would be based on the performances in *Giselle*. Being invited to join the cast was a long shot for me, and it would mean traveling for a few weeks, so I wasn't sure how Sebastián would react.

The coil of tension in my stomach tightened. Today could be a turning point in my career.

In the kitchen, Marcél was busy with something that smelled heavenly. He looked up and smiled with the usual warmth in his eyes.

"Good morning *ma chérie*. Sleep well, yes? Would you like your breakfast?"

"Just orange juice, I think. But I can get it." I stood, but he raised his palm.

"No, no, I will get it. You sit." His tone told me he was not to be argued with.

"Marcél, you don't have to cater to me. I'm used to taking care of myself."

"*Ma chérie*, it is my pleasure to take care of you when I get the chance. Please allow me. Sebastián won't be long. May I get you something else? I am making beef Bourguignon for dinner. A favorite of his."

"It smells amazing. I actually need to run to the theater to look at my schedule."

"Will you be back for dinner?"

I smiled. Nobody had asked me that since I left my parents' home. I loved how Marcél took care of Sebastián. He was overindulging, the way a grandfather would be.

"Yes, thank you. Wish me luck. They're announcing the cast today. I'm hoping for a big role."

"Ah. *Bonne chan*ce, ma chérie. I am sure you will get it." His smile was triumphant.

I sighed. If only Marcél could have switched bodies with Federico when he assigned the roles.

I texted Sebastián to let him know I wouldn't be back till later, then Nata to tell her to wait for me so we could go to the theater together.

By the time I made it to my apartment, it was one in the afternoon. My nerves were frayed. The roles were probably being posted at this very moment.

"There you are. I was worried you'd chickened out," Nata said from the couch, her languid body stretched out as she flipped lazily through the TV channels. I envied her. She had an almost sure shot at the lead role as Princess Aurora, and she was just...*ugh*. So freaking calm.

"You alone? Where's Alexei?"

"I told him to leave. He can meet up with me later." She swung her legs and ambled toward me. Her lips stretched into a wicked smile. Shit. I knew that smile.

"What is it?" I said. "I can't take any bad news right now."

"It's *good*."

"The last time you looked at me like that, you left for Russia with what's his name, and I didn't see you for three months."

"That was different. Besides, I did a two-month workshop there."

"Whatever. Spill'em."

"Okay. I didn't tell you before because I knew you would freak out—and you just confirmed I was right. But...I got *engaaaged*!"

"What? Why in the hell would you do that?"

"Because...Teo proposed to me last night." She squeezed my hands. "And I said yes."

"What the hell, Nata? What about your career? You're at the top."

"I know. But I want a family too. Not now, but in the future. We can't do this forever. Can you just be happy for me?"

"I am. It's just...I didn't realize you guys were *that* serious."

"I would've told you, but...with all this stuff between us, we haven't talked much. Teo is the *one*. He's very supportive of my career, and that won't change. I thought you would get it."

"I do get it. Come here." I pulled her into a hug. I loved this girl like a sister, but Jesus, *engaged*? "Just give me a few seconds to recover."

"I got your mind away from casting."

"Yeah." I chuckled. "Have you set a date?"

"Not yet. But I'd like to have the wedding in Punta del Este, at the beach."

"It's great. Really."

"Let's get out of here and go celebrate afterwards, whatever roles we get." She hooked her arm in mine and tugged me to the door.

Fifteen minutes later, we hurried down the theater hallway. A few dancers were gathered around the announcement board outside the studio. Two girls from the corps turned when they saw us standing behind them. One of them gave me a soft pat on the shoulder.

"Wow," she said.

I frowned and scanned the board for my name, my stomach tightening. My pulse halted when I saw my name next to the role of Princess Aurora on Second

Cast. Holy shit. And I would be partnering with Marcos. Nata would be Aurora on First Cast, partnering with Diego. I turned, unsure how she would feel about the change of partners.

"You did it," she whispered in my ear as she pulled me away from the other dancers. Casting was a sensitive issue. Nobody jumped up and down when they got a big role since it meant someone standing close by didn't get it. "This is it. Princess Aurora in New York City. You made it to the top, babe."

"You don't mind partnering with Diego?"

"Not at all," she said. "I love having Marcos as my partner, but I'm eager to dance with Diego. He's an exceptional dancer."

I nodded. Was this real? Marcos startled me wrapping his arms around both our waists, easily lifting us from the ground.

"My princesses." He kissed Nata's cheek, then mine. "This is going to be fun. Let's celebrate." He kissed my cheek again more intently, snapping me out of my daze. I blushed, trying to free myself from him, but he squeezed me against his rock-hard side. "I'm so fucking proud of you," he said into my ear. His warm breath tickled me, and I tilted my head away, but he didn't budge. "It was a matter of time, I told you."

"You're not bummed you aren't partnering with Nata?"

"Nope. This makes more sense because of your height. And Diego's a great partner." He gave me one more squeeze and let go. My stomach was in a nautical knot by now. The excitement about finally partnering with Marcos was tainted with the sudden angst of having to tell Sebastián. I still couldn't believe it. I never imagined this would happen so soon. But damn, despite all complications, it felt good. *Oh, Mamá, I did it.* I couldn't wait to tell her.

"Well," Nata said, "after Federico's meeting, Cami and I have some serious shopping to do for the cast party tonight. Unless you want to come with?"

"Nah, I look hot in whatever I wear." He winked, earning a full eye roll from Nata.

"What did Carla get?" I said.

"She's one of the fairies. That means I'll get laid tonight. Big time."

Nata made a puking gesture, and he grinned as he turned away.

My parents were thrilled at the news when I called. Mom cried as they congratulated me and wished me a successful tour. I hung up, feeling excited. Now, Sebastián. Clutching the phone in my hand, I locked it and slipped it back into my pocket. It could wait.

After the meeting, Nata and I left the theater and strolled for a few blocks to find a taxi.

"Let's go to the Alto Palermo Mall and do some damage. You're not saying no." She nudged my shoulder.

"You just went shopping."

"So? Thanks to your amazing intervention with Julián, I have money again. Besides, cast parties are always a good reason to go shopping. Don't be a buzzkill."

I rolled my eyes.

"Okay, what's going on?" she said. "Why are you not more excited?"

"I am excited. Just…shocked, is all."

"Every girl in the company would've killed for that role. It's the most important day of your career, and you look…stressed."

I let out a heavy sigh, running both hands through my hair the way Sebastián did when he was tense. We were by a small café, and I took a seat at a table on the sidewalk. I pulled up my legs and hugged them. Nata sat beside me. A waiter approached, and she ordered two espressos to get rid of him.

"You're killing me here," she said. "What could possibly be the matter? Did you fight with Sebastián again?"

"Not yet. But I don't think he'll be thrilled with my news."

"Why in the hell not?"

I chewed on my bottom lip.

"Camila!"

"He showed up at the bar the other night and almost went at it with Marcos."

"What? How do I not know this? Where was I?"

I shrugged.

"What happened?"

"Marcos and I were having a drink at the bar, and he was a bit…buzzed."

"Shit. I know where this is going. He had his hands all over you, didn't he?"

"Sebastián went nuclear. I had to stand between them. Marcos didn't back off, either."

"I'm sorry. That sucks. So now you think he won't approve of the tour because you'll spend all that time with Marcos. Look, you and Marcos work together. There's not a way around that. Sebastián will come around. He has to. Anyone dating a dancer has to understand that they need to be flexible, or things won't work." She squeezed my hand as the waiter appeared with our espressos. "You know that you dating Sebastián is a bit…tough for me to get used to, but I'm thinking of you right now."

"What do I do?"

She took a deep breath, thinking. "First off, you need to set boundaries with Marcos. He's your partner now, so that means you're equal. You're not his sidekick, so don't let him fool around with you. And with Sebastián…you have to be firm. Does he know about the tour at all?"

"I was waiting till I knew it was a sure thing."

"Tell him. Tonight."

I gave her an anguished look.

"This is important," she said.

I pressed my forehead to my knees.

She rubbed my arm. "You're not alone, you know? You have me, and Marcos. He can be an idiot sometimes, but he's also a professional and doesn't let things get in the way of work. We both have your back." She leaned over to hug me. "This is a big moment for you. You should be happy." Squaring her shoulders, she tugged on my hand. "Let's go buy something sexy and insanely expensive. That'll shake off your mood. We'll get you some indecent underwear for when you deliver the good news to the gangster."

"Nata!"

She laughed. "Come on. It'll be fun."

Four hours later, I slid into the back seat of a cab, shoving bags of stuff I couldn't afford. Nata made me buy a gray sequin dress with a very low back. It was scandalously short, but she assured me it would improve my chances of a good outcome with Sebastián. To top it off, I bought a pair of Ricky Sarkany sandals and obscenely expensive underwear. I wanted Sebastián to take a good look at me before saying no to anything I asked.

Marcél was watering the peonies in the front when my taxi pulled in. He approached and took my bags, letting me know he would put them in the guest bedroom. I found Sebastián at the kitchen bar with a glass of red wine.

"There you are." He pulled me into his arms. "Mmm...Hi, gorgeous. I've missed you. Where did you go all day?"

"I went home to get more clothes. Then Nata and I went shopping. I'm starving, can we eat?" I walked to the stove and lifted the lid on the pot with Marcél's beef Bourguignon. "This smells amazing." Not wanting to bother Marcél, I reached for plates and served us. Sebastián was lucky, Marcél could seriously cook.

After dinner Sebastián had to make a few phone calls, so I went to the guest bedroom to take a bath before the party. I undressed and was pouring in bubbles when a soft knock startled me. I snatched a towel and wrapped it around me. Sebastián opened the door and leaned his head on the frame.

"Why are you here? My bathtub's bigger."

"Oh, Marcél brought my shopping here, and I didn't want to invade your space."

"Don't be silly," he said. "I love the tornados of clothes you leave in my room."

I winced. "Sorry, I know I'm such a slob. It must drive you crazy."

He shook his head dismissively. "Maybe we could take a bath together?" He smiled suggestively.

I dropped the towel, and his eyes widened a fraction before he surveyed every inch of my body. I locked my hands on my waist, cocking my head as I waited for his eyes to meet mine.

"Like the view? *Helloooo*?"

"I *love* the view. Will never get tired of it. Come here." He pulled me to him and I kissed his chest. *Oh*, he smelled incredible.

"Hmmm…your clothes are still on."

He stripped off his clothes slowly, his eyes never leaving mine. It was sexy as hell. I ran my fingers down the chiseled muscles on his chest, and everything south of my navel clenched. He stepped closer and gripped my head at the nape, burying his fingers in my hair.

"What you do to me." His mouth seized mine and I melted. There was something carnal and, *oh*, so hot about the way he held me. I groaned into his mouth, and his hard cock pressed against me. Suddenly I couldn't kiss him fast enough, deep enough. My fingers moved to his waist, fumbling with the button of his jeans and undoing his zipper. On an impulse, I broke away and dropped to my knees, pulling down his jeans and boxers. His cock sprang free, hard, big, and beautiful. A flood of desire rushed through me, and I kissed his tip before taking him into my mouth. He let out a surprised, guttural groan as I wrapped my lips around him and ran my tongue along his length, slowly. My heart raced. I had never done this before, and I didn't really know what I was doing, but it felt right. So right. Shielding my teeth, I started moving, my tongue stroking him as I took him in deeper. He mumbled a curse through gritted teeth, and his fingers traced my jaw to my hair as I worked him. Restraint rumbled in his throat as he let me own him.

"You're going to kill me," he muttered, his voice hoarse and his breaths coming out in short pants. I looked up at him, his beautiful face and body coming undone as I sucked him harder. "Camila, fuck." His hands clenched my hair, bringing me to him as I took him in as far as I could. I felt powerful, disarming him like this. I worked my tongue and my lips around him, taking him deeper, faster. His hot, hard cock throbbed as his hands fisted my hair and his hips rocked faster, fucking my mouth. I moved around him, meeting his fastening rhythm. Then his grip on my hair tightened and his hips snapped twice, his whole body rigid.

"Fuck," he groaned, reaching his climax and spilling into my mouth. I swallowed him, owned him. My beautiful man. When I glanced up at him, his face was frozen in ecstasy.

Slowly, I stood, and he took me in his arms, his glorious body hard and misted with sweat.

"Where the hell did that come from?" he murmured, catching his breath. I bit my lip and gave him a small shrug.

"An impulse. It was my first time, but it looks like I did all right." I stifled a smile.

He took my face in his hands. "You are a goddess. Every fucking fantasy come true. I'm so goddamn lucky." He kissed me hard and picked me up in his arms before stepping into the hot, spilling tub.

"So what's this party?" Sebastián stood facing his floor-to-ceiling closet, wearing only boxers and a half-buttoned, blue linen shirt. His rolled-up sleeves showed a few inches of his tanned forearms, his raven hair a sexy mess. He was glorious sight. I watched the show from the bed, memorizing every inch of his body, and smiled. He was all mine. When he turned his head he caught me staring. "Like the view? *Hellooo*?"

"Oh, yeah. It's a fine view from here."

He winked and blushed a little. "You didn't answer my question."

"Um...come here." I patted the bed beside me.

"Everything all right?" He sat and caressed my face. I leaned against his palm, savoring the contact.

"I have some very...exciting news."

"Great. I'm in need of very exciting news. What is it?"

Scratching my temple, I shot a dirty look at the door where my courage had fled. Then I straightened my shoulders and took a settling breath.

"About a year ago the company planned a tour to New York, but then they canceled it because there weren't enough funds. This morning Federico announced that they received a very generous donation, so the tour is back on. He posted the roles, and I got the lead in *Sleeping Beauty*, with Second Cast. We leave in a month." I scanned his expression, but his face was impassive. Unease churned in my stomach. Shit.

"That's big, Cami...Congratulations."

"Thanks. It is big...huge. New York's what I've been working for my whole life."

He nodded. His gaze traveled around the room. Then he stood abruptly, running his hands through his hair as he walked to the window where he stopped, staring at the willows outside.

I waited. For a millennium, it felt.

He finally turned, letting out a heavy sigh. "How long will you be gone?"

"About two weeks."

He let out another heavy sigh. "I'm so proud of you, Camila. I am. It makes me happy to see you get closer to your dreams."

"But..."

"You can understand my apprehension." Worry lines creased his forehead. "Who's your partner on this tour?"

"Sebastián, I need you to be okay with this."

He closed his eyes, pressing his lips as he shook his head slowly. "You're spending two weeks in New York with a guy that's itching to get into your panties, and you want me to just be okay with it."

"Yes. This is work."

He rubbed the fatigue off his face and sighed. "I'm tired of arguing about this guy."

"Then let's not."

He looked at me for a long moment. I felt my muscles tensing, one by one, with every passing second.

"I would like to come with you," he said in a stern voice.

I frowned. "To New York?"

"Yes."

"Um...Sebastián, these tours are nonstop. Nobody brings anyone along. I mean, we rehearse, we perform, we eat, we sleep. There's no time for anything else."

"I won't get in the way, but I want to be there with you. I want to make sure you're safe."

Now it was me rubbing my face in frustration. This was an outcome I hadn't considered. Tension gripped my shoulders. I stood and headed to the closet. Shit. I took a long, cleansing breath. Okay, well...I would figure this out somehow. Later.

I startled when he hugged me from behind.

"I don't mean to make things difficult for you. I won't come if you don't want me to. But aside from my feelings about you being away with that fucker, this is a big moment in your career, your first lead role, and I want to be there for you."

I wrapped my arms over his, feeling the tension leave my body as I exhaled.

He kissed my head. "I can come for your first performance and leave after."

I turned, wrapping my arms around his waist and looked up at him.

"I would love that." Rolling onto my toes, I kissed him softly. "Now this party tonight"—I searched his eyes—"is for the dancers who are in the tour. If you'd rather not come—"

"I'll come. Unless you don't want me to."

"Don't be silly. I just…I need you to be nice. To the *other* dancers."

"If your friend keeps his hands off you, we won't have any problems." He kissed my head. "I've got to shave."

Chapter 32

Diego swung open the front door and greeted us with exaggerated enthusiasm, his eyes already glassy from his own pre-party, no doubt. I hugged him and he shook hands with Sebastián. I needed alcohol. My whole body was tangled in one hypertense knot. Diego waved us in and told us to grab a drink and have fun.

Girls in short dresses and guys in worn jeans and tight tees filled the loft in San Telmo that Diego shared with two other guys. It was spacious and simple: hardwood floors, leather couches, and massive windows to the street. The ultimate bachelor's pad.

I sighed in relief when I saw Carla. Tonight was my big chance to bring together the two parts of my life that were still disconnected, and I had a better shot at things going well with Carla present. She was already getting serious points for the Band-Aid dress she was wearing. She hooked a tanned leg in a four-inch heel around Marcos as she leaned in to kiss him. Perfect. The gap between Sebastián and my career was shrinking already.

We had all been asked to bring a bottle of booze, so every inch of the kitchen counter was covered with liquor. Sebastián said hello to a guy he knew, one of the dancer's boyfriends, and I went to get us drinks. I left the wine we'd brought at the bar and greeted Marcos and Carla with a quick kiss on the cheeks. Marcos lifted my hand up and whistled, making me twirl to get a good look at my new, super-short sequin dress.

"Baby, you look hot."

I blushed and glanced nervously at Carla, but she was nodding in approval. I pulled my hand away, feeling Sebastián's eyes on my back. It was a good thing I was no threat to Carla. She was the kind of girl that walked into a room and turned every head: blazing blonde hair, ice-blue eyes, plump lips. The works.

Marcos kissed my knuckles and nodded at her, letting out a long sigh. "Shitty luck of yours, Cams. I'm *very* taken. Your mogul boyfriend will have to do tonight."

Carla slapped his shoulder, raising her glass to clink mine. "Congrats, Camila. Aurora, huh? Pretty awesome."

"Thank you. Congrats to you too. And you get to take the prince home."

She smiled, giving Marcos a suggestive look. He pulled her against him and gave her a wet kiss on the mouth.

"Okay, you guys are too chummy for me." Just as I turned, Sebastián's arm snaked around my waist. Carla looked up at him and her cheeks instantly turned pink.

"Hey, nice to finally meet you. Sebastián, right? I'm Carla." She smiled broadly, showcasing perfect teeth.

Sebastián rewarded her with a full smile, causing her blush to deepen. "Nice to meet you, too, Carla." Then his smile quickly faded. "Marcos," he said icily.

"Sebastián," Marcos answered, mocking Sebastián's tone. Marcos's expression was impassive, but his eyes said, *Fuck you.* Sebastián's, *Fuck you back.*

Carla told Marcos she wanted to dance. He wrapped his arms around her while she guided him to an open space by the window.

Okay...round one.

Pretty soon the loft was swarming with people, most of them dancers with the company. Everyone was having fun, doing shots and dirty dances with each other. I waved at Nata as she made her way through the thick crowd, followed by Teo, to come and say hi. She was warmer toward Sebastián and introduced him to her fiancé. Sebastián shook Teo's hand, and after exchanging a few words, Nata said she needed a drink and they left to the bar.

As the night progressed, the tension between Marcos and Sebastián didn't ease. Sebastián shot him caustic looks, and Marcos smirked back or gave him a bored eye roll. It wasn't exactly progress, but at least I managed to keep them in the same room without a scene. Also, Sebastián had a first-row seat at Marcos with his bombshell girlfriend, and I hoped it would smooth some of the tension about the tour.

He left to the restroom while I went to the bar for a bottle of water. Marcos startled me from behind, buzzed as usual, and kissed my bare shoulder.

"You have to bring this dress to New York."

"Marcos," I scolded, wiggling away from him. "Stop it."

"What? I'm saying I like your dress. You used to like it when I gave you compliments. What's your deal lately? Is it this guy you're with? Is he giving you shit?" He scowled. His sandy hair was longer, brushing his forehead and giving him a rebellious teen look.

"Look, Marcos," I said, making sure Sebastián wasn't in sight. "After what happened at Isabel's the other night, I need you to chill. Sebastián's not exactly thrilled about us going to New York together."

"Tough shit."

"Yeah, well, tough shit for me too. He's planning on coming, so don't make things more difficult, all right? Go be chummy with your girlfriend."

"Wait. He's coming? To New York?"

"Yes, for my opening night, and it's sweet. Enough already, okay?"

"You'll be up to your ass with rehearsals. The last thing you need is this guy giving you shit because you're working late or he's waiting to go have dinner."

"Are you sure it's me you're worried about?"

"Tell him no, babe. It's fucking ridiculous."

"What is?" Sebastián said from behind me. Shit.

"You, crashing the tour to New York," Marcos said, pointing at Sebastián menacingly.

Sebastián straightened and took a step forward. "Fuck off, man. Remember you're all out of warnings."

"Shit, I'm almost scared," Marcos scoffed.

"Let's step outside," Sebastián said.

"Let's," Marcos answered.

I gripped Sebastián's shirt. "Cool down, Sebastián." He ignored me and kept his gaze on Marcos. Carla shot me a puzzled look when she appeared from behind Marcos and grabbed his bicep.

"Babe," she said to Marcos, "we're going to watch the film from opening night. Come on."

Marcos didn't flick a muscle, his gaze still burning on Sebastián.

Carla squeezed his arm. "Marcos, babe, let's go, they're waiting for you." She turned to me. "They're waiting for you too."

Marcos reluctantly followed as she tugged him to a back room where other dancers had gathered. I looked around for Nata and saw her approaching. I needed to get Sebastián away from Marcos. Nata motioned us toward the back room to watch the film.

I turned to Sebastián. "Let's just do this quickly and leave. I have to be present when they start the film from opening night. It's a tradition."

His jaw was set with tension, but he gave me a slight nod.

"What were you thinking going after him like that?" I said as we made our way to the loft's only back room.

"Your friend wanted my attention. I was just giving him what he wanted," he murmured.

I shuddered inwardly and tugged his hand to a stop. "This whole apartment is full of dancers. They would all stand with Marcos. And you can't ever, *ever* hit a dancer. If we're injured, we can't work."

Sebastián cocked an eyebrow. "Maybe you should remind *him* of that."

"Sebastián," I snapped. "I mean it. I've seen you fight before. Your jealousy could seriously hurt Marcos's and my careers. Promise me. Promise me you won't hurt him."

His eyes were etched in an icy glare as they met mine.

"Promise me," I insisted. "I know he's provoking you, but I need you to promise me that under no circumstances you will hurt Marcos."

He didn't answer.

"Sebastián?"

"Fine," he muttered. "Let's get this over with."

We followed Nata to the back room and stood close to the exit, on the far opposite side of Marcos and Carla. Someone dimmed the lights, and a giant flat screen TV showcased the opening night of *Giselle*. I watched, mesmerized, and for a moment, got completely lost in the performance. It all looked so different from the audience's point of view. Nata and Marcos were simply astonishing, making the most difficult steps seem natural. Then, I saw myself in my peasant costume, and my breath caught. I looked relaxed, happy, like I was having the time of my life. The tension and nerves inside me were invisible to the audience, and my movements were cheerful and graceful.

Beside me, Nata squeezed my hand. "You look great," she whispered. Smiling, I turned to Sebastián and my heart halted. Panic spread under my skin as I searched the darkness. He was gone.

And so was Marcos.

Chapter 33

A chill of horror flew down my spine as I hurried to the main room. I swept the ample space in search of Sebastián or Marcos, but found nothing.

I swung the front door open and looked frantically down the dark corridor, but there were no signs of either one of them. I was about to run back to get Carla or Nata when I heard the distinct snap of knuckles on flesh. My whole body tensed. From the end of the corridor, a few male voices cheered. Anger boiled within me. *Dammit, Sebastián.*

Rushing toward the sounds, I turned the corner and halted to a stop. My blood chilled.

Sebastián faced Marcos, surrounded by a group of Marcos's friends.

"Sebastián," I said, stepping forward, but two of the guys blocked me from getting closer.

"Sorry," one said. "Private party."

"Let me through! Sebastián, Marcos. For fuck's sake. Stop acting like children. This is a party."

Marcos took a swing at Sebastián and he dodged it.

"Marcos!" I snapped. "Cut it out."

"I told you," he said, "I don't give a fuck who your boyfriend is. He's got to fuck off. He doesn't belong here."

"Are we done?" Sebastián smirked. Marcos took a few swings, but Sebastián was quicker, and dodged him every time. Marcos groaned in frustration and sprung forward. He shoved Sebastián back, then clutched his shirt and punched his ribs. Sebastián gasped and gripped Marcos by the throat with one hand, but two of the guys stepped in and secured Sebastián's arms while Marcos swung another punch, this time at his mouth, then another at his ribs. Sebastián winced. Leaning back, he kicked Marcos behind the knee, causing him to fall on his ass. Marcos seethed. Sebastián took advantage of the distraction to jab a quick elbow at one of the guys holding him back, then the other, knocking out the air from their lungs almost simultaneously as he eased out of their grip. Keeling over, they gasped, their eyes drawn in anger and confusion.

"You're fucked, asshole," Marcos spat out as he stood. He nodded at the two guys blocking me, and they joined the other two, who were still recovering, then the four closed in on Sebastián.

"Stop!" I shouted as Marcos threw one, two, three punches at Sebastián's stomach while the others held his arms and head back.

Sebastián gasped in pain, but his eyes never left Marcos. "You're pathetic." Sebastián smiled.

Marcos took another swing at Sebastián's abs. Sebastián's expression tensed but he seemed to be just taking it. Why in the hell wasn't he fighting back? All of his moves were defensive. He wasn't even trying.

Boiling with frustration, I launched myself at Marcos, gripping his shirt and yanking him back as hard as I could, ire surging through me.

"Are you out of your fucking mind?" I yelled. "Get away from him."

Marcos stumbled back, panting. I pushed past him and lifted up my phone at the other four guys still holding Sebastián. "You step the fuck away from him or I'm calling the cops."

They gave me a rueful smile but let go of Sebastián, who straightened up painfully. I rushed over to him, my hands cupping his face as I wiped a trickle of blood from his lip with my thumb.

"You're lucky your girl has some chops," one of them said.

"You fucking cowards, all of you! What the hell? There's five of you." My hand slid down Sebastián's back and felt cold steel at the belt, under his untucked shirt. He reached back and pulled out a gun, letting it hang casually at his side. The guys took an immediate step back. My heart galloped.

"That's never comfortable," Sebastián said as he casually leaned down and picked up his coat.

"Who the fuck did we just mess with, dude?" one of the guys mumbled.

"Let's bounce," another one said. Marcos straightened and raked his hair back with his hand, a flash of anxiety crossing his eyes.

"You're an asshole," I said, glowering at him. "You stay the hell away from me, you hear me?"

"Stop fucking around, Camila," Marcos snapped. "This guy's a thug. He'll hurt your career. I'm not letting him fuck with mine. You get your shit together before the tour." He snatched up his jacket and walked away.

I bit back anger and frustration. What the hell had gotten into Marcos? I turned to Sebastián. "Are you all right? *Jesus*."

"I'm fine," he mumbled.

My blood boiled with fury, frustration, and guilt, but the ruling feeling was confusion. He was a black belt in martial arts and despite the odds, he could've easily had Marcos, even with those four guys holding him back. Plus, he had a freaking *gun*. I pushed the image away.

"What the hell happened, Sebas?"

"Hmmh," he groaned, easing into his coat. "Just a little disagreement over…boundaries. Nothing to worry about."

"Why didn't you fight them back?" I said, clasping his bicep gently. "I know you could've had them, you even have a fucking gun for fuck's sake, and you let them hit you. You didn't even touch Marcos."

"Nope." He smiled sweetly. "I promised you."

Chapter 34

We stopped at the top of the driveway to Sebastián's house, and he killed the engine. Leaning back against the window, he watched me with tired eyes. The moonlight filtered through the forest, casting shadows on his beautiful face. A pink scratch crossed his chin, and his lip was swollen, but I knew his ribs had taken most of the swings. That was how dancers fought. It was easier to deal with a broken rib or two than other injuries in your body. Guilt lanced through me. Part of me wished he had given it back to those assholes. He caressed my face and smiled.

"Don't sweat it. I'm fine," he said, reading my thoughts.

"I'm so sorry, Sebas. I never thought Marcos was capable of that. Next time you let them have it." I held his face in my hands. "I love you even more, if that was even possible."

In the bedroom, he pressed me against him. "You look beautiful tonight. I like your new dress." He slowly slipped the straps off my shoulders, letting the fabric slide down and pool at my feet. I stepped out, kissing him gently as my hands worked to unbutton his shirt. Without breaking the kiss, he shrugged off his shirt and climbed onto the bed, bringing me with him. He leaned back against the headboard and winced. I broke away, but he pulled me closer, locking me in his arms. I straddled him, wearing nothing but my new, overpriced underwear, his cock pressing from under the soft denim of his jeans. I kissed him sensually, relishing in the heady feeling of having him, like this. I wanted to devour him, show him how much I loved him. The kiss intensified, and he squeezed his arms, bringing me closer. Then he broke away.

"Will you do something for me?" he asked.

"Yes," I said. "Anything."

"Dance for me," he whispered against my lips. "Only me." He pulled his face away slightly, and his eyes darkened. The fire inside me flared. He made

343

me feel so wanton, so sexy. His fingertips grazed my back, sending shivers along my tingling skin. He traced the lacy outline of my bra. Then his thumb brushed my stomach to my panties. "Wearing *only* these."

I inhaled sharply. The thought of dancing only for him made everything inside me clench. "Okay."

"Oh, and put on your ballet shoes."

I arched an eyebrow. "Wicked fantasies we have. Anything else?"

He shook his head no.

I leapt off him and reached for my dance bag. He watched me from the bed as I pulled out my pointe shoes and slipped them on. Sitting on an armchair across from him, I stretched out my legs and tied the ribbons around my ankles, slowly, while he appraised me. A corner of his mouth pulled up, dark desire settling in his expression, but he didn't move or attempt to touch me. I bit my lip, my insides squirming with anticipation. How could he make me feel so sexy, so powerful without even touching me?

I searched for the music I wanted and linked my phone to the sound system. I had danced a brief solo to an aria from *La Wally* last year and was pretty sure I could remember it. Wearing nothing but black lace and silk underwear and pointe shoes, I stepped into the middle of the room where I had some open space. Maria Callas's heavenly voice filled the air, and I closed my eyes, letting the music seep into me. My body immediately knew what to do, and I dove into the variation, becoming one with the music. The piece was beautifully tragic, and it surprised me how well I remembered it. Every note vibrated through me as if the piece had been created precisely for this moment. I got lost in the melody, forgetting I was dancing practically naked and Sebastián was watching me from the bed.

I ended on the last note, and when I looked up at him, a new wave of emotion slammed through me. His eyes were moist, bright with love and admiration. Having done something that moved him that much took my breath away. I smiled broadly and he let out a heavy sigh.

"Cami, that was…the most beautiful, sexiest thing I've ever seen," he said in a hoarse, low voice.

Weightless wings fluttered in my stomach. "I'm glad," I said, catching my breath. "I don't do a lot of private performances." I winked.

"Come here." His pale eyes were suddenly afire and my blood sizzled. But…I pursed my lips.

"No."

His eyebrows shot up. "*No?*"

I slowly shook my head, stifling a smile.

Before I could blink, he was on me, forgetting his aching ribs and pinning me against the wall, his hot, hard body smoldering mine. He secured my wrists over my head with one hand, then lifted my ass with the other. I wrapped my legs around his waist, and he pressed his length against me. I moaned out loud, closing my eyes to savor the sensation. He ravaged my neck, his broken breaths colliding with my burning skin. Pinning me with his hips, he undid my bra at the front, trailing open-mouth kisses along my jaw. His hand moved down and slipped into my panties. I dropped my legs so he could pull them down, and I kicked them to the floor. His fingers slid between my legs and stroked my clit, moving around and around. I took a sharp breath as my insides quivered. The feeling was exquisite.

"Sebastián…" I moaned.

A low, deep growl vibrated deep in his chest. He let go of my wrists and, in two moves, undid his jeans and pulled them down with his boxers. I gasped out loud as he thrust into me, his hard, eager cock filling me. He paused to meet my hooded eyes, our mouths panting against each other as I adjusted to him. Then he eased in and out of me with a deeper, slower rhythm, again and again. *Holy shit.*

"You disarm me," he whispered in a low, husky voice as he moved inside me, never taking his eyes off mine. I climbed, following his accelerating rocking motion, letting him possess me, own me until I couldn't hold on.

"Sebastián," I breathed. "*God.*"

He slammed harder into me and groaned. I moaned out loud, gripping his shoulders as I exploded in a spiraling orgasm.

I drifted back to Earth as he gently pulled out and slid me to the floor with him. Enveloping me in his arms, he kissed my hair. "I love you, angel."

I pressed my face against his chest, breathing him in as his heart raced against my cheek.

"And I love you. So much."

We stayed like that for a few silent seconds, him gloriously naked, me only in pointe shoes. Our chopped breaths cut through the still vacuum of the room. Outside, the willows swayed in a sensual dance to the wind. Wrapping his arm around my waist, he stood, wincing at the pain in his ribs. A stab of anger pierced me. Goddamn Marcos.

"Let's eat something. I'm starving," he groaned and kissed my forehead.

"Wait. That's it? No *moment*?"

"Sorry?"

"No post-mind-blowing-sex moment, where you look into my eyes and tell me you want to grow old with me?" I smirked as I reached into the dresser for one of his T-shirts, quickly sliding it over my head. He grabbed my wrist and pulled me back into his arms, pressing his forehead to mine.

"Sorry. I'm an asshole."

"I was messing with you, but your guilty face is my new favorite." I pinched his chin and pulled away.

"Wait." Wrapping a quick arm around my waist, he locked me against him again, then winced.

"Sebas, careful."

"Let me take your shoes off," he murmured seductively.

"What?"

"Come." He took my hand and led me to the bed, then untied the ribbons of my shoes with careful diligence, caressing my legs as he did. It felt as intimate and loving as the moment we'd just had. Stinging tears threatened. I tilted my head to the side.

"Ay, Palacios. At this rate we'll be here all night." He looked up at me and I winked.

Without responding, he picked me up with one hand, threw me over his shoulder, and carried me into the kitchen while I squealed.

I popped the Chinese leftovers into the microwave and yawned. The wall clock said it was 4:00 a.m. I turned to get the dishes, and a yellow bakery box at the end of the counter caught my eye.

"What's this?" I reached over and opened it. My eyes widened at the single vanilla cupcake, the delicate swirl of frosting a perfect work of art. I looked up at Sebastián, and he was smiling.

"I got it for you earlier. Reminds me of our day in Colonia, sitting at the curb by that bakery while you devoured that vanilla cupcake."

"You are unnervingly romantic." I turned to him and kissed his lips softly. "Seriously, what did I ever do right? You know you're nuts by putting up with me. I'm disorganized, distracted, my friends are rude…What are you doing with me?" I whispered.

"I'm in love with you," he said, his expression serious. And I kissed him so hard I almost knocked him off the barstool.

We ate in comfortable silence, our legs intertwined under the kitchen bar. He wiped a crumb off my lip, and I kissed the pad of his thumb.

"So when are we leaving?" he asked.

"Where?"

"New York."

"Oh, the performance dates are in a little over three weeks. Will you be able to get away from work?"

"I do own the studio, Camila. I can take a few days off if I want to."

"Right."

"What is it?"

"Don't be mad," I said, looking up at him. "It's none of my business, but…"

He sighed. "What?"

"I overheard your argument with Julián last night."

He frowned. "And?"

"And…I don't know. Is it a good idea for you to take off while so much is going on at the docks?"

His jaw flexed. "This stuff with my father, it needs to end." He took my hand and kissed it. "It will all settle, soon."

An image of Marcos and his friends around Sebastián barged in my mind, then Julián's voice, *What did this girl do to you?* And the thought of anything settling anytime soon never seemed more impossible.

Chapter 35

I set the alarm to 6:00 a.m. that Monday. We had had two days to rest, and it was time to get back to work. Two days had also passed since the cast party and since I had last seen or talked to Marcos. I was still angry at him. Being Marcos's partner had always been a distant, elusive dream for me. The last few days, however, I wanted to kick him in the balls. But I had to fix things between us or our partnership wouldn't work.

I hurried into the studio, shrugging off my jacket as I dropped my bag by the barre where Marcos was already warming up.

"Morning," I muttered.

He looked up, assessing my mood. "Morning."

"I'm not going to give you a lecture," I said without looking at him. "Just cut the shit with Sebastián. Whatever your problem is, leave him out of it."

"Funny, I thought I was doing just that."

"I'm serious. Cut it out."

"I'm not afraid of him, Cams."

I looked up at him. "The only reason he didn't kick your ass last night was because I made him promise me he wouldn't. The last thing I expected was for you all to act like a bunch of fucking cowards. But if you or your boys go near him again, I won't give a shit what the outcome is."

"Is that a threat?" He smirked.

"Since you've met him, you've done nothing but provoke him. So stop. We're partners now, but it's not going to work if there's constant tension between us. Let's go back to the way things were at work."

He stepped closer. His gaze paused on my mouth before moving to my eyes. "That's what I want too."

The countdown to closing night for *Giselle* began, overlapping with the rehearsals for the tour in New York. Time was precious, and Madame warned every dancer that, for the next month, our time inside and out of the studio belonged to her.

The days became long routines of classes followed by rehearsals, followed by costume fittings and after-work meetings to address adjustments to the variations. We were all consumed by it. Balance went out the window, as it usually did during busy times at the theater. Sebastián was patient with the hurdles of my career and the little time it left for us.

It didn't help that my upcoming principal role ticked inside me like a time bomb. I was determined to seize the huge opportunity Federico had given me. Detaching myself from the world, I walked around like a zombie, mentally counting steps. Sebastián said on the nights I stayed over, I even mumbled them in my sleep.

Madame's voice took precedence in my head, her corrections replaying with no end as I obsessed to perfect the things she pointed out.

One morning, Madame and Federico called the soloists to run through their main variations alone. I was third in line and hurried to a barre in the back to warm up and rehearse. I looked around for Marcos—he was always here before me—but couldn't find him.

In the center, Nata and Diego performed the pas de deux while the others watched with the familiar glint of jealousy betraying the admiration in their expressions. Madame gave Nata and Diego minor corrections, but overall, they were flawless, beautiful. Nata wiped the sweat off her face as she listened to Madame attentively, her ivory skin misted with a sheer glow. My turn was approaching, and it was normally Marcos who eased my nerves before rehearsal runs like this one, but he was still missing. I pushed deeper into a split and squeezed my eyes shut to keep my insecurities at bay. Where in the hell was he?

A shadow came in my periphery. A body warming up. I immediately recognized the scent. *The venomous fragrance of lilies.* Beside me, Verónica propped a leg up on the barre, letting out an obnoxiously heavy sigh. I ignored her, keeping my eyes on the couple dancing in the far front.

"So, how's it going? Nervous?" Her voice was laced with the usual sourness.

"No. But you should be. Your développé is sloppy. You are screwing up the corps line."

"My form is perfect," she snapped. "It's yours that needs work."

"Don't project, it's pathetic. But hey, thanks for caring."

"Oh, I *do* care," she said, her voice lower but equally charged with detestation. "Your luck will run out sooner or later."

"Go be a better dancer. Maybe then you'll get *lucky* too."

She leaned toward me as I stretched into my other leg, her face uncomfortably close. "Myrta was *my* part," she hissed. "I worked my ass off for it. I don't know what you did with Federico to secure these roles, but things will change eventually. I'm a better dancer than you. Sooner or later you'll fuck things up, and I'll be waiting."

I fought the bile that rose to my throat and met her raven eyes straight on. "All you've got is venom," I said. "Spit it out on someone else." I stood and pushed past her, causing her to stumble back as I clenched my teeth to bite back my own venom. From the farthest entrance, Marcos walked in, followed by Andrea, the choreographer. Her face was flush.

"Where the hell were you?" I spat out.

"Got a little caught up in something." He grinned like the cat who just ate the canary. I glanced at Andrea, who was at the front, going through her notes, her hair slightly disheveled.

"*Her?* Marcos…" I frowned.

"Ah. Don't worry about it," he said, kissing my shoulder. I shrugged him off. "It's all good. Help me warm up?" He ushered me to the back while another couple took the floor.

I helped him warm up in silence. In the front, Federico leaned on the barre with his back to the mirror, his arms crossed over his chest. He watched the dancers intently, making suggestions here and there as each performer gave everything they had, pouring their hearts out to gain the approval of the man whose opinion mattered to us the most in the world.

Our turn came and we stepped into the middle, my pulse still charged from the exchange with Verónica.

We dove into the choreography for Aurora and the prince's wedding dance, and I focused on each movement. Flying through the steps I had practiced, I counted to stay precise, my body warming up as we danced the pas de deux. When we finished, my heart was flying. I wiped my forehead, catching my breath as Federico approached. He gave a few minor corrections to Marcos, then turned to me.

"Looks good, but remember to keep your shoulders down. I can see the tension." His hands clasped my shoulders gently and turned me to the mirror. "When you lock your shoulders, you can't engage your back," he said, lifting my shoulders slightly. "See? You also lose that beautiful look of a long neck. Use your abs more."

"Okay," I said. He must have seen the anxiety in my face, because he gave me a reassuring nod.

"Do some push-ups to improve your core strength and three minutes of planking every night before bed. Really focus on keeping your back straight. Think of your posture even when you aren't dancing."

From the mirror, Madame nodded knowingly, having corrected my posture a gazillion times. I knew it was just stress, but at this level, you were expected to manage it.

"I will. Thank you." We stepped away to let the next dancer get into position.

Marcos nudged my shoulder. "You're doing well. Relax." He ambled toward the back, and Andrea gestured for me to approach.

"Camila," she said. "There are a couple of things I want you to think about for this variation. For the wedding dance, remember that Aurora is a princess dancing at her own wedding. An aristocrat. It's important for that to come through in every step, even as you greet the guests. Keep working on the long port de bras sequence and the ménage at the end. Remember the king and queen are watching. As you finish, show confidence and humility. Aurora knows she's done well. She walks forward, carefully, with elegance. It would never occur to her to run." She demonstrated as I took mental notes, absorbing every move. Andrea was very good at her job, passionate. I could see why she had managed to turn Marcos's head. But a member of the staff? Did he have no boundaries?

"Let's work on this again later," she said. "But you did exceptionally well. Good work."

I thanked her and assured her I would apply her corrections to my variation. Madame caught me as I headed to my bag for water. She was all business. Notebook and pen in hand, spectacles halfway down her nose.

"Navarro, I want you to stay after class today. Andrea's schedule is very limited. She can stay late tonight, so I want you to start working on the changes she made for you. We are very short on time."

Fuck. "Okay, no problem." I let out a deep breath. Another night working late. Another evening I wouldn't spend with Sebastián.

At lunch break, I scurried to my apartment and sank into a cold bath. My body burned, and the pain in my ankle wouldn't let up. I had seen the sports medicine doctor, and he said to stay off of it. Right. I iced it every night and that helped, but I knew it wouldn't go away until the season break. Being in pain had me on edge. My phone rang as I was rushing back to the theater.

"Hi." Sebastián's deep voice lifted my spirits instantly. "Baby, where are you? I came to take you out to lunch, but you're not at work."

"Oh, no. I came to my apartment to take a bath. I wish you'd told me."

"I wanted to surprise you."

Tears prickled. "Shit. Sorry."

"Don't worry about it. I'll see you tonight. We have the dinner with the Germans. I'm looking forward to finally having an evening with you."

I stopped in my tracks. "Dammit. I totally forgot about that. I'm so sorry, Sebas, I have to stay at work tonight. Madame needs me to work on some last-minute changes."

He let out a long sigh. "Babe, you've been working long hours every evening. This is a huge deal for the studio. Can't you get a pass? Tell her you've had this planned for a month. It's important."

"She's staying after hours too. I can't tell her I have a *dinner*. Look, I'm sorry. Maybe I can join you later?" I hurried across the street.

"What time will you be done?" The strain in his voice was discernible even over the background noise of the city.

"I don't know. I'll call you, okay?"

"All right," he muttered, then hung up.

I now understood why most dancers didn't date outside of work. Our world was foreign, inhospitable. Like a planet where nobody could breathe but us. Blending it with Sebastián's world was like forcing two opposite ends of a magnet together.

I didn't make it to the dinner with the Germans, or to any of the other social events he wanted me to attend in the days that followed. Part of me was frustrated he didn't fully get it. Another part simply longed for our relationship to go back to a happy place, without hectic schedules and tension.

Thursday I was alone for lunch. I needed to boost my energy and decided to hit the smoothie place around the corner.

I winced at the midmorning sun. The air was dense, simmering into spring. I nodded at Alexei's oversized frame leaning on the wall. Tilting his chin up, he put out his cigarette. He was less distant now that things between the Zchestakovas and Sebastián's family weren't as tense.

"She coming out?" he asked.

"No. She has to rehearse through lunch. I doubt she'll come out at all till this evening."

He acknowledged with a nod and pulled out another cigarette.

"Alexei, those will kill you."

A tiny comma curved up a corner of his mouth. "You take care, *printsessa*."

I was about to cross at the light when two bodies eased out of a silver Audi a few steps ahead. I immediately recognized Julián's purposeful stride. Fuckdammit. What did he want? A chill slithered down my neck. The light changed, and I blended into the moving crowd.

"Camila," he said, catching up with me as I reached the sidewalk. I cursed inwardly and turned. He smiled widely, flashing his perfect teeth. His feline green eyes captured mine, confident, stunning. "Do you have a sec?"

"Um, I only have fifteen minutes to get a smoothie." Damn, why was my voice so small? I gestured to the shop a few steps away.

"I'll join you. I need to ask you a favor. It's important."

A favor? Me? What the fuck. "Oh…okay." Out of the corner of my eye, I noticed another guy following a few steps behind. His bodyguard?

"Look, this is going to sound weird…" We got in line at the smoothie shop, and he ran a hand through his hair the same way Sebastián did. A good fifteen people stood ahead of us. He pressed his lips then turned to his bodyguard. "Order her a…" He glanced at me. "What would you like?" I frowned and he sighed. "I need to talk to you and you don't have much time. Santi will get you whatever you want."

"Just a green smoothie," I said. I already didn't like where this was going.

Julián guided me to a table on the sidewalk tucked under an umbrella. He pulled out a chair for me, and I reluctantly sat, fighting the impulse to dash.

"I'll try to be brief," he said, taking a seat across from me and leaning forward like he was tackling a business deal. "Look, the studio needs Sebastián here for the next month. We may be in trouble if he's away."

"Okay?" I frowned.

"Sebastián told me yesterday he's planning on going to New York with you. You can't let that happen."

"I—Excuse me. What?"

"It's important. I need him here for the next month, and his father wants him here as well. We have some crucial shipments arriving, and Sebastián is key to things going smoothly."

"That's something you need to discuss with him."

"You don't understand. Don Martín won't let him walk away in the middle of all this. Not without a consequence. Our most affluent clients at the studio also do business with Don Martín. If he gives the word, they will pull out their accounts from our portfolio. If that happens, our business won't survive. Camila, that studio is Sebastián's dream. What he's worked his entire life to achieve."

"Then his father has to respect that," I snapped.

"Look," he said, reining in his impatience. "You don't know this family. In Don Martín's eyes, having his son at his side comes first. Sebastián's always kept a safe distance, but when he met you, he made the decision to finally walk away."

"Even if I wanted to help, I don't know what you think I can do. I have nothing to do with all this."

He watched me with a *How are you not getting this?* expression. "In Don Martín's mind, you're the reason why his son is distancing himself from the family business."

"Just in Don Martín's mind?"

He scanned the lunch passersby. "Frankly, right now, you're in the way."

A slow shiver traveled through me. "That's not...by choice."

"You can't let him go with you to New York."

"Look, I don't know why you're talking to me about all this. Sebastián is not a child that you and his father can manipulate. He's a grown man and he knows what's best for his business, just explain things to him the way you're explaining them to me. He's not stupid."

"Christ, have you not heard a word I've said? Sebastián's determined to do this. For you. And he's a Palacios. He would rather lose everything than back down. That's why I need your help."

"What do you want from me?" I sighed in irritation. I wanted to leave. This was nuts.

"Get out of the way," he said softly. "He needs to sort this out without you."

"That makes no sense," I said.

"Let me put it another way," he said more impatiently. "As it is now, things will never be smooth in your relationship. The family business will always interfere. Haven't you noticed by now? Don Martín will never allow Sebastián to leave the docks if he thinks he's being influenced by someone else, especially a woman. Sorry." He shrugged. "I know it sounds chauvinistic. But that's how things are."

"I still don't know what you want from me."

"For the moment you have to cut all ties with Sebastián. Don Martín has to be sure you're no longer in the picture."

"What? No, besides, Sebastián will never go along with that."

"You're right," he said, nodding like he had already thought of everything. "There's only one way Sebastián will let you distance yourself."

"And what's that?"

"You've got to convince him that's what *you* need. Tell him you don't feel safe."

"What? Why?"

"The Medinas saw you the day you and Sebastián delivered the soccer uniforms. They're not happy Sebastián no longer wants to mediate between them and Don Martín. They're dangerous and Sebastián knows it. If you tell him you don't feel safe, he'll immediately distance himself to protect you, trust me."

Trust you? I scowled. "I won't become Carolina, if that's what you mean. That's so...fucking manipulative."

"I know you care about him," he said calmly. "I'm going back to Germany in a few days. There's a group of investors there that could secure things for us at the studio. Until then, I need Sebastián to be in Buenos Aires to handle the shipments for his father and the Medinas. Once that's on track, we'll find a replacement and he can start backing out. The Medinas will be more agreeable once their business is secure. But, like I said, you can't be involved."

"I don't *want* to be involved." I grabbed my bag, but he stopped me.

"You're a distraction. We can't risk going to war with the Medinas. And it's not just them. There are others who won't like Sebastián leaving. You and your family will be in danger too."

It was as if he had kicked me in the gut. My family? Fuck. "I don't know what the hell you think I can do."

"This is not a game. Do whatever you need to do. Leave him if you have to."

I drew in a sharp breath. His deep green eyes seemed bottomless, holding dark secrets that would never see the light. The message was clear: *I order, you bow.* This was the businessman even the Russians feared. A King of Midnight bullying me into his plan, or Don Martín's plan, or the Medinas', or whoever the fuck's. It didn't matter. I clenched my teeth.

"This is not just about Sebastián, is it? It's about you too. Is it a power thing? You want your own *kingdom*?"

His expression hardened. "Sebastián and I have been friends since we were kids. He's like a brother to me. Don't you dare question my motives, girl." His words came out like a whip, as if he had slapped me. For the first time, he had lost his cool. Every cell in him radiated ire: his eyes, his jaw, his mouth, the way his eyebrows furrowed together. He looked away, then back at me. The anger had vanished, but the fire in his eyes flickered, pinning me to my seat. "I'll be fine no matter what. I've got enough money and contacts to start over if it comes to that. But Sebastián will risk everything if he goes against his father before the midnight shipments are in." His frown deepened. "You love him. You have to help."

"I have to go." I pushed my chair back and shouldered my bag. Santi finally appeared with my smoothie.

"Thank you," I murmured, grabbing it. Without looking at Julián, I dove into the crowd, letting it swallow me.

I felt like throwing up all day and couldn't concentrate. In the evening, instead of going home, I took a taxi to Sebastián's house. He was sitting under the pergola, strumming the chords of his guitar absentmindedly. The beautiful melody filled the air, somber, mournful, mirroring my mood. The weight of the conversation with Julián pushed down on my shoulders, seeping into every muscle like ink.

"Hey." I kissed his head and sank into a chair beside him.

He smiled and put the guitar down.

"I thought you weren't coming tonight. I would have picked you up."

I wasn't...but I've missed you."

"I've missed you too." His hand reached for mine and enveloped it. Suddenly I felt small, fragile. "You look beat, sweetheart. Want to go to bed?"

"Yes, that sounds great." I studied our interlaced fingers. Olive against sand.

"Did you eat?"

"I'm not hungry."

"Camila, you've got to eat, babe. You've lost weight."

"Please. I'm bone-tired. I'll eat breakfast before we leave tomorrow. I promise."

He stood and pulled me into his arms. I inhaled him: Heaven, sunshine, fresh laundry. My own personal oasis. I blinked tears that stung. How could I ever walk away from him? I pressed my face against his chest and squeezed him hard, unable to control the sobs that escaped.

"Hey," he said softly. "What's wrong?"

"Everything. I'm just...so tired."

His arms around me tightened. "Things will get better, baby. Don't cry. I've got you."

I cried harder, realizing how much I wanted that to be true. But Julián's words had tormented me all afternoon. I knew Sebastián would selflessly give up whatever it took to be with me. He would face his father and possibly lose his studio. I couldn't let that happen. Maybe Julián was right and this time it was I who had to protect him. But the idea of letting him go felt like ripping my heart out. I exhaled against his chest, too tired to think, relishing that one moment of perfect peace between us.

"You look like the Ice Queen." Sebastián smiled. We were in his bed, me dozing off in front of the TV while he shuffled through work papers. Ice packs plastered my ankles, feet, and knees.

"More like the abominable snowman," I muttered. "I'm in so much pain. My feet bleed constantly, and my ankle feels like I sprained it."

"Have you?"

"No, it's the same old injury."

Putting his papers down, he reached down to kiss my temple. "I know a way to make you forget about the pain," he whispered.

"Really?" I snapped. "Why do men always think sex fixes everything? The last thing I need right now is sex!" I readjusted my pillow and groaned.

He said nothing and went back to his papers.

"I'm sorry." I sighed. "I didn't mean that. I'm just so damned tired."

He nodded in understanding. "Anything I can do?"

I shook my head. He caressed my face, shoulder, then the length of my arm. Pulling the covers, he reached for my feet and moved down on the bed so he could give me a foot massage. His deft fingers worked gently around my blisters, slowly, diffusing the tension knotted in my battered feet. I closed my eyes and gave in to the heavenly sensation. Tears spilled before I realized. Fuck, I was crying again? I hated feeling this vulnerable. He pressed a soft kiss on the bottom of my foot, kissed the other, then scooted up and wrapped himself around me. We stayed like that in silence. I felt safe, loved. Then an image of Julián barged into my mind. *You love him. You have to help.* My heart constricted.

"Cami," he said softly, stroking my cheek. "I'm so proud of you. Of how hard you're fighting after your dream. You inspire me." I opened my eyes, and there was so much love in his expression.

Fuck Julián.

Kicking away the ice packs, I crawled onto his lap. "I love you, Sebastián. So much. I want you to know that."

"I love you too."

I tangled my fingers in his hair, ravaging his mouth. I kissed him with abandon, every part of me aching for him. A low groan vibrated deep in his throat. Our teeth clinked together, and I wanted that mouth on me everywhere. He lay back on the bed, adjusting me on top of him. I slid one leg between his, grinding against his thigh. His hands caressed my sides and my backside, exploring, kneading, memorizing every inch of me like it was the first time. I moaned as he peeled off my panties and stripped me of my camisole. His hands found my breasts and kneaded them softly. I seized his mouth again, rubbing my chin against his soft stubble. *Consume me*, I thought. *Make me yours. Over and over.*

Our bodies exchanged breaths, moans, growls. I melted in his hands as he possessed me, devoured me. I kissed the rippled lines of his stomach, following the happy trail down, the perfect V between his hipbones, then took him in my mouth, my tongue wrapping around the smooth silk. I looked up at him from under my lashes and imprinted his expression in my memory: eyes half open, mouth slack, surrendered. It made me giddy, drunk with power. I wanted to make him mine too. I swirled my tongue around and around, my lips shielding my teeth as I took him deeper into my mouth, and he let out a low growl. He was so beautiful. My king. And I couldn't help wanting more. I wanted everything.

"Camila, babe. Fuck." He tangled his hands in my hair, clenching it. I smiled and released him, then climbed back over the planes of his hard, chiseled body.

He clasped my hips and lowered me onto him. Slowly. Oh, so slow, making me feel every inch of him as he pushed deeper inside me. I threw my head back, riding him while he guided me. I moved faster, seeking the precious friction, and soon, I was lost. The room spun and I squeezed my eyes shut, gravity pulling me from shifting angles. He thrust harder and I moaned, collapsing on top of him, my hair dripping over him like ink, our chests heaving in a staccato of breaths. His heart pounded against my cheek while mine stuttered. High. Drunk on him. I pressed my face against his chest. We would find a way.

As I hurried down the theater hallways the next day, I felt a difference. The energy had changed. Or was I just now noticing? In the studio, we worked in silence, like oiled machines. The usual chatter in the background had faded, and every day we dedicated ourselves to our work and our bodies. The concern about possible injuries was high, so we all took special care. Late nights at the clubs were replaced by chiropractor sessions and soaking in the tub before the mandatory, ever present ice wrapped around old and potential injuries.

I couldn't attend Sebastián's social events that weekend because I was rehearsing, one more reminder that our worlds were incompatible, so he went with Julián and Mercedes. The thought of Sebastián at a party with Mercedes by his side or swarmed by other women stung, and I did my best to push it away.

On Tuesday, as I rushed out for my usual lunch smoothie, a text from Sebastián vibrated in my pocket.

I'll pick you up at eight tonight for the charity dinner. Let's talk dates for NY. There's a terrace in Brooklyn I want to show you. Cocktails, sunset, and you. I can't wait, love.

New York… It wrung my stomach as Julián's emerald eyes pierced my thoughts. Was I being selfish and delusional by ignoring his warnings? What if he was right? What if Don Martín and the Medinas did think I was the reason for Sebastián's decision to detach himself from his family business? *Wasn't I?* And my family…Was I putting them in danger? The thought sent a wave of nausea. That was nonnegotiable. Would Sebastián be able to protect them, or was I completely blind to the reality of all this?

The realization that Julián's plan of separating us might be the soundest option depressed me. Sebastián was a businessman, but he was also über protective and passionate, and this could all go to hell, and as Don Martín had said to me when we met, *passion can be a dangerous thing if it's not well directed.*

Since my conversation with Julián four days ago, I had felt a constant boulder in my chest. I hurried home and dressed for the dinner event with Sebastián, a gala at a house in Barrio Parque, one of the wealthiest, most beautiful neighborhoods in Buenos Aires. I was looking forward to a night with Sebastián, and away from a leotard.

The downstairs bell rang as I was slipping into my heels. I adjusted the gown I had borrowed from Nata. It was pearl-colored silk; long, elegant, beautiful.

Sebastián was breathtaking in a black tux. He pulled me into his arms, and I let the familiar warmth swallow me, lingering a bit longer than usual.

"Everything okay?"

"Yes." I mustered a smile, wishing we could freeze the moment and stay in each other's arms.

The party was an excess of wealth. Overkill in every aspect. Giant vases of fresh orchids dressed every table, waiters in white tuxes circulated, offering delicacies and champagne. Contortionists and entertainers from a world-famous circus meandered around the ample rooms, interacting with the guests and performing amusing tricks.

"What's all this for again?" I asked Sebastián as we walked in hand in hand.

"The Cornú Foundation for Autism. I've always been involved. They do a lot to fund research."

"Huh. Wouldn't it be easier if these people just *gave* the money directly to the foundation? I mean, how much does a party like this cost?"

Sebastián chuckled. "It probably would. But this is how charity functions work. The wealthy want the red velvet carpet rolled out for them. They want to toast with Cristal and be amused by the most expensive entertainment money can buy, and in return, they'll open up their wallets and fund a good cause."

I looked around in awe. The protocol of being rich. Could I ever get used to this? We mingled among Buenos Aires's elite, men in tuxedos and women wrapped in silk and expensive fragrances. Sebastián blended in easily. This was a game he knew well, and I understood it was because this was a part of him. He had been born among the rich, spoke their language, and charmed them with the manners of a perfect gentleman. I could see it on their faces, the way their mouths slowly curved up when he spoke, their eyes bright as they awarded him their full attention. He could probably ask anything of these people, and they would give it to him willingly.

I stood beside him while he conversed with an older couple with stiff hairdos. Both had more plastic surgery than I had ever imagined possible. They asked lots of questions about the new wing at the Malba museum, which Sebastián had designed.

"I told your father," the woman said in a voice worn away by whisky and too many cigarettes. "You see things differently than the rest of us. That's why your talent is so unique."

"Nora, You're making me blush." Sebastián gave her a full smile, causing *her* to blush. Mustering a polite excuse, he wrapped an arm around my waist and led me to the terrace. "I want to be alone with you," he said into my ear. "Let's get some air and talk about New York before another week passes us by."

"Sebastián…" I grasped his arm, but a young waiter rushing by abruptly bumped into me, spilling an entire glass of red wine on my gown. I looked down in shock at the ruined dress.

"I'm so sorry," he blurted. Then his face turned a bright magenta as we both took in the full extent of what he had done. "Shit," he muttered. "I'm so sorry, miss. I…" He quickly reached into an inner pocket and pulled out a handkerchief. Sebastián gripped his arm.

"She needs a goddamn *towel*. Look at her," he said through his teeth.

The waiter nodded, mortified. I almost felt sorry for him.

"It's okay," I said. "It's fine."

"Darling, are you all right?" A young woman in a long, black chiffon gown appeared from behind Sebastián.

"No, she's not all right, look at her, Juliana," said Sebastián impatiently.

She turned and smiled at him. They obviously knew each other. She was attractive, and an immediate protective instinct awoke in me.

"Come with me," Juliana crooned in a soft, low voice that was almost hypnotic. "We'll fix this." She then looked up at Sebastián. "My brother's looking for you, Sebas." She then hooked her arm in mine like we were close friends. I looked over at Sebastián. *Help?*

"Rafa will go with you," he said, but Juliana chuckled, rolling her eyes.

"For Christ's sake, Sebastián. It's a *party*. I will take care of her." She waved him off and quickly towed me through the crowd of guests to a back door. We then followed a long hallway leading to an opulent marble staircase.

"Let's go upstairs, much bigger bathroom," she said, gesturing to the upper floor without stopping. She let go of my arm, and I gathered my gown, carefully following her upstairs while balancing my weight on the stilettos. She knew her way around the house, and I wondered who this woman was and what her connection was to Sebastián.

365

Once we reached the top, she opened an ornate wooden door to a bathroom that was almost as big as my apartment. Everything was white marble. A colossal crystal chandelier hung over us, projecting rainbow patterns that gave the room a fairytale feel. We were in a sitting area with a double vanity framed by a large mirror. A long hallway led to an equally ample room with a grand shower, bathtub, etc. I looked around, mesmerized.

"What a mess," Juliana said, studying the dark burgundy spill on my dress. "I'll get you a bigger towel, wait here." She hurried down the hallway and disappeared through a door in the back.

I stepped to the vanity and tried drying the wine off with a hand towel. Shit, it was one of Nata's new dresses, and replacing it would surely cost me a fortune. I jumped when the door behind me opened, and a man in his thirties walked in. I expected him to apologize and leave, but he didn't. He closed the door behind him and smiled. His face looked vaguely familiar, but my pulse spiked in warning when he simply stood there, blocking the way out.

"Excuse me," I said, "I was just—"

"Miss Navarro, forgive the intrusion," he said in a low, raspy voice. "I'm deeply sorry about your dress. We'll send you a replacement. In the meantime, Juliana will get you one of hers. I believe you're the same size." He eyed me up and down slowly and my skin crawled.

"Do...I know you?"

"No. And I've been eager to meet you, but away from Sebastián and his entourage," he said with a lopsided smile.

A slow chill traveled through me. "What...do you want?"

"Sit down, please. We don't have much time." He gestured to the armchairs beside us as massive man in a black suit entered and blocked the door. Shit. Shit. Shit.

"It will just be a moment," he said. "There's nothing for you to worry about, sweetheart. Arlo is just ensuring nobody disturbs us."

Fear expanded in my chest as I slowly eased down on a plush armchair while he took the one across from me. I glanced down the hallway where Juliana had disappeared. Was she in on this?

"Juliana will be back later." He smiled smugly. My breath caught. *That Bitch.*

"Why am I here? Who are you?" I said with fake bravado.

He didn't answer right away. Instead, he let the moment linger and stroked his chin, watching me.

I straightened my back, tension coiling around my stomach as I racked my brain for a way out. "Sir, I—"

"Pedro. Pedro Medina."

The name immediately registered, drawing the oxygen from the room. A flashback of the incident with the black SUV barged into my mind. He was one of them. The Medinas.

"Like I said," he continued, oblivious, "I only want a moment of your time. You see, I'm a business associate of Sebastián's, and I hear he's making plans to leave the family business completely when, as it is, he's not as involved as we would like him to be." He waved his hand in the air dismissively. "He's always come through when we needed him. This time, however, he seems determined to cut ties. So, I ask myself, are you the reason?"

"Sir, I don't—"

He raised his palm. "No need to answer that, darling. I just wanted to chat with you, explain how important Sebastián's presence at the docks is to our business. We're about to bring in our biggest shipment ever. I'm sure you understand—"

"Mr. Medina—"

"Pedro."

"Pedro, I'm not involved with any of that."

"I figured you'd say that." He grinned. "But I'm a skeptical man, and I would like to make sure, so I need you to come with me." He nodded at Arlo who then swung open the door. Pedro reached his hand out to me. "Shall we?"

I scowled at his hand. What the actual fuck?

Sebastián appeared at the door. He froze when he saw me sitting next to Pedro Medina.

"What the hell is this?" he snapped. His jaw tensed as his gaze flew from Medina to me. "Cami, come here, love." He gestured and I stood, but Medina caught my arm and yanked me to him as he got to his feet, clutching me against his chest. I yelped and Sebastián pounced forward, but Arlo seized him and pressed a silver gun to his temple. I struggled under Medina's strong grip.

"Let go," I snapped.

"Pedro, I swear on my dead mother's grave, if you don't let go of her right now—"

"What?" Pedro said in a defying tone. "You'll do what? You know you can't touch me. You wouldn't break the pact, would you? For her?"

Sebastián wrestled under Arlo's hold, but the guy was huge, and pressed the gun harder against Sebastián's head.

"You can't touch her either," Sebastián said. "Let her go."

"Oh, yes, I can. She's not family. So she's free play. The other families aren't happy with this distraction either."

"I'll put a fucking bullet through your head if you don't let her go right now. She's not involved with my father. This will only make things worse for you."

Medina smiled. "Easy, now. You wouldn't want to start a war with my brothers. She comes with me until the midnight deal is finished at the docks next week. I'll keep her…safe." He ran his free hand down my gown to my hip. I fought him off, but his other arm tightened around my waist, my racing pulse hammering in my temples. Sebastián's jaw clenched.

Rafa burst through the door, startling everyone. Sebastián seized the brief instant to knock the gun out of Arlo's hand and shove him back against the wall. Rafa drew his gun and pointed it at the bodyguard's head. Arlo froze, glowering at Rafa while Sebastián picked up the gun and pointed it at Medina.

"Get your fucking hands off her. Now."

"Ah, such a hot temper, Sebastián. I'm unarmed."

"Now." Sebastián cocked the gun.

Medina ignored him. His stubble scraped my cheekbone as he pressed his lips to my ear. I darted a look at Rafa; frustration and rage darkened his eyes while he kept Arlo in place. I vainly tried pushing Medina back.

"Relax, sweetheart. I'll take care of you. And who's to say, you may not want to go back to him when this is over."

Sebastián fired a silent bullet, hitting Medina on the shoulder farthest from me. His body jerked back with the impact, his grip loosened, and I broke away. Medina stumbled back, his face a mask of anger and confusion. He scowled at Sebastián, then slowly dropped to the ground. His hand clasped the shoulder where the bullet had hit him, and blood dripped between his fingers, quickly soaking his shirt.

"You're fucked, Palacios," he growled. "Fucked!"

"Camila, baby. Come here." Sebastián gestured for me. I hurried to him, and he tucked me under his free arm, pressing me against him. He kissed my head, his other hand still aiming the gun at Medina. "You okay?" he murmured into my ear.

My heart raced, adrenaline and fear rushing through my veins as I tightened my arms around him. I closed my eyes, pressing my face against his chest, breathing in short, labored breaths.

"Cami." His arm squeezed me. "Are you all right?"

"Yes, yes," I said, nodding.

Rafa was already on his phone, and in less than a minute, Tano and another bodyguard burst in.

"Keep him here for a while," Sebastián said, nodding at Medina's bodyguard. "And take Pedro to see Dr. Zabala. He's on call. Use the side hallway that leads to the back house. Make sure no one sees you."

The men moved quickly and silently, clutching Medina by both arms to help him up.

"You're a dead man," he groaned as they ushered him past us. "My brothers will have your head for this."

Sebastián waited until he was gone, then, uncocking the gun, slid it into his waistband at the back and clutched me with both arms. "I'm sorry. Are you okay? This is my fault. Fuck. Fuck!"

"Sebastián, no. How could you know?"

"I should've come with you."

"How did you find me?"

"I told my men to keep an eye on Pedro, but they had lost sight of him, so Rafa was organizing a search. That's when I went looking for you. One of the guests waiting for the restroom saw you going upstairs." He took my face in his hands, his eyes drawn in fear and regret. "*Christ.*" He kissed my forehead. "If anything had happened to you. Anything at all. I just…" He wrapped me in his arms. "I am so sorry."

"I'm okay, Sebas. Really." But inside I was trembling.

He hugged me tight, his heart pounding hard and strong against my face. I had never seen Sebastián afraid before. He kissed my head repeatedly, murmuring apologies.

We left the party through a side exit and drove back to his house in silence, our hands interlaced, our thoughts lost in distant places. I rested my head against the cool window, staring at the taillights of the bodyguards' car ahead. Another car followed closely behind us, more men with more guns. Dread expanded in my chest as a realization sank.

Even a whole army of bodyguards wouldn't be able to save us from what the events from the night would trigger.

Chapter 36

I woke up in Sebastián's arms, his scent and traces of Ralph Lauren soothing my angst. We had slept like that, our bodies readjusting as we tossed and turned but never parting. His lips caressed my neck.

"I have the day off today," I said, stretching in his arms. "They're finally giving us a free Sunday. Should we talk about New York? Maybe you and I can leave this week, get away from all this. I'll talk to Federico."

He detangled from me and I turned to face him. His forehead was creased with concern. He traced my bottom lip with his thumb.

"What's wrong?" I said.

"I'm not coming to New York," he said softly.

"Why?"

He exhaled heavily, letting a long pause go by.

"Sebastián, what's wrong?" I sat up. "Is it because of last night?"

He nodded, sitting up and leaning against the bedframe. "They won't stop until this is over. Things are escalating, and I can't put you at risk again."

"It's okay," I said, reaching for his hand. "We'll lay low. If New York is not a good idea right now, you can just stay here and figure things out while I'm away."

"That's not enough. They've used you once to get to me, and they'll do it again."

"I'm not afraid," I lied.

He smiled sadly. "I won't take that risk with you."

"What do you mean?" I frowned.

"Camila, even with my bodyguards and my family's influence with the Families, I've put you in danger time and time again. We were followed to Luciana's house; the Medinas knew my bodyguards weren't with me. Ivanov is still after me after the incident with the girls, and he's a very dangerous man. Now this situation with Pedro...As long as you're with me, you're not safe. All this...shit, is something I need to fix, alone. You mean the world to me," he said, leaning closer and cupping my cheek. "If anything happened to you or your family because of me, because of all this crap that surrounds me—"

"It won't. You'll protect me, and them. I trust you."

"Last night was a close call. I won't let it happen again."

"What are you saying…" I muttered, breathless.

"I'm saying that I love you more than anything. So I have to let you go."

"What? No!" Tears rushed to my eyes. "No…"

"I'm sorry. But this is the only way."

"It can't be," I said, letting the tears spill. "You can triple the security, there's got to be something else."

His features tensed. "I shot one of them. They won't let this go."

"Please. I'm not Carolina. I know the world you exist in isn't perfect, but we can make this work, I know we can."

"I'll always be a Palacios."

"So what? I love you, just as you are. Give these people what they want, then end it, and we can have a life together. You have your studio."

He wiped the moisture off my cheeks. "I wish it were that simple."

"Why can't it be? Please don't give up on us, Sebastián."

He moved closer and pulled me into his arms. I let his warmth soothe me as I cried against his bare chest.

"Believe me when I tell you that this is the hardest thing I've ever had to do," he said.

"Then don't do it," I sobbed.

He pulled away to look at me. "You are not safe with me. Your family isn't either. I need to do this alone. I know you understand."

I shook my head no. He pulled me to him again, and I cried harder, breathing in short, shallow breaths. His arms tightened around me while, inside me, everything shattered like one of those safety glass walls, cracks spreading in every direction. He kissed my head, whispering soothing words until I could no longer bear it. I pushed away and stood, pacing the room frantically for my clothes. My eyes felt swollen and my throat hoarse.

"Camila," he said softly.

"No." I stopped abruptly and whipped around to face him. "You're a coward. You're giving up on us," I said, panting. He stood, walked to me, and reached his hand out, but I stepped back.

"Camila, please."

"Stay away from me," I said, my voice cracking, then turned and picked up my bag.

"Let me take you home."

"Hell, no. I don't want anything from you. This is what you want? You got it. Stay the fuck away."

Chapter 37

I walked into my dark, silent apartment. Inside me, loneliness spread like frost. I missed him already. It hadn't been an hour since I had left his house in a cab, and the pain was already unbearable.

I looked through the cabinets for vodka, bourbon, anything. I remembered Nata had started keeping chilled vodka for when the Russians came over and played cards. In the back of the freezer, I found a Russian label I recognized, *the good stuff*, and poured myself a shot. The alcohol scalded my throat, and I welcomed it as it burned its way down. I thought about the next day's rehearsal and poured myself another shot, then another. Before I finished the third, I dashed to the sink and threw up. *Loser. You can't even hold down a drink.*

I woke up on my bed ten hours later, still dressed and with my hair whipped around my face. Dim morning light filtered through the shutters, burning my eyes. My temples throbbed, announcing a hangover. I forced myself into a cold shower. It was a bitch, but it did the job and sobered me up some. Rushing quietly through my routine so I wouldn't wake Nata, I popped three painkillers and set off to work.

The morning was warm, the dense air brewing into a storm. My head pulsed with every car horn, every bus driver stepping hard on the gas. Dammit all. How would I get through today...*Focus on dancing,* I repeated to myself. I had to rise to the demands of Princess Aurora, the role every girl in the company would trade her soul for.

Madame's eyes were trained on me as soon as I entered the studio with my head down. I felt her gaze burning a hole in my back. She always knew when something was up. Well, I'd be damned if I was going to let things go to hell at work too. I slipped my ballet shoes on and took my usual spot at the bar to warm up. It was early, and the class was still filling. Marcos walked in a few seconds later. He nodded a greeting and joined my warm-up in silence.

I followed morning class like an automaton. My body knew every movement, and Madame's voice became a distant chant. *"Up, and down, and one, and two. Pa, pa, pa."* From the front, she surveyed me, suspicious. I had to fly under her radar, at least today. *Let me have today,* I prayed. *Tomorrow will be a new day.*

The class ended, and I ambled to my bag for a drink of water.

"Navarro." Madame's voice snapped in my ears like a whip. I froze in my spot and closed my eyes in a silent curse. Her quick, determined steps approached like the ticking of a bomb. I straightened my back and turned to face her. "You are lethargic today. Heavy," she said, eyeing me up and down as if I were an odd exhibit at the zoo. "Do I need to remind you the rules regarding partying the days before an opening night? I can smell the alcohol." Her mouth turned in disgust as she said it.

"No, Madame. I've been going straight home every night. I'm fighting a cold, that's all. But I've got good cold meds. Already on the mend." I feigned a smile, looking straight at her.

Her eyes narrowed a fraction, and after a brief moment she gave me a conspiratorial nod. "I'll allow a little leeway, but don't overdo it," she said, lowering her voice. "A single shot of good vodka before bed. It is the best remedy for the common cold."

I watched her, stunned, and had to almost repress a grin. As Nata's roommate, I had learned early on that, to most Russians, vodka was a sacred elixir against the flu. How had I not thought earlier of using this knowledge for hangover mornings?

During the afternoon rehearsal, Elena, my understudy for Aurora, sprained her ankle badly. Madame barked something in Russian and ordered Verónica to step in. *Fucking awesome.* My day was getting exponentially shittier. Verónica's exaggerated enthusiasm during the rehearsal got under my skin, and by the time we were done, I was ready for another date with the Russian bottle. The only thing that pulled me through was the thought of a massage I had scheduled for later that evening. But as I hurried down the theater stairs, my masseuse called to cancel because she was out with the flu.

Whispering a curse, I shoved my phone in my pocket and threw my dance bag over my shoulder, lumbering into the damp night air to hail a cab. The smell of wet asphalt drifted up from puddles painted with diesel rainbows left by an earlier rain. I headed toward Cerrito Street where I would have a better chance of finding a cab.

"Cami, wait up!" Marcos's voice called from behind. "You going home?" He jogged to catch up. He looked younger, chestnut hair tousled, gray sweatshirt cut off at the neck and sleeves showing off his roped biceps. When he reached me, his caramel eyes were bright, his cheeks still blushed from rehearsal.

"Wanna share a ride?" I scanned the street for a cab.

"Actually…" He scratched the back of his head and winced. "I was kinda hoping to crash at your place tonight. Is that cool?"

"Oh. Um…"

"Shit. You're still mad at me."

"No, Marcos," I said, hailing a cab. "I don't have energy to be mad at anyone right now, but it doesn't mean you can sleep over."

"Got it. No worries."

"What's wrong with your place?"

"Ugh. Carla's being a fucking pill. I need a night off."

I sighed. Part of me was glad I wasn't the only one with relationship issues. The cab pulled over by us. Fuck it.

"Let's go," I said.

"Thanks, Cams. You rock."

I showered after dinner and tied my hair into a messy knot. Marcos was already on the couch, pint of ice cream in one hand, TV remote in the other, feet on the coffee table. A spoon hung from his mouth as he surfed through the channels in boxers and a black T-shirt. His wet hair was whipped into a beautiful mess.

"You showered already?" I circled the couch. "Legs." I nodded, and he lifted his legs to let me by.

"Yeah, in Nata's. I like that strawberry shower shit she has." He stuffed a spoonful of ice cream in his mouth. I cocked an eyebrow, smirking at the ice cream container. "What?" he said defensively.

"Dude, you're a girl. Strawberry shower gel, ice cream, and a movie?" I plopped down next to him, propping my legs up next to his.

He wrapped his lips around the spoon and smiled as he pulled it out. "You—"

"I'll take it to my grave."

He eyed me and looked like he wanted to say something, and I took the remote from him. The heat from his body on my side was blazing. I was in pajama shorts, our bare legs almost touching. He placed his hand on my knee and it sent a shiver up my skin. I flinched and shifted, pretending to get comfortable.

"I've missed this," he said in a soft voice, and for a moment, I thought he would make a pass at me. He held my gaze, a snap of electricity sparking between us. Then with a swift move, he snatched the remote out of my hand. "But I'm picking the movie tonight." He grinned.

"You dick." I reached for the remote, but he lifted it up high, laughing.

"I'm teaching you valuable distraction techniques. You've got a lot to learn." He chuckled, flipping channels.

"I can still kick you out."

"Look, *Love Actually* is on. We can watch it, *again*." He got comfortable, and I laid my head on his shoulder. An image of Sebastián broke into my head, and my whole body tensed with guilt. I pulled away from Marcos, and before I realized, tears spilled down my cheeks.

"Ey…what's the matter?" he said softly, turning to face me.

I shook my head.

"What is it?"

"Nothing."

"Tell me."

"Sebastián and I…are having problems."

"Why?"

"It's complicated. I'm going to bed." I half stood but his hand grabbed mine.

"Wait." He tugged. "Come here. Talk to me."

"I don't want to talk about it. I just want to go to sleep."

His thumb stroked my hand. "I'm sorry."

"Are you?"

"I don't like seeing you like this."

I nodded. "Good night."

I lay in bed wide awake, going through the last month of my relationship with Sebastián: the hurdles of my crazy schedule, the tension about Marcos, Julián, Mercedes, Pedro Medina. But over all that was the boundless love I felt for him. What we had was real. Deep inside, I knew how hard this was for him, too, but admitting it meant willingly letting go of the best thing that had ever happened to me. Fuck if everything we overcame to be together in the last months had been for nothing, and in the end, Don Martín and his clan had won. Julián's torturing words circled in my head.

The family business will always get in the way.

Soft knocks on the front door woke me. I winced at my bedside clock— 7:00 a.m. Shit. Who in the hell knocked at this hour? Nata wasn't home and Marcos was a deep sleeper, so I mumbled a curse and kicked off the duvet.

From my bedroom doorway, I blinked a few times before the scene in the main room fully registered. My body instinctively froze while my heart kick-drummed my ribcage.

Marcos, still in his boxers and shirtless, was holding the front door open, rubbing the back of his head as he yawned. On the other side, Sebastián's frame towered over him. Even from where I was, the anger in Sebastián's expression was visible. Shit. Where the fuck was Marcos's shirt? Sebastián's gaze flew to me then back to Marcos, scanning him from head to toe.

"What the fuck are you doing here?" Sebastián's tone was low, charged. My pulse sprinted.

"Do come in." Marcos stepped aside and reached for his shirt, meeting my panicked eyes before turning back to Sebastián. "Don't worry," he said in a lower voice. "You didn't interrupt anything."

Sebastián's hand forcefully gripped Marcos's neck. "I said you were all out of warnings, asshole." He shoved him back and punched him under the ribs, knocking the air from Marcos's lungs.

Marcos gasped and doubled over. "Fuck."

"Stop!" I bolted forward, but before I could reach them, Marcos swung at Sebastián, who swiftly dodged it and threw another whiplash punch, this time on Marcos's chin, knocking him to the ground.

"That one's from before," Sebastián snarled. "Now get the fuck out."

Stepping between them, I gripped Sebastián's shirt at the chest, pushing him back and away from Marcos.

"Enough! What the hell do you think you're doing?"

Sebastián's eyes were trained on Marcos who was standing painfully.

"Are you okay?" I said to Marcos.

"Yeah," he said, wiping blood off his lip as he exhaled through flared nostrils. "I think your boyfriend forgot to take his meds." Picking up his jeans and shoes, he headed to the door, his eyes blazing as he darted a look at Sebastián, then me. "Catch you later, babe."

Sebastián's eyes stayed on the open door even though Marcos was gone.

"He spent the night?" A muscle ticked in his jaw.

"He just crashed on the couch. He needed a place to stay. Besides, that's no longer your business, is it?" I said acidly.

"Why is this guy in your apartment in his fucking *underwear*?"

"Like I said, no longer your business. What are you even doing here? And it's seven in the morning."

"I don't like the way we left things. I wanted to make sure you understood."

"Well, I don't."

"Camila, please," he said, standing closer. I leaned against the back of the couch, wrapping my arms around myself to somehow block him out. But I could feel him, the heat from his body, his scent, and it all worked in unison to torture me.

"Please don't," I said, looking down to hide the tears that threatened, the burning ache in my throat.

He let out a heavy breath. "This is a very important moment in your career. I know New York is what you've worked for every day since you first put on ballet shoes, to dance on that stage, walk the city streets as a professional dancer, the way your mother did. You need to be focused, or this amazing opportunity will pass you by while you get consumed in all this mess with my father. You have so many great things ahead, and right now I'm in your way."

I wiped the tears off my cheeks with the back of my hand. "Ironic, I thought it was me who was in your way."

"Come here." He pulled me into his arms and hugged me tight. I fought the sobs that escaped while a flash flood of anguish and loss washed through me. We stayed like that for a long moment, relishing the warmth of our bodies pressed together, unable to let go.

"I love you, Camila. Like I've never loved anyone. That's why I have to let you go."

"I'll wait," I said, not caring about how desperate I sounded.

"No. I can't ask you that. This war is far from over, and the farther you are from me, the safer you and your family will be. My brave, crazy girl. Go after your dreams." He squeezed his arms around me one last time, then kissed my head, and walked out.

Chapter 38

The next day I drifted through classes and rehearsals like a zombie. Marcos seemed sore but otherwise okay, and I was glad neither of us wanted to talk about what had happened.

I told Nata about my breakup with Sebastián that night. I must have been a real mess, because she cried about it. We ate frozen yogurt for dinner, and then I went to bed. Clutching my pillow, I let new tears soak the cotton. It was as if part of me had left with him, and all that was left of me was a shell, a snakeskin. I never imagined that much physical pain was possible.

That night a new routine began—I held in my feelings all day, and then at night, once I was alone, I cried myself to sleep.

In the days that followed, I poured my soul into dancing, repeating to myself it was all I needed. The only thing that was truly mine and nobody could take away. Outside of the theater, I was a ghost. I stared at the phone and contemplated calling Sebastián a thousand times, just to hear his voice. But what would I say? He didn't call either. Not once. Did he miss me as much as I missed him?

That week I saw black BMWs everywhere, mocking me. I had never noticed how many people in Buenos Aires drove one. Sometimes when I came home in the evenings, there was one parked in a far corner. Was it him? Was it Rafa keeping vigil? Or was my longing to see Sebastián playing tricks with my mind? Nothing seemed real, and the only thing that pulled me forward were my alternate lives as Queen Myrta and Princess Aurora.

Closing night for *Giselle* was three days away, and I took advantage of my newly found free time to stay in the studio after hours and work incessantly on my variations. Dancing to exhaustion felt good. It was the only thing that distracted me from the huge void left by Sebastián. I became a machine, focusing only on what I needed to be a better dancer. *Heart*, answered Papá's voice in my head. I squashed it. My heart was locked up.

Madame seemed pleased with my increased effort, and the excitement for the upcoming trip to New York was quickly building in the company. Still, a part of me felt empty. I missed him. Every night on the way home, I wished I could talk to him, tell him how nervous I was about New York. My dream was so close. He would be happy for me and rationalize my fears to make it all better. The memories of our time together haunted me: his smile when our eyes met at a pause in the soccer game with the kids, finding my clothes neatly folded on a chair after I had left them all over the floor the night before, a box from his neighborhood bakery with my favorite vanilla cupcake waiting on the counter, curling up with him by the fireplace while he massaged my battered feet. I missed him. I missed him so much.

Chapter 39

The moment the music stopped on closing night for *Giselle*, the crowd exploded in a deafening applause. We took our bows, and as the curtain closed for the last time, I hugged Nata tightly.

In the dressing room, she changed quickly into her street clothes. Knowing she had fans gathering at the entrance, I told her not to wait; I would take my time getting out of my costume.

Once I had changed, I scurried out the side door with my head low. Dodging the photographers, I scanned the familiar faces, searching for Nata to let her know I was skipping the celebration dinner. I froze when I saw Mercedes standing a few steps back. A tremor rattled me from inside.

With a bodyguard flanking behind her, she cut through the crowd towards me. A flicker of hope that *he* would be there tingled in my chest.

"He wasn't lying. You're very good," she said dismissively as she got closer.

"Thank you." I scanned the crowd behind her.

"He's not here," she murmured, reading my thoughts and watching my reaction.

"Well…thanks for coming. I have to go." I turned, but she caught my arm.

"Wait," she said. I glowered at her, and she let go. "I need to speak to you."

"About?"

"Not here."

"It's not a good time. I'm really tired."

"I need you to listen to me. Please." Her expression softened. Suddenly she looked desperate.

I let out an irritated sigh. "Make it quick."

"Sebastián got himself in a stupid war with his father. And it's not just Don Martín, it's the Medinas, too, and the other families. It's your fault," she sneered.

"*My* fault."

"Yes! He was never really serious about leaving until he met you. You changed him, and now, because of you, he's miserable. What the hell did you do to him?"

"I've got to go."

"Wait." She gripped my bicep again, and this time I yanked it away. "I need your help."

"*My help?* Fuck off, Mercedes." I pushed past her.

"Sebastián's life is in danger. He needs your help."

I stopped in my tracks and cursed inwardly. When I turned my head around, those emerald snake eyes met mine. There was a new, glassy sheen to them. Jesus, was she high?

"Just...listen, okay? Please," she said, sounding almost normal. She stepped closer, hugging her coat. "The head of one of the other families, a guy named Gabriel García, is blackmailing me. He says he's got information about a container of some Russian girls who went missing and it somehow implicates Sebastián and Julián. I have no idea what all that is about, but the container belonged to a guy called Ivanov, and he's a scumbag of the worst kind."

I shuddered inwardly at the mention of Ivanov. But Mercedes was a liar. I shrugged. "None of this has anything to do with me."

"Yes, it *does*," she spat out in a sudden burst of anger. "Gabriel is taking advantage of the situation between Sebastián and the Medinas. A pact prevents the Families to retaliate against each other. But, since Sebastián *shot* Pedro to save *you*, the pact is off for now, so we aren't protected, *Sebastián* is not protected if García puts us against Ivanov." She skeptically surveyed the dispersing crowd behind me, then pulled a tissue out of her pocket and dried her nose even though there was nothing there.

"What can you possibly want from me?"

She turned to her bodyguard, as if to check if he was still there. Then her gaze zoomed in on me. "I'm supposed to deliver half a million dollars to Gabriel on Monday at noon. That sonofabitch thinks he can get away with this."

"Look—"

"I want you to tell your Russian friends to intercept the delivery. I want them to take Gabriel out."

I chuckled humorlessly.

"I'm serious."

I scowled. "Are you completely *gone*? *Take him out*? Besides, what makes you think the Zchestakovas would ever get involved in that? For *you*? Your brother loathes them."

"He doesn't." She rolled her eyes. "And this is business. Gabriel's territory overlaps with the Russians'. They've wanted him out of the game for years. Believe me, your friends will jump at this."

"Yeah, I can't wait to tell them."

"You don't get it. My brother would open the borders to all the Russians' imports. They would have clear range to take over the Garcías' markets. Your friends hate García. He's the cause of all their problems. They've wanted his head ever since he pushed drugs through the docks and shot my brother's men."

"So it was him. Does your brother know?"

She rolled her eyes. "It doesn't matter. This is their chance. Everyone wins."

"Except the guy who gets *shot*."

"It doesn't need to come to that. He'll chicken out when he sees a pack of Russians coming at him, and he'll think twice before fucking with us again."

I looked at her incredulously. Was she fucking serious? A thread of crimson blood trickled down her nose. *Coke.* I had seen almost identical behavior among some of the dancers at the theater. But Mercedes? She quickly pulled out the tissue and wiped it off.

"Are you okay?" I said in an emotionless tone.

"Yes. This goddamn cold," she mumbled, avoiding my eyes.

"Why the Zchestakovas?" I muttered.

"Because this would benefit the Russians. Besides, they have a reputation for being...volatile. Even the most powerful among the Families stay away.

Your friends' network of hired guns is more extensive than most people imagine."

"You have money. Hire your own people. Leave my friends out of this." I turned, but she stepped ahead, blocking me.

"That's where you're wrong. Money isn't where the Russians' power lies. Your friends...they're ruled by loyalty. None of their people would hesitate to put a bat to your head if you crossed a Zchestakova." She sniffed. "If García has half a brain, he won't even consider going against them. He would be going against the whole clan."

"No. This is why Sebastián and I are not together. Find another way. Pay him off."

"You don't *pay off* people who blackmail you," she snapped. "It would never stop, and Ivanov is dangerous. Christ, don't you get it?"

"Then tell your brother...and Sebastián. Let them handle it."

Her expression hardened, her eyes scowling, incredulous. I wanted to take a step back but refrained.

"My brother and Sebastián *cannot* know about this. García was very specific, and he's got a rat infiltrated somewhere. Do not say a word to Sebastián, you hear me? You would be putting him in danger."

"*I* would be putting him in danger. Listen to yourself. Your whole plan is insane." Now it was me who took a step closer. "I won't be a part of anything that involves shooting anyone. If you think I would risk my friends getting hurt for you, you need to double up on your meds." I turned away, but she grabbed my coat. "Stop grabbing me!" I yanked my coat away and she almost fell back. Despite her abrasive words, she seemed weak, pale, and fragile. I almost felt sorry for her.

"*Talk to them,*" she sneered. "An opportunity like this doesn't come twice. It's in the Russians' best interest to help us. Here's my number." She slipped a card into a half-open pocket in my bag. I watched her skeletal hand retreat and narrowed my eyes.

"Is that a threat?"

"*Sebastián* needs your help, dammit. Do this for *him*. Here's your chance to prove you're more than the mousey little gold digger everyone thinks you are. Prove you belong in this family."

"Fuck you. And stay the hell away from me." I stormed off, clutching my bag tightly to rein back the sudden anger surging through me. My legs shook as I rushed to the corner where a cab waited for passengers. *That bitch.* I hurried into the back seat and gave the driver my address. Far behind, Mercedes got into a black Tesla.

On the short drive home, the conversation with Mercedes spun in my head. This was all too much. The images throbbed in my mind. Mercedes was on something. Was she a junkie? Jesus, what did I care? But Sebastián…Was he really in danger of Ivanov finding out it was he who helped those girls? Was Julián involved in that too? And Mercedes had mentioned an infiltrator… Someone had betrayed them? Who? I pushed the thought away. The whole point of our breakup had been for me not to be caught in the Palacios web anymore. Besides, I didn't trust Mercedes, and this could very well be one of her brother's schemes. I decided to leave the Zchestakovas out of it. Mercedes would have to find another way.

That night I dreamt of green snake eyes that watched me from the shadows as I ran for my life through a black forest. I woke up sore and exhausted, the sensation of the foliage scraping my face and legs still fresh on my skin.

I woke up at dawn, restless. In the living room, Nata sat on the couch, sipping her coffee. I poured myself a cup and plopped beside her.

"How was the dinner?" I asked.

"Long. Too much champagne. But it was nice to have a drink, finally."

"Why are you up?" I took a long sip of coffee to clear the fog in my head.

388

"I don't know...stuff. So, *Satan's sister* came to see you last night, huh?"

I glanced at her, suddenly awake.

"Alexei saw you two talking," she explained. "What did she want?"

"Nothing, that chick is mental. And I think she was high."

"And, naturally, she came to see you dance." She cocked an eyebrow. Did anything ever escape her?

"I don't know, she just came, all right?"

"You suck at lying. It's *that* bad?"

"She...I don't know." I sighed heavily. "She had some bullshit story about someone blackmailing her. But I don't believe anything she says."

"Why would she tell *you* that?"

"Nata...she's a lying bitch, okay?"

Nata gave me a scrutinizing look as she sipped her coffee. "Julián is being an asshole again. Does her impromptu visit have anything to do with that?"

"Why? What happened?"

"He's only allowing us to bring shipments through one border. It makes it very difficult for us to import high volumes because they have a cap on what they allow in at once."

"When did this happen?"

She shrugged. "A couple of weeks ago."

"You didn't say anything."

"I didn't want to get you involved again."

"Crap, I'm sorry."

"Don't be. It's how they are."

Shit. Shit.

"It will be nice to get away from all this for a few weeks. Pappa is so worried we'll go bankrupt. I haven't seen him like this since we left Russia."

A silent moment passed while we sipped our coffees and my brain worked overtime.

"Mercedes...wanted a favor." I looked up at her. "From your family, actually."

Nata put down her coffee and straightened up, giving me her full attention as I told her Mercedes's plan. She then reached for her phone.

"What are you doing?"

"Sergei needs to hear this. Keep going." She gestured quickly with her hand.

Ten minutes later, Sergei's trademark knock sounded on the door and he let himself in.

"So, what do those fuckers want now, ah?"

"Sergei, calm down," Nata scolded him. "Let's just listen. Camila's only delivering a message. She doesn't need to be mixed up with them anymore."

Sergei looked at me suspiciously. "Right. Get on with it, then."

I repeated Mercedes's plan while Sergei listened skeptically. Mercedes would meet with García the next day, and the Russians were supposed to show up minutes after. The idea was that, when García saw the Russian clan backing Mercedes and her family, not only would he *forget* his threats to release any information to Ivanov, but the new alliance between the Palacioses and the Russians would be enough to get Julián to redistribute the Garcias' territories at the docks.

When I finished laying it all out, Nata and Sergei stayed quiet in thought.

"Do you think it's a trap?" Nata asked him.

He sighed. "Could be, though I don't see the point. The De la Viñas profit from our business, and they know García pushes drugs. Besides, if they wanted us out, they could just cut us off like they did before. They don't need all this charade."

"Wait," I said. "You're not seriously considering this, are you?"

Sergei smirked.

"What if they're only using us to get rid of García?" Nata said.

"It's possible." Sergei nodded in thought. "Camila, do you think the girl was telling you the truth?"

"I don't know. I don't really know Mercedes, but I don't trust her."

"What is this information that García has on those two that would interest Ivanov?"

I hesitated for a moment. "She said it implicates Sebastián and Julián with some missing girls. But like I said, I don't know if she's telling the truth."

Sergei's eyes widened. "It was *them*? Palacios and De la Viña ambushed Ivanov's ship? Fuck me, that family never stops surprising me."

"You guys don't have to get in the middle of all this. You have no obligation to do anything."

"Camila," Nata said. "Those girls were trafficked, abused, beaten. And they were Russian. If it was Sebastián and Julián who saved them, Pappa will want to do this."

"There's no way to know," I said. "Mercedes could be lying. Sergei?"

Sergei paced around the room, his head down in thought. Guilt filled me. I didn't want any harm to come to the Zchestakovas, and things seemed to have gone south for them since I became involved with Sebastián.

"Don't worry," Nata said, reading my thoughts. "We were doing business with the Palacios and the De la Viña families long before you came along. This has nothing to do with you. We can say no."

"If we say no," Sergei said, "and Don Martín's son or his right hand, Julián, end up in Ivanov's hands, he will come after us for not helping. But if we do this and it goes well, we can get rid of García for good. He's a fucking traitor and our biggest barrier against expanding. We could more than triple our business. I'd love to see that fucker gone."

"Sergei, they're talking about *murder*. They can't ask you to do that," I said. My mouth was dry. How had I ended up in the middle of this?

Sergei waved his hand dismissively. "It shouldn't come to that. García's not stupid. Besides, if we side with De la Viña on this, we'll eventually gain the support of the other families, and Don Martín's. This could work out well for us."

"This is crazy," I said.

Sergei shook his head. "No. The De la Viña girl is right. This opportunity won't come to us again. I want García's head. We'll do it."

Chapter 40

I reluctantly gave Mercedes's contact information to Sergei. I was technically done with it, though I worried about the Zchestakovas and was anxious to know the outcome of this ridiculous plan Mercedes had weaved. Their business was suffering, but Mercedes's offer could mean their total downfall.

Sergei summoned his father's best men and arranged to show up at Mercedes's meeting with García the next day at noon. It would be Monday, so Nata and I would be at work and away from our phones until the break, and that had my skin on edge.

The next morning advanced at a snail's pace. Nata and I kept checking the wall clock and exchanging fretful looks. At lunch, we frantically checked our phones, but there were no messages. We sat at the back of the studio, picking at our sandwiches and not eating. It was 12:15 p.m. and we had still heard nothing. Nata checked her phone for the millionth time.

"I can't stand it," she said, and tossed her uneaten sandwich back onto the wrapper, wiping the crumbs off her hands. "They could all be dead by now."

"Nata! Don't say that. Sergei's smart, smarter than all of them. It's all going to go well. He's got Alexei with him, and your dad's most trusted men." I gripped her hand. Tears welled in her eyes and she let out a sob. I pulled her into a hug and squeezed her tight, fighting my own tears as I said a silent prayer for the Zchestakova clan and Alexei. "It's going to be okay," I whispered. "You'll see."

And I hoped I was right.

A torturous hour went by, two rehearsals in which neither Nata nor I was able to focus. When I came back from the bathroom Madame had pulled Nata aside, and judging by their body language, she was giving it to her. Nata listened with her hands wrapped around her waist and her head down. It was the first time Madame had reprimanded her. I had never seen my friend so out of sorts, and my heart ached for her.

As soon as they were done, Madame strode purposely to me. Shit.

"What is the matter today? We are leaving for New York in two days. *Two days*, and both my primas are on a mental vacation."

"I'm sorry, Madame. Some family matters. We'll sort it out."

She shook her head. "You should know that I warned Federico early on that you weren't ready for this. Don't prove me right." She clutched her clipboard and stormed off. What? Shit! I knew Madame was skeptical of my talent, but I certainly did not need her to spell it out for me. In the back of my mind, the bomb ticked faster on my role as Aurora.

I pushed the anxiety away and stepped out to look for Nata and see if she had news. She was leaning against the hallway wall, her hands wrapped around her stomach as she bent forward, breathing hard.

"Nata."

She suddenly raised her head and clutched me in a death grip, her slender frame trembling.

"What happened?" I pulled away, searching her eyes.

She shook her head. "I don't know exactly. García panicked when he saw Sergei and Alexei with all the others. He tried to run, I think, I don't know..."

"And?"

"He shot Alexei, and Sergei."

I felt the blood drain from my face. "Oh my God. Are they..."

"No, not dead. But Alexei's in critical condition."

"And Sergei?"

Nata shook with a sob. "He was shot in the shoulder twice and the leg. Shit, Cami." She pulled me to her and gripped me tight again. "If something happens to either one of them...Alexei's like my brother too."

"I'm so sorry. Do you want to go to the hospital? I'll come with you."

She shook her head. "Alexei's in surgery, and they said Sergei can't get visitors yet. Pappa wants me to stay here until he makes sure it's safe for me to come to the hospital. He'll call as soon as he can."

I nodded. Once again, her strength blew me away. Dread and guilt filled me, and I cursed myself for getting them implicated.

"This will never be over, will it?" I said to no one.

"At least García's dead. One of Pappa's men got him. That fucker."

I hugged her tight. Somebody had just been killed and I had been the one to summon the killers there. Sergei was badly wounded; Alexei's life was in danger. It was all my fault.

More than ever, I needed to get away.

Chapter 41

"Del Plata Airlines announces their flight 754 to New York City will board shortly. We will make another announcement as soon as we're ready to begin boarding."

I exchanged a look of disappointment with Nata as we browsed the gift shop for snacks. The company hadn't been able to get everyone in our group to fly together. Nata and I were on the first flight with a small group that would've been perfect if it hadn't included Verónica. Marcos was on another flight with the rest of the dancers. It had only been two days since the incident with the Russians, and the instant we found out that Sergei would recover and Alexei's life was out of danger, we packed our bags.

"Ignore Verónica," said Nata, trying on vintage sunglasses that made her look like Audrey Hepburn. "Nothing will spoil this for us."

"Yeah. You should get those." I nodded. "Chips or cashews?" I lifted both bags.

"Neither. They give you nuts on the plane, and I don't want the salt. It will make us bloated."

"You're so much fun sometimes," I muttered, sliding the packages back on the hook as they announced our flight would start boarding. "Let's go."

Thirty minutes later, we pushed our way down the narrow aisles to our seats in the back of the plane. Our boarding passes said we were sitting together, but as I followed the seat numbers, I realized we were in the middle section. Crap. Behind me, Nata inched forward, dragging her bursting carry-on.

Once we found our seats, we stuffed our bags into the overhead bins. Verónica appeared, hauling a pink hard-shell carry-on. She stopped next to Nata, arching an eyebrow.

"You're joking, right?" I scowled.

"I'm as excited as you are about this," she said, forcing her luggage into the bin.

I groaned out loud as we both stood to let her through. Shit. *Ten goddamn hours* sitting next to Verónica was a curve ball I hadn't seen coming. The familiar scent of her perfume announced a very long flight.

I did my best to ignore Verónica while the last of the passengers slowly filled the rows. A heavy lady with an equally giant handbag wobbled through, hitting people on the shoulder as she passed. We were turning our phones off when Nata's rang with a call from Sergei. She plugged her other ear with her finger to block the noise as she listened, her face scrunching in disbelief as she muttered something in Russian.

The plane was almost full when a flight attendant in an immaculate uniform and perfect makeup approached. She was young, and much prettier than the others.

"Miss Navarro? Miss Zches…" She frowned at the sheet of paper.

"Zchestakova," Nata corrected, angling the phone away from her mouth.

"Oh." She smiled, relieved, showcasing perfect teeth. "Your seat assignments have changed. Follow me please. You two are in first class."

"Why?" I blurted. Nata elbowed me as she told Sergei she would call him as soon as we landed.

We stood and quickly retrieved our bags. I glanced at Verónica, who had turned an ill green.

"Later." I winked.

The attendant led us back up the aisle to the first-class cabin, a small section with those individual thingies that look like mini-apartments. Holy shit. My heart pumped hard, and I turned to Nata who looked as stunned as I was.

"These are your seats," the attendant gestured. "Alicia will be back with champagne. Mr. Julián de la Viña wishes you a pleasant flight."

"Excuse me?" I frowned.

"Mr. De la Viña arranged for this last-minute change for you two. A token of his gratitude. That's all I know." She grinned her perfect smile and turned away.

"*Julián?*" I whispered at Nata. Dread churned deep in my stomach.

"Yeah. That was Sergei calling. He said Julián didn't know a thing about Mercedes being blackmailed. And get this: García was blackmailing her about stuff he had on *her*, not Julián or Sebastián. The little bitch lied to us."

"What?"

"Yeah, can you imagine? That chick has some balls for doing all this behind Julián's back. He and Sebastián didn't find out till it was all over. Man," she said, chuckling humorlessly, "I wish I could've been a fly on the wall in that conversation." She slid her carry-on into the much bigger overhead bin. "Either way, García's out of the picture, and Mercedes wasn't lying when she said Julián would give my family the green light to move into those territories. Though he wasn't happy to learn García tried blackmailing his little evil twin sister."

"So, what. Julián's *paying us off*? I don't want to sit here. I'd rather sit next to Verónica than accept favors from Julián."

"No," she said, stopping me. "We're staying. Those fuckers can go to hell. I'm taking their money and everything I can from them. Alexei almost died over this. We're staying here. Fuck'em, Cams."

Yeah, fuck'em. I scowled, plopping into the ample leather seat and caressing the armrests. "So, this is how the other half lives, huh?"

"More like the one percent. These seats cost seventeen thousand dollars each."

"Shut up."

"I'm serious," she said, taking a champagne flute from a tray that our assigned flight attendant, Alicia, extended. She handed me one, and we toasted to a kick-ass trip.

I had always dreamt of flying international in first class, but it was even better than I had imagined: champagne, fancy cheeses and snacks, filet mignon for dinner matched with a label wine. But I still couldn't help feeling dirty for taking Julián's charity. By now, Sebastián surely knew about Mercedes's meeting and the Russians' involvement. What did he think? Did he know I had been the messenger and the one who'd led the Russians to the lion's mouth? My heart constricted. I missed him.

I tossed and turned in the plush bed seat. In two days, I would be performing as a principal for the first time. At Lincoln Center. But all the champagne and luxury that first class had to offer couldn't soothe my nerves. As I stared out the window with my sound-canceling headphones and a chocolate dessert served on real china, I couldn't help thinking that, with every passing second, I was farther and farther away from Sebastián.

Chapter 42

I opened the window shade as the plane began its descent, and my breath caught. Nata stretched in her seat; I gestured for her to move over to my compartment to get a glimpse.

"That's beautiful." Her tone was charged with excitement.

"It is," I murmured, pressing my forehead to the cool panel while I stared at Manhattan's jagged skyline. Pink sunlight stretched behind the tiny buildings below, announcing a sunny day. I smiled when I spotted the Empire State Building splintering from between skyscrapers. In the distance, the Statue of Liberty glinted in the morning sun. A chill ran through me. God, I was really here. It was even more beautiful than in my dream.

We took a cab to our hotel located a couple of blocks away from the Lincoln Center. The concierge stored our luggage, and we went for coffee and a short walk until check-in time.

When we finally got our keys, Nata and I went to our shared room to get settled and crash for a quick nap. Marcos knocked on our door an hour later.

"Heeeey!" He high-fived Nata as he walked in. "Can you guys believe this place? Pretty sweet. My room's two doors down."

I groaned from the bed.

"What?" he asked, feigning offense.

"You two doors down means *parties* two doors down. Nata and I need a lot more sleep than you, so behave?"

"Sure." He winked.

"It's amazing," Nata said from the window as she gazed at the city far below. "The three of us here…it's a dream."

Marcos plopped on her bed while she unpacked the rest of her clothes. As soon as she finished, she unzipped my suitcase and began hanging my clothes and folding them neatly into a drawer.

"I'm top drawer, you're bottom," she said.

"You don't have to do that."

"If I don't, you'll live out of your suitcase and everything will be wrinkled. I can't stand it."

I rolled my eyes at Marcos, and he grinned, lying sprawled out with his hands locked behind his head.

"New York. This is awesome," he said, staring at the ceiling. He looked like a kid in Disneyland. It made me smile.

"You okay if I shower first?" I said to Nata, and she nodded. "I wouldn't mind going out for a quick bite afterwards. The meeting with Federico's not till seven. I need a hot shower, you guys. Then I'm all yours."

"*All mine*," Marcos said, tasting the words. "Promising."

"I didn't mean it *that* way." I tossed a shirt at his face and he caught it midair. "How's it that you can make the simplest things sound dirty? Shower. Go." I waved him off, wrinkling my nose.

He groaned, then leapt up and headed out.

Twenty minutes later, we were ready for a loop around the neighborhood. Nata dressed in warm, fitted black clothes, and I wore skinny jeans, boots, and a gray, cashmere turtleneck. Marcos knocked on our door, and when I opened it, his eyes quickly scanned me from head to toe. He smiled approvingly.

"Hey," he said softly as he tipped his head down to give me a soft peck on the mouth.

"Marcos…" A flash of heat rose to my cheeks. What the fuck.

"C'mon, Nata!" he called. "You look amazing. Let's go." Holding the door open with his foot, he waved at Nata to hurry. He smelled of fresh soap and his usual Calvin Klein cologne. He was a bad boy in faded jeans and a fitted, black sweater that did good things for what was underneath. "Move it, wenches." We slipped into heavy coats and wool beanies, and Nata pinched his stomach as she hurried out.

We rode the elevator down, and when the door slid open, Marcos clasped my hand, interlocking our fingers. *Fuckdammit.* I really didn't need this now.

A sudden lash snapped inside my chest, bringing a memory of Sebastián doing the same thing on our first lunch together. I instinctively let go, but Marcos grabbed my hand again, frowning when our eyes met.

He held the lobby door to the street, and we stepped out into a frosty early evening. The city was alive, cars, people, everyone in a hurry. Marcos strode between Nata and me, his warm, confident energy pulling me back to the present.

The first thing I learned was that New Yorkers aren't that different from Argentineans. They all had that *Get the fuck out of my way* look on their faces, permanent scowls sending a clear message that there's no time for conversation. Everyone minded their own business and looked cool in their unique way. A city made of trendsetters where nobody followed.

We strolled around the neighborhood, checking everything out. It was way too much to take in. I matched Marcos and Nata's quick pace. Marcos's eager eyes scanned the bars as we passed. With our huge grins, I was sure we looked awestruck as we made our way through the snow-brushed sidewalks. Mixed aromas of foods from all over the world welcomed us as we passed restaurants crammed against one another. The air was dense, like in downtown Buenos Aires, except much colder since December meant winter here, and was even colder than I ever imagined. A gelid gust of wind ruffled my hair, and I shivered in my coat.

"I'm freezing, you guys. Let's find a coffee shop," I said.

Nata nodded from inside her scarf. We settled on a café across the street and ordered lattes. It was a cool spot. The tables were recycled writer's desks from the 1900s, the wallpaper made of printed copies of handwritten diary passages from the same era. Recycled oil lanterns had been adapted as electric hanging fixtures, their amber glow adding to the charming atmosphere of the place. It was odd and foreign. I loved it.

We had our coffees and chatted about the week to come. An hour later, we were almost back at the hotel when Nata's phone rang. She pulled it out of her pocket with her gloved hand.

"Sergei. What's up?" She shivered. She had called Sergei as soon as we had landed, and they had talked for a while then. What now?

"*What?*" She skidded to a halt, covering her other ear with her free hand. The wind blew the hair off her face, and I realized she'd gone pale. Her eyes met mine, and my scalp prickled under my hat. "When did this happen?" she said.

"What?" I mouthed. She bit her lip hard and shook her head. *What the fuck,* what! My brain raced through the possibilities. Whatever it was, it wasn't good. The wind blew again, penetrating my bones. Marcos pulled his beanie down and ushered us inside the hotel as Nata said something in Russian and ended her call.

"Jesus, what, Nata? Tell me."

She gripped both my arms and looked straight at me. Marcos stood behind her, looking as concerned as I felt.

"Something's happened back at home."

"What? Who? Jesus, speak!" I snapped.

"I...Sebastián," she said, painfully. "He was shot outside his studio."

"What?" I mumbled. My lungs collapsed. The room spun. Nata swallowed hard as she looked for the right words. "Nata..."

"They injured him badly. I'm so sorry," she said softly.

"Oh my God." I brought my hand to my mouth, unable to breathe. "What...Will he be okay?"

"I don't know. Sergei couldn't tell me. They just took him to the hospital."

"No. No!" I gasped for air and Nata pulled me into her arms, but I stood, frozen. "What happened?"

"I don't know, Cami. Sergei thinks it was some kind of payback for García, but he doesn't know anything else."

I shook my head, tears streaming down my face. "Shit. *Shit.* This is all my fault. Fucking Mercedes. I should've never—"

"No," Nata snapped. "This is not your fault. This is how these things go, okay? Sebastián is surrounded by a lot of dangerous people. There's nothing you can do about that, you hear me?"

"I knew Mercedes was bad news. I should've trusted my gut. Shit." I wiped my cheeks. "I have to go, I have to…" Nata blocked me.

"No," she said firmly.

"I have to go see him! Don't you get it? If I hadn't gotten in the middle of all this—"

You have *nothing* to do with this."

"Cams, babe. Come sit down," Marcos said, clasping my shoulder.

"I need to see him. I need to know he's okay." Fresh tears followed the path of the old ones.

Nata took my hands in hers. "Call his bodyguard…what was his name?"

"Rafa?"

"Yes, Rafa. Do you have his number?"

I pulled my phone out and searched for Rafa's name. He answered on the first ring.

"Camila—"

"How is he? Please tell me he's okay."

Rafa explained Sebastián was in surgery and they wouldn't know anything for a few hours. He was curt and seemed to want to end the conversation, but I begged him for more information. I cried silently as he briefly explained Sebastián had been assaulted as he was leaving his studio for lunch, in broad daylight, and a bullet had pierced his lung. By the time the paramedics came, he had almost drowned in his own blood. Rafa had been called to a pickup nearby and suspected whoever was behind this expected Sebastián to be alone at that time. That was all he knew.

"I'll get on the next plane."

"No. Don't do that."

"I want to be there."

"Sebastián doesn't want you here. You'd be in danger, and he doesn't need anything else on his plate. I'll find out who's behind this. I promise." His voice was suddenly gruff. "I'm sorry to say it this way, but…you'd be…a burden here. I'll keep you informed. As soon as we know something, I'll call you."

"Rafa—"

"Camila. Please. Do not try contacting him, or me. I will call you as soon as I know something. Good-bye." The line went dead. Sliding down against the wall, I buried my face in my hands and sobbed out loud. People mumbled as they walked into the lobby, but I didn't care. Beside me, Marcos crouched down and kissed my frosted gloves.

In my room, I lay face down on my bed, gripping my phone so hard I worried it would disintegrate in my hand. Fuck. I had been dreaming to be here all my life, and now I would give my right arm to be back in Buenos Aires.

An hour later, the company gathered around Madame and Federico in a sitting area in the hotel lobby. Federico went over his expectations for the tour: no drinking before performances, no partying out late, blah, blah. All I could think about was Sebastián in the hospital.

Federico continued with the rundown: principals would be invited to a few parties, and attendance was expected to promote the tour. Meeting influential people was the most important thing after giving an outstanding performance. I should've been thrilled, but I just wanted to go home.

I tossed and turned all night, unable to sleep. The phone was by my pillow, and I tapped the screen every once in a while to make sure I hadn't missed a text. I knew I wouldn't be able to sleep till Rafa called. At 3:00 a.m., a text from Rafa came in:

He's out of surgery and in intensive care. The next 24 hours are critical. Will let you know as we go. Please stay where you are and don't try contacting him.

I let out a pent-up sob and couldn't stop till my eyes were dry and swollen. Sometime later, I sank into a disturbed sleep.

In what seemed a second later, Nata shook me awake. My forever present human alarm clock.

"It's late. Let's go. We have a warm-up class then tech rehearsal."

I rubbed the exhaustion off my eyes. That night she would dance as Princess Aurora with First Cast, and I would perform with Second Cast tomorrow. Thank God that wasn't till tomorrow. I felt as if a meteorite had smashed onto my head. Today would be tough to get through.

I dressed in a half dozen layers, then walked with Nata to the David H. Koch Theater. A layer of fresh snow glinted under the weak morning sun. People rushed down the hectic streets of the city. Most were dressed for work in suits and long overcoats. Nobody made eye contact as they strode purposely with their collars up and their chins down.

The morning blazed by with classes and people and coffee on every break to keep me awake. We had class with Federico and a chance to get acquainted with the stage. The theater wasn't as big as the Colón, but someone said it still held over twenty-seven hundred people. Everything was foreign: the smell, the cool drafts whenever a stage door opened, the lighting. I had never thought about any of it before. It was different, new, exciting. I kept my phone close and checked it incessantly. Why in the hell wasn't Rafa sending any updates? But then, no news was good news for now. Sebastián would need time to recover. He just needed time. *God, let him be okay.*

When the tech rehearsal ended, Madame gave us a couple of hours to rest and eat before coming back for that evening's opening performance. I couldn't stand still even though I wouldn't perform until tomorrow. Tonight, Marcos and I would sit in the audience with the rest of the dancers in Second Cast. I called my parents in Italy to check in. I knew Mamá was anxious to know everything about the tour and she shared my excitement for being in New York. They sounded so happy to be reunited with my siblings who had also traveled to see them. I didn't tell them about Sebastián. I didn't want to hear how my relationship with him had been doomed from the start. My parents would try to reassure me I was better off.

Back in the hotel, I tried taking a short nap, but my nerves were electric. I watched Nata, sound asleep, and envied her. Would I ever be able to reach that state of mind? I lay on my bed, staring at the ceiling, praying for Sebastián with my phone in my hand. But as the hours passed, Rafa didn't message me and my anxiety level rose.

That night I dressed in my finest gown for the first performance of *Sleeping Beauty*. It was a long, burgundy velvet dress that had cost me a month's salary, but that Nata had insisted I should buy along with a pair of high heels. I felt like a movie star as Marcos and I walked hand in hand through Lincoln Center. I was relieved to have his hand to hold on to. The night was enchanting, the lights illuminating the steps and the fountain glimmering under a soft layer of snow. I looked around, taking in all the beauty with a heavy heart. *If only Sebastián were okay, this night would be perfect.*

Marcos was breathtaking in a black tux he had rented for the week. I left my long coat at the valet, and Marcos escorted me to the main hall where we had a glass of champagne with the dancers in Second Cast. Everything was red velvet and glamour. People were dressed in the most exquisite gowns and gala attire. Heads turned when we walked past the waiting crowd. No matter where we were, Marcos always turned heads. My heart fluttered inside my chest like a humming bird's wings. I had dreamt of being exactly here, dressed like this, all my life. I looked around at everything with wide, tear-rimmed eyes. I thought of calling Mamá, but it would be four in the morning in Italy, so I sent her a photo of Marcos and me posing together, and a short text:

I'm here. Dressed in my red gown and the impossibly high heels Nata made me buy. Mamá, I'm here!

Then I tried Rafa's phone, but it went to voicemail. Damn.

The performance was spellbinding. Nata and Diego were flawless, raising the bar even higher for us. Nata looked carefree, weightless, her feet caressing the stage as an innocent Aurora celebrated her youth. Diego was strong and confident, his decisive movements contrasting with the delicate and sweet demeanor of Nata's performance.

I sat next to Marcos, clutching my phone so I could feel the vibration of an incoming message from Rafa. *Damn Rafa.* Didn't he know I was desperate for a call? A text? I knew it was selfish of me to expect him to send me regular updates, but I needed to know Sebastián was out of danger.

The cast met at a restaurant afterwards for a big dinner. Everyone was radiant. Nata wore a permanent smile as she clinked glasses with the other dancers. I felt as if I was looking at the scene through a glass window, my mind half-there and half-back at the hospital in Buenos Aires, with Sebastián. Surely, he would be under the best care the Palacios's pockets could afford.

Federico congratulated the cast and gave a small pep talk to Second Cast for the following night, things to focus on and things to be aware of. I zoned in and out of the conversation. From her end of the table, Madame watched me, vigilant.

I excused myself early, knowing everyone would understand. The next night would be my first performance as a prima, and I was obviously nervous. Only Nata knew that was only half of it.

On my way to the door, Madame intercepted me as I was bundling up in my multiple layers before facing the arctic evening air.

"Camila, wait."

I took a sharp breath and braced for the punch her words would deliver. And she hadn't said Navarro. But when she approached, her eyes softened.

"Is everything all right? You seem...distracted."

"No, Madame. Just nervous. I'm fine."

She gave me a small nod. "You are ready for tomorrow?"

"Yes, Madame. Of course."

"I don't mean to add to your pressure, but it's important that you know how much is at stake for you. Federico took a very big leap of faith in you by giving you the prima role. All his colleagues will be watching. I am saying this because you need to be a hundred and ten percent focused on this. If there is anything else in your mind...just clear it. You are a professional dancer, and no matter what our personal lives may have in stock for us, we must let it all go before we go onstage. Is that clear?"

"Yes, Madame." I dug my nails into my palms to stop myself from falling apart in front of her. My phone startled me when it vibrated in my pocket. I quickly pulled it out, and I darted a nervous look at Madame. "Thank you, Madame...Sorry, but I need to take this."

She nodded skeptically before turning away.

I pressed the phone to my ear. "Rafa. God, how is he?"

"The surgery was successful. He's conscious at times but needs a lot of rest. Time will tell. He'll stay in the intensive care unit for the next forty-eight hours, at least."

"Can I talk to him?"

"No, Camila. He can't talk much yet."

"Maybe tomorrow?"

"He's asked me to tell you not to call."

"What? Why?"

"Until we've got this under control, it's the best way to keep you safe."

"Rafa, I need to know he'll be okay. This was my fault. I should've never listened to Mercedes. This is all...a mess because of me." I wiped my eyes with my hand.

"Camila, this was my fault. But...you need to let him go. For good."

"What?" I was suddenly winded.

"I need you to listen, Camila. Do not call him, or even this number."

"I'm worried sick about him. Why can't I call?"

A long silence.

"Rafa..."

"We have a rat somewhere. The best thing is for you to be completely disconnected from Sebastián. He wants you to break all contact with him. He was adamant."

"He said that?"

"Yes. I'm sorry."

A pain I never knew existed cracked my heart in two. I closed my eyes and swallowed through the swelling in my throat.

"Please take care of him," I muttered.

"Good-bye."

Back in my room, I sank into the mattress, buried in a mix of despair, exhaustion, and uneasy anticipation as my heart broke all over again. I closed my eyes, and a myriad of images of my time with Sebastián played in my head. In the midst of all the adversities we faced were so many happy moments. My chest ached as if my heart had been ripped out. Nata eventually lay beside me on my bed and hugged me silently while I cried. I finally let fatigue win, and the darkness swallowed me.

I woke up physically restored but drained mentally. The adrenaline from the upcoming performance surged strong in my veins. I was in New York, dammit. Away from the Palacioses and the constant danger around them.

Later in my dressing room, I plugged in my phone to create a relaxing mood. I was in my first costume, a meticulously embroidered, soft pink work of art created for the *Rose Adagio* of Aurora's sixteenth birthday. I was finishing the last touches of my makeup when a soft knock on the door startled me.

"Come in," I said.

In the mirror, I watched a stagehand walk in, carrying a huge bouquet of tea-colored roses.

"These just came for you."

"Thanks," I said.

He placed the flowers on the dresser and scurried out. My heart woke. *Sebastián?* A little white envelope was clipped to the top of the bouquet. My pulse raced. Funny how hope could be a terrifying thing. I swallowed the emotions crowding my throat and, with trembling fingers, unclipped the envelope and pulled the card out:

We're so proud of you. You made it!

We wish we could be there.

Merde,

Mamá, Papá, Sofía, Javi, and Sabrina

The letters blurred as the last of my hopes faded. I looked up at the ceiling, pushing back the tears. Anger and hurt filled me. *Move on, dammit. It's over.* I straightened my back. Madame was right. As much as Sebastián's rejection hurt, I had to pour it all into my performance. I would make Federico proud, and I would put Madame's hesitations about me to rest, for good.

At the stage wing, a dancer from the corps fastened the back of my bodice as I bounced on my feet to stay warm.

"You look perfect, Camila. *Merde.*"

"Thank you. So do you. *Merde.*"

"Camila, Marcos, five minutes," the stage manager announced as Marcos stepped in from behind.

We waited, listening to the music as I marked my steps in place. Marcos reached for my hand and squeezed it. Our eyes met and he grinned.

"We're going to kill it. I just know," he said. "Let's do this. *Merde.*"

The overture began, and the familiar melody of Tchaikovsky's magnificent score filled the air. I took my first step and was immediately immersed in the performance. Marcos was an incredible partner on stage, making every transition seamless. His hands were strong and his movements confident. The world around us disappeared, and it was just the two of us on the stage, moving in perfect synchronization as only our bodies knew how.

Time flew by and I willingly got lost in the story, a world where everything was beautiful. As I whirled into a triple pirouette, my muscles burned with fatigue and ecstasy. My heart drummed against my ribs and I smiled, entrapped in that moment of happiness.

In the third act, Marcos and I danced the grand pas de deux for the wedding scene. It was enchanting, and everyone in the cast looked radiant, the costumes magnificent. We became the story, and it wasn't hard to leave the real world behind. We had worked so hard for this moment. This was why we forced our bodies to endure the constant pain, why we stayed late for endless rehearsals and said no to anything that wasn't ballet. This was why. And to us, it was worth it.

I took my last step and closed my eyes as the audience burst into applause. I blinked in the blinding lights of the stage, and the magic felt suddenly empty. Sebastián wasn't in the audience. *No, no*. I told myself everything was perfect. This was all I needed, all I ever wanted.

The last dancers took their bows, and Marcos held my hand as we bowed in unison. It was an amazing high. We had just performed on the New York stage. The applause continued even after the curtain fell. Then Marcos and I stepped out to the deafening cheers for one last bow. I pointed my left foot behind me, extending my arms to my sides as I bowed in a final grande révérance. The audience stood, cheering bravos while they showered us with flowers. Federico came on stage and handed me an enormous bouquet of flowers, kissing my cheek softly.

"You were magnificent. Well done," he whispered in my ear. Bright moisture swam in his eyes.

I grinned, ecstatic, standing on top of the world. Marcos squeezed my hand, his own happiness stretching across his face.

"We were amazing," he said. His tender hazel eyes were warm as he brought my hand to his lips. This was us. When we were on stage together, there was nothing else.

The back hallways buzzed with energy as the cast congratulated each other and scattered to get ready for a big celebration night in New York. Nata intercepted me backstage and pulled me into a tight embrace.

"You were perfect! I wish you could've seen yourself from the audience. You were magical, Camila." She blinked the tears and I couldn't stop mine.

"Thank you. It felt incredible. I can't believe it's over."

"Oh, it's *not* over. You get to do it again the day after tomorrow. And again, and again, and again."

Marcos appeared, then we stepped out into the frosted evening, and a shower of flashes exploded as a group of photographers crowded around us. Marcos wrapped his arm around Nata's and my waist, and we posed for the hungry cameras.

"One of you two," a reporter said. "The prince and princess!"

Nata stepped aside and Marcos pulled me closer.

"A kiss! Come on! Kiss her!" another voice shouted. Before I could blink, Marcos wrapped me in his arms and kissed me hard on the mouth, bending me backward like that famous New York photo of the sailor and the nurse. Another steady stream of flashes exploded. Unwrapping myself from Marcos's arms, I pushed away from him and turned to Nata. I ushered her toward the curb, away from the photographers.

"What the hell was that about?" I blurted.

"He's just playing along. Reporters *love* portraying the principals as real couples. It's part of the show. It sells."

"Well, I don't like it."

"Why?"

"Because."

"Of Sebastián…"

"He's in the hospital because of me. What's he going to think when he sees a photo of me kissing Marcos? It's cruel and totally insensitive."

"Cami." Nata held my hand and squeezed it. "Stop tormenting yourself about that. You're in New York! And Sebastián's got more important things to worry about."

Marcos caught up as we hailed a cab. "Ha. That was fun, eh?"

"Marcos don't do that again," I said as Nata scooted into the back seat.

"Ah, c'mon. It's all a show."

I frowned. "No, okay?"

"Lighten up, Cams, will you?"

During the cab ride to the dinner, Nata showed me all the photos she had taken before the performance: people dressed in their finest attire, the glow from the Lincoln Center fountain, the imposing light fixtures decorating the theater, the red carpet, selfies with the dancers drinking champagne. Everyone was smiling, and I was glad she had done it so we had memories of all this.

"Ah…our princesses and princes are finally all here. We can toast!" Federico stood from his seat at the head of an endless table. It was always strange to see him and Madame outside of the theater environment. Everyone filled their glasses and raised them. My cheeks burned and I quickly took my spot next to Nata and Marcos.

"You're cute when you blush." Marcos winked, handing me a glass of champagne.

"To the company," Federico said, raising his glass.

"To the company," everyone replied in unison. Champagne flutes clinked as the cast relaxed after a long week. Waiters appeared from everywhere with trays filled with different kinds of food: Korean barbecue, Thai curries, pasta, grilled seafood. I had never seen such variety before. It all looked delicious, but my stomach was the hub for all my tension, and it wasn't budging.

First Cast danced again the following night, and again, Marcos and I sat in the audience. I couldn't get over how different it was to watch from there. You didn't see how difficult everything really was, all the things we worried about when we were on stage. Nata and Diego made the variations look beautiful, easy, effortless. I was blown away that these people were my friends, my family, and from the audience, I could fully see how talented they really were. I felt proud of being part of the Colón company. Tears welled in my eyes. Marcos smiled at me and wrapped his arm around my back.

When we walked out to wait for Nata and the others, what looked like the same group of photographers from the previous night gathered around Marcos and me. Shit. Was this how it always was for principals? I had never gotten this much attention, and I wasn't sure I liked it. A few months ago, I would've thought it was flattering, but now it felt invasive. I thought of Sebastián and how he hated reporters. Maybe the best thing for the company was for me to go along with the charade, but I really didn't want people to think Marcos and I were a couple.

Back in the hotel lobby, after *another* dinner with the cast, Federico waved Marcos and me over to a sitting area on the side.

"I wanted to show you this." He lifted the Arts section of the *New York Times.* "You two made the papers."

My stomach turned as I took the paper and stared at a large front-page photo of the two of us in Marcos's dramatic kiss. The headline read: *Love on and off the Stage: Buenos Aires's Most Beloved Couple.*

"God," I whispered, bringing my hand to my mouth in horror. "No."

"Yes," Federico said, chuckling. "This is fantastic, Camila. Well done! It's a great way for us to get publicity."

"Through *gossip*?" I snapped, unable to unglue my eyes from the paper.

"Camila, it's the *New York Times*! The people that matter to us, the people *you'll* want to get exposed to as a performer, read this paper. The audience craves love stories. This is a great way for them to remember who you are."

I shook my head. Dammit, had Sebastián seen this already? *From his room in intensive care? Get a hold of yourself.*

"What's the matter?" Federico asked. "What do you care if people think you and Marcos are a couple? Believe me, any girl in the company would gladly play that role," he said, grinning smugly at Marcos, who looked at me with an *I didn't do it* expression.

"I just…" I sighed.

"Camila, sweetheart," Federico said, caressing my hair. "Just go along with this. Have fun. The company can use the publicity. Just smile and hug Marcos for the cameras, okay?"

I nodded slowly, thinking of what Madame had said to me at the restaurant. I couldn't worry about this now. Worrying about stupid gossip would only be a distraction. Besides, Nata was right. Sebastián had more important things to deal with than my fake romance with Marcos.

In the morning, Marcos, Nata, and I visited the studios of Manhattan Ballet. Andrew, their ballet master in chief, loved foreign dancers and had invited us to take a few classes with his cast.

Marcos strode in like he owned the place, aware of the usual looks he got from both male and female dancers. Beside me, Nata moved with silent confidence. She was used to being surrounded by dancers of the highest caliber. Russian dancers normally were, having had to deal with the pressure from a very early age.

Andrew had reserved some spots for us in the middle. I felt out of place as I peeled off my multiple layers of clothing, watching the Americans warm up on their portable barres. They looked more like Olympic athletes than ballet dancers. They were strong, athletic, muscular. No traces of the anorexic frames of ballet dancers that were popular in earlier years.

During the break, a few principals invited us to a juice bar downstairs. They were friendly, but I couldn't follow what they said because they all spoke quickly and had American accents. I had learned British English and never realized how different it was from the American dialect and pronunciation. Nata did better, though she didn't engage in the conversations too much, and Marcos…well, he always seemed to manage just fine. I felt disconnected, and after the news about Sebastián, an elephant foot had settled permanently on my chest. I wanted to be there, in the moment. It made me angry that after dreaming of this for so long, part of me still longed to be back at home.

When we arrived at the hotel in the afternoon, I was mentally and physically exhausted. Dancing normally took most of my energy, and now it was layered with worry, language barriers, and the constant social interaction.

One night, Federico brought the principals along to a gala at a penthouse on the Upper West Side. I wore a gown I borrowed from Nata and thanked her incessantly as I glanced around. I would've never been able to afford clothes for an event like this. I thought of Sebastián, how he would easily blend in with this crowd, mingling with the guests, looking dashing in his tuxedo.

At the party, we met Baryshnikov and famous actors like Matthew Broderick and Sarah Jessica Parker. It was like being part of a scene in a movie, and I was ecstatic to be able to share all this unbelievable craziness with Nata. Like most ballet dancers, we had both admired Misha since we were kids, and now we were here, sipping champagne with him as *he* complimented *us* on our performances. It was beyond surreal.

Everyone seemed interested in my "romance with Marcos." The women looked at him with starry eyes, some men with a mix of envy and admiration, others with lust. More photos, more reporters everywhere. And after a while, I no longer fought the charade. It was easier to go along, and it would all end soon.

The next morning, we met Christopher, Manhattan Ballet's new choreographer. A native of London, he was the ultimate principal dancer: strong, confident, and oddly, also straight. He strode into the class with his hair tied back in a messy knot. He wore torn jeans and a black sweater pulled up at the sleeves. His features were masculine and attractive, but not in the typical pretty boy way.

I could immediately tell people respected him. The moment he walked in, the class settled. Everyone stopped the chatter and hurried to their spots.

During class, Christopher stayed close to me and gave me minor corrections. His hands were strong but gentle. A chill ran through my back as his hands clasped my waist from behind, and his warm breath brushed my neck as he adjusted my form.

"See? When you straighten your back, you show the beautiful lines of your neck." He grazed the back of his fingers along my neck. I blushed and felt everyone's eyes on me.

After class, he waved for me to approach him. I told Marcos and Nata I would meet them outside and draped my towel around my neck.

"Great class. Camila, is it?" he said in his perfect British accent. I blinked, doing my best to ignore the blush that rose to my face. What was it about him that unsettled me?

"Um, yes. Thanks."

"You've got a very nice form. I would love to work with you sometime."

Was he joking? Me? But when our eyes met, he was serious. I blushed again. Up this close, his presence was even stronger. He had pulled off his sweater during class and was wearing only a fitted, black T-shirt. My eyes were doing a thorough inventory of his biceps and the roped muscles under his shirt. He smiled at my lack of response. Crap.

"See you in class tomorrow?" he said.

"Um, yes. Sure. Bye." I turned, cursing myself inwardly for the idiot I was. Two *um yeses* in two sentences. *Perfect, Camila. Way to make an impression.*

Outside the studio, Marcos waited for me while chatting with a couple of the American—*female*—dancers. When he saw me, he scooped me up and kissed my cheek.

"Let's go, princess."

The girls gave me a once-over: *lucky bitch.* As soon as we stepped out, two waiting photographers fired a steady stream of photos. This again. Marcos smiled and whispered in my ear, "Let's give them what they want. It'll be good for both of us. Yes? But I won't do it if you don't want to." His eyes were warm, his expression serious.

I gave him a skeptical look. But I needed to get over my constant longing for Sebastián. It was over. And if some stupid photos would help my career, so be it.

I nodded. "Let's do it."

He draped his arm around my waist and pulled me to him. *Click. Click.* We both smiled, leaning our foreheads together like a couple having an intimate moment. Then we grinned as we turned to the cameras. *Click. Click.* Marcos took my face in his hands and kissed me deeply on the mouth. *Click. Click. Click.* I closed my eyes and let him kiss me. It felt both familiar and foreign. *Click. Click.* For the first time, I wasn't really fighting him, and the familiarity I felt for Marcos, my friend, mixed with something sexier that was Marcos, the man. When he broke the kiss, I blinked at him and he smiled warmly. *Click. Click.* The photographers thanked us and scurried away to get a few shots of Nata and Diego.

"A few of the dancers said a hotel down the street has a killer happy hour. They'll meet us there later for a couple of drinks," Marcos said as we set off to get a cab.

I frowned. "Marcos, Federico said—"

"Ah, Cams. It's just a drink. Hey, I could see us here, you know? In New York..."

My mind drifted as he went on about how great this all was. I listened in a daze caused partly by the icy wind and partly by what I had felt when he kissed me. And...I had also felt out of sorts around Christopher. What was happening to me? Was this a subconscious attempt to get over Sebastián? Marcos seemed oblivious.

We made plans to meet at the hotel lobby in an hour, and I left to my room for a hot shower.

At the bar, a few of the dancers from Manhattan Ballet had already taken a whole section with high tables. The place was cool: exposed brick walls, dim lighting with low-hanging iron fixtures. Even the ceiling was intricately designed with those stamped tin tiles. It reminded me of an old train station. *Sebastián would've loved it.* I ordered a beer.

I sat at the bar, glad for a moment alone while Marcos went to say hello to Bridget, one of the Manhattan Ballet principals, a redhead with fit curves and long legs. A hand startled me when it squeezed my shoulder from behind. A second later, Christopher appeared beside me.

"Hi." He smiled, and his deep blue eyes crinkled at the corners.

"Um, hi." *There you go. Impress him with your extensive vocabulary again.* He looked around at the crowd, who was mostly made of people my age, though I didn't think Christopher was much older than thirty five.

"You here alone?" he said.

"No, I came with Marcos, my partner."

He nodded at Marcos. "Also your boyfriend, I hear?"

420

"Marcos? Oh, no. He's not my boyfriend. That's just...you know, for the media. Apparently, it sells."

"Ah, yes. Yes, it does." He ordered a drink, and I immediately felt self-conscious because I wasn't supposed to be drinking the night before a performance. I angled away from my beer, and he chuckled.

"I won't tell."

"Thanks," I said. "Federico is...rather strict about it."

"And yet, here you are. Rebellious. I like it."

I blushed crimson. "I—"

"I'm just teasing you. A drink always helps me relax."

He eased into casual chatter about the performances and the differences between our cultures. I was worried I shouldn't be out getting distracted, and almost excused myself to go back to the hotel, but the image of my tear-stained pillow stopped me. He was easy to talk to, and within minutes we were chatting about my life in Buenos Aires and his life in London. He had an intensity about him that was...sexy. Whenever he spoke about something he felt passionate about, a little V formed on his forehead. He used his hands a lot to explain things, and for some reason it made me feel comfortable. As I took a sip of my beer, he gently brushed my hair away from my face. Our eyes met, and the intensity of his gaze sent an electric shot through my already weakened system.

"I should go," I whispered.

"Let me walk you back."

"It's fine, I'm only a couple of blocks away."

"I insist."

"Okay."

I gave a quick kiss to Marcos and told him to stay. He glanced at Christopher and gave me a wary look, then nodded and told me to text once I got to my room.

I was glad my hotel was only two blocks away, because I was ready to throw a fit about the weather. How in the fuck did people function here? Even my brain was frozen. I couldn't think. A mother walked past us with a stroller. The poor kid was so bundled up you could only see his eyes.

In the hotel lobby, Christopher kissed my cheek softly.

"Good-bye, Camila of Buenos Aires. I thoroughly enjoyed talking to you. And I meant it when I said I'd love to work with you. Let me see what I can do."

"Thanks, Christopher." I smiled weakly.

"Chris."

"Chris. I'll see you tomorrow."

The next morning was our last class with Manhattan Ballet. I was excited, but as soon as I walked in, I felt the hostile looks from some of the dancers from the bar the night before. What was their problem? Chris and I had only been talking. Marcos walked in behind me and offered me his coffee as I finished peeling off the last layer of clothes.

"I had one already. This one's yours," I told him.

"You can have it. I get the shakes."

"Thanks," I said, looking up at him. He knew I loved those caramel macchiatos, but Marcos had never been the bring-you-coffee kind.

He kissed my cheek. "You look pretty today."

I sipped the coffee and looked around the room. Mmm. It was delicious. A few steps away, two girls from the Manhattan Ballet gave me a dirty look as they whispered something to each other. Chris called the class to their places, and the girls walked in my direction.

"*Slut*," one of them said under her breath as they walked past.

I frowned. I knew that word from the movies. Had I done something wrong? What was their problem? The girls glanced at Marcos, then back at me and turned away.

A one-day break between performances gave us time to recover. Some dancers left to see the city while others chilled at the hotel. I went to see the 9/11 Memorial Museum with Nata. It was stunning, and as I walked around in our guided tour, the heaviness of so many lives lost overwhelmed me. New York didn't forget, and this incredible tribute dedicated to so many for whom this city had been home, grieved for them in silence. My chest tightened. It was so powerful, moving, and yet, still uplifting, but it left me in a somber mood. Once again, I thought of Sebastián, wishing he could've been here. He would've explained every architectural detail, the passion bright in his eyes as he spoke while I listened in silent fascination.

On the way back, Nata left me to stop at the pharmacy. When I entered the hotel lobby, Chris approached me. What was he doing here?

"Hey, I was hoping to find you. They said you were out."

"Yeah, I went to see a bit of the city."

"Fancy dinner and a drink?"

"Oh, I—"

"Come on. Say yes. I meant to ask you after class today, but you left so quickly."

I thought of the girls in class and their dirty looks. More had followed after Chris had stayed longer to work with me alone.

Screw them.

"Okay…Let me change."

"Why? Darling, you look lovely."

We went to an Irish pub. Chris ordered an unfamiliar dark beer that at first tasted bitter but then soothed me into a state of pure sedation. We ate burgers and fries with vinegar, and for a few moments, I forgot Sebastián was in the hospital and that he had to completely cut me off from his life. Chris was charming, smart, and funny. If I hadn't been so heartbroken, I would have been really into him. We danced to a slow melody, and he wrapped his arms around me while he whispered sweet things in my ear in that sexy British accent of his. I closed my eyes and pretended that there was nothing else, no one else but the two of us in a bar in my dream city. His mouth slowly found mine, and I let him kiss me because I was kind of drunk and really exhausted from the constant loneliness and longing. I abandoned myself to the kiss and didn't notice the tears until he held my face in his hands and kissed my wet cheeks.

"My sweet, sad girl. There's something about you. A mourning in those eyes…I get it."

I looked at him, confused but also puzzled. A complete stranger had kissed me and it was comforting, different. Perfect, actually. He kissed me again, this time with all the passion and longing of lost, forgotten love. It felt good to be wanted, and I ignored the uneasiness unfurling inside me and pretended. This time for no other audience than myself.

Chris got us a room in my hotel far away from the cast floor. We snuck in, and he stripped my clothes while he kissed me adoringly. My head was foggy with alcohol and swirling memories, memories I kept pushing away. He laid me on the bed and I felt feverish and weak. *Damn alcohol.* But I had needed the courage to break away from the images of Sebastián.

He trailed kisses along my stomach from the line of my panties to the band of my bra. I closed my eyes and willed my heart to let go. It was strange to be in bed with someone I barely knew, someone other than Sebastián. How did Marcos do it all the time? He always said sex with strangers was so liberating. My body protested. Chris was without a doubt a good lover, but his touch felt foreign, and after Sebastián, to me sex and love had to be in the same package. I broke the kiss.

"I'm sorry…I can't."

Chris lifted his head, his forehead wrinkled with worry. "Something wrong?"

"No…Yes."

"Have I upset you somehow, darling?" he said, nuzzling my nose.

"No, no. It's not you," I said, sliding from underneath him and sitting up. "I'm just a mess right now. I'm so sorry."

"No need to be." He took my hands in his, and I gazed up at him.

"It's just...I broke up with someone before I came to New York. He was...important. I'm not over him. This wouldn't be fair to you."

"Listen, love," he said sweetly. "You don't have to apologize. We all have our sad stories."

Dread settled in my chest as we both dressed. Riding the elevator back to my floor, I wanted to feel relief for not sleeping with Chris. But instead I felt light-headed and heavy with a new sense of guilt. Chris would surely think I was a head case, and he wouldn't be wrong.

The next night at the theater, while I waited for Marcos to get me a glass of champagne, I saw Chris walk in a few steps away. He was pushing a young woman in a wheelchair and didn't see me as he approached a group of dancers from Manhattan Ballet gathered in the main hall.

"Let's go say hi," said Marcos, handing me a glass. But when I took a sip, the taste of alcohol turned my stomach. A lingering headache had stayed with me since yesterday, and the building fatigue was taking its toll. Marcos greeted Chris and the dancers while I considered going back to the hotel and going to bed. When my eyes met Chris's, he froze. An uncomfortable moment passed between us. *Yeah, Camila, the mental case.* Then I glanced down at the young, slender woman in the wheelchair. She was beautiful, her skin pale and delicate, her eyes large and black.

"Hello, I'm Ivette." She smiled, extending a slender hand with long fingers. "I'm Chris's wife."

Two dancers in the group stabbed me with icy glares. *Slut.* Guilt, betrayal, and disgust filled me. I scowled up at Chris, who looked like he had tasted something bitter, and I almost laughed out loud at the irony. Just when things couldn't get any goddamn worse. Just when I thought I was wanted and had almost given it a chance.

"Excuse me." I turned, hurrying to the exit.

Marcos caught up with me. "What are you doing?"

"I'm leaving. I don't feel well."

"What's wrong?"

I pushed the door, ran to a nearby trash can, and emptied the scant contents of my stomach.

"Shit, Cams. Let me take you back," he said, holding my shoulders from behind.

Back in my hotel room, Marcos took my coat off and dropped it on the bed. A memory of Sebastián hanging up my coat after a party punched me.

"How are you feeling?"

"I just need to go to bed. Thanks, Marcos. You can go. Nata won't be back till late, so I'll just go to sleep."

He left and I buried myself under the covers. I felt drained, my head ached, and I sensed the onset of a cold. I let my eyelids win and surrendered to unconsciousness.

The rest of the week dumped on me like a blizzard. I was grateful to have a fixed schedule, although it was hard to keep up with it. A head cold hit me full on, and I couldn't get over the insanely arctic weather. *How do people do this?* I asked myself every morning as I walked the two blocks to Lincoln Center.

The company had organized a few sightseeing tours in between performances, but I couldn't find the energy. It was a countdown to closing night, and I promised myself I would make it.

By the weekend, my head throbbed, and my nose was chapped from drying the constant drip. I made myself take a hot shower and drink herbal tea. God, I was sick of tea. Wrapped in a blanket, I stood by the window and watched the snow fall like moths in the wind. From our room on the fiftieth floor, the traffic sounds were faint, muffled by double-paned windows. As I sipped my tea, I watched the city I had dreamt of my entire life, and it seemed distant, foreign. Nothing like in my dream.

I thought about my first opening night at the Colón: Sebastián waiting with a huge bouquet of flowers, grinning proudly. But no flowers came now, and every night that week as I walked into my empty room, another petal of hope fell off, and the anguish that I had permanently lost Sebastián haunted me. I was tired of it, dammit. I had to do something. My head was foggy from the cold. I shivered even though the heater was cranked all the way up. Stumbling to the dresser, I grabbed my phone to call him.

Chapter 43

My phone was dead, and Marcos had borrowed the only power cord we hadn't lost yet. I did my best to dress quickly, but my body complained from the incessant hours en pointe, and I was pretty sure I was running a fever. Pushing the discomfort away, I slipped into a pair of UGG boots Nata had forced me to buy, put on my coat, and rushed to the elevator.

The front desk loaned me a charger, and after a few minutes, my phone screen lit to life.

"The number you have dialed is no longer in service." The automated recording played the message over and over. I tried Rafa: same answer. What the hell.

Nata could help. Sergei could get me Sebastián's number somehow. Remembering she was with Diego at a café across the street, I rushed to the exit. But when I stepped out, the gelid air slapped me like a mother would an insolent child. I stumbled forward, the world spun, and it all went black.

I shivered. Why was it so cold? I tried stirring, but my body was numb, my muscles rubbery and heavy, as if they belonged to somebody else. I opened my eyes to an unfamiliar room. My arm itched. When I tried scratching, my hand met a plastic tube taped to my skin. I stared at it, not understanding.

"How are you feeling?" Nata said from the foot of my bed. She sat on a corner of the mattress, her face worried.

"What...where am I?"

"At the hospital."

"What?" I looked around at the stark white of the walls, trying to summon the memories. "The hospital..." My throat burned with thirst, and my mouth felt sandy and dry. Nata reached for a water cup on my bedside and handed it to me. I emptied the cup in one long gulp. Water never tasted so good.

"You fainted." She stroked my hair gently. "I saw you from across the street but couldn't get to you in time. You hit your head," she said, her voice laced with remorse.

I reached up to my temple. It felt as if a searing iron had branded me there. "Ough."

"Take it easy, Cams. The ambulance brought you here. You were burning. They said you had an infection, and they gave you antibiotics. The doctor wanted to keep you here overnight to rule out some other things."

"What time is it?"

"Seven."

"At night?"

"In the morning," she said, carefully brushing the hair off my forehead. "Listen, I've got to go, but I'll come check on you at the break, okay?"

"Wait, no. I'm coming."

"*No.* You stay here and rest. They said they'll dismiss you later today if your fever breaks. Rest."

"I'm fine." But as I tried pushing myself up, an invisible mallet pounded my forehead. I plopped back into the pillow. "Shit."

Nata pressed the back of her hand to my cheek. "You still have a fever. Here." She refilled the cup and I downed it.

"Nata…closing night is three days away. I can't be sick."

"You need to rest. Verónica will take your place tonight and you're off tomorrow. Get better." She kissed my forehead. "Christ, you're burning. I'll have Marcos check on you after his rehearsal, okay?"

No, no. Not Verónica. Please, wait. A wave of fatigue washed through me, and my eyelids fell closed. Everything shut down.

A second later, I blinked at the light. Nata was gone, and Marcos was stretched out on a small armchair beside me, watching an American football game.

"Marcos, what time is it?"

"Hey, sleepy." He glanced at his watch. "One. In the afternoon."

"Seriously?"

"Yeah, you've been out cold. The doctor came a while ago and gave you a shot. How are you doing?" He winced at what must have been my haggard appearance.

"Shit," I groaned and squeezed my eyes shut, threading the images together. "I slept for a *whole day?*"

"You did. Slacker." He chuckled. "Looks like you're on the mend. The antibiotics worked. They said they kept you another day because your fever wouldn't break, and they wanted to rule out a very aggressive virus that's hitting New York. Bummer you were out. I wanted us to do this whole tour together."

"What do you mean?" I realized it as soon as I said it. "Verónica danced in my place?"

"Yeah." He sighed. "Like I said, it sucks."

Shit. I tested my limbs against the mattress. They were stiff, unresponsive. I pointed my toes, stretching my feet until a sharp pain burned up my calves. *Focus.*

"What time is the next rehearsal?" I said.

Marcos yawned as he glanced at his watch. "In forty-five. We're still on lunch break."

I rubbed the grogginess from my eyes and slid off the bed, scanning the room. The IV line pulled on my arm. I scowled at it, and ripping the tape off in one solid tug, I slid the needle out, then pressed the tape back where the needle had been. "Ouch. Where are my clothes, do you know?"

"Your clothes? What the hell, Cams, you can't pull that thing out."

"I don't need it." I met his eyes. "Are you going to help me get my clothes or not?"

"Cams, you can't dance like this. Verónica can cover you."

"No!" I whirled around and the room spun. I gripped the bed rail just in time. Marcos frowned and tilted his head, watching me as if I was some odd experiment he didn't understand. "Tell me," I said. "Was she good?"

"Nope. Federico's in a shitty mood. It sucks overall, but what are you gonna do...And she's put on weight too. My arms are killing me from carrying her fat ass around."

I stared down at my white knuckles wrapped around the bed's metal rail while a new determination expanded within me. I thought about that day in the studio, a million days away now. The day when Madame kicked me out because I couldn't keep going. I had obeyed and gone home, feeling defeated and beaten up by the injustice of it all. I now realized she had been testing me. Sure, an ankle injury was tricky, it could go either way, and handling it right required maturity. But for the first time since I started ballet, I knew. I really understood the life I had chosen. The right choice was to always keep going, to do what reasonable people weren't willing to do. To keep pushing, keep dancing. I thought of all those nights at the studio rehearsing until my muscles burned, all the painful hours I had spent coercing my battered body to cooperate while other girls my age had fun, and parties, and friends and boyfriends. No. *No*. This was it. The threshold. The hell if I had come this far to let Verónica take my spot at the final hour. I had already given up everything for my career. I was here to perform.

"Help me find my clothes." I turned unsteadily to the small closet.

"Cams, babe. Nobody wants you to come back more than me, but this...is nuts. They said to wait till this evening."

I ignored him and pulled up my jeans. They were looser.

"Are you listening?" he said.

"Tomorrow's closing night," I said as I stepped into my UGGs.

"You can't dance. You're sick." He squeezed my shoulders gently.

I met his eyes. "Oh, yes. Yes, I can." I shrugged his hands off and pulled on my sweater.

His expression changed and he nodded slightly. It was as if he were looking at a stranger. "You sure about this?"

"Let's go."

Deciding to skip the paperwork, we scurried down the hallway. I had no idea what releasing yourself from the hospital would involve, but I didn't want to find out, and time was slipping through my fingers. Marcos's muscular arm held me against his torso. I kept my chin down as we hurried to the elevators. My head was spinning wildly and my pulse raced. I focused on each step, using the lines of the floor tiles for guidance. *One more step, one more, keep going. You can do this.* I felt so weak. My legs were about to give when Marcos finally opened the exit door, and the gelid noon air of New York shook me awake.

After a quick shower at the hotel and a heavy dose of ibuprofen, I walked into rehearsal, still holding onto Marcos's arm. Verónica's eyes narrowed, scanning me. I made sure I kept my shoulders back and my chin up. I had concealed the circles under my eyes, but I still felt weak, my stomach swimming in a mixture of drugs and acid from the coffee I had downed at the hotel lobby. At least the pills did their job, and my headache was now a dull pain. I looked around for Federico and Madame, but they were nowhere in sight. I hurried across to the dressing room, waiting for someone to grab my arm and tell me to go back to bed, that obviously I wasn't up for it. But no one did. And it occurred to me that everyone in the cast was likely focused on concealing their own injuries. There was a lot at stake for them, too, and nobody would question whether or not I was fully recovered. It comforted me to think I was simply a part of this huge puzzle, and they needed me as much as I needed them. Except for Verónica. She wasn't having it, and as soon as I stepped out of my dressing room, she intercepted me.

"You're back?" she spat out, trying to mask her infuriated tone. "We have tomorrow covered. Federico's decision," she reinforced. "Just...chill."

"No. *I've* got it covered. *You* go chill." I grinned. "Excuse me," I said, stepping around her.

The next evening, armed with cold medicine, Papá's pills, and a few shots of wheatgrass, I sowed the ribbons on the unique custom shoes embroidered by Anna. I had been saving them and, finally, it seemed like the perfect night to honor her and all my hard work to become a prima. An image of Sebastián pulling me off 9 de Julio after I bolted across to save them crossed my mind, and I smiled. It seemed like a million years ago.

I gave my last time on the New York stage everything I had, my bottled-up dreams spilling free.

I went through every variation in a sort of drug-induced trance, except it was my adrenaline that kept me going. My head burned and every muscle ached with fatigue, but I fought hard so no one would see it. As Madame always said, our own suffering was private. The audience wanted perfection and smiles.

At the wings, between dances, I bent over, my temples pulsing as I caught my breath. A girl from the corps handed me a chilled bottle of water, and I downed it.

"Are you all right?"

"Thanks." I said, nodding, then leapt back onto the stage in sync with the music. An overall fire ran through my muscles. I ordered my body to obey and followed the variations without stopping to assess the pain that screamed from my ankle or the feverish sweat that covered my limbs. *I* was in charge.

The final act came, and Marcos and I danced one last time for the scene of Princess Aurora's wedding. He smiled, and a feeling of triumph sang in my veins. We had done it. I smiled back, on a high of adrenaline and meds. It was as if I were dancing in someone else's body.

When the curtain finally fell, I bowed to the audience, bursting into applause from behind the lights of the stage. For the first time, I truly felt like a professional dancer. Pain ravaged my muscles, but I had pulled it off. This was the life of a dancer. The public didn't pay to see that you were just like them. They paid for the illusion, the dream that you were untouched by the ugliness of the world.

For our last night, Federico had organized an over-the-top farewell that said, *Oh yeah, I'm at the top.* Everyone in the ballet world was there. Baryshnikov greeted us and Nata and I joked: *You again?* It was a grand party. The tour was over, and it was time to go home. A sense of nostalgia flashed through me. Despite the hurdles of the trip, this was New York City. Being here kicked ass.

Madame intercepted me as I stepped out of the ladies' room.

"Camila, do you have a moment?"

"Of course." I had noticed that since we had gotten to New York, she no longer called me by my last name. Had I earned her respect? She ushered me to a small sitting area in the corner, away from a group of tipsy guests. She straightened invisible wrinkles on her black velvet gown, and her steady green eyes gazed into mine.

"Sit," she ordered, and I obeyed. "Andrew, Federico, and I have been talking with Manhattan Ballet this week. Andrew is quite impressed by your potential."

"Really? I'm...flattered."

"You should be. Andrew is a great director. This is out of the norm during a tour, but Andrew is thinking about asking you to join Manhattan Ballet."

"What? *Me?* Why?"

"Why *not* you?" She frowned. I searched her eyes. Was she delusional?

"B-because...there are others that are so much better. Nata—"

"Nata is an established principal at the Colón. She's part of our legacy," she said calmly. "Your career, on the other hand, is just starting. This would be the right time for you to make a move like this."

"I...I don't know what to say. I'm...stunned."

"Camila," she said, placing her languid, gentle hand on my shoulder. "Professionally, this is a unique opportunity for you."

"It's huge....But what about Federico? He's given me a chance, I can't walk away like that."

Madame shook her head. "He and I have talked about this. The Colón can't offer you the same exposure as Manhattan Ballet, and though he resists, he knows that."

I chewed on my bottom lip, processing.

"If this was happening to me at your age, I wouldn't hesitate," she said.

"I just..." I looked into her deep green eyes. The usual hardness was replaced by a new sense of respect, as if she were no longer talking to the struggling dancer with incorrigible habits. "Madame, I thought you didn't think I really had it."

"I'm hard on my dancers, hardest on the ones with the most potential."

"But you don't mind if I leave the Colón? You're letting me go?"

She placed her hands on mine and gripped firmly. "Foolish girl. I will miss you dearly. It's not every day I get to work with a dancer with your determination. You have grown tremendously. But I know what this will mean for your career. I have to let you go."

My throat tightened, the ache strangling a whimper that was fighting its way out.

"I would have to move here." I wrinkled my forehead.

"Oh, for Christ's sake, child. Of course you would have to move here. Listen to me." She squeezed my hands again. "You have been preparing for an opportunity like this your entire life. You work harder than most dancers in the company, and you just proved it yesterday by fleeing the hospital to rehearse and perform on closing night. Or did you think I wouldn't realize you were dancing with a fever?"

I looked at my feet to hide the burn in my face. Did anything ever escape this woman?

"What does Federico think?" I said.

She waved her hand dismissively. "Federico is like most ballet directors. Territorial, narcissistic. I love the man, but it's the truth. This is *your* chance, Camila. And you can't let guilt or fear decide. But if you don't take this, then you are not the dancer I thought you were." She gave my hand one last pat and stood, turning back to the party.

When I finally got to my room that night, I felt completely drained. I had briefly spoken to Andrew during the party, and we had made an appointment for the next morning.

I was up most of the night thinking, imagining myself as a New Yorker, walking the city streets to work every morning. But as I considered the great career path this could mean for me, a part of me still felt hollow. Was I not ready? Was I being a coward? This would be a big change. Maybe I had to just go for it, maybe these feelings were normal, and they would eventually settle once New York became my home. I tossed and turned. But the more I envisioned my life here and the more I tried to convince myself this was the obvious next step, the heavier my chest felt. For everything New York had to offer, Sebastián wasn't here.

"It will mean hard work," Andrew explained after laying down his proposal from behind his large, mahogany desk. "You would be starting slow, I'll be honest. Most of the main roles will go to the principals this year, but we can arrange some solos for you until we post casting for the new season. We can formalize things then." We were sitting in his office, a corner space on the fourth floor with a stunning view of Central Park.

If I accepted, I would join Manhattan Ballet right away. The season was half over, so I would only have a few days to fly home to get my stuff. In Buenos Aires, the Colón ballet was off for the summer, and Federico wouldn't offer contracts for another month.

"It's such an honor to even be considered." I bit my lip, my pulse sprinting. "Would it be okay to have a day or so to think about it? It's a big decision."

"Absolutely. I'll be out tomorrow, so why don't we touch base Tuesday morning?"

I agreed.

My heart pounded against my chest as I closed the door behind me and pulled out my phone. There was only one person who could help me think this through.

"Is it normal that I'm freaking out, Mamá? What should I do?" I said as I dodged a group of tourists dressed in Hawaiian shirts of ridiculously bright colors over their winter clothes.

"It's a fantastic opportunity," Mamá said. "And, honestly, it may not come around again. Some dancers wait years for a chance to dance in New York, even as a starting soloist. But only *you* can make the right choice for you. You have to listen to your gut, Cami."

"But *you* did it. New York was home for you."

"Yes, it was. For a few years, anyway. But this is about you. Ever since you were little, you've told yourself and everyone else that once you made it to New York, you would be a professional. I know how much this means to you. How much it always has."

"I know. And now that I'm here…I'm not sure what comes next."

"Look. Every once in a while, it's good to stop and reassess your goals. This is the time to do that. Think about what you want to get out of your career, honey. New York is no longer the last stop, now it's a diving board. What is it you want? That will give you the answer you're looking for."

"I'm scared, Mamá. The truth is, I hate it here. I thought it would be fun, that I would love everything about Manhattan. But it's cold and gray, and everything's different. I really don't see myself here."

"Cami, there's always an adjustment period. Besides, it will be spring soon." I heard her smile through the phone.

Later that morning, I told Nata and Marcos about my conversations with Madame and then with Andrew. As it turned out, Marcos had also been offered a position as a principal with Manhattan Ballet.

"And?" I said, sounding harsh without meaning to.

Marcos shrugged. "Don't know yet."

Sitting beside me on the bed, Nata reached for my arm. "What do you want, Cami?"

That question again. "I'm not sure anymore. I was convinced this was what I wanted, to live in New York, dance for Manhattan Ballet, but now I don't know. It doesn't *feel* right to be here, you know?"

"I do know," Nata said. "I was terrified when I first came to Buenos Aires. I cried for days. I hated it. Now I wouldn't go anywhere else."

I went for a walk in Central Park, but after ten minutes, I couldn't feel my toes, so I grabbed my swimsuit and switched to the hotel's Jacuzzi. As I swirled my toes in the steaming water, I let the thoughts loose in my head. Why was it suddenly hard to just say yes to New York?

Staying here would also mean working with Chris. I was relieved I hadn't let things move forward that night, but interacting with him on a regular basis would be awkward. Shit. I had no clue what to do. What I did know, though, was that my career choices couldn't be about Sebastián, or Federico, or Chris, or anyone else. What did *I* want?

Tuesday morning, I sat facing Andrew, the massive width of his desk separating us in space and in rank.

"What do you think?" he said, leaning back in his chair and interlacing his fingers behind his head.

"I think..." I spread my palms on my lap and took a deep breath.

"I know it's a bit of a slow start, but you can grow. It *is* a great opportunity. But, if you're not ready..."

"I would be honored to join Manhattan Ballet. *Christ*, this..." Tears of overwhelming joy and exhaustion rushed to my eyes and I didn't bother stopping them. "This has been my dream ever since I can remember. And now...it's finally here. I'm sorry." I wiped my cheeks with my hands. "I sound like a little girl."

"Not at all. You've got talent, but you've also worked hard. Or you wouldn't be here. You have every right to enjoy this moment. So, is that a yes?"

"Yes. Yes! I would *love* to dance for Manhattan Ballet. Thank you so much, Andrew. I'll give it everything to make you proud."

"Fantastic. I'll see you back here in two weeks. Eight a.m. Go ahead," he said, nodding. "Go celebrate."

I stepped out in a daze and bumped into Chris, who was waiting outside of Andrew's office. "Pardon me." I looked down as I sidestepped him, angling to the exit.

"Wait," he said. "I was hoping to have a word with you."

"I...I have nothing to say to you."

"Please."

"Sorry, I've got to go."

"One minute of your time, is all. I just need to say something to you."

I gave him a stern look. "What can you possibly say that would make what you did—what *we almost* did—any less horrible?"

"Nothing," he said, hanging his head. "But I need you to understand. Please, have a coffee with me."

"Another time." I turned, hurrying to the exit.

"Camila." He caught up with me. Dammit. "We can't leave things as they are…We might be working together. Am I wrong?" That stopped me in my tracks. Crap. He had a point.

We sat at a small café around the corner. It smelled of freshly ground coffee and chocolate pastries. I avoided his eyes and focused on the people coming in. *Mm, cute top.*

"Camila, I love Ivette," he said softly.

"You have a funny way of showing love. And commitment."

He sighed. "I deserve that. Look, I've never loved anyone like I love her. She used to be a dancer with the Royal Ballet, and we fell in love quickly. But five years ago, she fell during a rehearsal and that was it. Her spine suffered severe injuries, and after three surgeries, they told her she would never walk again."

"I'm sorry," I said sincerely.

"The thing is, I still love Ivette as much as I did when she could walk. But she's changed. She's not full of light like she used to be."

"That's understandable."

"When I met you, you reminded me so much of her. There's something pure about you. Despite the sadness I saw in your eyes the other night, you're so full of life, and genuine. It's almost as if the ugly parts of the world can't touch you. And I…I was selfish." He focused his eyes on his empty cup. "For one moment, I wanted to feel that joy again. I'm so sorry. I would understand if you reject Andrew's proposal. It would be…inconvenient, I guess, to see each other every day." He looked down at his interlaced hands on the table. He seemed vulnerable, hurt, and I understood the sadness I had seen in his eyes before. He was just a man, someone in pain, and the anger and disgust that I had felt for him dissipated.

"All right. I accept your apology. And...I also accepted Andrew's proposal."

He looked up at me with a mix of shock and fear.

"That's right. So be professional, and don't make this any more...*inconvenient* than it already is." I picked up my bag. "See you in a few days."

Chapter 44

I hugged Nata hard when she left that morning. Marcos and I would stay a couple more days.

The two of us toured the city, and I hoped our time together would persuade him to stay in New York too. We hit some of the typical sights like the Statue of Liberty and the Chrysler Building. We walked around Broadway and took selfies by the knick-knack shops that sold everything *I Love NY*. It was fun, and for the first time since I had arrived, I breathed the energy of the city and let New York in. I bought a down parka that went all the way to my feet, and as I zipped it up and stepped out into the frosty air, the winter didn't seem unbearable anymore. The trick, I learned, was to have good quality gear and to keep the walks short.

We wandered along the High Line and had sushi inside the Chelsea Market, where the old Oreo cookie factory had been recycled into a cool shopping area. We strolled across the Brooklyn Bridge and around the Williamsburg street market. Artisans displayed antiques and original works of art on a grassy area by the Hudson shore. From there, the view of Manhattan was spectacular.

On the way back to the hotel, we walked into a funky bar with live music. It was still early, and the place was fairly empty. The bartender greeted us with a "Hi there," her eyes immediately trained on Marcos. We scooted into a small booth by the window and glanced around. At the bar, a few people our age sipped beers. On a stage a few feet back, a live band played a slow tune, the singer's voice deep and sexy. Marcos signaled to the waitress.

My English was decent, and Marcos's entire vocabulary consisted of no more than five sentences, which included *Where's the bar?* and *Beer, please.* But he managed just fine.

The waitress took our order while her eyes devoured Marcos. I leaned back in my seat, witnessing for the umpteenth time the reaction women always had to Marcos, relieved it wasn't something I would ever have to worry about.

Our drinks came, and we clinked bottles to this amazing city and a successful tour. Marcos gulped his beer with a long swig and signaled to the waitress for another.

"Little Camila, a Manhattan Ballet dancer. I knew you'd kick ass. You're an exceptional dancer."

I smiled because Marcos could always take my ego from the basement to the penthouse, just like that. It was one of my favorite things about him.

"Thank you, but the truth is, I'm scared to death. What if I don't measure up? The dancers here are exceptional. I'm worried I won't have what it takes."

"Ah, this again. I remember a young girl at the Colón auditions, a million years ago, it seems, with the same fears."

"Oh, my God. That's right." I smiled. "That does seem like a million years ago, and yet, the fear I feel now is as real as the one I felt then."

"Hang on," he said, then disappeared to the back of the bar, where he exchanged a few words with a bartender, who glanced over at me and nodded. Then Marcos was back.

"Let's dance," he said, taking my hand. But our timing was bad, because when we reached the little dance floor, the band announced they would take a break.

"Maybe later," I said.

Marcos shook his head.

"What?" I frowned.

"I remember I did a pretty good job in easing that girl's nerves back then. I'm convinced I can do the same for this girl right now."

"Marcos, what—"

That same song from the morning of my first audition at the Colón, the energetic Colombian tune by Juan Luis Guerra, "*Me Sube la Bilirrubina*," blasted from the speakers. My hands flew to my mouth as I burst in laughter. Marcos took my hands, just like he did back then, and we set off to the trumpets of the salsa number. Marcos pulled me against him, then pushed me away. It was sexy, fun. The liveliness and tropical melody instantly lifted my spirts and, just like it had done back then, erased my fears. Everyone in the bar clapped when the song ended. We were both panting and bowed our heads in response. I wrapped my arms tight around Marcos's neck.

"I love you, Marcos."

"I know," he said ruefully.

The band came back, and they started playing a slow song. I didn't unwrap myself from Marcos when he began swaying to the melody of the acoustic guitar. A young couple next to us joined us and started making out, oblivious that they were in public. Marcos's thumb caressed my cheek, and unease fluttered in my stomach. We danced together every day, but it had been a while since we had been out alone, and it felt like unfamiliar territory. The hollowness that occupied my heart since Sebastián and I broke up, expanded. Marcos tightened his arms around my waist, bringing me close like he had done so many times in the past. Everything about him became familiar at once: his warmth, his scent, his perfectly carved body. It all worked in unison, every inch of him exuding confidence and masculinity. It was hard to think of any woman resisting him. It hadn't been that long since *I* was convinced Marcos was the love of my life. But after Sebastián, I wasn't sure I would ever love anyone else unconditionally again, not even the beautiful package that was Marcos.

I rested my head on his chest, feeling his heartbeat. Another memory of Sebastián haunted me, and my shoulders tensed. Marcos's arms squeezed me tighter.

"Let it go." His lips brushed my ear, and when he pressed me against him, he hardened. "Oops," he whispered.

"Marcos…"

"I'm sorry, babe. I can't help it. I just…We've got so much pent-up chemistry." Cupping my face, he brought it to his until our lips met. It was gentle at first, but then I closed my eyes and kissed him back. What was happening? In the back of my mind, I knew this was somehow wrong. Or was it? I was single, he was single, and we were here, far away from our jobs and our lives and everything that was real. On their own accord, my lips parted wider, giving his tongue access, and the kiss deepened. Tears prickled in my eyes. The wound inside me bled, and the old loneliness throbbed and burned.

I was tired of it.

I clenched his hair in my hands and kissed him harder, kicking the burning away. This was Marcos, my old, unreachable love, and he was kissing me like I was the only woman in the world to him. Marcos, Marcos. *Jesus*, it felt so good to be in his arms. And who knew? Maybe there was still a chance for us. Maybe we would dance in New York together, turn the fantasy into a love story like those reporters had. *Our* story. We both let go of everything, kissing each other deeply. *Marcos*, I was kissing *Marcos*, my friend, the man I once loved.

"Wait. Stop," he said, pulling back, but I gripped him tighter.

"Let's go back to my room," I said in a husky voice, our breaths mixing. His eyes met mine, then traveled to my mouth, and I felt it everywhere.

"Cams, no. You're not *one of my girls.*"

"What if I want to be? Please, Marcos. I need this. I need you. Please, take the pain away."

Back in my room, I let him peel off my clothes. He grabbed my hair at the nape with one hand and kissed me hard. He was decisive in everything he did, a bit rough, but in a way that was sexy and masculine. I let my hands explore his ripped body, trying to connect with all the things I had once felt for him, willing them to overpower the emptiness left by Sebastián. Marcos threw me back on the bed and interlaced his hands with mine, pulling them over my head while his mouth ravaged me. The rock-hard muscles on his chest rippled against mine, his jeans scraping the satin of my panties. He broke the kiss to look at me, his hot breath blending with mine.

"Cams. You're so fucking beautiful, babe." He kissed me again, exploring my neck, then undid my bra and kissed each one of my breasts slowly, adoringly, then harder. An image of Sebastián barged in my mind, and I forced it away. He's gone. I closed my eyes and focused on Marcos's mouth as his teeth grazed my nipple and then sucked hard. I moaned out loud and felt him everywhere, and suddenly it was just the two of us, the ghost of Sebastián almost exorcized. Marcos was an incredible lover. He fucked me hard, then slowly, taking me to the brink with his deep, smooth rhythm. I trembled around him, and my muscles clenched, welcoming him while our bodies melded in the sexiest, most intimate dance yet between us. I dug my nails into his back while his pace accelerated, his pelvis slamming against me. I climbed high, higher, until I couldn't tell anymore what was him and what was me. And then I was lost. It was all him, it was *us*.

I woke up in his arms with the faint morning sun on my face. I blinked at the rose dawn sky, and the familiar emptiness left after Sebastián tugged at my heart. Turning around to face Marcos, I took in his handsome face. He looked so peaceful. He stirred sleepily and I smiled, surrendering back to a deep, peaceful sleep.

When I opened my eyes again, the room was bright. What time was it? I was tangled in my sheets. Alone. There was no sign of Marcos, and the bedside clock said it was eleven. I plopped back on the pillow and rubbed my eyes. I hadn't slept till eleven in…months. I felt restored, good about my decision to move to New York. This would be a new, exciting stage for me.

I showered and dressed in jeans and a sweater and knocked on Marcos's door. A minute later he opened it and invited me in.

"I was thinking we could hit the Guggenheim today," I said. "What do you th—" I froze at the sight of his suitcase on the bed, his wrinkled clothes carelessly tossed in it. "What's this?" I turned to him without hiding my disappointment.

He rubbed the back of his neck. "I meant to tell you last night, then—"

"Then you thought you would *fuck* me first?"

He cocked an eyebrow. "I'm pretty sure it was the other way around."

My eyes burned and I clenched my teeth. "You don't have to leave."

"I spoke with Federico yesterday. He offered me a position as a choreographer. It's what I want."

"But your career's thriving as a *dancer*...Why?"

"I'll still perform as a principal. But I'll also work with Federico on some of his ideas. It's an amazing opportunity for me."

"What about Manhattan Ballet?" I snarled with a mix of anger and betrayal. "It's a great opportunity also."

"It is."

"Then what? Why leave?"

"Cams." He paused. "If I stay here, I'll fall for you. And you're still hung up on the gangster."

"Don't be ridiculous. That's over."

He half smiled. "You can't bullshit a bullshitter. And I'm not good at coming second."

"You're not going to fall for me. You're Marcos, for fuck's sake. You don't *fall*."

"You changed that. And now I want more. I want all of it. But I want it with someone who's all in."

"Marcos, stay. New York will give you more than Federico."

He let out a long sigh. "Federico's been a good mentor for me, and we work well together. It's the right thing for me long-term." He looked calm. He had made his mind up.

I clenched his biceps with my hands. His muscles tensed between my fingers.

"Please."

"Cams..."

"You're my partner. I thought...after last night, I thought you would stay. I thought we would do this together."

"I can't. I'm sorry." He pulled me into his arms, and I tried pushing him off, but he was much stronger. He pressed me against him, and I hit his chest with my fists, pounding as hard as I could. He didn't fight me, and as soon as I stopped hitting him, he pulled me into his arms again. Anger and frustration soaked my cheeks as I sobbed, beaten, against his chest.

"I hate you."

"No, you don't."

"I don't want to do this alone."

"You *have* to do this alone. This battle inside your head between that part of you that wants things and that part of you that says you're not good enough has to end. *You* have to end it. And you have to do it on your own. Just like you did when you got up from the hospital bed. That strength is inside you. It's time to let go of the rest."

I cried and he hugged me tight. I felt like a castaway, alone, stranded.

There was only me now.

Chapter 45

The season with Manhattan Ballet had ended, and we were off for the summer. It had been an uphill four months, working triple time to earn my place in the company. Andrew had promised me a few good soloist roles for the coming season, so things were starting to brighten up.

The July heat in New York was stifling, and the few friends I had made at Manhattan Ballet had fled out of the city, so I packed my bags and bought a ticket to Buenos Aires. I hadn't been back since I had first left for the tour. I hadn't wanted to. I just had Nata send me some of my things and bought what I needed after my first paycheck came.

I felt it the moment the plane touched the tarmac. The longing, as if it had been waiting for me. A fist gripped my heart when a myriad of images of Sebastián flashed in my mind.

Outside the sliding doors of Ezeiza International Airport, Mamá and Papá welcomed me in their arms, and I inhaled their familiar scent. I squeezed my eyes shut, letting the familiarity of our group envelope me.

We sat under the shade of the vines in my parent's backyard, chatting about my life in New York and Papá's new wing at the hospice. The mayor had changed his mind, and the city was funding the project for two more years.

"Palacios wouldn't have anything to do with this, would he?" Papá asked, his tone skeptical.

"I doubt it. I haven't heard or spoken to him in over five months."

"I'm sorry, you're right." He gave me an empathetic look and quickly changed the subject. But in the back of my mind, I wondered idly if Sebastián did have something to do with the mayor's sudden change of heart. Dismissing the thought, I listened to their stories about their trip to Europe and the reunion with my siblings, and felt truly grateful for my family. I had taken it all for granted.

After just a few weeks at my parents', I was ready to go back to New York. It was mid-season at the Colón, so I was only able to see Nata and Marcos in the evenings, and they always looked exhausted. For the first time, I understood what dating a dancer meant to an outsider. It sucked. Ballet always came first.

On my last morning in Buenos Aires, I decided to go for a walk in the city and say good-bye to some of my favorite spots. I stopped for an espresso and croissant at Plaza Vicente López, then meandered among the pedestrians flooding Florida Street. Everything was familiar: the street sounds, the horns in the distance, the buses breaking nearby. I was at home here. I sidestepped a couple dancing the tango, the iconic melody of "*Por Una Cabeza*" funneling out from the speakers that sat on the sidewalk. A vivid memory of my tango performance with Marcos at Vladimir's party had me smiling…Then it quickly vanished behind another image of Sebastián and me dancing barefoot on the beach in Colonia, a wedding in the distance, laughter, sailboat lights blinking in the rose sky. I doubled my steps. Everything here was also another scene of the complex production that had been us.

On the train ride to my parents', I leaned my head against the window, watching the city blaze by. As we approached the station, I hesitated for a moment, then sank back into my seat and let my stop pass. There was one more thing I needed to do before going back to New York, and it could change everything.

I knocked on the door I had come to know so well, my nerves pulsing as I waited for the familiar fragile frame to approach and greet me. My heart kickboxed my sternum. I squeezed my knuckles, waiting.

Dammit. *This is it.*

I looked around impatiently, and it struck me that everything looked exactly the same, as if no time had passed. The peonies in the flowerbeds by the windows, the treetops swaying to the afternoon breeze.

The door startled me when it swung open. Mercedes's feline eyes bore on mine.

"What do *you* want?" She scowled. She was thinner, pale. Not the stunning woman I had once met at her party. I wondered vaguely if she had a drug problem.

"Mercedes, it's been a while."

"Yeah. What are you doing here?"

"I need to speak with Sebastián."

She eyed me for a moment, then raised her chin as if resuming a script after a short pause. "He's not here. I'm house-sitting."

"Oh. When will he be back?"

"Not for a long while. He's in Spain…with Carolina."

It was as if she had slapped me. Hard. She noticed, because her mouth stretched into a serpent grin.

"You're lying," I snarled. Then Rafa appeared behind her. His eyes widened a fraction.

"Camila. What…are you doing here?"

"Rafa," I said in a brighter tone. "I came to see Sebastián."

"Sebastián's in Spain," he said a bit more somberly.

"I told her," Mercedes said, curling her arm in Rafa's. He darted a look at her hand and tensed. "She thinks I'm lying. You tell her, Rafa. Tell her Sebastián went to see Carolina."

Rafa frowned deeply.

"Is that true?" I searched his eyes.

"I'm sorry. May I offer you a ride home?" he said.

"No," I murmured, and he nodded, his expression remorseful.

"I'll be out back," he said to Mercedes before glancing back at me. "Take care of yourself, Camila." And before I could respond, he was gone.

"Apparently, they reconnected," Mercedes went on, leaning on the door frame. "You didn't think he would be waiting here like an idiot, did you? After you paraded around New York wrapped around your dancer boyfriend? It was all over the papers. 'A Dancer's Love Tango,' they called it." Her eyes narrowed. "How dare you show your face here after doing that to him? He almost died while you were in New York living your little romance, did you know that?"

A rush of rage surged in my blood. "He almost died because you're a lying bitch. You lied to me so I would get the Zchestakovas to help you. *That's* why Sebastián got shot. Don't think I've forgotten."

"Listen to you. So ballsy. As far as I know, this worked out fine for your friends."

"You're a pathological liar," I said between my teeth. God, I wanted to strangle her.

"You're not welcome here, and I've got things to do." She slammed the door in my face leaving me there, like the idiot I was.

I slumped into the worn-leather seat of the train that would take me back to my parents'. I wiped my face with the back of my hand. What did I expect? Nata had nailed it from the beginning: *A Palacios doesn't take the back seat.* It hurt to have been discarded so quickly, so efficiently, a used Band-Aid. Nata had also said that there was something very unique about a first love: pure, innocent, without the barriers we build after a broken heart, and I understood. That's what he and I had.

Now it was gone.

Chapter 46

I walked along the streets of Manhattan, following what had become my favorite route to work. It was only June, but the city air simmered in warning of an early summer. I didn't hurry; I was never late for work anymore. More than a year had passed since I had moved to New York, and I was no longer the mousey corps girl chasing the clock and shrinking under Madame Vronsky's scrutiny.

Rearranging my dance bag's strap over my shoulder, I leapt up the familiar steps of Lincoln Center, admiring the straight, clean lines of the buildings. Paying attention to architectural details was one of the many marks Sebastián had left in me. I suppressed a smile at the massive banner hanging on the side of the building. My image as Juliet in the arms of Jonathan, my partner, made my pulse race.

The role of Juliet was one of the most meaningful ones I had ever undertaken. Not just because of the physical demands of the part, which were many, but because I felt as if my life experiences had somehow been preparing me for this performance. Juliet loved Romeo the way only young lovers did. To the two of them, it didn't matter that everything worked against them: family, friends, the time. As I learned the steps of my variations, I reached deep inside, unlocking all my memories of loving Sebastián, the good times, the struggles, the heartbreak. The images blended with the earlier love, or infatuation, I had felt for Marcos, then the loneliness when he left New York. Although I didn't drink poison like Juliet, I understood her heart completely.

Jonathan held my hand up as we bowed in unison under a shower of white flowers and deafening applause. After so many weeks of hard work, we had pulled off a successful opening night. My cheeks hurt from smiling. Jonathan kissed my temple while someone handed me a giant bouquet of flowers and congratulated me. The bows continued as the maestro came on stage. More applause.

My body buzzed with adrenaline and fatigue as we gave a final bow and hurried back to the wings. In my dressing room, a wardrobe assistant helped me out of my costume, and I hung the items diligently, leaving everything ready for the next performance. I wasn't a clothes-piling slob anymore. New York's space-constrained environments made neatness crucial. Order also brought peace of mind. New York had taught me that.

A crowd gathered outside the stage door. They spilled everywhere, rounding the dancers for autographs and photos. As I exited the building, a group of young girls ambushed me.

"Camila, Camila. Here, please!" They closed in around me so I would sign their copy of *Pointe* magazine featuring my photo on the cover. I quickly signed one, two, three, four, five, so many. But I didn't mind. Now I was a prima. It was *me* on that cover. Andrew had said my rise to principal had been one of the fastest he had seen, but no matter how many magazines I signed, I still couldn't fully believe it was me. My hand cramped as I scribbled my name on the last two. Then one last hand held a notepad forward.

"One more, please?"

That voice.

It stunned me. I looked up and suddenly I couldn't breathe. Jesus. *Jesus.* It was *him. Here.* How? And dammit, he looked breathtakingly handsome: tall, well groomed, his skin a golden tan that made his ash-colored eyes paler. He was impeccably dressed in a black tux. Heads turned to us, to him. I blinked off the stupor.

"You're here," I mumbled.

"I am." He smiled. That beautiful face. Goddamnit, I knew every inch of it: the square lines of his jaw, his straight nose, those lips. Okay, so maybe I melted a little. How many nights had I spent lying awake, remembering every inch of him, imagining he was there with me? The bastard. I looked over his shoulder, scanning the faces of the women in the crowd. Was *she* one of them?

Carolina? Or was she waiting for him in her expensive negligée in some hotel room? *Stop.* I straightened my back.

"What are you doing in New York?"

He shrugged and gave me a lopsided smile. Dammit, I wanted to kiss him, tangle my fingers in his hair. It was longer now, and it made him look mature, even sexier if that was possible. I hated the fact that I wanted to jump in his arms and kiss him, bite his bottom lip, smell him. A tug on my gown snapped me out of my daze.

"Can you sign, Camila?"

I signed my name on the little girl's magazine while Sebastián waited, watching us. She then smiled and ran to a waiting couple a few feet away. They waved, thanking me.

"You were phenomenal," he said.

"You saw me dance?" I blurted, hating the enthusiasm in my tone.

"I did. I'm so proud of you. You made it. All the way."

"Thank you." I let myself smile for the first time. His eyes appraised me with longing. I looked away at the traffic behind him, remembering we were strangers now. "I should go."

"Wait. Do you…have plans?" he asked.

"Oh, I…" Was he kidding? "I have the celebration with the cast. You know…"

"Ah. Of course." He nodded in understanding. An ambulance passed, the siren deafening, then fading away. The crowd had dispersed now, and it seemed like it was only the two of us left. Somewhere behind, the splashing sound of the fountain filled the silence. I couldn't tear my eyes away from him. The glowing lights of Lincoln Center cast shadows on his face. He was even more beautiful than I remembered.

Christ. What did he want?

"I came to New York to see you," he said, answering my silent question. His voice was low, guarded. "There are things…to say." Those dreamy eyes could still see right through me.

My lungs stopped. A war had launched inside me: the young girl I once was still wanted him while the new me wanted to punch him in the chin for all the scars he had left in my heart.

"Maybe a drink after?" he said. "Or tomorrow night?"

I glared at him. "She won't mind?"

He frowned. "Who?"

He didn't know I knew already, and that bothered me even more. His face looked puzzled. He was a good liar, apparently. I shook my head, deciding I didn't want to put myself through this reproach, rehashing our past. It was done. I glanced behind him at the traffic. Looking at him was way too difficult, and risky. A sudden lash of anger flicked me. Why did he have to show up in my new, happy bubble of a life and disturb the peace? I had finally stopped thinking about him every second.

"It's important," he said, interrupting the tornado in my head. "I'll wait as long as it takes."

Wait. Yeah. Wait for fucking *ever*. But I knew after tonight he'd be all I would think about. My anger flared. His presence had that effect on me, of wanting to rip off my own clothes. God, I hated him.

"I can't. I'm sorry."

His brows raised in surprise, or disappointment.

"I've got to go. You take care, Sebastián."

I was about to leave when Jonathan startled me by wrapping his arm around my waist from behind and kissing my cheek.

"Here you are. My bride in the afterlife," he said in his British accent and that low, slightly hoarse voice he often used to seduce everyone around him.

Sebastián's eyes narrowed a fraction, his jaw locking in disapproval.

"And who's my opponent, may I ask?" Jonathan asked.

"Jonathan, this is Sebastián. An old friend from Buenos Aires."

"Ah. A pleasure. Jonathan Stanton. Her partner on stage." Jonathan shook Sebastián's hand, awarding him a supermodel smile with slightly crooked teeth, his secret weapon.

Sebastián shook his hand firmly.

"You're coming to the party with us, yes?" Jonathan gave me a fleeting look that told me he was dying to know who Sebastián was. As a dance partner, Jonathan was confident, tall, masculine. In real life...well, we shared very similar tastes on men.

"No, he can't. He's busy. Another time." I glared at Jonathan, and his mouth stretched into a devilish grin.

"Oh, come on. What could be more important than going to one of New York's most exclusive parties as the prima's date? And you're already wearing a tuxedo. Believe me, these parties are *divine*. You won't regret it."

Sebastián responded with a broad smile, having figured out Jonathan wasn't at all an opponent.

"He *can't*, all right? Go! Shoo. Get us a cab. I'll be there in a minute," I said, waving him off.

"Camila, you're being bossy and it doesn't suit you."

"Jonathan," Sebastián said in a confident tone. "You've convinced me. There's nothing else I would rather do than spend the evening with Camila."

Chapter 47

Two doormen dressed in black tuxes greeted us at The Top of the Standard, a rooftop restaurant in the Standard Hotel with an unobstructed 360° view of Manhattan. Andrew always picked striking venues to reward the cast after an opening night, and tonight was no exception.

I walked in with one hand in the crook of Jonathan's arm. Sebastián took my other hand, but I let go. He frowned.

We hadn't been there for a minute, and the two of them had already captured glances from several guests. A waiter paused by us with champagne flutes. Sebastián handed me one, gave one to Jonathan, and took one more for him.

"To dreams that came true," he said, raising his glass with a pointed look.

"To dreams that did," I said coolly.

Two of the principals approached us, and I introduced them to Sebastián. It was so strange to have him here, in the world I had built so far away from him. I was going to kill Jonathan later. Sebastián wasn't my *date*. He wasn't mine and that was fine, but I didn't want him here, barging into my lovely new life with memories from the past. Happy memories that made me feel more alone.

Interrupting my thoughts, Andrew greeted me, then Sebastián. I did the mandatory introductions, and he told Jonathan he wanted him to meet someone. As he turned to go, Jonathan leaned down to kiss my cheek.

"Where the hell have you been keeping *him*?" he said. "Call me after. I want every detail."

I glowered at him and he grinned.

The next half hour was all about exchanging congratulations with other cast members and greeting contributors to Manhattan Ballet, who were always at these parties. There were also the usual celebrities, reporters, the drill.

Two photographers fired a stream of snapshots while asking me about the challenges of my role in Juliet, what advice I would give to aspiring dancers, and all that. Sebastián stepped back, but I snatched his arm, pulling him to me as we smiled at the cameras. The scene had a strange sense of déjà vu: Sebastián and I surrounded by photographers and reporters. Except this time, *I* was the target of their attention and he was my anonymous date.

After what seemed like an eternity on my four-inch heels, my feet weren't having it, and I whispered to Sebastián that I needed a break. We sat on a plush sofa facing the window wall, Manhattan glimmering at our feet. In the distance, the Empire State Building glowed in purple and white neon. I sipped my cocktail, unsure where we would go from here. So many questions circled in my head: Why was he in New York? Was he just passing through? Alone? Was this simply a drink between old friends? And where the hell was *she*?

I decided I didn't want to know. What difference would it make? After tonight we would go back to our separate lives.

"Where are you staying?" I said distractedly.

"A little place nearby, a few blocks from the Park," he said, scooting closer to let a couple go by. I hated that my body was aware of every one of his movements and the close proximity of his. I felt the heat radiating from him. The lethal mix of warmth, suede, Ralph Lauren, and that unique scent that was just him was messing with my senses. Memories of another life ambushed me: his huge bed, sheets of the softest Egyptian cotton wrapped around our tangled bodies, his hands in my hair, his mouth everywhere, and sex, so much sex. *Jesus.* I gulped my drink. This was a runaway train.

"You look stunning, Camila. So grown up."

"I do?"

"Yes. New York agrees with you."

"Well, how long has it been?" I said casually. "Over a year now?"

"Fifteen months, one week, and two days," he said assertively.

"Oh." I downed the last drops of my drink.

"Do you have a performance tomorrow?"

"No, just afternoon classes."

He nodded, letting a silent moment pass. "It's really good to see you," he said. "So much has happened since you left Buenos Aires." He rested his hand on mine, wrapping his fingers around it. The heat was electric and it expanded up my arm. I closed my eyes. *Shit. No.*

"I don't know what this is…" I said, pulling my hand out from under his. "What are you doing here?"

"I needed to see you."

"Why?" I glared up at him. "Why now?"

"Why *not* now?"

"Seriously?"

"Yeah." He frowned. "Is that so hard to believe?"

I pressed my lips and looked around the room, at the people smiling and having fun. This was my world now. I didn't have the friendships I had in Buenos Aires, but I had built something for myself here. Things were good for me, finally. All that time trying to forget him. He had no right to come here and wreck it all for me again. He had left me. That was his choice.

"Camila…" he said softly. I shook my head, forcing back the tears, but when I met his eyes, the hurt and emptiness that filled me suddenly strengthened my spine.

"It's been over a year. We had our chance. You chose," I said bitterly. "Speaking of which, where's Carolina? Waiting in a hotel nearby?"

"Carolina and I are not together."

"Didn't work out?" I said sardonically.

His expression softened. "We only met for a coffee, and it was good to see her after so long. She's happy."

I gave him a look that told him to cut through the bullshit.

"I'm telling you the truth." He frowned.

"Either way. It doesn't matter."

"Camila." He reached back for my hand, but I pulled it away. "Look at me."

I reluctantly did, reining in the last of my patience.

"It wasn't until recently that Rafa told me you had come to see me." He shook his head in irritation. "I was very angry with him, and with Mercedes for telling you I had gone after Carolina."

"Why would Rafa do that?"

He sighed. "He wanted to protect you. Things at the docks were still a mess then, and he knew how hard it had been for me to let you go the first time. But tell me, why did you come to see me?"

"What does it matter?"

"It matters a lot, to me. Tell me."

I shrugged. "It was an impulse...I don't know, I guess I wanted to see if there was still a chance for us to work things out somehow."

He looked around the room, his nostrils flaring, his lips pursed in disapproval. Then his eyes met mine, the pale background blazing. "I'm sorry. Mercedes has a twisted mind. There's nothing between Carolina and me. She's happily married. She has a family."

That lying bitch...My pulse quickened.

"She's in rehab now," he went on. "Coke."

I knew it!

"Well...it doesn't matter anymore. And it doesn't change the fact that you erased me from your life." I said bitterly.

"I wanted to protect you." He reached for my hand again. "I have a lot to tell you. Being away from you has been, by far, the most difficult thing I've ever had to do. But it was the only way to keep you safe."

"Safe?"

"Things were very unstable back then. After the shooting, I didn't know whom I could trust. Turns out Tano was the rat. He was an informant to Medina *and* García. Anyway, it's a long, fucked-up story."

"What about Ivanov?"

"We got lucky. In all the chaos, he went after the wrong people and it ended badly for him. I must say, he won't be missed."

"Jesus..."

"He was a very bad man. He hurt a lot of people."

"So what held you up this long?" I pulled my hand away and brushed invisible dust off my silky gown, avoiding his eyes. So much was different now. Even my dress. It wasn't borrowed, it was mine. The old me would've had a stroke at the price tag. He watched me patiently.

"What?" I said sarcastically. "No reason?"

He hurried his drink. "You seemed busy."

"What the hell does that mean?"

"'A Dancer's Love Tango. Buenos Aires's Beloved Couple,'" he said in a clipped tone. "The headlines were everywhere, online, on the papers, but it was the photos that sealed it. Even I am not that hardheaded. Your message was very clear."

"It was all a show," I snapped. "For the papers. You of all people should know better than to trust the media."

He shrugged. "You seemed happy. And I had no right to mess that up for you. I knew the pain I'd caused you. I felt it too."

"If you wanted to know, you should've asked me," I murmured. An awkward silence went by. I finished my drink.

"So you and Panty Hose Boy. It didn't work out?"

"Panty Hose Boy?"

He smiled sardonically. "It suits him. So, what happened? Please tell me he sucks at sex—it would make my day." His tone was humorous, but I still saw the pain in his eyes.

"Why do you want to know."

He roughed an anxious hand over his jaw. "I just want to know. I know I have no right to ask you."

"You don't." I let the seconds pass, debating if telling him was a good idea. He didn't look away, his intense gaze waiting.

I sighed. "We were only together once."

A flash of hurt crossed his eyes, and he nodded. "Just once?"

"Yes, okay? Now drop it. I'm not discussing this with you."

"Why just once?"

"Sebastián!"

"I won't ask again, I promise. Why just once?"

"Because he wasn't you, okay? Now drop it."

His expression softened. "Okay. I'm sorry. It was eating me up. I know you said it was a show for the papers, but from where I sat, it looked very convincing. I needed to know."

"And now you know. It's in the past."

He interlaced his fingers with mine, and we both watched our hands fusing together. I swallowed the lump in my throat. What was this? Where did we go from here? Maybe it was just too late. Too much had happened. We were strangers now.

"Dance with me," he said, tugging on my hand. "Please."

I followed him in a sort of trance, to a quiet spot by the window, away from the party. For the first time in months, I felt out of my depth. I had sworn nobody would ever put me through what he had again. I wouldn't allow it. His arms wrapped around my waist, and all at once, the memories of the past thrashed in my mind. Dread filled me and I thought of Juliet. I felt her loneliness. Sebastián's world and mine would never mix. I inhaled him and pressed my face to the lapels of his tux, relishing in that fleeting moment that would soon become a new wound. Every second I spent in his arms pushed the knife deeper, and I knew the new memories would rip me apart later. I took a long, deep breath as my throat swelled painfully. I needed to go.

"I've left my family's businesses," he said, as if he'd heard my thought, but in my foggy mind, the words barely registered. He took my face in his hands so I would look at him. "All of them," he said. "Except for my studio. I've finally cut all business ties with my father."

I blinked. "What?"

"It took a while. It wasn't just about a separation from my father's businesses. It was complicated, lots of interests at stake. You can't simply walk away from the Families. But it's done."

I frowned. "You gave it all up? Seriously?"

"It cost me every penny I had." He gave a small shrug. "But my studio is all I need…That, and you."

My chest tightened, the walls around my heart thickening protectively. I opened my mouth and closed it. It wasn't this simple. It couldn't be.

"I've missed you," he said, so close I could almost taste him. "So damn much." His mouth found mine, and everything south of my navel coiled. His lips were soft, laced with vodka and mint. His arms tightened around my back, bringing me closer. My emotions thrashed through my chest like a tornado. When we broke away, we were both breathing hard.

"Why are you here, Sebastián?"

"I'm here for you."

"It's been too long," I said, fighting the tears. "And it's been hard, but I'm finally okay."

"Camila," he said, taking my face in his hands. "A single moment hasn't gone by when I stop thinking about you. I've never lost hope."

A stray tear rolled down my cheek, and his thumb wiped it.

"My beautiful, crazy girl. I've never stopped loving you."

I gripped his hair at the nape and kissed him hard, and in that moment, the past faded. Was this my revenge? Having him one more time? Whatever it was, I didn't care. I wanted this. Him. The rest could wait.

We took a cab to his hotel, a quaint boutique remodel a few blocks from Central Park. I wondered idly if he had chosen that location to be close to where I worked.

Inside, the building was quiet, the faint sounds of the city distant. He led me to an old elevator that looked like an antique birdcage. As soon as he slid shut the door, I gripped the lapels of his tux and kissed him, ravaging his mouth. His arms closed around me and lifted me, pressing me tightly against him while his tongue explored my mouth. I tasted the urgency on his lips, the longing, and

I was sure he tasted mine. I was out of breath but couldn't break for air. I didn't want to let go. I was afraid that if I blinked, it would all vanish. I would wake up back in my room and throw a pillow at my roommate, Julia, for snoring and tearing me from this incredible dream.

He pinned me against the elevator wall, the *ping* of the passing floors muffled by our desperate breaths, the sound of lips crushing.

"God, I want you," he groaned against my jaw. The elevator finally came to a stop, and he opened the door behind him without breaking away from my mouth.

In his room, I took off my coat and draped it over the back of a chair. His lips curved, amused, as he undid his tie. Facing him, I pulled off the spaghetti straps of my dress: first one, then the other. The silky fabric slid down, pooling around my feet. Sebastián's eyes traveled slowly down my body as if he were memorizing every inch of me.

"Holy shit." He shook his head slightly. "Do you have any idea how sexy you are? You're even more beautiful than in my dreams."

I helped him unbutton his shirt and kissed the rippled muscles of his chest. He smelled like heaven, Ralph Lauren, *home*. He clasped my chin and kissed me hard while his other hand moved to my ass and lifted me. I had to hold on to his shoulders and wrap my legs around him. The skin-to-skin contact unleashed a chemical frenzy inside me, my dormant hormones couldn't keep up.

I clenched his hair between my fingers, devoured him, our teeth clinking together in desperation. We wanted everything at once. He threw me back on the bed, and I crawled backward, my eyes trained on him, my mouth half open while my chest heaved up and down with panting breaths. He stood at the foot of the bed, a six-foot-five Adonis. He was hard, and his boxers did nothing to hide it. He watched me with hooded eyes, and I bit my bottom lip, admiring him. My insides ached with need. His open shirt fell to the ground, unveiling a pale line that followed his ribs from the center of his chest to the back, disappearing under his arm. I inhaled, bringing the tips of my fingers to my lips

465

as I winced. He gave me a sideways smile, assessing my reaction. Our eyes met and I smiled back at him. Somehow that scar made him more beautiful. It marked the new man he now was, a self-made man who went after what he wanted.

Without taking his eyes off mine, he finished undressing. Climbing onto the bed, he crawled over to me, sauntering like a predator about to devour his prey. My breath accelerated, desire soaking my panties. *Dear God.* This was happening.

His fingers grazed my leg up to my knee while both my palms splayed against his sides, sliding up. My fingers met the rough surface of the scar, tracing it.

"Does it hurt?" I said against his mouth.

"No. It's just ugly." He smiled.

"It's not. It's beautiful." I pressed my hands against his chest to take a better look. Rolling him over, I sat astride him, examining the scar as the tips of my fingers followed it. Sliding down, I pressed my lips against it, tracing kisses along the slightly rougher line of patched skin. I felt powerful, in control. God, he was beautiful. His chest heaved up and down in broken breaths while my mouth and my tongue traced this new part of him, a new part I had already fallen in love with. Then his fingers tangled in my hair and brought my mouth to his. I melted in his hands.

He rolled me over and his knees separated my legs. He kissed my neck sensually, moving down to my breasts, then down to my stomach, trailing the familiar path. My skin combusted. Closing my eyes, I threw my head back, savoring the sensation of his hot lips against my navel. His thumbs hooked on my panties and pulled them down, his breath mixing with the warmth between my thighs. I clenched my teeth, watching him through squinted eyes.

"God, how I've missed you," he said, kissing the most intimate part of me. I bit my lip till I tasted sweet rust. His tongue circled around, teasing my clit. I lay back and clenched the sheet at my sides, moaning while my body turned to melted iron with a mind-blowing orgasm.

I groaned and he smiled, his breath brushing my wetness, teasing my control. He lifted his head to look at me. His eyes were the color of steel, his eyelashes dark and endless, his expression almost boyish. Placing his palms on each side of me, he pulled himself up, the rippled muscles of his chest sliding over me, pinning me down against the mattress. I welcomed his weight, almost smothering me, and caressed his hair, smiling at him.

"My turn to be on top," I said. He raised a curious eyebrow, then slid his arm underneath me, and with one move, sat up, bringing me with him. I hugged his back with my legs, squeezing him, my arms loose around his neck. His cock was hot against my thigh. I wanted him so much, desire was now an ache deep in my belly. I felt powerful. I loved letting my body surrender to Sebastián, but it felt good to take control.

"You're mine now," I said.

He smiled seductively. "At your service."

I readjusted so he would slide into me, and then I lowered myself slowly, so slowly it was torture, but I made myself wait, savor it. His breath was heavy and hot against my neck as he struggled with his own control. My mouth was slack and he kissed me, biting my bottom lip between his teeth. I let myself sink so his whole length was inside me, filling me completely while I moaned out loud, my skin sizzling, my blood singing. His hands gripped my waist, and we danced to a slow rhythm, sliding up and down. I panted against his face, our foreheads pressed together. We didn't kiss, we both relished the moment, it was too intense. I moved faster, digging my nails into his shoulders, our bodies slick with sweat and sex. I closed my eyes as the heat expanded inside me, the tension coiling, building.

"Sebastián. God…" I exploded as I came hard around him, a long, blinding flash of light that left me breathless. His pelvis slammed against me, and he groaned, gripping me hard as he buried himself deeply inside me, riding the spasms of his orgasm.

My hands made their way to his hair, raking it back, and I finally kissed him. There was no desperation; it was soft, gentle. My mouth tasted like his and his like mine. Our tongues played, caressed. It was soothed, patient. It was love.

He rolled me down onto the bed and lay beside me. Our hands found each other. Our fingers tangled. The minutes passed in silence, our slowing breaths the only sounds filling the room.

"I want to feel like this every day," I said. "Even if this is just a dream."

He turned to look at me. "It's not a dream."

I propped myself on my elbow, letting out a long breath. He brushed a loose strand of hair off my forehead.

"What's wrong?" he said softly.

I shook my head, searching for the right words. "It's just… seeing you here…" I sat up. "Forget my French, but it's a major mindfuck. You still have a hold on me. I don't know what this means or why you're here."

"I told you, I'm here for you. I love you, Camila." He smiled shyly. "My heart is still yours if you want it."

I shook my head, appeasing my racing pulse as I summoned all my strength.

"I'm not going back to Buenos Aires with you, Sebastián. I'm not that girl anymore. There was a time when I would have done anything to be with you. Anything. But letting you go… coming here… It changed the way I see some things. My life is here now, and I—"

He pressed his fingers against my lips. "I wouldn't ask you to change one thing for me. I knew you loved me when you left Buenos Aires. What we had was real. And as hard as it must have been for you, you did it. You left it all behind and came here. I had a lot of time to think about things when I was in the hospital. My own life, what I wanted." He propped up on his elbow. "It was your strength, the courage to follow your dreams, that inspired me to finally go after mine. I want to be with you, Camila. If this is where you are, then this is where I want to be too. I love you."

"You would leave everything behind and move here. For me?" I said incredulously.

"Yes," he said without hesitation. He leaned over, and his lips brushed mine gently. I let out a stuttering breath.

"But your studio, all your clients are in Buenos Aires."

"We can make it work." He pulled away to look at me, his hand stroking my cheek. "Do you still love me? Do you want me here?"

"I...Yes, but..."

He grinned. "Then I'm staying."

Chapter 48

That week we hunted the city for an apartment. After seeing over a dozen overpriced tiny places with no view, we settled on a month-to-month rental on the second floor of an old building in Little Italy. The apartment was no more than a small studio, and the rent was scandalous, but it had a window to the street and lots of light, and it was all we could afford. Life in Manhattan was beyond expensive, and after covering a full rent, my salary wouldn't allow for extravagances. But I didn't care about any of it. It was our new chance at a life together.

"Kind of feels like home, doesn't it?" I said to Sebastián as we ate sandwiches at the scanty kitchen bar of our apartment. I leaned over and kissed him. "Thank you for doing this. It means so much to me."

"It will be an adventure," he said.

"I'd say…" I picked at the crust of a ham and cheese that was a sad emulation of Marcél's version. "Going from an estate in San Isidro and your own studio in Puerto Madero to a one bedroom in a shabby part of town."

"Are you trying to talk me out of it?"

"No! Of course not. But I know that this 'adventure' comes at a high price for you."

He leaned over and kissed me. "Stop worrying. We're okay."

"Are we? Your clients must want you there."

"Cami, stop. It's my decision to be here. Can you just tell me I'm *awesome* and go with it?"

"You're awesome," I said. "I'll go with it."

"That's better." He kissed my forehead and moved to clear the dishes.

"Speaking of Buenos Aires and your connections…There's something I've been wanting to ask you for a while."

"What's that?" he said from the kitchen sink.

"Do you remember my dad's hospice project? The one the mayor was threatening to close?"

"Yeah…"

"Well, this was over a year ago, but the mayor changed his mind overnight and decided to completely fund the project."

"That's great," he said without looking at me as he filled the sink with water.

"Sebastián…did you have anything to do with that?"

He shook his head. "Your dad asked me not to get involved, remember?"

"Look at me," I said. He turned to me and I searched his face, but his expression gave nothing away. "I know it was you."

"I have no idea what you're talking about. And if your dad asks you, you tell him that."

"I will." I smirked. "But off the record, thank you."

He glanced over at me, suppressing a smile.

I watched him from my seat as he rinsed the last of the dishes and I couldn't help a smile. Back in Buenos Aires, I had never seen him do domestic chores. There would be no more Marcél or five-star lounges now, no fancy cars or expensive restaurants, or people opening the doors for him because they knew who he was. Here, there wouldn't be privileges of any kind. Period. Just a studio apartment with no AC and a hefty rent. All for a girl who could only offer to love him back with her whole heart.

One morning, after going on an early run, I quietly snuck back into the apartment so I wouldn't wake him. But as I closed the door behind me, I stilled at Sebastián's voice coming from the bathroom. Without making a noise, I sharpened my hearing and stepped closer. The door was ajar and Sebastián was shaving. He had the phone on speaker, and the other voice was distinctively Julián's. They were arguing.

"I need you here. There's a shit pile a mile high and all the other architects are up to their neck in projects."

"I can be there in a few days. We'll sort it out."

"Give me a goddamn date, Sebastián."

"I don't have a date. I'll let you know once I have my flight."

"For fuck's sake, man. How in the hell is this going to work for you? You've spent every last penny you had on this shit with the Families. Your father's still pissed that you're gone. He wants to know what the hell you're doing there."

"What I do is nobody's goddamn business," Sebastián growled.

"Bullshit. You know how things work. You're a fucking Palacios. You don't just walk out from all that. No one does."

"Well, I did. It's over."

"Your name is still tied to *every* transaction that goes through the docks."

"Every transaction, huh?"

"It was the only way your father could assure the Families that you won't leak anything to the police or the press."

"I wouldn't do that. My father knows it."

"Well, nobody gives a fuck. The only thing that matters is that you vanished. That makes our clients nervous. So cut me some slack and show your face sometime soon."

A pause followed. With my heart in my throat, I hurried back to the front door, opening and closing it loudly.

"I'm back. You up?" I called.

"Morning," he said, stepping out from the bathroom and wiping his freshly shaven face with a towel.

"Everything all right?"

"Yeah." He kissed my forehead. "How was your run?" He looked glorious, his eyes were a clear blue, the color of the shallow ice of a glacier.

"Good." I waited for him to say something about the conversation with Julián. But he just kissed my lips chastely.

"I made coffee."

472

"Sebastián I heard your conversation just now," I said as he turned to get dressed. He stopped for a second, then reached for his shirt and pulled it over his head.

"What about it?"

"Maybe you should go home for a while."

"Camila," he said, running his fingers through his wet hair. "This is where I want to be. I'm not going anywhere."

"But it sounds like you're needed. I'll be fine. We'll be fine."

"Sweetheart." He pulled me into his arms. "I love our life here. I have no interest in going back to Buenos Aires. I'll fly down to pick up some of the projects, and I'll work from here."

"You're doing this for me, and I don't want that."

He exhaled. "At first I was. But now I like it here. I really don't want to leave."

That night, I lay next to Sebastián as he slept peacefully. I tossed around, restless, recapping his conversation with Julián that morning. Julián had a point. He was still a Palacios, a King of Midnight. He would always be tied to their net somehow.

Maybe being here was best. I stared through the window at the neon sign from the deli across the street, and thought of those late-night shipments, clandestine cargoes that would never be tracked by paperwork. Here, Sebastián was just a normal guy. No bodyguards, no Don Martín, no Medinas. And I understood giving it all up to be with his girl, in this hallway of an apartment a million miles away from home, was the only way he would be free.

While I was at work that week, Sebastián painted the old walls of the apartment, built new shelves and a bookcase, and re-sanded the old wood floors, all at a minimal budget. The projects he brought from the studio in

Buenos Aires started bringing some money, but I insisted we saved it for a bigger apartment. Besides, manual labor seemed to make him happy. In just a few days, our dingy studio had been transformed into a beautiful mini-loft where every space was usefully repurposed with a designer's eye. Our landlord was stoked and even offered to hire Sebastián on a cash basis to redesign some of the other units.

When I came home one night, I was welcomed by the mouthwatering aroma of empanadas that Sebastián was pulling from the oven.

"You remembered." I raised my eyebrows in excitement. "That's why you asked me to get wine?"

Throwing the dish towel over his shoulder, he shook his head in amusement. "How can I forget the day when a gorgeous, suicidal girl fell into my arms in the middle of 9 de Julio Avenue?"

"I was not suicidal! I was *rescuing* one of Anna's shoes."

"Hmmhm."

"They cost a fortune!"

"So naturally, you dove into traffic."

I unwrapped the scarf from my neck and threw it at him. "You're infuriating. You just…don't understand. Some things are worth diving into traffic for."

He grinned. "I couldn't agree more."

From the corner of my eye, I spotted a little table set for two in our tiny balcony. I squinted at him. "I only forgive you because you're so disgustingly romantic. And all I did was get this cheap bottle of wine." I slid it into the freezer.

He pulled me into his arms. "Everything I need is right here." His mouth found mine, and I wrapped my arms tightly around his waist. His ripped back muscles flexed under my hands. All this remodeling work he had done at the apartment was a bonus.

After a dinner of empanadas and salad, we sat side by side with our feet up on the balcony railing. Sebastián poured the last of the wine into my glass.

It was a very expensive bottle of Sauvignon Blanc and the last from the few he had brought from Argentina. It was crisp and delicious. Realizing there wasn't enough to fill his glass, I stood.

"You stay. I'll get the other bottle."

In the kitchen, I pulled the Chardonnay I had bought at the liquor store on the way home. I filled his glass, and we toasted to happy moments in Manhattan. As he took a sip, Sebastián's mouth curved in distaste.

"I'm sorry." I smiled guiltily. "It's bad, isn't it? But the wine at the Greek brothers' is so expensive. It was all I could get for ten dollars."

He refilled both our glasses and raised his. "To happy moments and bad wine."

Standing, I moved to his lap and kissed him. "I love you, you know?" I leaned my forehead against his. He smiled and kissed me fervently, sending tingles everywhere. I would never tire of this, of him, and the way he made my body come alive as soon as he touched me. It was ethereal, even more so than the high dancing gave me.

New York was our bubble of happiness away from the world. But as we lay in bed at night, I worried that this domestic life away from his studio might soon not be enough for Sebastián.

Chapter 49

The following spring, an early heat wave slammed Manhattan. Even the tourists flooding the streets sought relief inside museums and shops. The air was stifling, and without air conditioning in our apartment, my nights were restless.

The stench of rancid garbage greeted me as I made a slow way up the subway steps, leaving the cavernous cool air behind. We had been rehearsing tirelessly for *La Bayadère*, and my muscles were tight and battered. Sidestepping a group of teens, I hustled inside the building hosting the Manhattan Ballet studios, desperately longing for the relief of the air conditioner.

But the oppressive climate would not be limited to the weather.

"People, gather around." Andrew gestured as he walked in, followed by a young couple: a male and a female dancer I had never seen before. The air in the studio instantly changed, conversation ceased, and everyone stepped to the front, all eyes on the two newcomers. The couple's expressions were stoic, their complexions pale and the lines on their faces well defined. She had red hair pulled tightly into a bun and all the features of a traditional ballet dancer: long neck, skeletal but muscular body, and the demeanor of someone who knew what they had been born to do. He was tall, languid, his posture perfectly straight, exuding confidence that perfectly matched his partner's. The couple focused on Andrew, oblivious to the burning scrutiny directed at them.

Jonathan, my partner, appeared next to me.

"What's this?" I whispered.

"Hmm. Andrew's new find."

"What?" I turned to him, and he shrugged.

"Last year it was you, this year it's Russian prodigies. Andrew likes keeping the pool fresh. Look at them, they're preschoolers. Christ."

"People," Andrew started again, "you've all heard the rumors, and I am now in a position to confirm them: Effective next week, Alphonse Bordieux, from Paris Ballet, will be the main choreographer. And that's not all, I have more exciting news for you today. This is Mina and Nikolai. They're just visiting us now, but they will be joining Manhattan Ballet as principals in the fall. Be warm, be helpful, and show them around. They're our guests of honor this week. Now let's get started." He clapped once and everyone took their usual places, the new couple at the front. I looked around, breathing in short, shallow breaths. Nobody else seemed to care, or maybe they were used to it, because this was simply how things were. Nothing personal, move over, make room for the new. A sense of loneliness invaded me as I took my spot at the portable barre. It was just like my first day at the Colón, and for a moment, I was that girl again, with a lot to prove and a long road ahead.

Andrew walked by me without pausing. His attention was on the new couple. It seemed as if he were only walking around so he could watch them from different angles. I told myself it was normal, he was evaluating them, but deep down I knew that over the last six months his initial dedication to me had slowly faded. Maybe this was how it was for all dancers at some point. When you know you've stopped learning.

Andrew turned, this time facing me directly, and I purposely tensed my shoulders. I knew it dramatically affected my posture, and I wanted to see if he noticed. Back home, Madame used to torture me about it. Andrew smiled with a small nod and walked past me to the front.

At lunch, Jonathan and I sat side by side on the steps of Lincoln Center, eating egg salad sandwiches. The sun was high and baking, but anywhere was better than inside the studio today, watching Andrew parade his new Russian pets around.

"Who in the hell came up with an egg salad sandwich?" I tossed my half-eaten sandwich in a nearby trash can and wiped my hands. "I miss choripanes. I miss all the food in Buenos Aires."

"You were spoiled. This beats the hell out of the Marmite sandwiches I had in England."

"I miss fresh pasta shops, Freddo's ice cream, and dulce de leche. I really miss dulce de leche. In Argentina, we put it in everything. There's nothing like it."

"Well, it wouldn't be as good if it wasn't forbidden." Jonathan winced. "Having dulce de leche whenever you want sounds much more tempting if it comes with a price tag of letting your boyfriend go back to being Tony Soprano."

"Yeah. Except Tony was violent, fat, and a brute. Sebastián is sweet, handsome, eats with his mouth closed, and doesn't have a closet full of two-toned, short-sleeved shirts."

"Yes to all. But I still had a crush on the total mindfuck that was Tony. He was a fat thug, but his sense of chivalry made you pull for him no matter what. Your beau, though... Bloody eye candy."

"You should see him in an Armani suit."

"I'm perfectly happy watching him shirtless, fixing stuff around your flat. Besides," he said, taking the last bite of his sandwich and crumpling the wrap, "he could make a fucking burlap sack look sexy, babes."

I laughed.

"But what was it really like? I mean, being Sebastián Palacios's girl?"

I shrugged. "In many ways it was really nice. We would walk in anywhere, and people would actually move out of the way to let us in because they knew who he was. They respected him. I don't think he'd ever stood in line anywhere before he moved here. But then, there were also the bodyguards, the guns, his father."

"Must be some change."

"Yeah. I don't fully understand yet how he was okay giving all that up."

Jonathan nudged my shoulder. "Because he loves you. You two have the real thing. He's a lucky bastard and he knows it."

"And yet, here I am, back on square one. You know, I never thought about it until now…"

"Thought about what?"

"I came in last year just like them, Andrew's Russian preschoolers. Why did I think I was special? I mean, is it always like this? Do you ever really feel like you've made it?" I tore a corner of leftover bread and tossed it at a pigeon nearby. "Will there always be a skinnier, younger, red-haired Russian breathing down your neck?"

"Do you really want me to answer that?"

I shook my head. "I miss home," I said, staring at the new pigeons gathering in anticipation of more leftovers. "I always thought that once I got to New York, it would all fall into place. That all the insecurities I had as a dancer would just…go away. Because being here, doing what my mother didn't get to do, would mean I was a real dancer, you know?"

Jonathan smiled, shaking his head. "Let me guess, you still feel the same. No matter how many times your name is up there." He nodded at the sign announcing the upcoming opening night for *La Bayadère* with Jonathan and me as the leads.

"Exactly." I took a swig of my bottled water and wiped the sweat gathering on my forehead. "At home Madame kicked my ass daily. God, she would just be on me some days like a goddamn virus…there was no hiding from that woman."

"Funny, the things we end up missing."

"Yeah. What's really funny is how miserable I felt then. I didn't get it. I thought she hated me. And now, I would give anything to get that kind of attention. 'Navarro, zat is not your color, girl.'" I let out a long sigh. "Plus I've been here for almost two years, and you're still my only friend." I leaned over and rested my head on his shoulder. "You're my rock, Jonathan."

"I'm going back to London in the fall," he blurted.

I straightened immediately, searching his eyes. This was a joke, right?

"Royal offered me a position as principal, and I said yes." He turned to look at me. "I'm sorry."

"You're serious," I said, mostly to myself. A flashback of Marcos telling me he was going back to Buenos Aires almost two years ago slammed me like an avalanche. It had been a crucial point in my career because it had meant I would have to go forward alone. No Nata, no Marcos to lean on. Just me.

"Say something." Jonathan reached for my hand and interlaced our fingers. I leaned my head back on his shoulder.

"Dammit. Congratulations."

That week a guy in a hoodie followed me all the way to the studio. I brushed it off, but the next day he appeared out of nowhere and followed me again. It creeped me out, so I asked Sebastián to start walking me to work.

Jonathan waved at me one morning as I walked in.

"Okay, it's been a week," he said. "Enough already. As much as I love watching your hot boyfriend's arse leave every morning, you need to get a grip."

"Leave me alone. I'm fine."

"You lost weight again, I can tell. You're messing with my balance."

"I always thought Sebastián's bodyguards were a pest. Now I miss them."

"Leave it to you to protest two bouncers flanking you like you're royalty. Maybe I'll get myself one in London." He grinned.

"Screw London."

He reached for my hand and tugged me down so I would sit next to him. "Stop all this whining," he said. "You're not going to get mugged, and this is not the end of us. It's a step forward for me and for you. It's time to grow again. And you never know, we may partner again someday."

"You're right. But I'll miss you."

We never talked about Jonathan leaving after that. In the midst of so much change at work, we both needed something to stay the same. We dove headfirst into the season with an unspoken promise to make it our best.

Inside the walls of our studio, time moved with the precision and predictability that gave Manhattan Ballet its reputation. To the world, we were a well-oiled machine of professional dancers, a family with solid ties, a unit. But what they didn't know was that we were really a group of well-trained strangers. Our bond didn't extend beyond what was written in black and white on our contract for the year. At the Colón, we sweated, bled, hated, and loved together. We constantly measured ourselves against each other. We may have not always been the big happy family we portrayed on stage, but at least we were aware of each other's existence. Everyone's presence was acknowledged one way or another. Americans were less dramatic and less socially intense than Argentineans. Here, we didn't hang out after work. Most dancers took college classes or worked to pay for Manhattan's astronomical rents. An image of Marcos and Nata making plans for hitting clubs after work flashed in my mind, and I smiled. But as I looked at the dancers vacating the studio, my smile faded, and I wished I was back at home.

As I stepped out into the evening, I pulled my phone out of my pocket and searched for the number I wanted.

Chapter 50

I stood at JFK with my arms wrapped around Jonathan's neck. The ballet season was over. It was time to say good-bye.

"Let go. You're going to give me a neck cramp," he said.

"I can't. Don't go."

"You'll be fine." He pulled away. "Liam will be your partner next year."

"I hate Liam. He has bad breath."

"You'll learn from him. Give him a chance." He took my face in his hands. "Take care of yourself. Go take a holiday with your knicker-scorching boyfriend and forget about all this for a few days. And when you come back, don't get lost in all this cosmopolitan bullshit. You know who you are. Here or on the moon."

I walked into my little loft feeling beat and aching for a cool vodka tonic, but the sight of a suitcase by the door stopped me cold.

"You going somewhere?" I looked up at Sebastián as he approached, his face pale and somber.

"My father had a heart attack. I'm going home tonight on the eleven o'clock flight."

An hour later, Sebastián had us both packed. Whatever awaited, I wanted us to be together. Besides, the July heat threatened to swallow Manhattan whole, and I couldn't wait for a break from it and to be surrounded by familiar faces. The thought of reentering the Palacios turf made me a bit anxious, but I couldn't wait to go home. At the Colón, the season would be in full swing, and I could go see as many performances as my time in Buenos Aires allowed. I wasn't due back in New York for another two weeks, when I would meet with Andrew to discuss my contract renewal.

Sebastián carried our bags downstairs, and I was doing a quick last-minute check before I locked up when my phone rang. The familiar voice greeted me, and I sat on the stairs, holding my breath.

Chapter 51

The flights to Buenos Aires for that night were sold out, so we had to fly to Montevideo, then drive to a nearby airport, where Julián's jet waited.

As soon as we landed at the small private hangar outside Buenos Aires, I felt in my bones that I was back at home. The morning air was damp and heavy, mixed with the smell of fresh hay. The place was a modest ranch in a remote, rural area. Outside the hangar, two bodyguards waited, casually dressed in jeans and white T-shirts and leather jackets, both armed with handguns tucked at the waist. *Home sweet home.*

An arctic winter breeze brushed through me, and my body shivered with fear and anticipation for seeing everyone I missed. In the distance, I recognized Rafa's silhouette standing still by the car.

"Welcome home, Sebastián. Camila," he said as we approached. His eyes assessed mine with apprehension.

"It's all good, Rafa. You were just looking out for him. No hard feelings."

He answered with a nod, instant relief easing his expression.

I sank into the familiar back seat of the BMW as we made our way to Sebastián's home, and Sebastián sat next to Rafa up front.

"How is he?" Sebastián asked.

"Stable, but the cardiologist said the next twenty-four hours are critical. He'll be glad to see you."

"Yeah…"

"Straight to the hospital?"

"We'll take Camila home first."

"I want to come with you," I said.

Sebastián turned his head, and Rafa's eyes met mine in the rearview mirror. They both answered in unison, "No."

"Just in case," Sebastián said, reaching back and placing his hand on my knee. "I would feel better if you went home. For now."

I nodded and sank back into the seat. It seemed as if every time we entered his kingdom, we were torn apart.

The car sped across the countryside toward the city, and I felt bone-tired. Staring out the window, I let the fatigue from the last twenty-four hours sink me deeper into my seat. My mind drifted while the green scenery blazed by. I couldn't wait to see Mamá, Papá, Nata, and Marcos. I smiled, imagining their faces when they saw me here. I was pretty sure my parents would be at home the next day. I could show up at lunchtime. Then in the evening, I could swing by the theater to surprise Nata and Marcos after rehearsals and lure them out for drinks like old times.

Marcél appeared at the door as we pulled into the driveway, his fragile frame a little less straight. New creases on his face formed as his mouth stretched into a welcoming smile. I undid my seat belt and stormed out to greet him with a hug.

"Welcome back, *ma chérie*."

"Oh, Marcél. How are you?" I squeezed him tight.

"Older. Crankier. It's good to have you both back. The willows have missed you. The house is somber without you here."

Sebastián left for the hospital, and I sat at the kitchen bar while Marcél chopped vegetables for a stew that smelled delicious.

"*Ma chérie*, lunch is ready whenever you want. Would you like to eat now? I'm almost finished with the lamb stew for this evening."

I smiled warmly at him. "I'll wait for Sebastián. Do you think he'll be safe?"

Marcél's expression softened. "Don't fret about that, sweet girl. Monsieur Sebastián is with Rafa, you have nothing to worry about."

"But he got shot once, and all this thing with the Families... Marcél, I'm worried about him."

Marcél's warm hand patted mine gently. "He will be just fine, I promise. Why don't you go take a bath? It will help you relax. Your things are already in your bedroom. Go, sweet girl. Try and rest. You must be exhausted after that long flight. Sebastián will be back before you know it."

"Okay," I said, and reluctantly peeled myself off the barstool, then lumbered to Sebastián's bedroom. The scent of fresh paint lingered in the hallway, and I vaguely wondered if he'd had the house painted recently. My phone buzzed with a message from Sebastián:

All good. I saw my father and he's stable. I'll be home in a little over an hour.

I let out a long sigh of relief.

After a long bath, I lay face down across Sebastián's massive bed, relishing the luxury of the extra space. Next to our flat in New York, this house was a palace. Burying my face into the pillows, I surrendered to the familiar scent of lavender and fresh sun and fell into a deep slumber.

I woke with a start and blinked in the light. I looked around, disoriented, then remembered where I was. Bright sun filled the room, and the bedside clock showed I had slept for over an hour.

With my heart galloping, I hurried down the hallway without bothering to put on my shoes, grateful for the radiant heating that kept the floors warm.

At the kitchen island, Sebastián stood with the phone to his ear. Relief washed through me at seeing he was back at home, safe. He turned, and when our eyes met, I noticed the exhaustion in his. Hanging up the phone, he gave me a tired smile as I wrapped my arms tightly around him.

"How's your dad?"

"He was awake when I got there. They'll move him out of intensive care today, but the doctors are keeping a close eye, and he needs to rest."

"I'm glad," I said, loosening the embrace. "How's...everything else?"

His forehead creased. "Two of the family bosses showed up while I was there."

"Shit. And?"

"It was civil. I told you, It's over." He rubbed the fatigue off his eyes. "Julián's coming by in a couple of hours."

Great.

"Don't scowl. He's helping more than I deserve. He's kept things going while I've been away. It was a lot to pile onto someone else."

I kept my thoughts to myself. If Julián was helping, would there come a time for him to collect his favors from Sebastián?

After lunch, we stretched out under the pergola, and I tightened my New York down coat around me. Despite the cold air, it felt good to be outside. I took a deep breath, savoring the musky scents of the forest in winter. Beside me, a full fire crackled in a massive outdoor fireplace. Only a few crumbs of Marcél's lemon meringue pie were left on my plate. I smudged a bit of meringue and sucked on my fingertip.

"I miss Marcél."

"He misses you," Sebastián said. "I've never seen him this happy."

After the long flight and Marcél's coma-inducing meal, I needed another nap. I glanced over at Sebastián and told him to join me.

I followed him through the familiar hallway. Everything seemed the same except that lingering smell of paint...I wrinkled my nose. "Did you have the house painted?"

"Nope..."

"Why does it smell like paint?"

"It doesn't. You're imagining things."

I stopped and winced. "No…It's coming from there, I think."

"Camila, wait—"

But before he could reach me, I was already opening the door.

I gasped.

The room—a once bare-boned space which, on my first visit here, he had told me was his favorite room in the house—was now a full ballet studio. *A full. Ballet. Studio.* In his house! I opened the door all the way and walked in.

"Holy shit. What is this?" I looked around wide-eyed, scanning every inch. Seamless mirrors paneled the walls from floor to ceiling, and a ballet barre cut across the middle. I turned to Sebastián, and he was watching me from the door with a guilty expression.

"When did you do this?"

He rubbed the back of his neck and stepped in. "After the shooting."

"But…why?" I said, unable to tear my eyes off every detail. "We weren't together."

"I was hoping one day that would change. I don't know…Doing this made me feel closer to you somehow."

"Holy shit, Sebastián." I looked down at my feet and bounced once. A top-of-the-line sprung floor, the kind that absorbs even the slightest of shocks. I walked around dumbstruck, taking it all in. In a far corner, there was a sitting area with a mini fridge and freezer with glass doors. It was stocked with drinks and what looked like ice packs. Beside it was a basket with fresh towels, a cubby with yoga mats, stretching bands, and other gadgets, including foam rolls and an exercise ball. On the opposite end, a side door was open to what looked like an en suite bathroom. Every detail of the design was immaculate, clean, modern, and elegant. Still, the most breathtaking feature was the window wall: floor-to-ceiling glass overlooking the forest underneath, an endless collage of gold and green at my feet with every sunset.

"I'm speechless."

He hugged me from behind. "It will always be here for you."

This man.

I could dance here in the summers and watch the sunset mosaics of magentas and blues. Sunset was my favorite part of the day. He knew that. I wiped the tears off my cheeks and hugged him tight, making him stumble back.

"I love you, Sebas."

Chapter 52

"Good morning," Sebastián whispered against my neck, kissing the crook under my ear. His muscular arms tightened around me, and a delicious shiver ran through me. Reaching back, I raked my fingers through his hair and turned to kiss him. His mouth was warm, welcoming. It was sexy as hell. I pulled away, breathless, and bright, clear eyes smiled at me with mischief.

I narrowed mine. "What?"

His grin widened.

"I know that look, Sebastián. You're up to something."

"I have…a surprise for you."

"You've already given me *my own* ballet studio. And all I gave you was that stupid snow globe." I glowered at the little Manhattan souvenir on his bedside table. I had bought it at a knick-knack store in New York after we had moved in together. Since then, he always brought it with him on his trips. He reached for it and shook it, and we both watched the snow slowly drift over the city skyline.

"I love my snow globe." He shook it again. "Reminds me of when you gave me another chance." He looked over at me, and I wrapped my arms around his neck, rolling onto him and pinning him under me.

"You are one sweet, sweet boyfriend, Palacios." I suggestively pressed my hips onto his, awakening him. "Hmmm. I think I should thank you properly."

His hands gripped my hips. "If you do that now, we won't leave this bed for hours."

"Sounds like a good plan to me. Got anywhere to go?" I rubbed my hips against his again, and he groaned. His grasp on my hips tightened, and he moved me aside. *What? No!*

"Where are you going?"

"We can do this later. Now I need you to get up." He gave me a chaste kiss and grinned.

"Sebas!"

Standing swiftly, he fished his clothes from the floor. I admired him from the bed, thinking about how the scar across his chest made him look even sexier.

"Can't we do this later?" I pouted. "We have to go see my parents in a few hours, and I'm not ready to detangle from you yet."

"If you're done pouting—which, by the way is fucking sexy—put this on because what I want to show you is outside." He tossed me one of his sweatshirts and quickly slipped into his jeans.

I reluctantly put on my jeans and UGG boots, then shrugged on the sweatshirt that went down almost to my knees and pulled my hair into a messy bun. He took my hand and led me past the kitchen to the...dining room? *Whoa.*

I gripped his arm. "Wait. I need coffee."

"Nope. Sorry, no time."

I scowled.

"Come on." He wrapped his arm around my waist and pressed me to him, kissing me swiftly. "You're a moody little thing this morning."

"You're seriously pushing it. This better be good."

Clasping my hand, he unlocked the French doors and led me to the garden. It was like walking into a movie set. The enchanted sounds of the forest surrounded us: birds of all species welcomed the new day, the cicadas announcing a bright morning, and in the distance, the treetops sneaking from under the morning mist. The air was cool and damp. I inhaled deeply, letting it fill my lungs. Sebastián tugged on my hand.

"Can you tell me where we're going?"

His mouth curved into a smug smile as he guided me down the winding trail that disappeared into the forest. He then stopped by a willow where a bike waited.

"Um...what are we doing?"

"Patience and faith, sweetheart. Come." Sliding onto the bike, he gestured for me to sit sideways on the bar between the seat and the handlebar. I reluctantly obeyed, watching him warily. What was he up to? Our lips were inches apart, and his eyes locked on my mouth like he was considering kissing it. Desire swirled deep in my belly. He smiled wickedly, then kicked his feet backward, propelling the bike to roll downhill on a dirt trail. What in the hell could be so important?

We traveled deeper into the forest, the trees growing bigger and closer together. Faint sunlight filtered through the branches. The air was crisp, scented with the pungent aroma of pines and fresh dirt. I shivered as the cool mist brushed my face. At the end of the path, the forest opened abruptly into a grassy area by the riverbed.

"We're here," he said and kissed my cheek softly.

I slid to the ground, and he dropped the bike, taking my hand in his. In the soothing tranquility of the morning, a young sun stretched over the rippling surface of the river, glistening into a million golden sparks. Soft waves lapped against a white-sand strip. The view from here was breathtaking.

To the right, a cabin on stilts stood over the shallow of the river. It was bare wood with large windows and a deck wrapping around the whole perimeter. I had never been to this part of the property before. It was beautiful. An oasis.

"Is that a guesthouse?" I said, leaning against him as he hugged me from behind while we took in the view. He kissed my temple, hugging me tighter when I shivered.

"More like a retreat away from the house. My parents used to come here in the mornings to have breakfast and watch the sunrise."

"It's beautiful," I murmured, admiring the whole scene with fascination. There was something incredibly enchanting about this place. I kicked off my shoes and velvet grass threaded between my toes.

"Come." He unwrapped himself from me and led me up the steps to the cabin. As we reached the top, the whole surface of the deck came into view.

My heart stilled.

I looked up at Sebastián, and my jaw dropped.

He grinned. "Now you can have your coffee."

I blinked away the stupor, holding my breath in fear I would break the spell.

An immaculate breakfast table set for two awaited on the deck under an oversized umbrella. Everything was crisp white linen, fine crystal and silver, and a delicate vase of white roses in the center. A smaller table with silver domes and pitchers of orange juice and coffee was set to the side. Two pedestal heaters framed the breakfast table on each side, gleaming bright red. All around us, the river shimmered in the morning sun. It was a dream.

"This is…this is so romantic."

"Come." He took my hand and led me to the table.

Pulling out my chair, he picked up a napkin, snapping it playfully in the air before placing it on my lap. He then poured coffee in our cups, and I downed mine in two long sips. It was Marcél's coffee. I recognized it immediately and it tasted heavenly. I was about to refill my cup when Sebastián reached for a bottle of champagne and filled two crystal flutes.

"Enough coffee. We have a lot to celebrate."

"We do?"

"Yes." Putting down the bottle, he squatted down beside me and smiled, tucking a strand of loose hair behind my ear. He caressed my cheek, watching me, his eyes wide and loving.

"I know that if you had your way, you would have a vanilla cupcake for breakfast every morning." Standing, he reached to the side table and picked up one of the silver domes and placed it in front of me.

"We're having *cupcakes*? Well done, Palacios. Scoring high." When I reached to lift the lid, his hand covered mine.

"This is not just *any* cupcake." His voice was low, seductive. I bit my lip as a surge of heat ran through me. Slowly, he lifted the silver dome, and the world around me froze.

A single vanilla cupcake sat in the center of the silver plate. It was frosted with delicate white seashells. And he was right. This was no ordinary cupcake.

An emerald-cut diamond ring peeked from the top, sparkling in the bright morning sun.

I drew in a sharp breath as he dropped to one knee.

Holy shit.

"Camila," he said, taking my hand. "You're the only woman I will ever love. You make me happy, every day. You surprise me, every day. Since I met you, you've grown into an amazing woman and have taught me so much about myself, and what believing in yourself can help you accomplish. When I'm with you, I'm the man I strive to be. You've always believed in me. You're fearless and passionate, and full of light. I love you, sweetheart, and I want to give you the world. If you let me, I want to spend the rest of my life doing everything I can to make you happy." His clear, bright eyes bore into mine as tears spilled down my cheeks. "Marry me."

"Sebastián," I whispered.

"We'll live in New York, or Paris, or wherever you want. I know that I come with a lot of baggage, but I promise you that I will follow you to the moon. Marry me. Say yes."

"Yes." I launched myself into his arms. "Oh, God, yes!"

Standing, he wrapped his arms tightly around me, spinning me around. I giggled, and he suddenly stopped and kissed me deeply.

"I love you, my future Mrs. Palacios. You sure you're ready to bear the weight of the name?"

I took his lovely face in my hands. His eyes were bright, blazing with happiness.

"Your *name* is part of the man that you are, the man I love so much. You're generous, and kind, and selfless, and nothing would make me happier than spending every day with you. Now…I have a surprise for *you*."

"You've already given me what I wanted." He pulled me onto his lap as he sat. I smiled at him, running my fingers through his silky, raven hair, and the morning sun sparked against the stunning diamond on my ring.

"A few weeks ago, I called Federico."

He searched my eyes. "Oh?"

"I needed some career advice. The truth is... with Jonathan gone, it feels like the end of a cycle for me there. I'm done with New York, or it's done with me, I don't know. Andrew's constantly grooming new dancers. And honestly, I feel like I'll always be a guest there. I miss Madame, and Nata, Marcos, and Federico. I miss learning. So, Federico and I discussed the possibilities. And...last night, when I was locking up the apartment, he called to offer me a permanent position with the company."

He listened thoughtfully. "Okay...What about your contract?"

"I'll talk to Andrew."

He let out a long sigh. "Camila...is this what you really want?"

I pressed my forehead to his. "I miss home, Sebas. I want us to live here. Would that be okay with you?"

"Sweetheart, I told you, I'll live wherever you want. But are you sure you're not doing this for me? I know you worry about me traveling back and forth."

"I promise. It's not just that. This is home."

His brow furrowed in thought, and he took in a long breath, his eyes focused somewhere in the distance.

"I thought you'd be happier," I said, brushing a few strands of hair off his forehead.

"In New York, we can be normal people," he said sternly. "Here, I'm a Palacios. Even after walking away from the docks."

I rolled my eyes. "Oh, for Christ's sake, you can switch the tux for a burlap sack any day and you would still be a Palacios. And I love that about you. *We* decide, not them."

His arms wrapped around my waist. "Our life will change. We won't be able to escape the public eye. It will mean having protection wherever we go. Photographers." His mouth twisted in disgust. "It will be a constant fight for privacy."

"It would also mean an air conditioner in the summer, and your *huge* bed every night, and this house, and being close to my parents and Nata and…" My eyes widened. "Marcél!" I held his face in my hands and kissed him. "Marcél would spoil us, and you'll stop complaining I don't eat enough."

His eyes assessed me with a doubtful expression.

"This is what you really want?"

"Yes! Can you just tell me I'm *awesome* and go with it?" I said, quoting his very words to me when he decided to move to New York.

"You *are* awesome." He smiled. "Okay. Home it is, then." His arms tightened around me, and he kissed me deeply. "My beautiful, brave wife-to-be." He smiled wickedly. "You know…the cabin has a *very* big bed too. Let me give you a tour." He gave me a soft kiss and lifted me up with him, then carried me into the cabin.

"I guess we'll see how brave *you* really are," I said, grinning.

"Why is that?"

"Because in a couple of hours, you'll have to tell Papá that you're marrying his favorite daughter."

FIN

Acknowledgments

I have many people I want to thank…

First, my husband and kids. My husband is my rock, my lifeline, and my best cheerleader. Your endless support kept me going, especially when I wanted to give up, all those times. My appreciation to you, and to the kids is endless. Your unconditional love, your wicked sense of humor, your joy, and your big hearts, have been my inspiration to go after my dreams. You make me believe anything is possible, and for that, I am grateful every day.

Thanks to my virtual writing group, the originals! Lavina, Jamie, and Carol. You cheered me on and taught me so much! You will always have a special place in my heart. And yes, I still hear your voices and corrections in my head!

Another big thank you to my writing group at San Diego Writer's Ink. You guys have been my teachers throughout all the versions of this book!

Special thanks to Tammy G.'s contribution. Thank you for your editorial reviews, your feedback, and your endless knowledge of the world of ballet.

Thank you, Leslie, you are the best beta reader! Your feedback made me rethink key things in this book, and you helped me make it better.

Huge thanks my editor, Chih. I am so grateful for your thoroughness, your skills, your input, and your manner.

A big thank you to all the professional ballet dancers, from the Colón theater and from around the world, who shared insider's tips and their knowledge of a dancer's life.

And lastly, to my family and friends, in Buenos Aires and the U.S., for your enthusiasm and support along this journey. I love you all!